Praise for
The Silence of Trees

"In *The Silence of Trees*, Nadya, the astonishing matriarch, war survivor, and narrator, weaves a remarkable life centered on fate, love, luck and choice while honoring the ghosts of her past. Her voice is an important and unforgettable addition to the post-war immigrant experience in this highly impressive and exquisite debut by novelist Valya Dudycz Lupescu."
—IRENE ZABYTKO, author of *The Sky Unwashed*
and *When Luba Leaves Home*

"Valya Dudycz Lupescu presents us an impressive novel debut with *The Silence of Trees*, in which she conjures a captivating story of the heroine, Nadya, across more than fifty years of secrets, truths, tales told and untold, quiet sacrifices, as well as memories of a difficult personal history she left behind in Central Europe. While letting go of her ghosts during her final years, she came closer to what was painfully lost to her and her people, even closer to the many small measures of happiness awaiting her . . . Will she embrace a present that renews and honors a heavy past? Like an enchanting tapestry of Ukrainian magic and folkloric images, this is a thoughtful and beautiful work."
—FIONA SZE-LORRAIN, author of *Water the Moon*

"Lupescu weaves a magical tale in two senses: first, from the perspective of the craft of writing and, second, from that of sheer entertaining storytelling. It is the rare book that can bring the reader into the mystical side of folk religion without engaging the fantastical. Lupescu has done so. She has given us a window onto Ukrainian folk traditions that elegantly reveals the complexity of spirituality as it intertwines with politics, economics, folk traditions and formal or institutional religion. The story is captivating. The holocaust and the attempted demolition of the Ukrainian people is not an easy subject but Lupescu deftly frames her contemporary story against those shadow times without losing sight of the hopefulness, the determination and the spiritual faith of the survivors evidenced in their struggle to sustain their culture in America. This is a story that may make one laugh and cry, but, in the end, inspires readers to remember there are many ways of "knowing" and many perspectives on the notion of truth."

–MONICA M. EMERICH, PhD
President, Groundwork Research & Communications
Associate Researcher, Center for Media, Religion and
Culture, University of Colorado, Boulder

The Silence of Trees

What is remembered —lives!

Valya Dudys Lupen

THE SILENCE
OF TREES

A Novel

VALYA DUDYCZ LUPESCU

Wolfsword Press

Chicago

2010 Wolfsword Press Trade Paperback Edition

Published in the United States by Wolfsword Press.

Cover Illustration by Madeline Carol Matz (www.mcmatz.com)

The Silence of Trees

ISBN 978-0-9821261-3-4 (pbk)
LCCN: 201093304

Printed in the United States of America
www.wolfswordpress.com

For my grandparents:

Parunia & Iwan
and
Maria & Petro

PART ONE

Stories

In our own society today, fortune/telling serves much the same purpose as it has long served in traditional cultures, offering a chance for dialogue, for sharing, for objectification, for hope and drama and revelation. As a way of telling about fortune, Tarot reading offers the opportunity to cultivate our natural narrative abilities and endow them with deeper resonances and broader meanings.

—Cynthia Giles
from *The Tarot: Methods, Mastery and More*
(Fireside, 1994)

CHAPTER ONE

THERE IS A UKRAINIAN LEGEND THAT ONCE EACH YEAR, on the night of Ivana Kupala, a magical flower blooms in the heart of the forest. Anyone who finds it will be granted their heart's desire: the ability to hear the trees whisper and watch them dance, the power to make anyone fall in love with them, the magic to make barren lands bear fruit and barren women fruitful. It is a single red flower with several names: tsvit paporot, liubava, chervona ruta. The legendary bloom can grant wishes, open the doorway to the past, and awaken spirits to visit with loved ones.

I looked for the tsvit paporot when I was a young girl. I searched for it in many places, in different countries, over a lifetime. I eagerly went into the unknown, looking for magic, for mystery, for adventure. But sometimes magic finds you. Sometimes it comes in the least likely of forms: in a small black river rock, a deck of hand-painted cards, a sprig of purple herb or an envelope from home.

Just when you think that life is slowing down, magic happens. The universe sends you a message, like a tsvit paporot on your doorstep. The question is: what do you wish for?

At the age of sixteen, more than anything, I wanted to have my fortune told by the mysterious vorozhka, the Gypsy woman who camped with her people on the outskirts of our Ukrainian village. Mama disapproved, but so many young women had gone before me and come back with astonishing stories. The vorozhka told Mariyka that she would travel across the sea in search of kisses heavy with perfume. She told Darka that she would find many children gathered around her feet on her father's farm. Even Olena —who dreamt of going to school in Lviv to study languages—went to see the vorozhka. She told Olena that she would soon ride a train heavy with hope. After finishing my chores, I would sit with Khvostyk purring in my lap and dream of the vorozhka's predictions.

After my best friend, Sonya, went to see the Gypsy, I thought Mama would finally agree.

"Mama, Sonya's mother let her see the vorozhka. Her brother even kept watch as she walked through the woods to the camp. And do you know what the vorozhka told her? She told Sonya that soon she would see everything lit up around her. That the night would be broken by light, and she would run into the arms of her husband. Who else could this be but Yaroslav? He often tends his father's sheep at night and carries a lantern. Mama, I need to go see the vorozhka to learn about my future. All the other girls have gone."

Mama never looked up from the bread dough. Her strong hands squeezed the dough even harder as she said in that tone reserved for scolding little children:

"Nadya, you will not go. I forbid it." Mama bit down on her lower lip—something she always did when concentrating. "Gypsies are dirty. They steal, and they lie. What kind of life is that? They have no home. No home, Nadya. Why do you think this is?"

Mama rubbed her brown eyes, leaving flour on her brow. She looked me in the eyes. "Why? Because they take all they can and leave before people realize they have been fooled. We are not fools. This vorozhka is a fake. She performs tricks, uses pretty words to steal money from hardworking people."

Mama returned to her kneading. "When I was a girl, they came too. Marko Pavlyshyn had two cows and one horse stolen. Marusia Ivanovych had five chickens stolen that same night. The next morning when they went to find the Gypsies, they were gone. Coincidence? No, Nadya. Gypsies are dirty; they ride on a bad wind. You stay away from them and their enchantments."

I ran to the barn in tears and hid behind the cows. I wanted to learn about my future. I wished to experience magic and mystery, as in the stories where the young girl, Vasylyna, would go to see the witch, Baba Yaga, in the forest. Yes, like Vasylyna the Brave, I wanted an adventure.

So on the night of the new moon, I had Gypsies on my mind as I walked to the barn to leave an offering for the dvorovyi, the yard spirits. The early spring sky was heavy with stars to light my path. Around me, the howling of wolves and whirr of bat wings traveled on the wind. It had just become my task to leave the offerings, and even though I had watched Mama many times before, I was nervous. What if I did something wrong and the spirits allowed harm to come to the cattle?

I pushed open the heavy door and peered into the blackness, permitting starlight to wrestle with the shadows. Each corner held secrets: each shape shifted in the light. I could feel air on the back of my neck. Breeze or breath? I didn't check. As I walked through the barn, I cursed the crunch of my feet on straw. Sleeping spirits did not like to be disturbed. I did not want to find their glowing eyes peering at me in the darkness.

At the eastern corner, I stopped and knelt on the dirt floor. Hay cut into my bare knees; the smell of manure stung my nostrils. I lifted three slices of Mama's morning bread out of the napkin I carried and from my pocket, pulled out the sheep's wool I had gathered earlier that day. I cleaned a spot on the ground and set down the napkin, carefully placing on it the bread and wool.

I opened my palms above the offering. Then I focused for a moment on my breath, steadied my heart, and collected my voice. "Dvorovyi, friendly neighbors, I offer you these gifts."

I folded my hands, placed them in my lap, and closed my eyes. "Be kind to the cattle and sheep, and watch over them. I thank you."

I knelt in silence for a moment, hearing the scurrying of feet or claws or paws on straw. I listened to the door creak and bang against the barn wall, the soft neighing of horses, the distant chorus of creatures awakened by darkness. I could feel movement all around me.

A gust of wind rushed into the stable and caught in my hair, tossing it up and into my face. Still I remained seated with eyes closed, my hands motionless in my lap. Only when the wind ran away to other farms, when I felt the calm restored—only then did I open my eyes and rise to my feet.

I locked the door behind me and stepped toward the house. My fingertips tingled, and the air seemed lighter, brighter than before. I could not see the house from the barn. It was set back under the trees, but I saw smoke from the stove above the treetops. Mama was probably brewing tea. My stomach growled, and I hurried toward home knowing that Mama would be preparing a snack. But before I reached the house, the winds returned carrying with them beautiful violin music—music that suggested mystery and evoked the vorozhka and the magic of her camp. The music tempted me to follow. Tato and Mama would expect me to linger outside. "Our Nadya lives in dreams," they always said. So I could probably steal away unnoticed for a few moments. I turned away from the house and toward the wind, urged on by the music.

Running quickly through the trees, I found myself at the edge of the forest. As I stood hidden by thick branches, I saw a woman dancing in the shadows, a whirlwind of long layered skirts. Her blouse was buttoned to the neck, and rows of beads caught shades of crimson, copper and gold from the flames as they rose and fell in rhythm. The music mingled with the cries of the forest, carried by the winds into the trees to blend with the running waters of the nearby stream.

In the distance, a man stared into the woods and sharpened his blade, which shone ruby red in the firelight. Although I knew he could not see me, I suddenly remembered the stories Mama had told me about Gypsies who kidnap young women to sell into slavery in far away lands. I shivered, savoring the thought of strong arms carrying me into a Gypsy wagon filled with perfumes and silks and furs. I would be forced to travel to exotic places where people played with monkeys and rode on elephants. They would teach me to dance and dress me in long flowing silk gowns and gold chains. People would watch me and other women perform seductive dances, and they would shower our feet with coins and pearls. I would never have to dig in the dirt or clean up after the horses and cows. Mama and Tato would never again tell me what I could and could not do.

Mama and Tato! They would soon notice that I was gone. I turned away from the camp and faced the woods, angry for having to leave. How could this beautiful music be evil? This sad melody, so soft and familiar, that slid across my body and pulled at my chest with bittersweet secrets ... how could the music be "bad" when it filled me with dreams of dancing and adventure? And how could the woman who danced like flames on the wind be "dirty"?

Straining to keep the music with me as long as I could, I stumbled through the forest. It seemed to take twice as long to get home as it had to find the camp, but I wanted to remember each turn so I could find my way again. I went to sleep that night planning my visit to the vorozhka. My dreams were filled with clapping hands, stomping boots and music so powerful that it painted pictures in the clouds and lifted me to dance on air.

Intoxicated by the chords that danced in my memory, I waited impatiently for the next full moon, watching for the crescent to fill. When it finally absorbed all the milk of heaven, I lay waiting for my parents to go to sleep, watching as shadows poked their heads out from corners and then disappeared when I blinked them away.

I watched Mama and Tato's nightly rituals from across the room, all the while pretending to be asleep in the bed my sisters and I shared. At one time, four of us had shared the bed—before Maria, the oldest, married and died in childbirth. The little bed was still tight with three of us tucked inside, and I was always stuck in the middle.

Mama let down her hair and brushed it gently. Tato sharpened his knives for hunting. After he finished, he read Mama one of her favorite poems: "Seven Strings" by Lesya Ukrainka. Lesya's words gave me courage as I waited for my parents to sleep:

"I have faith in that magic, faith in those powers,
    Because with my heart I know them as true,
As oracle for these mysteries, these precious fantasies
    With my sincerest heart, I welcome ..."

My eyes grew heavy as I struggled to stay awake, lulled to sleep by Tato's voice and the sound of weary fingers rubbing against onion skin pages.

When I awoke, the room was silent except for occasional sighs of sleep. I carefully disentangled myself from my little sister Halya's embrace. She clung tightly to my waist, her head against my shoulder, as if I could keep her safe from the dreams that left her whimpering. I eased out of her arms and stepped onto the floor. Our little house had no room for secrets, so I moved with cat's feet to gather everything I needed. A cloud slipped away from the full moon and her light shone bright on my sisters' faces.

Laryssa lay on her side, facing the window. Little moans escaped her lips every few minutes, and she unconsciously wiped away strands of hair from her mouth and nose. Her beautiful long hair—brown with golden streaks from the sun—lay around her like Aunt Katia's hair when I found her drowned in the river. I shook away the memory and crossed myself for luck.

Halya lay curled in a ball, filling in the space I had left. Two tight, thin braids poked out from her head. She was sad that her hair was thin, like Tato's. I hoped she would not be troubled by the nightmares that usually interrupted her sleep. I wouldn't be there to hold her while she trembled, to sing her back into dreams if she awoke screaming.

Deep in my stomach I felt a tugging toward them, back into the warmth of the down blanket Mama made for us last Christmas. I had never disobeyed Mama or Tato before, and I hoped to return before they awoke. I had a question that drove my feet into boots warm from sitting beside the fire, a question that compelled my hands to wrap my babushka tightly around my head, a question that drew me deep into the night.

I stepped outside, clutching in my mitten the small black stone I had found on the riverbank after we buried Mama's youngest sister Katia. The night after her burial, I had convinced my older sisters, Maria and Laryssa, to take me to the river to offer flowers to the rusalky. According to legend, all drowned women would be transformed into one of these river spirits, beautiful maidens who bewitched passersby with their voices. I imagined Aunt Katia as a rusalka, face aglow with moonlight, delicate shards of music slipping off her tongue to pierce their hearts and lure them to their deaths.

While Maria and Laryssa leaned against the trees talking about how Mama could not sleep from grief, I set the flowers on the water. Then I saw the glittering stone on the bank, a piece of night sky filled with stardust that settled perfectly into my palm when I lifted it from the river. I felt Aunt Katia near me and heard silver bells on the waves, so I carried the stone home and set it beside our bed.

Although she did not tell me until I was older, Mama had a dream that same night. In it, Aunt Katia's ghost stood over my bed, touched my forehead and said, "This one hears my voice on the night air. I will watch over her."

Mama said that Aunt Katia would do all she could to protect me. I need only follow the river.

So I kept the stone with me for good luck, which is why I carried it the night I went to see the vorozhka. It rested in my palm beside a tiny gold earring I had found along the path to Sonya's house last month. The earring was going to be my payment for the vorozhka's fortunetelling.

After a last look at my sleeping family, I turned away, tightly clutching my black stone. I focused on that stone and on the moon lighting the path as I walked past the barn toward the woods. I remembered the stories Baba had told me while I sat on the floor watching her embroider beautiful red and black patterns on cloths; stories about the lisovyk who lived in dense forests. I could still hear her voice in my ear:

"Little Nadya, you must always be careful in the woods, because that is where the lisovyk lives, and he is a tricky spirit. Why, he casts no shadow! The light of the moon is swallowed in his long white beard. His blood is blue like the winter sky, so his skin glows with a deep blue light that you can see in the heavy darkness of the forest. His big green eyes will open wide when he sees you, and if you see him they POP out!

"Yes, yes, the lisovyk is tricky. He changes his size a hundred times in one night. One minute he is tall like the oak, and the next minute, he hides behind a mushroom. You will see the light flicker from his skin as he runs around the trees. He wears his clothes backwards and puts the left shoe on the right foot and the right shoe on the left.

"But do not laugh, my little mouse, because the lisovyk is proud. He will lead you in circles and make you lose your way in the forest. If this ever happens, listen to me, this is what you must do. Sit down on the trunk of an old tree. Take off all your clothes and put them on backwards. Put the left shoe on the right foot and the right shoe on the left. This is important, little one, do not forget the shoes. Only then will the lisovyk lead you where you want to go. But do not laugh at him if you see him, or you will be lost in the forest forever."

I smiled, remembering Baba Hanusia, Mama's mother, who lived with us until she died. I missed her stories and her warm hugs. As I passed the creek, I heard the murmur of water against the rocks, like whispering voices. I began to hum softly to myself so the rusalky who lived in the creek would not enchant me with their songs. Aunt Katia could not protect me from the spells of her watery sisters.

Luckily, Sonya had told me I would need to bring the vorozhka an offering. She also told me that the Gypsy woman would be sitting near the fire during the night of the full moon, because it was her job to keep the rest of the Gypsies safe on nights when magic was very strong. I clutched the stone in my mitten, trying to avoid the dark corners of the forest, which seemed to swell against the glow of the moon.

The hairs on the back of my neck rose, and an eerie silence grew from the shadows, broken only by my quiet humming. As the leaves broke their hold on the sky, I saw the shudder of a campfire, but no beautiful woman sat beside it. My eyes adjusted to the light as I watched flames twist around the wood. Smoke smeared my view of the camp into a haze. I tried to blink into clarity the smudged impressions of ragged horses beside wagons, paint flaked and peeling. In my ears, neighing blended with snores and sighs from nearby tents. I closed my eyes to savor the spiced breath of the night: spilled wine, woodsy musk, and budding night flowers.

Then behind me, fingers dug into my shoulders and spun me around. I struggled not to fall. I opened my eyes and saw the face of the Gypsy woman; the one I had seen dancing several weeks before, but somehow she looked different. Where were her beautiful clothes? She wore mismatched rags, like those my mother would sometimes wear around the house: a torn shirt of blue and white flowers, a skirt of red and yellow stripes. The colors, which may have once been bright, were now muted by blotches of dirt. Her hair hung in heavy clumps around her thin face. I dropped my gaze to her bare feet, so tiny. Smaller than little Halya's feet. How could a grown woman have such small feet? Then I noticed the blood.

Her feet were covered with scratches. The stains on her clothes were a mixture of dirt and blood, fresh blood that continued to spread across the dull patches of color. Her torn blouse revealed bruises on her neck and chest. And her face! Even in the dark, I could see blotches covering her cheeks, forehead and chin. What had happened to this woman? We had both walked alone through the woods.

I wanted to ask if she had been hurt, offer some kind of help. Should I extend my arm for her to lean on or give her the handkerchief tucked inside my boot? Instead, I stood in silence, staring into black eyes that watched me with contempt and rage.

She pushed me, then dropped her hold. Stepping back, she wrapped her arms around her chest and raised her head to stare into the night beyond my right shoulder. Firelight caught her features, and beneath the dirt and blood, I saw a plum crescent birthmark that stretched from the corner of her left eyebrow to the crease of her lips. I took a deep breath, and the Gypsy brought her hand to her face, catching my stare.

Baba told me to respect those who had been marked for a special life, even if the rest of the world hated and feared them. Baba would stretch the neck of her blouse open to show me the tiny brown foot-shaped birthmark on her shoulder—caused by the "guardian angel who stood there when she was born." The Gypsy had also been born with a sign setting her apart from the others, marking her for a life of fortunetelling and magic.

Russian words heavy with a foreign accent seemed to grow in her mouth until she was forced to gasp them out: "Why have you come here?" Avoiding my eyes, she stared above and beyond me. The only words I could mutter in my Ukrainian tongue were those I had practiced every night for two weeks while lying in my bed.

"I came to have my fortune told. Can you h-h-help me?"

The wind shifted, bringing her smell to me: sweat, blood, urine. Heavy scents, sour and metallic like those that filled the barn after Tato butchered runts of the litter. She exhaled deeply and rubbed her hands along her arms.

"Of course." She laughed to herself and looked up to the moon. "Of course that is why she came. To see the 'Gypsy' in the forest." Her hands smoothed her skirts and settled into fists.

"Are you frightened? Scared of the lady covered in blood?" She began to wave her hands in circular motions and lowered her voice to a raspy whisper. "Ooh, this 'Gypsy' must have been doing something 'bad' in the woods. Black magic. Maybe dancing with the dark god?" She stopped for a long second, then looked into my eyes.

"Are you sure you should be here, *gadji*?"

Fear blew through me, catching the cold in my bones, strengthening my shiver. For a moment, I heard Mama's voice as if she stood beside me: "Be careful, Nadya. Come home. Don't trust her, she is a Gypsy. It is all a trick. You will disappear into the night, and I will never see you again." I clenched my fists and bit my lower lip.

The vorozhka raised her eyebrows and took a step toward me. "What is the matter, peasant girl? Are you scared that I am going to have my brothers steal you?" She wiped blood off her lips, rubbed her eyes.

Then she stepped around me and closer to the fire. She was shivering. Dark circles hung under her eyes, and blood streamed in thin lines from the right side of her temple down her face. Her Gypsy face: hollow and full of shadows ... and young. Not much older than my Ukrainian face: lighter and rounder, surrounded by brown hair woven into one neat braid.

"That is all you girls come here for. To see the mysterious Gypsy camp. To have your fortunes told." She spit on the ground. "Your people only come here when they want something. Or someone to blame."

I stood watching her as she rubbed her hands up and down her arms, arms covered with fine, black hair. I whispered, "What happened?"

She lowered her eyes. Her voice angry as she mocked me: "What happened?"

Looking around, she calmed herself and lowered her voice. "What happened? New soldiers arrived in the neighboring village. They decided to explore the woods—"

"Soldiers," I interrupted, "What kind of soldiers?"

She looked into my eyes. Again the hairs on my neck rose.

"Soldiers are soldiers. They fight. Their life is war. And we ... what are we in war? Things to be moved, broken, used, thrown away, claimed by whichever side comes through our camp.

"My family, we travel far. We see how this war breaks people and land. We pass empty villages. We see pits they dig for bodies. We know the death smell." She rubbed her hands together. "We come here . . . to seek a quiet place. I went too far from camp."

She laughed bitterly. "I thought I would be safe in the woods."

I shook my head, not comprehending. She almost smiled.

"Poor stupid girl, you don't understand." Sighing heavily, she turned around to face the fire. I gasped when I saw the gash that divided her blouse in half, lines of blood criss-crossing like embroidery on silk. She continued, "Five of them. They threw me on the ground. Laughing. Shouting, 'You like it, Gypsy bitch. Bark for us. Lick it. This is your lucky night.'" Her voice cracked, and she shuddered. "I tried to bite them. Hit them. Scratch them. They beat me. Two held me down. They—"

Suddenly she turned around to face me, tears in her eyes. "Now do you understand?" She shook her head. "Probably not." The Gypsy picked up her skirts in her left hand and turned toward the river.

"Wait here, peasant girl." She wiped her face. "I am *drabarni*, a vorozhka. I will read your fortune." She looked around the camp. "But first I need to clean myself in your river. Be quiet. You do not want to wake my brothers."

She walked away.

I held my breath, feeling my chest tighten as I watched her walk into the forest. When she finally merged with the trees, I exhaled, my hands cupping my nose and mouth, afraid even to whimper. What if the soldiers were still nearby? What if her brothers awoke?

I sat down and looked around. Each time the moon crept out from the clouds, shadows darted along the campsite. Light would linger on dirty clothes and dishes arranged in strange, neat little piles. Firelight blurred with moonlight on the dull surfaces of the metal washtubs stacked beside an old maple tree. I looked around for cut wood for the fire but could not find any.

Such a woman, this Gypsy. So strong that she could gather up her skirts and walk to her family's camp with her head up, wiping away blood. Who was I next to her? She was right: I was only a peasant girl. What could have brought me away from the safety of my family?

Then I remembered why I had disobeyed Mama, why I had crept through these woods. I needed to ask the vorozhka if Stephan and I would marry.

He seemed so far away from me as I sat in the Gypsy camp, and I knew he'd be furious if he knew I'd come alone, especially if he knew about the soldiers. They must have been Russian. Tato had said he'd heard rumors that Russian soldiers planned to reclaim our land from the Germans, but he'd shrugged them away. Ever since the Germans had closed the schools and libraries, information from the outside had become more and more difficult to learn. So rumors hung on every tongue. But if they were Russian soldiers, I wondered how their return would affect Stephan.

I remembered how the German soldiers had come to our village two years ago during the hot summer. They gathered all the young men, including Stephan and his brother, for three weeks of "training." When he returned, Stephan wore a German police uniform, his eyes darker, heavier; scars on his hands and face. His brother never came back.

When Uncle Vasyl spat at him and called him a traitor, I could only clench my fists. Stephan's skin had lost its rosy color; the laugh lines had vanished from around his eyes, his lips. His "training" had silenced the music that once filled his face. After putting on that uniform, he never again picked up his guitar. I can't even remember him laughing. Never aloud, only chancing a few careful smiles with me. Stephan would not tell me what had happened then. Nor did he talk about his missions, when he would be gone from the village for weeks. I searched his scars for clues, peered into his eyes for pictures, but they never came. He was closed to me.

The flames began to die down to a flicker, and I thought perhaps I could gather wood for the fire. No sooner had I lifted myself up than I saw the Gypsy returning from the river, carrying firewood. As she walked to the camp, I was mesmerized by the thrusting, swinging motion of her hips. She led with her pelvis, in a motion both awkward and graceful. Small feet followed her hips through the grasses; her shoulders and arms an afterthought in movement. She was beautiful and terrifying. The vorozhka had a warrior's spirit. Baba had talked about it, told me stories of women who once rode the steppes with long swords strapped to their backs. After dying in battle, they would return to live a new life fighting for their freedom and their families. This Gypsy was such a woman.

She stopped beside me—near the dying embers—and put the logs on the fire, blowing the flames into life. Her clothes were wet but rid of most of the blood. Her hair smelled of the stream. I wondered how she had escaped the rusalky but did not ask.

I was puzzled by her calm. She stood aglow with fire that shimmered in her skirts, her fingers, her eyes, her hair. I wanted to touch her to see if she was real, embrace her and tell her that I was sorry for what had happened to her, but she frightened me. And she was proud . . . a vorozhka with the spirit of a warrior. I was only a peasant girl.

She leaned over me and pulled an embroidered shawl out of a dark satchel hidden beside a log. I was struck by how the scarlet and silver flowers on the black cloth shimmered in the light. She pulled the shawl tightly around her shoulders and picked up the satchel, tying it to her waist. Only then did she turn her gaze to me. "So, you are still here," she said bitterly. "My brothers did not find you and take you into the woods."

I stumbled on my words. "I'm sorry. I-I came to ask—"

She interrupted me. "About love, yes? All you girls running into the night aflame with love. Do you know that all around you trains carry people away? To be shot, burned, tortured." She sat in front of the fire and motioned for me to sit next to her. I could smell a perfume, like berries and mint, on the shawl. She continued. "Each girl thinks that time stops death for passion. Well, I will read for you, but my hands shake with what I know. If you saw with my eyes—" She sighed. "If you saw with my eyes, then you would seek different answers."

She rubbed her hands together over the fire. "First my payment, peasant girl."

I gave her the gold earring. She put it between her teeth, biting down. Then she lifted it closer to her eyes.

"This is all you have for me?"

I nodded, panic spreading through me.

"Very well. I will read for you."

She pulled a bundle from the satchel and unwrapped the scarlet silk cloth to reveal a deck of cards. She placed the silk on the ground in front of her and handed me the deck. I began looking through the cards, pausing to admire each one. They were beautiful, covered in pictures of kings and queens in fancy clothes. Only the icons in St. Sophia's Church could compare with the bright colors and gold on these hand-painted cards. Each one told a story, and looking at them, I felt carried away into another land.

The vorozhka placed her hand over mine and said, "No. Not for your eyes to admire. You would get lost. Just shuffle them back and forth, placing one hand over the other. Think about the question that drew you here."

I closed my eyes and pictured Stephan in his uniform swinging me around, his arms at my waist. Shuffling the cards, I remembered how he would wait outside my teacher's house to walk me home. I could feel my cheeks in a half grin as I thought of how handsome he looked in his crisp, dark uniform; his dark brown hair tossed about like stalks of wheat in the wind. I could smell his leather holster when I threw my arms around him. As he whirled me around and around, he would say in that deep voice, "My precious Nadya. What have you to share with me today?"

He would set me down and take my books in his arms, watching my lips as I told him the day's lesson, interrupting me with quick kisses, then urging me to continue. The right side of his lips would hint at a smile, the small hidden dimple almost revealed as I jumped about with excitement because I had learned a new thread of history or a new poem by Taras Shevchenko.

"Your face is on fire when you come back from your studies, Nadya." And he would draw in a deep breath. "You are so beautiful."

I would blush under his dark brown eyes. Baba used to say that dark eyes were enchanting; they held the magic of the night. Would I marry this man, spend my life with him?

The Gypsy again put her hand on top of mine, took the cards and started to lay them out on the silk in a pattern of lines and crosses. When I began to ask her a question, she looked at me sternly and put her finger to her lips.

"I need silence to tell your story, peasant girl."

I grew braver. "My name is Nadya."

"You are gadji, not Gypsy." She didn't look up.

I watched as the cards transformed into story on the silk before me, stained glass gods and goddesses glowing in the fire's light. She spoke their names as she turned each card over. They sounded like poetry or a prayer.

"Lovers. Queen of Swords. Star. Emperor. Page of Cups. Devil. Seven of Cups. Tower. Sun. Ten of Coins."

Then she closed her eyes. When she took my hand, I jumped. Her palm was cool and dry; mine was sweaty and warm. I realized I was holding my breath when my lungs began to hurt. I exhaled, watching her. The smell of coming rain hung in the air.

The vorozhka finally opened her eyes. She ignored a tear that fell down her cheek.

"My name is Liliana," she said. "I will read your fortune."

CHAPTER TWO

Liliana peered into my eyes. "Understand me, these are not tricks. Not games I play to take your riches." She held the gaze in silence, and then continued. "This is the story of your life. A story that unfolds in these cards painted for my mother by a man who loved her many years ago. A story that I see in these images, in your eyes."

"Let me explain this story as simply as I can. Nadya, your heart is filled with love and dreams of romance. You live in a world of fantasy, but your beliefs will soon be tested. Lurking nearby is tragedy, separation. Loneliness will chase away your hope. This is true, this will happen.

"In the future, I see warmth, stability, a large family. You will cling to them and give your heart to those you love. But first, there will be death and deception. A breaking away from your past.

"Nadya, you will need to walk away from here, but do not forget where you came from. You will need to learn how to open your heart again once the silence slips in. Remember how to forgive. Others *and* yourself."

Liliana squeezed my hand gently. "In the future, you will have a choice. You will find yourself completely shaken. Stand still, and you will die. Move forward, and you will find happiness."

I looked again at the cards before me, and out of the corner of my eye, I noticed rose streaks creeping from the east across the sky amidst dark clouds, violet in the light of the coming sun. If I didn't return home quickly, Mama and Tato would know that I had been gone all night. I stood up.

"Liliana, thank you."

She opened her eyes and nodded in my direction.

"Be careful, peasant girl. Yours is not an easy path. Those boots brought you here. They will carry you far away, but the steps you walk are familiar. Remember the roots of home, or you will always be searching. Remember, sometimes to leave is to find yourself."

We looked at each other in silence before I turned and walked quickly toward the forest. A few steps into the woods, I caught the smell of something distant burning and began running to my parents' farm.

I strained to see the source of the smoke, my heart beating fiercely in my chest. What could have happened while I was away? I left no candles burning. I had shut the door behind me.

My hand reached up to clutch the crucifix I had been given at my christening, and I gasped a prayer as I ran: "Guardian Angel, please watch over my family. Please keep them safe." I watched the sky through the leaves grow brighter as the sun began rising.

I smelled burning wood and flesh before I reached the end of the forest. Then I saw the barn being devoured by fire. Flames shot up from dark pools that reflected the sky. The barn's sides and bottom were already black; large holes revealed animals on fire. I watched smoke rush out; I saw cows and sheep trying to get through the flames. Those that tried to escape were pierced by sharp pieces of burning wood planks. Those that remained collapsed from the smoke. I could smell them as the flames consumed their flesh.

I stood paralyzed, listening to the animals scream. The deep moans of the cows as they fell to the ground. The cries of the sheep, like children. The sound of flames like raging, angry winds filled my mind. Where was my family? Why didn't they come to stop the fire?

Thoughts raced through my mind. Then I heard a voice like Aunt Katia's say: *Run away from there. Now! Get help.* And so I ran back into the woods. I headed south to the Bilyks' farm. They had five brothers who could help put out the fire. They would help us.

But when I got there, only ashes and the charred frame of their house and barn remained. I found no trace of the Bilyk family.

My knees collapsed, and I fell to the ground and wept. Even before I felt the rain, I heard large drops falling around me. Then cold taps covered me. I wanted to scream, to wail, but fear of more soldiers nearby held my voice in my throat. Instead, I clenched my fists and pounded them against the ground. Why had my prayers gone unanswered? Was it because I had disobeyed?

Thoughts kept rushing through my mind: pictures of Mama dead, blood trickling from her lips, clotting in her soft, brown hair. I had to get home. Why hadn't I checked on my family first? Why wasn't I thinking clearly?

My head was pounding, my stomach curling up. I felt like the world around me had become one of Halya's nightmares. Where was my family? Would I never see them again? Never feel Mama hug me, never hear her quietly sing, never see the wrinkles in her eyes when she laughed? A scream welled up in my throat, but I forced myself to stand up and walk back toward the house, hiding in the trees on the side of the road.

Maybe if I hadn't gone. Maybe if I had stayed awake, watching the moon, I could have seen the soldiers. What if everyone was dead? What about little Halya? Oh, God. Halya. I brought my hands up to wipe away the tears and the rain.

Suddenly I saw Stephan ahead of me, blocking the road to

the house. He stood in his uniform, his hands open to me, and I ran to him and collapsed.

"Oh God, Stephan . . . the fire, the barn." I couldn't get the pictures out of my head. I couldn't stop shaking. "Soldiers are here. Mama . . . she's dead. I know it. Stephan. Mama. Halya. Help them . . . we have to help them."

He stood there without words, holding me, but his arms felt stiff, his embrace not tight as usual. I pushed myself away and looked into his eyes, struggling not to fall, the mud slippery, my legs trembling.

"Say something." I threw my arms into the air and brought my hands down in fists. "Say something. My family is dead or dying, and you haven't said anything. We need to help them, Stephan. What should we do? Where should we go?"

"Nadya, we need to leave." He avoided my eyes. "The Russians are coming."

For a moment I stood there, not understanding his words. Coming?

"No, Stephan. They are already here. The barn, Mama—"

He shook his head and looked down at his boots.

"Oh, God." My stomach cramped, and I turned away to throw up into the bushes. I bent over clutching my stomach, the throbbing in my head even louder. If the Russians were not here yet, then it was the Germans who had burned down the farm. The Germans! I started to scream and beat my fists against Stephan. He grabbed me tightly and cupped his hand over my mouth. I bit him, tasting blood, but he continued to hold back my scream. I shook my head back and forth trying to free my voice.

"If you scream, then they will come for both of us." He waited a moment before releasing me. I stepped away from him.

"Why didn't you warn us? Why didn't you stop them? You wear their uniform. You must have known. How could you, Stephan? I—I could have been inside." I watched his face.

Nothing. No expression even in his eyes. Anger clenched my jaw and tightened my chest until I was speaking in gasps. "*I could have been inside, Stephan.*"

He went to hold me.

"Don't you touch me," I said, pulling away. "I don't know you."

"Nadya, I didn't know. They didn't tell us. As soon as I saw smoke, I ran to find you. When I saw the barn and house on fire—"

"The house? Oh, my God. I only saw the barn on fire. I have to get them out." I made a motion toward the house, but he grabbed my left arm.

"Nadya, I looked inside the house. I looked for you. Your family was taken away. There's nothing for you there."

"You saw them being taken away? Why didn't you stop them?" I tried to shake off his grip, but he held my arm firmly.

"I'm one man against twelve. I could do nothing. When I didn't see you being led away, I thought they had killed you. I thought you were dead, my Nadya." He pulled me to him, holding me tightly, but I stood there stiff. My head against his chest, I listened to his words, hearing his heart beating through his jacket, hating his uniform, and trying not to hate him.

"I looked in the house," he continued, "but you weren't there. I was going into the woods to look for you when I saw you coming down the path. My beloved Nadya, I'm so glad that you're alive."

I could say nothing. An emptiness settled into my chest that swallowed all the pain. I could only stand there and be held as the rain pounded on my face.

The line of time blurs with age, leaving only certain points pronounced in memory. The road from my parents' home is a fog of bitterness and regret, but the day Stephan was taken is painfully clear. We had been given shelter in a small Slovak village by an elderly couple who had lost their own son in the war. Jan and his wife Bozka allowed us to sleep in their barn in exchange for a few days' labor on their farm.

The evening before his capture, Stephan and I sat sipping burned coffee in the old couple's home. Until then, neither word nor affection had passed between us since we'd left my family's farm. He begged me to go outside with him, to talk away from the old couple's ears. How he pleaded, and he looked so ragged, stripped of the polish of his uniform. His pants were ripped at the knees; his shirt soiled down his back and under his arms.

When I finally agreed, we went outside and sat beneath a large fir tree. I was so afraid and felt so alone. I wanted the nightmare to go away.

Stephan had taken my hand. "Nadya, what would you have me do? I love you. I couldn't have stopped them. Are you going to damn me like everyone else?"

He looked so broken, so vulnerable that I wanted to kiss him then. Bury my face in his chest, have him hold me as everything else faded away.

"Nadya, did I choose to wear that uniform? Even though we buried it, I still feel it. I can't get rid of it."

He stroked the beard brought on by weeks of travel. I had never kissed him with a beard; he had always been cleanly shaven, his face smooth. This was not a face I knew. Everything was foreign now.

"Do you hear me? You just stare at me with those big green eyes like I'm a monster. I didn't kill your family. I have enough guilt without that on my head."

I clenched my fists. My family. Killed. As he watched. I wanted to spit in his face. Curse him for not saving them. Curse him for taking me away from everything.

"God, you can't imagine what I've seen. What I've been

forced to do. Nadya, I am so ashamed. I try to escape in dreams, but even they are filled with blood. So much blood on my hands." He buried his face in his hands, his fingers pulling at his hair. I wanted to scream and weep at the same time. Cry in his arms. Push him away.

I could smell his breath: mint and coffee. I wanted to take his hand, trace the scars on his wrist with my fingers. Rub my lips against the soft hairs of his arm.

"If there is a Hell, this war will fill it with people like me." Stephan looked at me. He had such long eyelashes for a man. I knew he wanted me to say something, do something.

But I did nothing.

Instead I watched the shadow of leaves on his thigh, his hand resting there, scars on his knuckles, his fingers. Scars he could not cover. The winds brushed through the long stalks of grass; they sounded like hushed murmurs. Like prayers.

While I sat staring into the hills, Stephan's fingers brushed against my lips. Part of me lay buried under the ashes of my family's barn. Yet, no matter how much I had tried to hide inside myself, I wanted so much to be touched, to feel alive. He was all I had now.

When I felt his fingers on my lips, I kissed them despite myself. Closing my eyes, I bent back my head and inhaled deep and long, taking in the sweetness of raspberries crushed underfoot and the dark, moist smell of sweat and dirt. His fingers lingered on my lower lip before sliding slowly down my chin, down the center of my neck, stopping at the hollow above my collarbone.

He leaned over and kissed me in a moment I wished would last forever because everything else faded away, but the old couple shouted for us to come back inside the house. Then the soldiers came. We tried to hide Stephan under the table, but they found him.

Laughter. Loud laughter as Soviet soldiers stood inside the old couple's house. Their faces were like my brothers. Not the angled, blond faces of the Germans, but brown Slavic faces: thick eyebrows, full lips, black hair. Calloused hands, nails caked with dirt. Smell of sweat and manure worn into their skin. Faces like Tato's. Like Stephan's.

Mixed up words in the Russian tongue: "Punish traitors . . . abandoned Motherland . . . liberate . . . dog hiding under table . . . worthless . . . traitor . . . good dog . . . broken but useful."

Then a whirl of fists and blood. Stephan thrown around the room, his face battered, his body beaten.

There is a story that some men have inside them a beast that comes out in rage or on nights of the full moon to eat human flesh, to terrorize villagers. I remember watching the soldiers' straight postures transform into those of bears and wolves as they pounded Stephan's face again and again. They grunted and growled, hitting Stephan in the chest, the belly, the back. And when he fell to the ground in pain, all three soldiers—snarling and spitting—continued to kick him.

Then the soldier with the crooked mouth slithered toward me. His breath was foul: alcohol and garlic. His lips were caked with food, spit, and dirt.

"Pretty little bird . . . hold her tight . . . good hips . . . firm breasts . . . fine stock . . . hold her . . . that's a good girl . . . open your eyes . . . such nice skin . . . I'll be back for you."

I watched from the doorway as the soldiers dragged Stephan down the path. The hair over his left ear was matted with blood, which trickled down his neck and soaked through his shirt collar like sloppy embroidery.

The last to leave was the commander, who turned and smiled at me. "We'll be back for you, little bird." Then he slammed the old wooden door behind him. I stepped up to open it, but Jan reached across me and bolted it shut.

In shock, I stood for a moment looking at the wood grain. There were faces and animals. I could see an entire story hidden in the tree that became the door of this old couple's home. I wondered if either of them had ever seen the characters in the wood.

"Come, girl." Bozka put her arm around my waist and nudged me gently to the table. "Poor girl. Come sit down, and I will brew you some fresh kava."

As I walked, I cradled Stephan's overcoat. It was all I had left of him.

Jan sat down at the table and turned to his wife.

"Let her be," he said, shaking his head. "They take her husband out to be killed, and you serve her coffee?"

Not my husband, I thought. I had used Stephan's name so they wouldn't separate us. I decided then to never again use my father's name. I wanted no harm to befall my family if they somehow survived. The Russians would not connect them with a daughter who had run away with a German policeman. Even if that police officer was later taken away by Soviet patriots in a remote Slovak village. How could they know?

I allowed myself to be led to the table by the old woman and sat down in the same spot as before. Before the soldiers came. Before they took Stephan away.

Bozka glared at her husband. I looked at Jan, who had seemed to shrivel as the soldiers exited. His shoulders slumped, his head sunk down and his hands trembled even more as he pulled out his pipe.

"You do not know that they will kill him," Bozka hissed while preparing the coffee. "They talked of digging ditches."

Jan began to refill his pipe. "Don't talk fairy tales, wife. You know what it means. We've seen the graves. You've seen them." He looked at me. "You should know what happens. So you don't wonder. Forget about hope."

I felt a chill. The icy wind still circled even though the door was shut.

"First, they tell the men to dig deep ditches. Next, they order them to strip—"

"Jan! This is not the time—"

Time. I had no more time. Soldiers took that and everything else away from me. And always excuses to cover the graves. First, the Russians killed Dido and Uncle Ivan. Not starvation, they said. Collectivization. A plan. Always a plan. What excuses for the Germans who murdered Mama, Tato, Laryssa, and Halya? And now, again, the Russians. Now they took away Stephan.

Time. Where was my past? My future? The vorozhka was right. What are we in war? Things. To be used. Broken. Thrown away. I had no more time. I had nothing. I couldn't even feel anything. Just dead inside.

"Shut up, Bozka. She should know the truth. She is alone now." Jan stared at me.

I looked down at Stephan's coat. Why did I let him leave it with me? He would need it out there. I was warm in this little house. I pulled at my ripped blouse trying to bring the two sides together.

"I'll sew that for you, dear," the old woman said, noticing my efforts.

"Don't interrupt me, wife," Jan said. "Listen to me, girl. The soldiers will order them to strip. Then tell them to turn around and face the ditches—"

Feeling the ache in my right eye, I gently touched the bruise on my cheek. There was a little blood on my hand when I pulled it away.

"Then they are shot. They have dug their own graves. Unless the soldiers use their swords. That is how they killed our son. But he was one of the Hlinka Guards."

I looked under the table and realized what a tiny spot it had been for Stephan to hide in. He must have been cramped, especially with his bad knees. How could we have thought they wouldn't find him there? Even with the tablecloth, it would be the most obvious hiding place. Poor Stephan.

Jan pounded his fist on the table, "Listen to me, girl. Listen to me because I know about war and death. The man you love is gone. Forget him now, or he'll haunt you forever."

He shook his finger at my face, "You can sit there silently for now, but you better let that pain out. Cry if you have to. Scream if that's what's inside. Don't let those bastards take away your voice."

He glared at me, then reached out for his wife's hand. Bozka walked over and took it.

"War brings death too soon," he said. "Get used to it. You are alone now."

I rested my elbows on the table and buried my face in my hands. I had been alone since I left Mama and Tato to see the vorozhka. Even on the long road here to Slovakia—even with Stephan walking beside me—I was alone.

Bozka whispered, "Jan, enough."

I saw the spilt coffee on the ground, coffee the soldiers had spilled when they ripped the cloth off the table. I reached over to lift up a rag from the corner. After carefully hanging the overcoat on the back of the chair, I knelt down beside the table and dabbed at the small puddles.

The cottage air suddenly seemed too thick, the tobacco too heavy, the voices too familiar. I stood up, reaching again for Stephan's coat.

"I need to go outside." I said, aching for the openness of sky.

"It's the middle of the night; you shouldn't go alone," Bozka said in protest.

"I am alone." I unlocked the door and walked outside.

I spread Stephan's coat beneath the silver fir and lay on top of it, curling into the fabric, the smell of him mixing with grass and raspberries. It was all I had now, all that was left of him. We had shared our final kiss in that spot.

Out of the old couple's cottage came the smell of boiling raspberries and coffee. I watched a black griffin fly overhead, toward gray branches on the hillside, standing out against the sky like poetry. Baba said that Mother Earth gave us messages in her work, omens in her creation. Most people just didn't read the signs, she said. But what of those gnarled letters against the night? I looked longer and they spelled my mother's name. Or was it mine?

I lay my cheek upon the earth, listening. Around me grasses whispered, winds exhaled through leaves, bushes shook off heavy sighs. The gentle hush . . . a lullaby. Like the songs my Baba used to sing. To make me feel safe. To chase away my night frights. To remind me that death could have a gentle face.

When Baba Hanusia was dying, she came to stay with us. I was young and didn't really understand. I knew Baba was sick, but I thought she would get better. One night, after everyone else had gone to sleep, I jumped out of bed and crept over to Baba, who lay sleeping—still except for the deep cough which scratched through her throat every few minutes. Slipping under the warm blanket made for her by her mother, I tried to wrap my arms around her but I could not reach. Instead, I wrapped my left arm lightly around her neck. I lay my head on her chest and listened to her heartbeat. The sound was so big, like the rumble of a warm summer storm. It was everywhere. She was everywhere, and I was safe.

As she opened her eyes and felt my hug, Baba smiled.

"Why aren't you sleeping?" she asked, brushing her hand against my long hair.

"Because I wanted to sleep with you," I whispered. Then I began to cry.

"What's the matter, little mouse?" she asked, then coughs shook her body.

Trying to hold the tears back with tiny fists, I said as calmly as I could, "Mama said you're sick."

"Shh." She pulled at my chin. "Stop crying. Sit up and look at me. Sit up."

I pulled away from her and tucked in my knees, my fingers tightly clenched together. The silence of the room brushed up against my bare arms, my neck, my chest, and I missed the drum beat of her heart filling up my ears.

Baba sat up a little in bed and reached her arm around my waist, pulling me closer.

She cleared her throat and whispered, "Little mouse, I've told you a lot of stories, no? Stories of princes and devils, foxes and bears. Stories of rusalky and werewolves and Baba Yaga."

"I love your stories, Baba. Please tell me one now. Tell me a story to make the bad dreams go away?" I asked, nuzzling into her neck.

"Nadya, I don't have time—"

"Baba, please," I begged. "Just one. A quick one, please."

"All right," she sighed, "but it will have to be very quick. Now listen carefully, this is the story of Valentyna and the mountain.

"Once there was a young girl named Valentyna, whose family lived beside a large mountain. Every day before she did her chores, Valentyna would stand at the bottom of the mountain and wish that someday she could reach the top.

"All day while she worked in her Tato's fields, Valentyna would sing songs about the mountain, about how she could kiss the moon and touch the stars if she reached the very tip. Her sisters would laugh and make fun of poor Valentyna, because all they thought about was playing games, singing and dancing with boys."

Baba stopped for moment as coughing once again shook her.

"As she grew up, Valentyna never lost her dream. She would tell beautiful poems and stories about the people who lived at the top of the mountain, about the strange animals who would dance with the cloud spirits when no one was looking. People would come from all the nearby villages to hear her songs and poems. They would sit around a campfire at the foot of the mountain and listen as Valentyna painted pictures with words."

Baba's voice was soft, like her round cheeks, like the hanging skin beneath her chin that I liked to touch. And when she spoke, the air seemed lighter, the room less frightening.

I waited for her to continue, but when she didn't, I asked, "Baba, how does it end? What happened to Valentyna? Did a prince find her? Did she meet a bear? What happened?"

Baba smiled at me. "Because Valentyna found her voice, she told beautiful stories that brought magic into the lives of the villagers. Soon many people began to dream about climbing the mountain."

"Did they? Did she? Did Valentyna climb the mountain?" I asked, squirming with anticipation.

"Valentyna did climb the mountain, and others followed her." Baba stopped to cough again.

"But what did she see? What did she find at the top?" I asked, impatient for the ending.

"What do you think she saw?" Baba asked me in return.

I closed my eyes for a moment and imagined the top of the mountain.

"She saw a horse with wings dancing with a dragon. And on top of the horse sat a beautiful prince, the prince of the mountain. He married her, and they lived in a beautiful castle. They had lots of cake and coffee. And she didn't have to do her chores because he knew magic. Oh, and her whole family came up to live with her, even her mean sisters. And her Baba, too."

Baba laughed and laughed. "Very good, Nadya."

Then her heavy coughing rocked against my small body. I opened my eyes, suddenly scared.

"Baba? Baba, are you okay? Stop coughing. Stop it!"

Her coughing fit ended and she frowned at me, but her voice was gentle. "Nadya, I can't stop it. I'm dying. I'm going away. Just like my own Baba had to go away."

I wiped sweat off her brow with the cool rag that lay beside the bed.

"Then I'm going with you," I said stubbornly.

"No, little one, you can't come. Not now. But I want you to know a part of me will always be inside of you, right here." She tapped against my chest.

"But who will tell me stories?"

"Nadya, I've told you many stories. Someday you will tell them. But remember. Remember that stories are more than just words, more than fairy tales. They are magic."

Her voice grew softer, and she looked behind me to a dark corner of the room where Dido Mykola's fiddle sat against a pillow. "Stories, they are songs that carry us to dreams."

Then her eyes opened wide. I heard a quiet thread of violin music coming from the corner.

Baba smiled and hummed along with the melody. Then she spoke in the direction of the violin: "Mykola, welcome. How handsome you look." She stared off into the dark corner. "Ah, how we used to sing under the stars. You would smile at me while you played, and I would dance with my sisters. But really only for you. My dance was only for you."

I suddenly smelled lilacs, but there were none in the house.

Baba's face flushed pink. "Thank you, they're lovely. You always brought me lilacs. Oh, their smell would fill Mama's house. And I knew I loved you when you first said my name, and then we danced. I loved to dance with you."

For a moment, she seemed to remember that I was there and

looked toward me and said, "Your Dido Mykola. Remember. Remember us." Then she looked back toward the corner and whispered, "I will dance with you, Mykola."

Her head fell to the side, and the music stopped, but the smell of lilacs lingered. I lay down beside her again, my head against her chest, listening. But the silence had filled her up inside.

I cried myself softly to sleep.

CHAPTER THREE

The morning after Stephan's capture, Bozka woke me with the gentle nudging of her slipper. I had fallen asleep outside, curled in Stephan's coat. Sometime during the night, someone had covered me with a warm, woolen blanket.

"Wake up. Wake up. It's morning. The soldiers will be back soon. Come inside and eat." She held up a string of sausage and some cheese. "You have a long day ahead. You need to wash and eat."

"Thank you, but I'm not hungry." The thought of food brought clenching pains to my belly.

"Really, you should eat." She shook the sausages closer to my face. The smell of garlic . . . her face shifted for a moment. It changed into the soldier's face, spit clinging to his lips and stretching from my cheek. I sat up quickly, wrapping my arms around my chest.

"Stephan? The soldiers." I shook my head as images flashed before me. Mama? Baba? I wanted to go home.

"Gather your wits about you. I'll pack this food for later."

Bozka then sat down across from me on the grass and began to explain her plan for my escape. She had a rich cousin who had married a German merchant at the beginning of the war. They lived in a large house a few miles away. The cousin's husband had connections in Germany with several work camps that were looking for young women to work as housekeepers and in factories. Because I was young and pretty, she was sure that I could get a job working in one of the German officers' homes. In a few hours, the old woman would take me to her cousin's house, and from there I would board a train to Germany. Even further away from home.

I allowed Bozka to usher me onto the train car without even thinking about where I was going or what I would do, but I left the sack of food behind. I didn't want anything from that place, nothing to remind me.

The train to the camps was filled only with women. The one I remember most was an old Ukrainian they called Baba Lena, who sat across from me eating a loaf of bread that she had pulled out from under her skirt. From a crack in the wood behind me, moonlight slipped into the car to light up Baba Lena's face. She cradled the bread, rested her hands on her knees, her legs drawn close to her chest, her shoulders hunched over, and eyes staring only at her polished black boots. Man's boots. Soldier's boots.

She ate without a breath, without offering to share even as the young mother beside her cradled her starving baby and whimpered. Baba Lena took no notice of the other skeletal shadows, the growling bellies, the smell of urine and vomit, the cries of the young children. She sat eating the small loaf for hours, taking the tiniest bites and chewing each one many times. Never lifting her head above the bread. Never lifting her eyes. Sometimes in between bites, I saw the saliva between her lips catch the light and glisten like a web.

When only crumbs were left hidden in her palms, I watched her tongue, cat-like, dart out and lift the smallest specks into her mouth. And after they too were gone, she licked her palms over and over and over, in between each finger, sucking on each fingertip. Then she licked her lips and lifted her head up and back against the wall of the train car.

"I have lived long enough to be selfish," she said to no one. To everyone.

The young mother beside her cursed her and wept. I tried to see her baby, who had stopped crying a short time earlier, but the darkness kept her hidden. When a bump bent the moonlight in her direction, I saw that the child's eyes were open, staring but not blinking. The mother continued to cry and coo.

I turned back to Baba Lena, who was now staring at me from beneath large white eyebrows that stood out against her dark skin. She smiled. Once again licking her lips, she asked aloud: "You think I'm a witch, a Baba Yaga, for eating while babies die of hunger?"

Baba Lena scratched at the babushka that covered her head and answered herself: "No."

She stopped and closed her eyes. After some time, she fell asleep, her lips open to release a series of gurgles and rasps. Another large bump woke her, and as she shook her head, she continued: "When you are old, you deserve to eat and sleep. You earn this with age; you earn this with all your deaths."

As she spoke, Baba Lena bobbed her head back and forth with the rhythm of her words. "You are young, all of you. Death is still new, still fresh. I have died hundreds of times. With my parents, my brothers, my sisters, my husband, my sons, their sons. I died in the first big war when my brothers never came home. I died when they took away our land. I died when soldiers stole our cows, our pigs, our barley. I died when they shot my granddaughter for trying to pick up a single grain of wheat in the dirt. They hung her on a fence post as a warning.

"I died when we had nothing left but the cats. I died when the dead filled the streets with stink. I died when no one was left alive in the village except for me and my son, who was blind.

"So I fed him the only meat there was. The only food the Russians left for us. This was before the second war. My son did not know what he ate. I choked down the flesh I cooked. There was nothing else left. Then some people came and told us it was over. Stalin had had enough. They asked how we survived. I lied.

"I have died hundreds of times. I died when this war took my last son. Yesterday, soldiers took him from the Slovak village. Then they raped me, again and again. An old baba is still a woman, they said. So again I died.

"This bread I ate, they spat on and threw at me when they were finished."

She began to laugh over and over again. I closed my eyes and tried to think of something else, but she kept cackling. I covered my ears, and even that did not stop the laughter. Eventually she fell back asleep.

"I sat bundled in Stephan's overcoat, my arms wrapped around my stomach trying to still the rumbling of my belly. Why had I refused Jan's wife's bread? Reaching into the tiny secret pocket in my skirt, I pulled out my good luck stone. I placed it in my mouth, trying to remember not to bite down and break my teeth.

The black stone felt cool and smooth on my tongue and tasted of the spring water from where it came. I could taste the sweat from my own hands, having held the stone for hours and hours. It was all I had left from home. The Russian soldiers had ripped the crucifix from my neck after they tore open my blouse.

When the young mother began to eye me suspiciously, I slipped the stone from my mouth and replaced it in its hiding place. I could not fight her for it.

I became aware of a quiet shuffling sound. I looked to my right, where another young Ukrainian girl sat. Blond curls lay flat against her face, her cheeks round in contrast with her thin body. She sat with her eyes closed, head leaning against the train wall. Her clothes were dirty and ripped—like those of many women on the train—but she wore a pair of dainty black gloves. The rustling came from her hands, which she kept rubbing together over and over again. A sound that became soothing, and when it stopped, I noticed she had fallen asleep.

Soon she began to cry out softly, mumbling, "No, Juliek . . . Papa . . . come with us . . . not without you . . . "

Baba Lena opened her eyes and glared at the sleeping girl, who continued to whimper quietly.

"Jewess." Baba Lena sputtered. Then louder: "Jewess!" She pointed and stared. Around the girl, people began to pull away until only Baba Lena and I remained sitting near her. The others sat even closer together, smashed to one side of the car to stay away from the sleeping girl. Under her breath Baba Lena began to chant "dirty Jewess, dirty Jewess, dirty Jewess" over and over and over again.

A Polish woman on the opposite side of the car shouted, "Shut up, old woman! They will take us all away." Baba Lena stopped but continued to glare.

I looked over at the girl, who was finally awake and staring at the other women. "I am Ukrainian," she whispered. Still the others stayed away from her.

Then she looked at me, eyes pleading. "I am Ukrainian." She couldn't have been much older than Halya, maybe thirteen or fourteen years old.

Not knowing how to respond, I nodded.

Baba Lena laughed, a loud laugh that shook her old body.

Suddenly, something in the girl snapped. I recognized the look in her eye, and the hairs on my neck rose, a shiver on my shoulders. Her eyebrows gathered together, thick wrinkles formed on the bridge of her nose. Her lips curled and pulled back to show perfectly straight, white teeth that she gritted tightly together. She stared at the old woman.

"You are not the only one to face death," she said slowly, each word heavy in her mouth. Then she brought her lips together and spat in Baba Lena's direction. Baba Lena just smiled.

The girl straightened her thin shoulders and looked at me.

She motioned for me to move closer. I was terrified.

"Sit here," she said.

When I didn't move she said "Please" and motioned for me to face her, my back to the other women. "Please block them from my sight."

For some reason I did, although I hated to have my back to anyone. Maybe it was because she reminded me of my sister. Maybe because I was drawn to her strength, that flash of warrior spirit in her eyes as she faced Baba Lena. Maybe I did it because I was so lonely.

After I sat down, something in her face softened. Again she looked so young, so frail.

"Thank you," she said, and tears began to stream down her cheeks. She didn't move to wipe them away.

"I am ... so tired ... of fighting." She shook her head. "So tired ... of all this."

She coughed and turned her head away. The coughing didn't stop, and she lifted to her mouth a discolored handkerchief with "Miriam" embroidered on it in tiny blue stitches. When she took it away, it was stained dark red.

"Will you listen?" she whispered. After looking behind me around the car, I nodded.

"I'm dying," she said. Again I nodded. I could smell death on her now. It clung to her, sweet and metallic.

"I want someone to know." She brushed damp blond curls away from her face, and then began rubbing her hands together. Again the soft rustling sound.

"So much," she exhaled. "So tired."

She looked at me for a moment, at my face, and frowned. "I'm called Miriam," she said.

Cocking her head to the right, she stared at my eyebrows, my forehead. How hard she stared with those deep blue eyes. Then she looked down at my hands. The rustling stopped as she reached out to take my hands in hers, holding my palms upward. The gloves were stiff and coarse against my skin.

Time passed, and all she did was look down, exhaling heavy breaths and shaking her head.

"Ukrainian hands," Miriam said. "Ukrainian hands. Calluses on your fingers, your palms. Strong hands." She held them, but her grip was so weak. She kept her eyes on my palms and said, "You see, everything can be seen in the hands. Future. Past. It's all there. If a man's hands are graceful and thin, his nails too long and well-groomed, if he always rubs his thumb against his fingers, then his nature is that of a fox. He will be crafty and cruel." Miriam continued to stare at my fingertips.

"I saw it when he pushed open the door," she continued. "His hands were thick and hairy like a black bear. After he entered, they rested always in fists."

"They took me and Mummy outside. The one with bear hands tried to kiss me. I spat in his face, tried to gouge his eyes. I had long beautiful nails, strong. They left a deep scratch on his face. He slapped me, grabbed my wrists, and walked me over to the fire."

At this she let go of my hands and pulled off her black gloves. The effort brought tears to her eyes. She winced and asked, "Do you see? Look at mine, do you see?" I stared at the black wrinkled flesh. It didn't look like skin at all. It reminded me of burned meat, dry and dark.

"He held my hands in the fire," Miriam said. "I saw skin melt away . . . the smell . . . then pain. I fainted. When I woke, I was naked . . . bleeding . . . burned. Mummy lay next to me . . . dead."

"Your hands." She looked first at her own and then mine. "I can see so much in the way you keep them in your lap, fingers curled round each other, the way you were cradling your stone. You have gentle hands, small but strong; your nails short but thick. Yours are the hands of a female wolf, loyal and fierce, and kind." Miriam reached for her handkerchief and coughed again. More blood.

The wind carried wisps of thick black smoke through the car, the scent of death. It was like the smell around my parents' burning barn, but stronger, thousands of times stronger. Even the sleeping women gasped and coughed.

Miriam stiffened and put the gloves back on her hands. We took turns peering out through the crack in the wall. I saw only the sky filled with thick black smoke. Miriam shuddered and began to rub her hands together again.

"It's just a factory," I said.

"No, it's not," she whispered.

We sat there in silence for what seemed like hours, the only sound the rustling of her gloves and her occasional coughs. Only after the smell finally faded away did she speak again.

She told me about her rich family in New York City, America. Her mother used to write letters to her Uncle David, who owned his own business. Miriam told me about this strange new place. To pass the time. To keep our thoughts away from death and darkness.

"How wonderful it is there. Everyone is rich. They have stores filled with fruit and vegetables, apples and pears and exotic fruits, like oranges and coconuts. They have moving pictures, fancy cars. You can go to dinner and sit next to a movie star or the president. Everyone is equal. It's heaven." Miriam got very quiet, spoke in a tiny voice. "I can get my hands fixed there. I can play piano again. Draw. Feel things."

She blinked back tears. "I miss feeling things."

I held her gloved hand as she talked. I had never known anyone who lived in America. I didn't know much about it, except for rumors about Hollywood that Sonya had heard from her Aunt Sophia. As long as Miriam talked about this magical place, she filled my head with new dreams to replace the nightmares of the past few weeks. As long as she kept talking, I didn't have to think about Stephan or Mama or Halya. I could live in her words.

Miriam died in my arms the night we arrived at the camp. What had the vorozhka foretold? Tragedy. Loss. Separation. It all came true.

CHAPTER FOUR

When I rode away on that train, I vowed never to return to Ukraine. I arrived in Germany with the understanding that I would find a new life somewhere else. I had no idea what that new life would look like, but I knew it could not include my past.

I never imagined that fifty years later, someone from home would try to find me. I never anticipated that anyone could be alive who would remember.

"What's that burning, old woman?" Pavlo asked, shuffling up behind me, "One would think that after seventy years on this Earth, you would know how to cook eggs without burning them."

The ham and eggs on the stove were ash shadows of breakfast. Again my daydreaming had distracted me. I reached for the spatula to scrape the charred bits into the trash as my cat, Khvostyk (named for the cat I had had as a child) stood by and waited for me to drop bits of ham on the floor. After thirteen years, he knew that I hadn't the best aim.

"Old man," I said without turning around, "one would think that after more than fifty years, you would give me at least one morning of peace and quiet. These eggs are not for you; they're for me. I like my breakfast crispy, or have you forgotten?"

He chuckled and smacked me on the behind before sitting at the kitchen table. Knowing he would reach for the basket of pompushky I had baked the night before, I turned around and said sternly, "Those are not for you, Pavlo. Taras and the kids will be coming by after church tomorrow, and I want to have some treats and coffee ready for them."

He put back the pompushok and reached for his lighter. "Well, how much longer then?"

"Long enough for you to slowly kill yourself with your morning cigarette. I've always wanted to be a widow. So glamorous, like Elizabeth Taylor." I knocked on the wooden cutting board beside the sink; better not to tempt fate. But Pavlo didn't react, and I watched him slowly rise from his seat and walk to the washroom. "Besides," I continued, "it's been one year since Marko Somovych's wife died, and he'll be looking for another bride soon. He says I make the best varenyky."

"He wouldn't have you, Nadya." Pavlo reached for the blue and yellow bathrobe hanging on the inside of the door—a gift from the grandchildren last Father's Day. "Marko's looking for a younger woman, not an old bag like you. Besides, all of your junk wouldn't fit in his tiny house." He winked at me and went out onto the porch.

"Pat down your hair; you'll scare the neighborhood kids." I shouted out the window, but he didn't hear me. I saw his new hearing aid sitting on the window sill.

Of course his "morning cigarette" was really three or four, so I had plenty of time to cook up his breakfast before he began to get anxious again.

I cracked two more eggs into the skillet, put on some ham, and placed rolls to warm in the stove. After a restless night, I had overslept and felt unsettled. I usually woke long before my husband and savored the time to myself. Instead I felt rushed trying to prepare his breakfast when I hadn't even had my first cup of coffee.

I didn't like it when my morning routine was interrupted. It made me feel anxious. Each morning, I would brew a pot of coffee, then walk to my icon corner, where Pavlo and I had hung the icons we bought with our first paychecks. In the Ukrainian tradition, a couple's parents usually gave them a set of icons for their wedding and new life together, but all of our parents were dead when we married, and we never had a blessing ceremony. I had embroidered ritual towels to drape over the icons, each covered in black and red stitches that formed the Tree of Life. This little corner was the heart of our home, a spiritual connection to Ukraine and the life we had left far behind.

I walked to the icon corner, lit a candle in front of Mary, and thanked her for my health and the health of my family. I asked her to watch over my children, and then reflected on an upsetting dream that lingered in my memory. When I was a child, my mother taught me that dreams carried messages. As I stood before the icons, I recalled my dream about three spiders weaving a web in the corner of my bedroom. I had watched the spiders work together to create a beautiful web that eventually stretched from one side of the room to the other. When they were done, the smallest spider ate the larger two, landed on my chest, and stared into my eyes. She was crawling toward my throat when I woke up.

What was my message? Clearly I was being warned of something.

I stood for a moment in silence, offered thanks, and then chose my hand-decorated "Baba" mug from the cupboard—a gift from one of my grandchildren. I didn't always pick the same mug; it depended on my mood. I had a few to choose from. If I needed strength, I chose the Kitchen Goddess mug that my best friend, Ana, had given me. When I was feeling sad, I drank from the grey, chipped mug I had "accidentally" taken home from my first job at the factory.

Checking back on the eggs, I thought about Pavlo, who was smoking his precious cigarettes in his beloved garden. I thought about his kiss and crooked smile, the raised mole on his shoulder and the way he lifted his eyebrows when he was being coy.

Sadness made my breath catch in my throat because I remembered what it was like to be in love. I remembered another man, another lifetime, another passion. I remembered how that ache hollowed me out inside. How different from the quiet, comfortable affection I felt for my husband.

I brewed some coffee and turned the flame off the eggs and ham. I didn't want to risk another burned breakfast. I had so much cleaning and cooking to do before Palm Sunday. I looked back at the pile of papers on the table. No matter how much I cleaned and sorted, the pile kept growing.

There were bills, a letter from the church, and some advertisements. Underneath them all was an envelope addressed to me. The return address—scribbled in faded blue ink—was a village in western Ukraine; it did not include a name. The tiny farming village was not on many maps, but I recognized it because it was where I was born. My hands shook as I turned the envelope over. It was opened; the letter missing.

Stephan?

He was dead. I tried to push the name, the face, and the emotions out of my head, as I had done for half a century.

But who? I couldn't imagine who had sent it or why. No one there knew me anymore. No one had seen or heard from me since I was sixteen years old. There was no one left alive to remember.

I ran my fingers along the edge of the envelope, tracing the letters: my name, my address, VIA AIR MAIL printed on the front. I put it between my hands and closed my eyes. I slid the paper in between my palms, trying to feel something of the hands that held it, that wrote my name. Who could be left alive to remember me?

I assumed that the Ukrainian Post must have opened the letter, suspecting that its contents somehow threatened the Russian Mafia? Or perhaps money or secrets being transferred?

Neighbors who had recently traveled to Ukraine had talked about the Black Market and about Communists afraid of Western interference. Anything evoking suspicion could trigger their wrath. Some things don't change much, even after fifty years.

I worried that whoever sent it was in danger, although that was probably why they hadn't written their name on the envelope. The question remained: Who could have sent the letter?

The coffee maker dripped and sizzled, releasing wisps of earthy scent, like honey and burning wood. My hands shook a little as I carried the envelope to the cabinet above the coffeemaker, and hid it inside the cedar box I kept next to the tea boxes. The box was a handmade gift from Pavlo on the one-year anniversary of our arrival in America. Inside it, I kept a few precious objects: some seeds, my black river rock, and my son Mykola's dog tags.

Pavlo would be finished with his cigarettes at any moment, and I didn't want to share the envelope with him. What would I say? What could I say? I had never discussed my past with him. He knew only of my time in the camp, the time right before I met him. It was enough.

I put Pavlo's food on a plate and said a tiny prayer over his breakfast. The prayer made me feel better, especially after the letter. I found comfort in rituals—small acts repeated with intention to remember, to reflect, and to renew. Some were traditions that I had learned from my Mama and Baba; others I adopted on my own over time. I realized long ago that rituals made me feel connected when I otherwise felt alone. They connected me to my family, to my homeland, to God, the Blessed Mother, the saints, and all the spirits and angels. I tried to share my rituals with my children and grandchildren, but I'm afraid that most will be forgotten. So much will be lost.

I set the plate on the table and sat down with my coffee. I was fighting my urge to rush back to the cupboard and pull out the envelope again. I wanted to see if I missed something, a clue or an echo. Who could have sent it? Why now after all this time? So much had been lost. I stopped myself. What difference did it make? It was just an empty envelope. Nothing more. It didn't mean anything.

On Palm Sunday, I expected all our kids and grandkids to pour through the house after church. Except for my youngest daughter, Ivanka, and her husband, Roman, who were on their honeymoon in Germany. A honeymoon in Germany seemed to me as ridiculous as a vacation in Siberia, but it was their life, not mine. I had never had a honeymoon, never took a vacation. The only trips I had made were running away from the past, away from home, and away from myself. But maybe the past had finally caught up with me.

Pavlo tapped me on the shoulder. The familiar musty smell of Marlboros should have alerted me to his return to the kitchen. Hopefully his breakfast wasn't too cold.

"Nadya, what's the matter?" He patted the top of my head before sitting down at the table.

"Nothing; I'm fine. Just thinking."

Pavlo took a bite of his ham. He nodded with approval.

"Perfect," he said.

The smell of cigarettes was heavy on his breath. Although I would never tell him, I was thankful for the familiar scent—earthy like bark and grass and mud, thick and rich. It was a smell that grounded me.

My mother once told me that you know you are in love when you can watch a man eat heartily and not get disgusted. I watched Pavlo eat over the years, shoveling forkfuls of potatoes and beef, bowls of borshch and rye bread, handfuls of chocolate and ice cream into his eager mouth. Between bites of food, he shared with me the loss of factory jobs, the death of our son, news from home. Sometimes I was annoyed by the bits of food that revealed themselves amidst his words, aggravated by the blend of colors that settled in the corners of his mouth. But he never disgusted me.

I would add to my mother's wisdom that the key to love is in the breath. You know you love a man when you can stand his breath in the morning after a night of drinking and cigarettes. When you can kiss him after he finishes a garlic and butter sandwich and still enjoy the feel of his lips. When he looks into your eyes, tells you he loves you—and the pickled herring and onions are stronger than his voice—yet you still smile. You still want to be close to him. Yes, then you have found love. My Baba used to say that the breath is a taste of the spirit. When two spirits recognize each other in memory and future, then love grows.

I leaned over and kissed Pavlo gently. The coarse hairs on his chin scratched my face and his lips were dry, like crumpled paper. I drew back and took a sip of my coffee. Pavlo took another bite of ham.

Yes, I had come to love Pavlo, but love and passion were not the same. I looked toward the icon of Mary, and shrugged. What more could I ask for at this age?

Later that morning, I received another surprise. My daughter-in-law Anna and my granddaughter Lesya stopped by to drop off empty coffee cans in which I would bake the sweet babky for Easter week. My other daughter-in-law, Christina, arrived a few minutes later, carrying even more tins. Christina always asked me to bake extra Easter bread for her office; she liked to share her "ethnic pride."

I had them sit at the dining room table while I went to boil some water for tea. I heard the door slam a moment after I walked out of the room. I figured that Lesya had had another argument with her mother. She was at that age when mother and daughter seem to clash at every turn. I continued to prepare a tray of cups and cakes in the kitchen while my daughters-in-law gossiped. I kept thinking of the envelope and tried to think happier thoughts.

My Mama always said that when you cook or bake you should think of happy times or the food will be spoiled. I had a busy afternoon ahead. The water for the potatoes came to a boil, so I turned down the flame on the stove. Outside, the sky looked like shades of ashes and coal. I leaned toward the open window and smelled rain coming. In the backyard, I saw Lesya's shoulders slump as she sat down on the bench and wiped her eyes.

Anna, walked through the kitchen and then outside, but as soon as she sat down next to her daughter, Lesya rushed back inside the house. Her mother followed behind, her hands waving in frustration.

"Do you have to announce it to the world? Why does my life have to be everyone else's business?" Lesya shouted at her mother.

I was amazed that children spoke that way to their parents. In my day, I never—

"Lesya, I was only telling your aunt. Not the world. Besides, this is family. What's the big secret? People will have to find out eventually. Especially if you want to bring him to Palm Sunday Mass tomorrow." Anna looked at me apologetically.

"Find out what?" I asked, pouring the boiled potatoes into a strainer. I needed to make a big batch for the next day's varenyky. "What is all this running around slamming doors? And why are you talking like that to your mama? She is your mama, Lesya. You give her respect."

"It's nothing, Baba. I don't want to talk about it right now." She folded her arms and leaned against the refrigerator. "Besides, you wouldn't understand."

"Anna, leave us alone, okay?" I turned to her and winked.

Anna shrugged and returned to the living room to talk with Christina. I heard her say, "I don't know what to do about her."

I smiled at Lesya. "Okay, it's either them or me. You choose."

She almost smiled and leaned over to pet Khvostyk, who collapsed at her feet. Lesya was Khvostyk's favorite grandchild; she had been since he was a kitten. He tolerated my other grandchildren, but he was always fond of Lesya. Whenever her parents went out of town, she and her two sisters, Natalie and Tanya, spent the night at my house, and the cat would not leave Lesya's side. He used to sleep on her knees. If she rolled over, he would sleep on the pillow beside her.

"Now, Lesya, come here and make yourself useful. Chop these onions for me." She came closer and stood beside me at the counter, rolling up her sleeves.

"I really don't want to talk about this right now, Baba." She chopped the onion in half with a precise whack. "You'll only get angry with me, and I don't want to spoil the day. Can't we talk about something else?"

"All right, all right. Your Tato told me that you have some project at school, some paper you need my help for? What is all this about?" I put the potatoes in a big bowl and started mashing. I tried to catch her eyes, but Lesya kept staring at the cutting board.

"Oh, it's a paper that I need to write before I can finish my Master's."

"In literature?" I asked, knowing very well that it's in history. We've had this joke since she was a little girl, when I would ask her about her favorite subject in school.

Little Lesya had looked precious in her First Holy Communion dress, white with a little blue embroidery around the edges. She looked so much like Halya, except that Lesya had my thick brown hair.

"Baaaba. Nooooo. I like hiiiis-stooor-reee." Little Lesya answered in that sing-song voice, stretching out her words.

"Not English?" I asked again, patting down her brown bangs, frizzy from the heat.

"Noooo." She giggled. *"Baaaba. You're not listening."*

"Why history, Lesya?"

"I like stories that are true." She giggled. *"And my memory is good. History is just remembering, Tato says."*

Lesya stopped chopping for a minute and looked up at me with a full grin. "History, Baba. Very funny. You *know* it's history."

"Ah, I'm an old lady. My memory is not so good."

She laughed and leaned an elbow against the counter. "You can pull that with Tato and everybody else, but I know that you remember everything. Where do you think I got my amazing memory from?"

"Hmm, I don't know," I said, unable to resist. "I forgot."

She groaned and went back to her chopping.

"I'm writing about the immigration of our family from Ukraine to Chicago. The factors that brought you here; the problems you encountered: World War II, the DP camps. Why you left Ukraine, how you got to Germany, what it was like for you.

"Well, that's only part of the paper: the personal narrative section. It's more than just personal history; it's also a study of the immigration patterns of Eastern Europeans over the course of the war. But I'm using my family history as a springboard—"

Lesya kept talking, but I stopped listening and began to panic.

I couldn't possibly talk about it.

I couldn't tell her how I got to Germany. What if word got back home? But everyone was dead. But the letter? Maybe someone? No; no one was left alive. But still, I couldn't tell her. Why was the past trying to resurface? What would be next? What other messages? What other messengers?

I glanced at Lesya, who stared at me over the onions.

"Hello? Baba? Where did you go?" she asked, folding her arms. Lesya pressed her thin lips together—just like her father, that same stubborn look. He used to do that when I told him he couldn't stay up to watch late-night monster movies on the television.

I smiled at Lesya "Sorry, dear. Mention the past, and you send an old woman into daydreams. The past is heavy for an old lady like me."

"Ah, you're not old. But what were you thinking about?" she asked.

I looked at her plate. She had finished chopping the onions, and there I stood with half-mashed potatoes.

But I couldn't tell her.

I put more energy into my mashing, adding salt and pepper.

"How are those onions coming along, Lesya? Would you get me the butter from the icebox?"

She brought me the butter and stood staring at me.

"Why don't you ever want to talk about the past, Baba?"

"What nonsense are you saying? I talk about the past all the time. I tell you about when your father was a little boy. About your Dido and I, when we came to Chicago and worked in the factories. I tell you about when you were a cute baby. The smartest I have ever seen. But don't tell your sisters or cousins. I'm not supposed to have favorites." I winked at her. "Why do you say I never talk about the past? When you're old, that's all you have."

I took the butter from her and put it beside my bowl. Adding salt and pepper, I remembered too late that I had already added some. Ah, in my haste I put in too much. And I was supposed to be watching Pavlo's "sodium," the doctor said. Pavlo always put too much salt on his food.

"Ah, now see what I've done! Go sit and talk with your Mama and Aunt. Let me finish my varenyky in peace." I motioned toward the dining room, but she didn't leave. Instead she pulled out a kitchen chair and straddled it like a horse. I hoped she would tell me what was bothering her.

"That's your Dido's chair, and he'll be right back," I said. "He just ran out to get some more milk from the co-operative." I turned around and tried to ignore her, although I felt her staring at me from behind. I added the butter and kept mashing.

"What? What is it?" I asked without turning around. "It's obvious you want to talk with me. So talk."

I heard her take a deep breath, but only silence followed.

"Well? Are you scared to talk to your Baba, hmm?" I turned around and looked at her. Her arms were folded on the back of the chair, and her left cheek rested on her forearms. Her eyebrows were gathered together; her lips pouting.

"What is it? Are you pregnant?" I asked, turning back around to the potatoes.

"No, Baba. I'm dating someone."

I sighed with relief. "That is good news. Who is it? That nice boy, Myron? Or maybe that young Nosenko boy from Detroit? He really liked you. At Bingo, his Baba told me that he thought you were the prettiest girl at the New Year's Eve Dance."

"Baba, no," she softly muttered.

"You're definitely not too young to be dating. I already had three children at your age. Is your Mama giving you a hard time? You know her; she is very protective. Now, I'll talk with her."

"Baba."

"Oh, maybe it's that man—what's his name? The Professor. Yaroslav Somebody. Of course you would like an older man. I'll talk to your father. It's okay if the man is a little older—"

"Baba, listen to me." She stood up and walked to the icebox again. "He's not Ukrainian. He's . . . German American. I met him in school. He studies history like me." She said this all in one breath, then looked at me, eyes wide and defiant. She was ready for a fight.

"What?!" Pavlo's voice boomed as he came in from the porch. He walked toward Lesya, and slammed his umbrella on the table, raindrops scattering.

"What?! Who is German?" He looked at me. "Nadya, what is she talking about?"

I walked toward Pavlo, holding my hands out in front of me. I didn't need him having a heart attack. I said softly, "Calm down, Pavlo. Just calm down. We were just talking. Now go change out of your wet clothes."

"Don't tell me what to do," he said between clenched teeth. "Who is German?"

Anna and Christina came and stood in the archway between the dining room and kitchen.

"Dido, my boyfriend is. Well he's American, but his grandparents—"

"No." His face was blood red; the vein on his forehead throbbed. "I forbid it. No blood of mine will mix with German blood!"

"Pavlo, your blood pressure. Please." I laid my hand on his arm and then turned to Lesya. "What are you saying?" I asked her while lightly stroking Pavlo's arm. "Are you forgetting where you come from? Your roots?" I threw a glance in Anna's direction. "How have you been raised?"

Pavlo shrugged my hand away and stepped up to Lesya. His face red, he pulled back his shirt sleeve and pushed his arm in her face.

"See this? See these numbers? Your boyfriend's grandfathers did this to me." He grabbed his umbrella and left the house, slamming the door behind him.

Lesya stood against the fridge, tears in her eyes, her arms folded at her chest.

"That's not fair," she whispered. "It's not fair. This is America. Those aren't my grudges. The past is the past."

"Leave us," I said to Anna and Christina. They didn't move, so I repeated louder, "Leave us."

As they retreated to the front room, I sat down and motioned for Lesya to join me.

"No, Lesya. You listen to me. The past is not the past. Especially not for your Dido and me. You're a student of history. You know better."

"But Baba, listen. His grandfathers weren't even soldiers."

"No. You listen. The Germans came to my home. They killed everyone I loved. They destroyed my country. Your country. They destroyed everything. Can you imagine having everything taken away from you? Everything? But not my memory. This I have.

"It is easy for you to keep the past on paper. For us, the past is alive, breathing down our necks. When we see an old woman on the street that looks like our sister. When we hear songs our Mamas used to sing. When we smell tobacco our Tatos smoked. When we taste sausages seasoned with garlic and pepper that are so much like the ones our Babas once made. When we dance the dances of home. When we celebrate the old traditions. The past is there with us.

"It is understood. We don't have to say anything to each other. We kept ourselves safe with silence. To speak the words is to somehow make it more real. To make it more painfully real."

I tried to stay calm. She was still young; I needed to explain.

But she didn't look me in the eye. She stared at the photographs I had taped next to the calendar: photos of her and her sisters, my other grandchildren, my sons, my daughters.

"Baba, I understand the past is painful, but this is America—"

"I know this is America." I was so close to losing my temper. I took a deep breath, then continued. "I came here so I could raise my children in peace. So I could save our traditions, keep our culture alive. That's why your father learned Ukrainian. That's why you speak it. That's why your mama took you to Ukrainian School on Saturdays, Ukrainian dancing, Ukrainian church. So everything the Germans and Russians tried to destroy would not die. So it would live here, in America. So our traditions, our ancestors, our history would live in you."

I paused to catch my breath. She didn't look at me, so I continued, "Lesya, I know this is America. Don't tell me about this country. Why do you think the Ukrainian community is so close, so united? Because we all share the need to keep our traditions alive. Is it so easy for you to turn your back on all this? To throw it all away for a stranger? He is not one of ours. He can't understand."

I went to the kitchen cabinet and pulled out the cedar box. I sat back down with the box in my lap; my fingers traced the beautiful carvings. "This box was made in America. But the hands that created it are Ukrainian; the style is Ukrainian. These patterns: Ukrainian. The stars for hope, the moon for dreams, the egg for new life. These symbols are very old. Your Dido remembered them and carved them for me. It is a message in wood.

"This box is like you. Like the tree, you were created and grown in foreign soil. But like the wood, you were transformed by the magic of memory. By family, school, church, traditions, you were shaped. Carved inside of you are ancient patterns: songs, stories older than me. They make you something very precious.

They are carved into who you are. You cannot erase them. But you choose what to carry."

Lesya didn't look at the box. "Baba, America is not just a place for Ukrainian culture; it's a place for many cultures to live together. To learn about each other. To share—"

"Learning . . . learning is okay. You go to school for that. But remember where you came from."

"I am not forgetting, Baba. I was born here."

I didn't know how I could explain it to her. She was so smart; so good with words. I placed the box on her lap, but she didn't touch it.

"Lesya, to bring him into the family is to say that what the Germans did in the war was okay. Can you do that?"

"Baba, no. To date him is to date one man, not a country. He should not be condemned for things done over fifty years ago in a different place by different people."

"One man? Not a country?" I tried to catch her eye. When she refused, I picked up her chin with my hand. "What about you? Are you just one woman? Is being Ukrainian not important to who you are?"

For a moment she didn't answer. Then tears. She placed the box on the table and said calmly, "You don't understand. I love him. I'm not turning my back on who I am, but I refuse to condemn someone because of his grandparents. I believe that in this day and age we need to forgive and understand. I'm not saying forget—"

"It is so easy for you to say that, Lesya. It is so easy for you to say." I thought of the empty envelope inside the cedar box and shook my head. The past did not stay buried.

CHAPTER FIVE

The only person I could have discussed the envelope with was Ana, but she had died the year before. I still felt her presence, and I would often sit among the plants in our garden and talk to her. It had been our special place—beside the fence where we had stood and chatted for years when we were neighbors. I wished I could have talked to Ana then, but I had the entire family coming for Palm Sunday lunch, and there was no time for such an indulgence.

As I was staring out the window, I felt a swift whack on my behind. I turned to find Pavlo grinning sheepishly, his left eye brow raised in mischief and a long pussy willow branch in his hands.

"It's not I, but the willow, that taps you on this week of Easter," Pavlo said the traditional Palm Sunday words and tapped me once more; this time lighter. "Nadya, this is the only time each year when I can smack your behind all I want, and even the priests approve."

When he tried to hang up his coat, it fell to the floor. I picked it up and hung it on the chair. Of course, he hadn't noticed. For him, things miraculously appeared in their place. Maybe he thought it was the domovyk, the house spirit, who kept the house in order.

"And where is my pussy willow, Pavlo? Did you bring me a few blessed branches, or did you give them all away to the old widows at Slavko's Bar?"

"What?! And risk your wrath?" His grin widened. "Besides, you don't need a weapon; your words are enough." He shook the pussy willow playfully in front of me.

"You're not funny, old man. It's Palm Sunday. The kids and grandkids will be here any minute, and I still haven't set out the sweets and coffee. Stop playing your games and give me my branch." I quickly reached for the branch, but he lifted it high into the air above me. Even though age had taken inches off both our heights, he was still a head taller.

"No," he said and took a step back. "You can't have it."

"Fine." I walked to the icebox to get out the milk and butter. "One of my children will bring me one." I was not in the mood for his childish behavior.

Another smack on the behind, and then the doorbell rang. Pavlo shuffled onto the back porch to answer the door. I heard voices repeating the traditional Palm Sunday greeting, accompanied by hearty taps on body parts. I quickly tried to make everything ready as my daughter Zirka and her husband, Peter, filed into the kitchen.

"Hi, Mama." She tapped me lightly on the shoulder. "It's not I but the willow that taps you on this week of Easter."

"Yes, yes. But did you bring me a branch?" I motioned toward the table. "Peter, sit down and have something to eat. You look too skinny. Doesn't my daughter feed you? I taught her how to cook, but she must have forgotten." I glanced at Zirka. "I've told you many times, a skinny husband is not a happy husband."

"Mama, I know how to cook. Peter eats plenty at home." She took a plate and knife and began to peel an apple plucked from my fruit basket, carefully cutting off the skin, then slicing it into eight even pieces. She handed it to her husband.

"Enough for a pigeon," I mumbled. I put some varenyky in the frying pan on the stove and added onions and butter.

"Where are the twins? Soccer practice again? Kung Fu?

Hockey? Chess Club?"

"Mama, they have an important game tomorrow. They need to rest and practice." Zirka began to peel another apple.

Peter leaned against the fridge, and I watched him pick at the fruit. Maybe he's sick.

"Have some coffee, Peter. Help yourself. Are you feeling well? I have some vitamins that Dr. Shelepko gave me. I'll give you some to take home—"

"Mama. No vitamins." Zirka poured coffee for herself and Peter. "We have vitamins. Besides, you *know* how I feel about Ukrainian phy-si-cians."

I smiled as she said the word in the sing-song voice that she used to use as a child. For a minute, I saw my little girl beneath her fancy clothes and hair. But only for a minute; then she was back to her "professional" tone.

"Peter is not sick; he's in excellent shape," she said.

"All right, all right. I'm sorry for worrying about my kids." I took the pork chops off the stove and set them on the table. "When will I get to see my handsome twin grandsons? Are you hiding them from me?"

Zirka glared at me. "I am not hiding them from you—"

I interrupted. "Eh, you know those boys are going to forget what their Baba looks like."

""You'll see them next week for Easter," Zirka said in between careful bites of her apple.

Peter leaned over to me and whispered, "I tried to get them to come, Mama, but you know Zirka. She wants the boys to get scholarships to college."

I smiled and patted his arm. Poor man. My daughter could drain the energy out of any healthy husband; no wonder he was skinny. He had more meat on his bones when they married.

The doorbell rang again.

"Are you going to come by later tonight? Your sister will be painting pysanky. It's been so long since you've painted them, and you have such a gift. Why don't you stop by?"

"Mama, Peter and I have tickets to a show. We're going out to dinner with clients."

"My daughter . . . the big important business lady, but she doesn't have time to paint eggs with her sister." I looked at her new suit: very fancy. Everything neat and in its place. Not a wrinkle in her clothes or on her skin. Zirka once tried to convince me to cover my face with some of her anti-age cream, but I told her that it was not natural. Women today worry so much about looking old. What did I have to look young for?

Zirka walked over to Peter and put her manicured hands on his shoulders. "No guilt today. Please."

Guilt?

Honesty.

My son Mark and his wife, Christina, stepped into the kitchen carrying a white box and several stalks of pussy willows.

"Hello, my beautiful mother," Mark said after kissing both my cheeks. His eyes looked tired; playful, but still tired. Work was stressful for him. Setting the box on the table, he took all three branches and smacked Zirka on the behind. So much like his father. I looked around for Pavlo, but he must have stepped outside.

"Mark, you always overdo it." Zirka pinched her brother until he yelped.

"Hi, Mama. We brought a chocolate cake." Christina opened the box and pulled out a beautiful torte covered with strawberries and whipped cream.

I sighed. "Christina, I have food here. I know how to bake. Save your money. You don't need to bring me gifts. Just come and visit. Bring my grandchildren."

Mark awarded me a light smack on the behind.

"How could I resist such a target?" he said, stepping away.

"Are those pussy willows for me, son?"

"Uh, they will be," he grinned sheepishly. "But not yet. I'm waiting for Katya so I can give her a proper welcome. I haven't seen my sister since Christmas." Yes, so much like his Tato.

He nibbled on a piece of coffeecake. I looked back at the torte he brought; it did look delicious, but I had to watch my weight. It was bad enough that everything was beginning to sag.

"Can I slice this? Or will you be angry?" Christina asked while carefully measuring the slices for the torte.

"Cut, cut. It's too late now. But you must take the leftovers home with you. Pavlo and I are too old to eat so many sweets."

I looked down at the table. No one had touched the babka I baked that morning.

"What! No one wants my babka? It's fresh and sweet. You eat coffeecake and torte, but not my babka. Do not insult me. Eat."

I walked into the living room to find Mark and Christina's daughters.

I found Pavlo asleep in his recliner, a Ukrainian newspaper in his lap, and the willow still clutched in his right hand. Mark's two daughters, Tamara and Petrucia, sat on the couch watching television. Catching the girls' eyes and bringing my finger up to my lips, I stepped behind Pavlo and carefully eased the branch out of his hands. He let out a snore, but didn't wake up. I saw that he was not wearing his hearing aid again.

The girls giggled as I tiptoed over to the chair next to them and sat down. "Now, tell me why you come to Baba's house and don't come into the kitchen to say hello."

"But Baba, Dido was telling us a story," Tamara, the youngest, said while turning off the television.

"Funny that your Dido can tell a story while he's asleep. Come give Baba a kiss." They jumped up, and I tapped each one lightly on the behind with the pussy willow.

"I'll tell you a quick little story. Do you know why pussy

willows have these fluffy white buds?" I asked them. They shook their heads. "Well, once there lived a mean old farmer who had a pretty little brown cat—"

"What was her name?" Tamara asked.

"Her name was Kasha," I answered, "and one spring day, Kasha had nine beautiful baby kittens. But the mean old farmer didn't want the kittens, so he took them all and threw them into a great big sack."

"Oh no," the girls said in unison, looking around for Khvostyk, who stared at them from under the table.

"Well, he took the sack down to the river and tossed it in, waiting for it to sink to the bottom. Kasha sat on the riverbank mewing and crying for her lost babies until a willow tree nearby asked her what was the matter. Kasha told the willow what had happened, and because willows are naturally kind trees, the tree plunged her branches into the water and pulled out the sack. Kasha ripped a hole in it to free her babies, but all but one of the kittens had drowned. Ever since, willows everywhere bloom with kitten-like buds in memory of the drowned kittens and their sad mother."

The girls sat wide-eyed, staring at the pussy willow in my hand. I smiled, remembering that I had first heard that story when I was Tamara's age.

The doorbell rang, and Pavlo's eyes opened wide. He looked toward me, and then toward his empty hand. "Nadya," he growled playfully, "you give that back. I need it to greet my children."

I rose and walked toward the door. "No, I will greet them. You get some coffee so you don't spend all afternoon sleeping."

At the door, my son, Taras, held little Pavlyk, his grandson and my first great-grandchild. "Hi, Mama."

He was beaming with pride. I still could not believe that my son was a grandfather.

Taras kissed me on the cheek. "Natalie and Jerry should be along in a second. I'm going to go show this little guy off."

Taras walked into the kitchen while I waited for his wife, Anna. After hugs and more willow taps, I followed her into the kitchen. Everyone cooed at the baby, passed him around, and exchanged observations. He was only nine months old but already a big boy, round and healthy for his age. He definitely took after Jerry.

When it was my turn to hold Pavlyk, I took him into my arms, rubbed my face against the top of his head, and inhaled his smell. Baby powder and apple blossoms after the rain. Sweet and soft and delicious. I rubbed my cheek against his soft black hair.

At this moment, Jerry came into the kitchen carrying the diaper bag and beaming his usual toothy grin. "Hi, Baba," he said giving me a quick kiss. "He's getting heavy, be careful."

"All these warnings," I said, "You forget I had six children." But I did sit down because he was getting heavy.

Little Pavlyk settled into my arms, and as I bounced my knee up and down, I whispered to him the lullaby my Mama used to sing to me and my sisters:

"Liu li, liu li, liu li, sleep my little Pavlyk,
Soon the dawn will bring new hopes.
Now the night promises new dreams."

I looked up and saw that my Pavlo was watching me from across the room, his thin lips in a soft grin. I blushed, caught in a private moment.

My oldest daughter, Katya, burst into the room. Pavlo and I looked away from each other, embarrassed. The air tingled with Katya's fiery presence. I felt her even before I looked in her direction.

"Well, hello! I guess you're all tired from whacking each

other with willows. I think this is the first time I didn't hear arguing when I walked down the gangway." She rushed over to Pavlo and gave him a big hug and then to me, sweeping little Pavlyk out of my arms.

"My turn, Mama." She kissed him on the top of his head, then spun around, the baby giggling in her arms.

Suddenly everyone began talking all at once. I looked at Christina and tried to focus on her face, but her words began to run into each other. My daughter-in-law loved to talk. I remembered the first time I met Christina. I thought she was so quiet. I could not imagine how she would ever communicate with my son. Mark has the temper of a bear and a loud growl to match. But apparently she talked loud enough to get a few words in, because they've been married for twenty-eight years. But oh, how she liked to talk.

"And Darka's daughter is engaged to a concert violinist from Toronto. His mother used to sing opera in Europe. They have a lot of money, I hear. He stands to inherit . . ."

Still, she was a good mother. She gave me two beautiful granddaughters. Mark, certainly enjoyed talking as well, especially about things he was passionate about, like computers.

"You know, Taras, you wouldn't have so much trouble if you got yourself a real computer," Mark said, smiling smugly as he reached for another slice of babka.

I gave up trying to make sense of it all. My mind wandered. The month before, when I was at Mark's house, he tried to show me his computer and explain all that it could do. He tried for such a long time to explain it to me. All I know is that it's some kind of electronic magic, like a television that listens to your requests. But Mark told me he has conversations on the computer. I watched as he typed in questions and someone named Shorty31 answered back. I knew Mark didn't do it because I watched his fingers carefully.

Maybe it's not so different from the way my Baba used to gaze into the stream and talk with the rusalky, or the way Mama used to talk with the domovyk, the house spirit, to ask them to keep us safe when Tato would go to the city to trade. Back home they were called spirits; here, they are called "modems."

My sons' voices were getting louder, but they blurred together. Both Mark and Taras had the same sort of growl, which they had inherited from their father.

"See, if you have a slow network connection . . . it's harder to surf the Web."

This Web, Mark tried to explain it to me. But I told him that I already understood. Finally computers are teaching people what my ancestors have known for hundreds of years. My own Baba taught me many years ago about the invisible threads that connect everyone. They are made from the holy waters that became the Universe. These threads connect us with the people who came before us and those who will follow us; they also connect us with all living things. Bright like moonlight, this essence flows from inside us to everything else, because we are all made of the same waters: the waters of our souls.

I looked at Pavlo, but he sat quietly, ripping apart pieces of kolach—Ukrainian braided bread—and dipping them in a puddle of honey on his plate. He was watching his family, a grin on his face. I don't think he understood it all either, but he liked to have them around.

But for me, at that moment, it was too much. Too many voices. Too loud.

I stood up and walked onto the porch, grateful for the break. I sat on the sofa and gazed through the doorway into the kitchen. My family.

I watched as my young granddaughters rushed into the kitchen hitting each other with willows, each saying over and over "It's not I but the willow . . ."

Their mother grabbed the branches. "Girls, you stop that right now. Shame on you. Those pussy willows are blessed. You should not be fighting—"

They ran back into the living room, laughing. I smiled to myself; this house needed more children's laughter. It kept the domovyk happy.

Taras walked over to the bathroom armed with his willow, waiting for Katya to walk out. Mark and Peter talked about houses. Anna and Christina washed dishes, and Zirka stood beside them showing off her new anniversary ring. Pavlo sat back in his chair, closed his eyes and smiled. In a moment, he would be snoring, unnoticed by his children who sat engrossed in conversation, gossip, and disagreement.

This house had been the backdrop for most of our life together. Sitting there, watching my family framed by the doorway, I watched time shift with each breath, bringing me back through the many memories these walls have witnessed.

I was twenty-six when Pavlo carried me over the threshold of our first house in Chicago. I placed bread outside the door and a candle in the window to welcome our ancestors. Pavlo chuckled at my superstitions but didn't resist. That night, as the children slept on the queen-sized mattress we had been given by friends, Pavlo and I scrubbed the floors stained with dirt and cat urine. In the weeks that followed, we stripped the blue-gray paint off the doors and windows and laid new lemon yellow tile in the kitchen. A little work each day made it our home.

I taught all my children how to make bread. Elbows deep in dough, they stood on chairs and kneaded. "Don't sneeze into the bread," I warned, "and never wipe your noses." That night we ate their loaves. The children beamed with pride, flour still on their faces.

Once, while waiting for Pavlo far past the time when work was done, I embroidered a blouse for Katya's school play, sitting beside a candle to save electricity. He staggered in, cigarettes and alcohol trailing behind. Before I could yell, he collapsed in front of me, head in my lap. He wept silently. A whisper: "Laid off."

A scream froze in my throat. Hands stained red from shredding beets, I stood staring at the door after the chaplain left. Mykola, my youngest son, was dead. Vietnam. No more hopeful morning candlelight vigils. I made the necessary calls. My heart sank beneath the house, buried with his uniform. Somehow the other two boys came back alive.

Girls drifted in and out of the kitchen, trying to win my boys, impress their Mama. Sofia, tall and blonde, laughed loudly at Pavlo's jokes. I caught her smoking outside of church. Tatiana, tiny and petite, smelled like baby powder. She chewed her fingernails and washed dishes with gloves. Alexandra, round and pretty, never stopped talking. She kept touching Mark's knee. Christina, bubbly and strong. She brought me a cake and served me the first piece. Anna, pretty and quiet, with the eyes of a doe. She washed the dishes and put them away. She listened to me.

Katya and I sat in the kitchen after she moved her books and clothes into her tiny apartment. We drank tea together; she twirled her curls around her fingers. We had so much silence between us. I gave her a wooden cross for her bedroom. I didn't know how to keep her safe.

The wheel of life turned on and on, and just as I thought I

began to understand, everything changed again. My Baba always used to say "the past is present," but I never understood until recently. She would explain that stories are the connection; they are our way of touching those invisible threads that connect everyone. Stories are our hope for the future.

But what then of the missing letter? What of that empty envelope that sat so heavy on my thoughts? I tried all day to keep busy, to chase away the ghosts. Still it sat inside that box, taunting me with possibilities, haunting me with questions. I thought about my family, safe in my kitchen. Unaware that something was creeping toward me, threatening to shake my world apart. But then again, maybe it was nothing. Maybe I should not allow myself to bring the dead to life because then I would have to bury them again.

"Mama? Are you okay?" Katya put a hand on my shoulder. "You have tears in your eyes. What's the matter?"

"Nothing," I snapped. "Can't an old woman just weep sometimes? I've lived a whole lifetime, you know. I have a lot to cry about."

Katya stepped back and walked back into the kitchen without a word. I had pushed her away. But how could she understand? How could anyone understand? Ana would have understood, but Ana was dead. Amazing that in a house so full, I felt so alone.

I looked again toward the kitchen. My mama always called it "the heart of the home." As children, we sat around the hearth fire, huddled together under Baba's blanket, her scents captured in the fabric: thick and sweet, lilacs and mint, coffee and onions. Mama would tell us stories to chase the cold into the farthest corners of the cottage.

Because of the harvest, Tato had gone into town to try to sell our wheat and potatoes. He had left before dawn. I remember standing at the window with my sisters, waving goodbye. The sky had been heavy, the air still. Mama whispered, "A storm is coming. Quick, girls, back to bed."

As we ran to our bed, she said a prayer and made the Sign of the Cross in the direction of town, "Guardian Angel, help keep him safe on his journey."

Mama then crawled into bed with us, and we lay curled together in sleep for a few more hours until it was time to wake up and do our morning chores. The rains came at midday, so we stayed in the house, cleaning to pass the time. Laryssa and I scrubbed the stove. Maria and Mama washed the walls and floors. Halya collected any feathers that were falling out of the blanket and pillows so Mama could sew them back inside.

"Just think how happy your Tato will be when he comes home to find such a clean house," Mama said, resting her chin on the broom.

"Girls, it's important to have a clean house. That way you keep your husband satisfied, and you keep the evil spirits from entering. They don't like a house whose table has no crumbs. But they love a house filled with lazy children." She lifted the broom over her head and made a face, chasing us around the house, while we hid giggling.

By the time we had finished eating supper, the night was heavy with thunder. Little Halya was afraid to go to sleep, so Mama gathered us near the hearth and heated milk and honey for us to drink.

Mama sat down in Baba's old rocking chair, picked up Halya and placed her on her lap. Maria, Laryssa, and I sat together, Baba's blanket covering the three of us. Mama gave Halya a squeeze and looked at Maria.

"Maria, you're already a little lady. Would you pour the sweet milk into mugs for your sisters?"

At thirteen, Maria already looked just like our Mama. She was tall and thin like a young birch, with light olive skin and hazel eyes like Mama's. Maria always wanted to mother us, making sure we did our chores if Mama was away. Giving us lessons if we had nothing to do. Whenever we played, Maria would have to be the mother and we were her children. We always misbehaved, and she would punish us by making us stand on our knees and say the Hail Mary. More than anything, Maria wanted to get married and have a lot of babies.

After she carefully poured our sweet milk, Maria settled into the spot between me and Laryssa. Mama began to rock back and forth.

"Halya, my sweet little rabbit, I'm going to tell you and your sisters a story that my Mama, your Baba, told me when I was a little girl. Once upon a time before people lived on Earth, there was a glorious garden filled with beautiful flowers and plants. There were fields of poppies and lilacs—"

"Baba's favorites," I whispered, and Laryssa shushed me.

"—raspberry bushes and dewberry," Mama continued. "So many flowers of all different shades and scents. But the most beautiful of all was the single white Rose that grew in the center of the garden, a queen among the others. She would rise each morning while the other flowers slept, and tilt her head up toward the Sun so she could feel his warm rays upon her petals.

"Well, the Sun had watched the Rose grow from a tiny blossom, and each morning when she stretched out her petals, she grew even lovelier. The Sun slept each night dreaming of her and arose each morning to shine even more brightly. You see, the handsome Sun had fallen in love with the pretty young flower, but he could not gather the courage to even whisper a hello. Instead he sat in the sky, shining brightly above her. Each time she tilted her head toward the sky, he would send all of his rays to dance upon her milky white petals.

"One day, when the Rose awoke, threw back her head and tussled her leaves, the Sun was so overcome by her beauty that he could no longer keep silent.

"'Hello down there, lovely creature,' he shouted in his deep, warm voice.

"The Rose, however, was taught not to speak with strangers, so she coyly looked down from the Sun's bright gaze.

"'Lovely Rose,' he continued, 'Do not look away. For if I could no longer look upon you, my heart would break and the world would forever be covered in darkness.'

"The Rose quickly looked up in alarm. She could not imagine a world without the Sun, for she too had long been admiring his handsome face, rosy cheeks, and long yellow curls that stretched toward the earth.

"'Lovely Rose,' the Sun said, 'I have watched you for many long mornings, and now I have something to tell you. I have seen beauty throughout the world, but never have I seen a more radiant creature than the one white Rose in the heart of this garden. I could gaze upon you for all eternity. You are the most beautiful of all the Earth's creatures. I have fallen in love with you.'

"At this, the Rose began to blush, and as the color spread through her petals, it stained them bright red. This is how she remained forever, blushing with love for the handsome Sun. And when her daughters were born, they all carried the mark of their parents' love: bright red from the true love their mother and father shared for all eternity. This, my daughters, is why roses are red."

I slept that night, my face buried in Mama's shoulder, dreaming of a magical Sun and true love, certain that both existed.

CHAPTER SIX

"Why are you smiling, Baba? What are you thinking about?" Lesya came inside and stood behind me. I worried that she wouldn't come after our big fight, but there she was. She slipped her arms around my waist. "You're so lost in thought these days."

I turned around and looked at her in her green suit, her hair in long brown curls. She smelled like sandalwood.

"My, you look pretty today. Your mama said you had a meeting." I smoothed away the hair that always fell into her eyes.

"Some students got together to study for a big exam that we have tomorrow morning. On the politics of the Middle East." She pulled off her black leather heels and took a step toward the kitchen.

"Thank you for not slamming the door," I said. "I hate that sound."

"Sure," she said, and shrugged her shoulders.

I watched as she went to Pavlo and kissed the top of his balding head, but he stiffened.

"Hi, Dido," she said, giving him a hug, but he ignored her and reached across the table for the butter.

"Hey kiddo, where's my hug?" Katya asked, and Lesya walked over and gave her aunt a hug and a kiss. Katya had always been perceptive, sensing things that others did not. Like my Baba. When Katya was born in Germany, somewhere in the distance outside the barracks, I heard the chiming of tiny bells. Still wet with birth, Katya watched me closely even though newborns weren't supposed to be able to see much. I saw the birthmark on her right thigh, and I knew that hers was going to be a different kind of life. I named her for my Aunt Katia, Mama's sister, the one who drowned. I hoped this Katya would have a happier life.

Lesya walked around to greet everyone else, then sat down across from her grandfather, avoiding his eyes. I walked back into the kitchen, pulled out her favorite mug from the cupboard and poured her a coffee, with two spoons of sugar and just a touch of milk. I set it down in front of her along with a slice of my kolach.

"Eat up, skinny one. There's not enough meat on these bones."

Katya nudged her. "So, are you going to stay and paint pysanky with me today? Maybe we can convince your Aunt Zirka to join us. How about it, Sis? Can you fit us into your busy schedule?"

Zirka looked over at her husband, who raised his eyebrows and pointed to his watch.

"Sorry, Katya. Pete and I have a business thing."

I looked again at Peter, who was nodding. So fragile for a man. If his ulcer wasn't acting up, then his teeth were hurting. He was always on some kind of new diet. No milk, no cheese, no butter, no eggs, no wheat. Lately it was no gluten. At least I didn't cook with gluten, whatever that was. No wonder he was so skinny. My children ate everything, and they never got allergies. America. Suddenly everyone has food, but they can't eat.

"I'm not sure if I can stay," Lesya said into the coffee cup she was holding up to her mouth. She hadn't even taken a bite of the kolach.

"Why not, Lesya?" I stood behind her, playing with her hair. "You said last week that you would stay. I don't know how many more Easters I'll be around for. Maybe one more, maybe not."

"Oh, Baba. You've been saying that for the last fifteen years."

She reached over to pet Khvostyk.

"If you don't want to stay, then don't," I said.

"Lesya, you can stay for a while, can't you?' Anna asked, although it was more of a demand than a question.

"Fine, Mom, but just for a little while." Lesya cut the kolach on her plate into tiny pieces before eating them one at a time. I smiled. That's exactly how her father, Taras, ate his breads and cakes: cutting them first into tiny squares, so they lasted longer.

I wondered if she knew how much they had in common. My son would have loved to have gone to college. I wondered if she realized how lucky she is. Probably not, I thought. The young are anxious and never really satisfied. That's what keeps them always reaching forward, trying to change things.

If only things had been different, maybe I could have gone to the university. If only things had been different. But then I would not have them all here, my children.

All at once, everyone began glancing down at their watches, making excuses for why they had to leave. So quickly the spell was broken. Reaching over, I kissed little Pavlyk once more on the head, then stood up to prepare care packages. As usual, I had too many leftovers.

"Christina, don't forget to take your torte," I said.

"My hands are already full of Ukrainian newspapers for recycling," she replied. "Mark, grab the torte."

I saw Anna trying to get away without a care package.
"Take something, Anna. I have too much and it will go bad." I piled pompushky on a plate and covered them with aluminum foil. "Here, take these for Tanya." I divided up the rest and handed out plates and plastic bags.

Then they were gone. Even Pavlo snuck outside, no doubt to have a cigarette or to play in the garden. Katya went to her car to get the supplies for painting pysanky. Only Lesya remained seated in the kitchen, drinking her coffee. I began to wash the dishes, waiting for her to speak first. I learned long ago that silence could be the strongest prompt.

But she didn't say anything; she just stared into her coffee cup. Katya came in and placed a large box on the kitchen table.

"Katya, not on the crumbs," I said. "I haven't wiped down the table yet. Please put that in the dining room."

When she came back, she helped me dry the dishes.

"So, Ma, are you going to help? It's been a long time since you painted eggs."

"No, Katya. Pysanky are not my art. I thought that I would embroider while you and your niece painted." I motioned toward Lesya, but Katya just shook her head and shrugged her shoulders.

After the dishes were done and put away, we moved into the dining room. Katya took charge, clearing the table of my vase of dried flowers, my favorite blue glass candlesticks, the faded leather photo albums. I let her do this; it was her ritual.

"Mama, do you mind if I cover the table with this cloth? It will protect the wood from the melting wax; plus I like to work on it." She pulled out a beautiful yellow cloth embroidered along the edges with an elaborate design of trees and birds.

"Did you embroider these?" I asked, running my fingers along the delicate green and blue threads.

"No, my friend Robin did those for me. It was a birthday present." She carefully spread out the cloth and set cast-iron candleholders—heavy bowl-like containers—upon it.

"Are you sure they won't scratch the table?"

Katya groaned softly. "No, Mama. They will not scratch the table."

In each iron holder, she placed a thick white candle. "Sit down, Mama, Lesya." She went into the kitchen to prepare the dye in glass jars. I rummaged around in my cabinet for my latest embroidery. A blouse for Lesya, but she didn't know about it yet. Lesya went to the porch and came back, having changed into jeans and a bright green sweater. The color made her eyes glow.

She sat at one end of the table and began to braid her hair. I sat down across from her, watching her lips pouted in determination. How much she reminded me of my littlest sister, or at least how I imagined Halya would have looked if she'd lived into her twenties.

Katya was still mixing dyes in the kitchen. When she returned, she sat between us. We were three generations, a triangle of women.

She placed the three jars on a tray in the center of the table. Orange. Brown. Black. She always liked the earth tones best. I preferred the rich reds, blues, and greens that shone like jewels. Beside the jars she placed a carton of raw eggs. She then arranged it so one candle was directly in front of each of us.

"Mama, are you sure that you don't want to paint?" she asked while handing Lesya a kistka, a little wooden tool topped with a copper cone.

"I'm sure, Katya." I scanned the cloth for my last few stitches.

"You know, Lesya, I can't remember: have you done this before?" Katya asked, pulling blocks of beeswax out of a wooden box.

"It's been a while. I think the last time I made pysanky was in Saturday Ukrainian school, maybe third or fourth grade. You can refresh my memory."

Katya stood up to dim the lights. In silence we watched as she lit the candles with a silver lighter engraved with her name. I was struck by the beauty of my oldest daughter. She looked a lot like her namesake. Ah, my daughter would have liked her great-aunt. But she knew nothing of her ancestor, the one with her name. I never told her.

My Baba always told me to be careful of the names I would someday choose for my children because the name invoked power from those who had the name before. Names made connections between the dead and the living. But it gave me hope to see the shades of the dead in my flesh and blood.

Katya was small-framed, compared to Lesya and me. Short with long brown hair full of red highlights. She looked so much younger than her fifty years. She always looked young for her age; but unlike some girls, she never minded. Zirka always wanted to grow up so fast. Katya savored her childhood, held on to her fairy tales and fantasies.

Katya sat back down between us and pulled an egg out of the carton.

"First, you need to choose an egg. The egg symbolizes the return of the sun, the coming of spring, the renewal of life."

She was in her "teacher mode." That's what her brothers and sisters called it when Katya was a little girl playing "school" with her siblings. She did go on to teach. I smiled at her, but Katya was looking intently into the candle.

Lesya plucked an egg out of the carton and set it down in front of her. I heard the cuckoo clock in the kitchen. Five o'clock.

"Then you need to find a pattern," Katya continued. She pulled some books of designs out of the box and handed them to Lesya. "Here, look through these for some ideas."

"It helps to divide the egg into quadrants. It makes it easier to design the rest, Lesya," She turned toward her niece and furrowed her brow. "You need to really think about what you want this egg to mean. What story you want it to tell. You see, the patterns are ancient symbols. Even the colors have meaning. Our ancestors would carefully choose these symbols and colors because the images they chose would tell a story. The story of their past, present or future. Sometimes all three."

Katya smiled, that devilish, faraway look in her eyes. When she turned toward me, I quickly looked down at my embroidery. "The colored eggs were also used to cast spells, "she said, "fulfilling the secret wishes of their makers—"

"Aunt Katya, if you're going to tell me that the eggs are magic, you can stop right there."

I looked up from my red cross-stitches in surprise. "This from the girl who used to tell me that she could see fairies in her bedroom?"

"I was a kid, Baba." She looked up for a moment, then back to the book. "A kid with an overactive imagination."

Back to my embroidery. I would let Katya handle this one. Khvostyk purred beside my leg.

"Well, kiddo, the eggs were believed to hold magical powers, carrying with them the energy of creation. Each painted symbol was charged with magical energy. Each animal, flower and geometric shape had layers of sacred meaning.

"Older people were given pysanky with rich designs and dark colors because their lives deserved the ornate patterns. They had lived those patterns. You'd have quite a decorative pysanka, eh, Mama?"

I ignored her and kept stitching.

"Young people's pysanky had a lot of white and sparse designs because their lives were still new," she continued.

"Okay, no disrespect," Lesya said, "but the origin of the word pysanka is pretty ordinary. The root is pysaty, 'to write,' and writing seems pretty logical to me."

"Sure, but writing was once considered magical," Katya said.

I looked up and watched her hands. Tiny hands with long, strong fingers. Gentle hands. Her left one held the raw egg while her right hand gently sketched. Soft, scraping sounds.

"Is it such a stretch for you?" she asked. "Writing in so many cultures was considered magical. Think about ancient Egyptian hieroglyphics or the Hebrew Kaballah. I know you studied some of these in college."

"Stories, too," I added, lowering my eyes to my embroidery.

"Stories have been considered magic."

"That's why I study history and not mythology." Lesya said, yelping as her egg cracked. She must have pressed down too hard with her pencil. Yolk flowed over her fingers as she jumped up and ran to the kitchen.

"Lesya, you need to be gentle with the eggs," I shouted into the kitchen.

"I know, Baba," she shouted back, her voice irritated. I added a few more red crosses to the cloth.

"Maybe you can talk to her, Katya, about this boy she likes," I said quietly, glancing toward the kitchen where Lesya was wiping egg yolk from her shirt.

"Mama, she needs to live her own life, and you need to learn how to let things go."

"Let things go? Let things go?" I felt the anger rising in me, "I have been letting things go my whole life, Katya. If you only knew what I have had to let go—"

No. I decided not to do this now. She didn't understand. How could she? What would she think? I took a few deep breaths, concentrating on my embroidery.

"Mama, I hate it when you slip into your head like that. When you censor yourself. I just know you're having conversations with yourself; you've been doing that my whole life." She stretched out her hand to touch mine. "You could try talking to me."

Lesya came back from the kitchen, and Katya quickly pulled her hand away.

"Everything okay in here?" Lesya asked.

"Fine," I said.

"Fine," Katya echoed. She took a quick breath. "After you've done a basic sketch on the egg, you heat the wax over the candle." Katya held the kistka over the candle. The wax in the copper cone slowly melted. "Next, with the wax you cover everything that you want to be white. You need to cover up what you want to preserve."

I felt her staring at me.

"But you have to trust that the truth is right there under the surface. Right, Ma? You have to trust that when you eventually burn it off, the truth will come through?"

I ignored her and kept embroidering.

"Keep in mind that white is the color of innocence," she said. "Purity. To use white is to invoke its powers. The power of cleansing, or starting fresh."

Lesya held the second egg more gently, quickly sketching a pattern. I looked over at Katya's hands. She was covering her egg with circles and dots.

"The circle is the most powerful symbol you can put on an egg. A circle is a symbol of protection, to keep away bad thoughts or spirits. The dots possess magical powers of prediction. Together, they represent eternity. The universe."

I watched as red stitches became flowers on my cloth.

Katya's hands moved skillfully across the egg. "So, what's this about a new boyfriend?"

I looked up at Katya, who winked at me. Lesya cast a glaring look in my direction. I shrugged.

"Oh, just a guy I met in my 'Leaders of the Second World War' class. He's gorgeous. He loves all the same things I do. He's interested in World War II history just like me—"

At this I had to interrupt. "Yes, but his grandparents were not on the same side as we were? Stalin and Hitler! What a perfect setting for a budding romance. You are both interested in World War II. Perfect, just perfect. As if a war could keep you two together."

I felt the anger rising again, but this time I did not stifle it, "World War II separated people. It did not bring them together. What are you thinking, Lesya? I thought you were a smart girl!"

"Mama! What's gotten into you today? Why are you so angry? Calm down, okay?" Katya put her hand on my elbow to try and calm me, but I shrugged her away. I was tired of staying calm. After fifty years, a fierce storm was building. I stared at Lesya, waiting.

"Baba, World War II brought you and Dido together. You found love during the war."

I felt my cheeks flushing, and I was grateful for the candlelight. My hands settled into fists, and I tried to calm the rage that I felt spreading out from my chest. I exhaled a long breath.

"What do you know of it? Nothing! You know nothing of what I lost. Nothing." I pounded my fist on the table. "For all your schooling, you have not learned about life. You can't learn history from just a few books. History lives in the people who were there, not in numbers. Not in names of battles. Not in 'Hitler and Stalin,' but in me, in your Dido. In the people who died in nameless graves. What about their history? You meet a boy and read some books and think you know everything. You know nothing."

Lesya's eyes squinted and her lips tightened. She had her father's temper. My temper.

"Then tell me, Baba," she said, choosing her words carefully, "Tell me about your history instead of keeping it hidden inside your little wooden boxes."

I tried to calm myself before I said something I would regret. She was young; she didn't understand.

"Lesya, my Mama and Tato, my sisters died in that war at the hands of German soldiers. They burned my entire village because the Russians were coming back. Can you understand that? They were killed in their home in a country that I had to leave forever. I have no cemetery where I can visit with my dead.

"I tried to honor them by teaching my children and

grandchildren about their homeland. Would you disgrace your heritage? Would you throw this all away?" I motioned to my cupboards filled with framed photographs of our family, painted pysanky, Ukrainian books and records. "All I've worked for."

How could I convince this stubborn child? How could I show her, tell her?

"This is America, Baba. Their memories live in me, but I have to make my own future."

Oh, she loved to argue with me, this one. Lesya should have been a lawyer.

"I will teach my children our traditions, our language,"Lesya said. "I don't need a Ukrainian husband to do that."

"You say this now. You will see that it is not so easy to do all by yourself." I stood up. "I have to feed Khvostyk."

I walked into the kitchen and poured him some cat food. Then I turned on the faucet and ran my hands under the warm water, splashing my face. I heard my own baba whisper from my memory: *Anger has its place, Nadya. It's not bad, but it is deadly, like fire. Raging out of control, it can kill and destroy. It is hard to heal a bad burn, sometimes impossible. When fire begins to grow, you can use water to control it. Same thing with anger. Turn to water to soothe you.*

How was she so wise? And she was younger when she died than I was today. When I turned toward the dining room, I heard Katya steer the subject back to pysanky.

"And once you have everything covered in wax, then you need to dip the egg in the lightest color. In this case, orange. Orange is the color of endurance and strength."

"All right," Lesya said, still irritated. "I don't need to know their 'magical' meanings. It's not like you believe it anyhow. It's interesting and all, but you can save it for your class lectures. We've moved beyond those supersti—"

She stopped when she saw that I had come back into the

room. I quietly sat back down in my chair.

"Ma, why don't you tell her a little about the war. Help her to understand. It's not something you usually talk about," Katya said while staring at her egg in the orange dye. Clever woman to put me on the spot.

"No," I said avoiding both their gazes. "I will not share the history of my life with someone who does not respect me or my so-called superstitions."

I turned my attention back to my embroidery. Let them talk; I was going to embroider. Katya reached over and pulled out her egg, bright orange from the dye. Lesya placed hers in the jar.

"Now you take the wax and cover everything that you want to keep orange in whatever pattern you've chosen." Katya explained and then began to draw three snakes winding through the quadrants. She looked at me. "The snakes are for protection from disaster." She turned her eyes back to the egg, still talking. "Snakes are an ancient symbol of the Goddess, who was worshipped on our lands for thousands of years. The snakes are a symbol of feminine power."

Lesya played with the kistka in her hands. "Baba, don't prejudge him. You spent time in Germany; you know that they're not all bad people."

"Lesya, they killed my family. Who knows what else they did to them first? I've had fifty years to imagine all kinds of cruelty." I threaded my needle with black thread. "It's even harder for your Dido. His experiences were more horrible than mine. Talk with him, Lesya. Hear his stories."

"What about your stories, Ma? I've been waiting to hear your stories for most of my life. It's ironic that the woman who gave me my love of storytelling refuses to share any of her own." Katya tried to catch my gaze.

Impatient, Lesya took her egg out of the dye and began to

trace her next pattern in wax. Her egg was a pale salmon color, barely there.

I ignored her question. But I knew Katya: Once she started something, she would want to finish it. Snakes wound around Katya's egg, entwining around the circle. Her hand was so still. She almost didn't have to look at the egg, she drew with such assurance.

She started again: "What was it like in Germany? I know I was born there, but I don't remember anything."

I tried to think of something safe to share. Something that would show them that I understood, that I was not too old to be right.

"It was not all horrible," I said. "We had some good times. Did you know that my first assignment in Germany was to work as a housekeeper in the home of an Oberst, a German colonel?

"The Oberst was unmarried and lived with his parents in a beautiful mansion. I had never seen such wealth. Gold and silver. Art on the walls. Fancy furniture. He was even given a medal for bravery. It was a clasp with oak leaves and swords, decorated with fifty diamonds. It was amazing. He kept it locked in a safe when he wasn't wearing it. The wealth he had amassed was unbelievable, like a dream.

"They gave me a small room. I had never had my own room before. Never since. It had a small bed with white sheets and a white pillow. The sheets were so soft, and the room always smelled like pine. There was a painting of sunflowers on the wall. I would stare at them while lying in bed and dream of my Mama's garden at home, her sunflowers.

"In return, I would clean the house, bring them their meals if they ate in their rooms, attend to them at the table if they ate in the dining room, mend the commander's uniforms and wash clothes. I helped the cook and gardener and did many other small tasks.

"The Oberst's parents were nearly blind, so I would read to them from books written in German. I had learned to read a little German at home, and some more on the trains, but that was where I really began to learn the language.

"The old woman liked me and treated me like a daughter. Her mind was falling apart and she would sometimes confuse me with people from her past: her sister, her mother, her baby girl who died in childbirth. She would sit and talk with me, telling me stories of the time before the war, before the First World War, when Germany was still great. With frail fingers, she would point at portraits on the walls, identifying the men and women who watched me as I washed the floors and dusted. Once I baked her a medivnyk, my Mama's recipe for honey bread, and she said it was the best bread she had ever tasted."

Katya reached over and placed her egg in the brown dye. She rested her chin in her palms, elbows on the table, watching Lesya.

"But her husband, the Oberst's father, only grumbled," I continued. "He did not like me, but had no choice but to tolerate me. The old man was ashamed that he couldn't take care of himself, that I had to clean his bedpan and bathe him. He always avoided my eyes and muttered under his breath in German. Most of the time he was silent, lying in his bed and staring out the window at the gardens. On sleepless nights, when I wandered the halls, I often caught a glimpse of him weeping in forgotten corners of the house.

"The Oberst was kind to me. He was handsome and tall, very strong, and even spoke a little Ukrainian from having been stationed near Rivne for almost a year. He was smart, spoke five languages and had a deep raspy voice that made the German girls swoon. When I would go to the market with the cook, the German maids of other soldiers would curse me out of envy. You see, the Oberst had fallen in love with me."

Both women looked at me, eyes wide with disbelief. I smiled,

"He would bring me bouquets of flowers for my room and tried to find me books in Ukrainian or Russian that I could read before I went to sleep. He was kind. He told me how grateful he was for my service, praised me for the kindness I showed his parents, told me how beautiful I was. But I could not forgive him for what his kind had done to my family. When I told him, he begged me on his knees not to blame him. He said he had nothing to do with it. He begged me to stay with him, to marry him after the war was over."

"Wow," said Lesya, shaking her head.

"You see," I continued, "I was once young and beautiful. There have been many men who have fallen in love with me. Not just your Dido. My life could have been so different." I laughed to myself.

"But after I rejected him, I couldn't stay there much longer. He would come home after being gone for a week or two, and he would stare at me with broken eyes. It hurt my heart, made me uncomfortable to receive his kindness without giving him what he wanted.

"Many Ukrainian girls would have stayed. Many did. Others had a much more difficult time; their soldiers were not as kind. Taking what they wanted, not asking. But after that, I stayed in the work camps. Well, until the Americans came. It was later, at the Displaced Persons Camp, where I met your Dido.

"Lesya, you're not working on your egg," I said. "That's enough of the past for now."

"But Baba, I can't believe it. I never knew—" Lesya said, picking up her egg.

"Well, there is much that you don't know about your Baba."

I watched as Lesya tried so hard to draw straight lines.

"Don't be so concerned with perfection, Lesya," Katya said to her niece. "It's not about the perfect line; it's about the emotion behind the symbols. Let the egg tell your story."

I stood up. "Does anyone want coffee or tea?"

Both shook their heads. I sat back down again. No use brewing just for one cup.

Katya reached over and took her egg out of the brown dye. Lesya handed hers over, and Katya placed it in the dye.

"Brown is a symbol of the Earth and the harvest," she explained. "After you take out your egg, Lesya, cover in wax everything you want to stay brown."

Lesya looked over at me. "But Baba, you saw that all Germans were not cruel. You know that they are not all the same."

"Lesya, I left him. You see, I could have had it easy, living there with the commander. I would not have had the kind of hard life your Dido and I had here in Chicago when we arrived. Then again, who knows? With the way the war ended? We cannot predict our futures. We also cannot go back to retrace paths we did not choose.

"Sometimes the easy choice is not the right one. You know that. We all have to make hard choices."

I looked toward Katya.

Her kistka gently resting in her hand, Katya began to evoke small waves in wax on the brown egg, surrounding the snakes with swirling waters. Katya saw me watching her and grinned.

"The water is for purity of thought and action. These are the Waters of Life. They are filled with the energy of Creation. When I finish with the brown color and put the egg in the black dye, everything that isn't covered in wax will turn black. It will form a sort of reverse meander, spirals that shadow the earlier brown ones. Waves of the Waters of Death to match the Waters of Life." With that, she placed the egg in the final dye: the black.

Katya then pulled Lesya's egg out of the brown dye and handed it to her.

"Don't rush," she told her. "This isn't a race. I've been doing this for a long time."

I turned back to my embroidery. Katya began to sketch her next pattern on a fresh egg. The silence was too heavy.

"Embroidery has symbolic meaning too," I said while stitching. I'm the grandmother. Wasn't I supposed to be the one imparting wisdom? "Red is for vitality and love. Black is for the *chornozem*, the rich black earth. Sometimes it is also the color of sadness."

More silence, except for the scraping of copper on eggshell, the whirr of thread through cloth, and Khvostyk crunching on his cat food nuggets in the kitchen.

"On pysanky, black is the color of eternity. It represents the past, present and future, where they connect and overlap."

I wanted to tell them it's true. The past and present and future did overlap. The dead could haunt you even when you tried to keep them buried. I was going to try and forget about this envelope. I was going to pretend it never came. After all, what else could I do? I didn't know who it was from. Maybe it was a mistake.

"See, it's the black that unites all the other symbols. They may seem disjointed when you first paint them on one color at a time, one line at a time, a bunch of separate shapes."

Could Pavlo have opened it? Could he have removed the letter? No. He would never have done that. It must have been the post office in Ukraine, always looking for money, always looking for a conspiracy.

"But when you look at them all together, they tell a story. You need all of them to get the entire picture."

Katya pulled her egg out of the black dye and put Lesya's egg in. This part always amazed me, from the time I was a young girl. The egg always looked so ugly when you took it out of the black dye. Covered in thick layers of discolored wax, you would never think that underneath it all there was a beautiful pysanka.

"Here comes my favorite part of all." Katya peered at her pysanka. "The unveiling." Katya smiled and glanced over at me. She held the egg gently next to her candle flame. "If you put the egg directly above the candle, it will burn, so be careful."

Katya took a soft cloth out of her pocket and gently wiped away the wax that had melted from the heat. A beautiful design began to emerge. "After it dries, I'll cover it in varnish." She held it up.

"You see: Now the egg is whole. You never really know what it's going to look like until you melt away the wax. Then all the parts come together, and the story is revealed."

PART TWO

Roots

A tree uses what comes its way to nurture itself. By sinking its roots deeply into the earth, by accepting the rain that flows towards it, by reaching out to the sun, the tree perfects its character and becomes great. . . . Absorb, absorb, absorb. That is the secret of the tree.

—Deng Ming-Dao
from *Everyday Tao*
(HarperOne, 1996)

CHAPTER SEVEN

As the months passed, I tried to go on with my life, but there was a heaviness on my heart that I could not shake. Each morning, I took the envelope out of the cedar box and searched for clues. It had grease stains in the corners and a coffee stain on the back. Each day, I scanned the mail for a new letter. Part of me felt like I was dying, and I began to withdraw more and more from my family. I lost weight and didn't get my hair cut or styled. I had little energy and stopped taking my daily walks.

I kept thinking about my parents, about my sisters. Was it my fault they died? What if I had never gone to see the vorozhka? What if I had stayed home that night? Could I have saved them? Who found me? Why now?

My daughter Zirka believed I was "depressed" and needed medicine. Taras thought I was tired from working so hard and offered to buy us a dishwasher. Katya made me beautiful, brightly colored pysanky, no doubt trying to use her creative magic to effect a positive change.

Only Pavlo didn't seem to react. As long as I made his meals, washed his clothes, and kept a clean house, his world was secure. He visited with friends, went to church, watched soccer at Slawko's Bar. I did nothing to interrupt his routine, so he noticed nothing out of the ordinary.

Honestly, I was relieved when Pavlo left the house each day. I could then sit on the couch and stare out the window or watch television. Unless interrupted by the phone or guests, I would fall asleep for hours in the afternoon.

On mornings when Pavlo didn't leave the house, I would escape to the garden. As the weather grew warmer, he spent more time in the air-conditioned house, leaving me to my sanctuary. On the Feast Day of St. Yuri, I went outside with the excuse of tying crimson and gold ribbons around the birch tree in the backyard. I secured the bow and then sat down in the grass, leaning against the garage for shade and support. Flakes of blue-gray paint crumbled under the pressure of my back. Pavlo had been saying he would repaint the garage for the last two years, but still I faced that peeling paint each time I stepped out of the back porch. And what an awful shade of blue. I didn't know what he was thinking when he chose that color fifteen years ago. It must have been on sale.

But the garden, the garden was Pavlo's art and passion. Each dusk since spring's arrival, he was out there whispering Ukrainian love songs to the peas and potatoes. He gently checked each new leaf, each new bud. The tomato plants got more affection than I did. I reached over and plucked off a leaf, brushing it against my lips.

Andriy Polotsky.

Something about the smell of the tomato plant always reminded me of Andriy Polotsky. Not the tomatoes, which were still green but growing larger. No, it was the smell of the leaves. Deep green in color, covered with fine white hairs. A clean smell . . . like lemon rind or fresh-pressed paper or mornings when the rains begin to gently fall just as the sun is rising.

Long before I met Andriy, I met his mother. After I left the household of the German Oberst, I was re-assigned to a machinery parts factory. My hands went from healing and household chores to assembling intricate pieces of metal that we were told would be used for automotive parts. One of the girls swore that a German soldier told her we were assembling parts for weapons. The thought that I could somehow be helping the German cause was too much to handle, until I concocted my revenge. I decided that I would curse every piece of metal I touched, so the weapons would all backfire on the soldiers who held them.

As I worked, I would imagine all kinds of violent malfunctions: guns exploding, tanks firing inward, grenades detonating in hands and pockets. I invoked all the spirits of fire to help me in my vengeance. I went so far as to imagine graphic deaths for Hitler and his henchmen. Only these daydreams helped pass the time and made life bearable. Every night when I left the factory, I would try to stop thinking about the soldiers and my revenge. Baba always said that once you uttered a prayer or a curse, you must trust that God will make it so.

When I was placed in the factory, I was also transferred to an all-women's barracks in a German work camp. The oldest woman in the barracks was Andriy Polotsky's mama, and she took it upon herself to mother the rest of us, most of whom were half her age. Paraska Polotsky was her name, and she was the shortest woman I had ever seen in my life. I was nearly a head and a half taller than she was, and I had not yet stopped growing. Her long blonde hair was woven into a single braid that she wrapped several times around her head. When she let it down before going to sleep, it reached the floor, a single streak of silver spreading down the center. She wore tiny oval glasses—without which she could not see—and her cheeks were always flushed.

She asked us to call her Mama Paraska, because she had no daughters, and so we did. Many of the girls had lost their mothers in the war, and Mama Paraska filled that void in our lives. If we felt sick, she knew the herbs to prescribe and they always worked—when we were lucky enough to find them around the

women's barracks. When we had nightmares, Mama Paraska
made us satchels stuffed with sweet grasses to chase away the
demons. Often, one of the girls would cry on her shoulder at
night, falling asleep in her strong arms.

I had been lucky enough to get the bed next to hers, so on
nights when she had no weeping visitors, she and I would talk in
the darkness. Sometimes I would watch her brush her long blond
hair with its streak of gray, her cheeks flushed with exhaustion,
eyes puffy and tired. Her hands would shake, knuckles swollen,
fingers bruised. I was amazed at how old they looked compared
with her beautiful face. Her skin was so smooth, the only deep
lines settled in around her eyes and the creases of her smile.
From laughter, she told me, because of the joy her son, Andriy,
had brought into her life. When I asked her about her husband,
she would only furrow her brow and say, "Men are worthless."
Then remembering her son, she would smile. "Except for my son.
Andriy is an angel. All other men are worthless."

Mama Paraska winked her right eye. She always did this to
emphasize a point, so her right eyelid permanently drooped a
little lower than her left, giving her face a soft and sleepy look.

"Nadya, the only thing certain in life is children," she said.
"Men, they come and go. Friends, they come and go. But
babies–" She took a deep breath and smiled. "–babies are your
life, your future. They are the ones who will take care of you when
you are old. They are the ones who will tell your stories when you
are gone. Your children will keep you alive."

She stopped and handed me her brush. I moved closer to
her, smelling on her skin sweat and garlic from her kitchen
duty. As I began to brush her hair, she continued, "Children
hold inside themselves a piece of your soul. There is no stronger
connection."

When I brought the brush up to the crown of her head, she
sighed. Her shoulders relaxed a little as the tension began to slip

away. Sometimes she would hum songs from home under her breath, but this time we sat in silence.

The sound of the brush crept into my memories, tempting the past to rush into the present: my own mama's hair, thick and brown; the dimples in her cheeks; the sweet, burnt smell of cinnamon; the circle-shaped scar on her left arm that burned white against her tanned skin; the way she tapped her foot when she was angry and clicked her tongue when I disobeyed.

Mama Paraska turned around and looked at me through the darkness.

"Now you are my daughter," she said. She brought together her thumb and first two fingers, kissed them and then lifted them up to my cheek. "I give you a piece of my soul."

She took back the brush, put it away and settled into her bed. I heard her breath fall into the rhythms of sleep; but for me, sleep never came that easily. Instead I lay back and stared up at the ghosts gathering around all our heads.

Sleeping around me were twenty-three broken hearts. Like mist, heartache hovered above the floor. Guilt slept in tight shoulders, clenched jaws, fists. Fear filled the room with whimpers and silent trembling.

Above hovered spirits. Slipping through cracks, they came each night. I grew to recognize those closest: Maria's father, who smelled of the pipe and played violin over and over again—the same song each night as she wept into the wood, whispering his name. Olena's sister, Ivanka, who ripped at her clothes, tore at her face. Tatiana's lover, who watched from near her head and hummed a song I did not know. Even Mama Paraska's husband came to her side. He sat on the bed beside her, his hands on his heart, tears in his blinded eyes.

All their voices began to mingle into a rich, deep hum. I kept my eyes closed tight once their chanting began to thicken. Names were whispered and repeated. Their tone grew more anxious as dawn crept close—these were the names of those hoping to breach the veil of dreams, to reach the memories of dreamers. These dead were afraid to be forgotten: Hanusia Dzyuba, Franz Foter, Vasil Zinoviev, Marusia Vishnevsky, Kolia Dombrovsky, Lyda Lukich, Anna Katz, Pavlo Romanchuk . . . so many names. They whirled and swirled until they formed a hum like a factory, a tired machine, a hum that drifted away when the sun slipped through the windows.

Never my ghosts.

Each night, I waited. I looked. I listened. Perhaps others saw my mama, heard her sing a lullaby. Perhaps others could not see their own dead either. We never spoke of it. But in the mornings, I was not the only one with tired eyes and dark shadows.

We tried to hide our fears beneath our clothes, inside our fists and tight jaws. We even took comfort in those blue identification patches that we were forced to wear, emblazoned with the "O" for Ost, for East. They united us, reminded us that we were not alone.

Some nights, when the moon was bright enough to light our beds, and the nightmares were fierce enough to combat our exhaustion, we would lie there and confide in our sisters beside us. We never sat up, never looked to claim whose story rushed by our ears, never had faces to connect with the whispered histories. On those nights it was the living, not the dead, whose voices floated thick around us. Our living voices—to keep away the crying, pleading voices of the dead. And as we spoke, it was one voice truly. One story with different names but filled with ripped blouses, swollen bellies, bloody lips, tattered hands, broken hearts and corpses. Always corpses.

But in the mornings, we needed life, not death. Laughter, not tears. In the darkness we spoke our truths, but in the light we spoke of hope, of love, of an end to the war. We looked to each other for signs of life, and we treasured Mama Paraska for her affection, her stories, her support, her vitality. She was our second mother. Twenty-three daughters in that bunkhouse would have died for her, and I was somehow blessed to be her favorite. So she took it upon herself to try and seal my fate with a happy ending.

Mama Paraska's husband had been killed in the war after joining the Cossacks in the Austrian Alps to fight the Germans. Her son, Andriy, had left their village before the Germans came, fleeing North to join the Russian army. Mama Paraska decided that my happiness was dependent upon her son. She spent most of her time bragging about Andriy and trying to convince me that I should marry him.

"Ah, sweetie, how you would love my Andriyko. Everybody loves my son. In the army, he proved to them how smart he was with their machines. He always had a special touch with things mechanical. The big army generals will thank him generously. So by now, he must be very rich, and when he finds me, he will buy us a nice house on the Black Sea where you can have lots of babies and take care of me when I am old."

Because there was no way for Mama Paraska to send letters during the war, she would kneel by her bed at night and pray, convinced that God would forward her messages to Andriy.

When I asked her about it, she explained, "Nadya, God and I have a good relationship. My father was a priest, as was his father before him. So God listens extra special to my prayers. That's why he keeps my son safe, and that's why I know I'll see him again after the war."

Then Mama Paraska got down on her knees beside her bed, and after crossing herself three times, she said, "Hello God, this is Bohdan Shupinski's daughter, Paraska, praying to you, so listen carefully. I am sending this to my son, Andriy, who would have also been a priest if it were not for this war. Please send him this message in his dreams:

"Hello, my beloved Andriyko. This is your Mama. I love you

very much. I have found a nice girl for you to marry. I'm looking at her now, so you will see her in your dreams."

At this she opened her eyes, took my hand, and stared at me for a long time. Then she continued, "You see, Andriyko. She is beautiful and smart too. You will like to talk with her and dance with her. Hurry and find your Mama so I can introduce you, before somebody else steals her heart. Don't forget to say your prayers, and be good: God watches you extra close. Time for me to sleep. I love you.

"God, that is my message. Please have the Angel Gabriel deliver it for me. Keep my son safe, and he will make us both proud. Amen and good night."

Then she crossed herself three more times and laid down in her bed.

Those nights and days stretched on and on in a pattern of working and eating and sleeping and working and eating and sleeping and working. We barely ate, seldom slept, and always worked. Then one day, the Germans fled and the Americans arrived. The war was over.

Peace.

We were left without orders, without guidance, without purpose.

It happened so quickly. One day we had received our usual dose of ridicule, abuse, and violence. The next morning we awoke to the sound of a loud shoom: the sound of cars and tanks and trucks all fleeing without us.

We stood there until even the dust stopped swirling. We stood there in shock, uncertain what to do next. We stood there until one woman let out a loud whistle. Then we all charged the square, the center of the camp where we had so often stood for inspection. Every soldier was gone.

Many women wept, some fainted, others yelled and cheered.

I hated them for their happiness, for their relief. What did peace change for me? Nothing. I lay down in the sun and took in a long, deep breath.

This peace was not mine.

"Freedom" they shouted. "God Bless the Americans!"

Freedom? I could not go home. What good was this freedom?

The American soldiers arrived that afternoon and moved us into the old Neustadt tank center. We were not the only work camp to be emptied into the maneuver field. Hordes of people came from nearby camps, combined with displaced crowds rounded up as the Allies swept through Germany. We were all brought to that dusty place where the soldiers took inventory.

Refugees. Displaced persons.

That was the first time I heard those words.

I stood holding Mama Paraska's hand and stared out at the hundreds of people gathered there. The field was a silent still life of questions. Unspoken questions that brought breath to gray faces and skeletal bodies. They emerged everywhere, growing out from the sun-baked field, creeping out from behind yellow and blue and red patches, painting the moment with a painful, strained hope.

And fear.

Faced with the chance to find those we had lost, we were frozen with fear. Childish hopes had kept so many of us alive during bloody days and hungry nights: the thought that someone lost could someday be found. That someone believed to be dead could somehow have been spared.

But the possibility of undeniable truth was more terrifying than our nightmares. If not hope, what would we have left to hold onto in sleep, in quiet moments when the ghosts would come?

With questions ultimately came answers, as the first brave few crossed over invisible boundaries to connect with strangers–

once family and friends. Some lucky ones looked around the field to find a wife, a brother, a daughter, a neighbor. The rest watched in envy.

I had no one left to look for.

The soldiers called for order, and somehow received enough of it to begin the process of registration.

After those first moments of careful questioning, after the soldiers had taken all our names and given us general assignments, something wild swept through the camp like fire. Emotions stored away during the past few years rushed to the surface and burst out as people began to run about the field. Hands outstretched, they moved through the crowds. Some found lips, sweaty palms, lonely flesh. Others found fists, clenched jaws, angry glares. As the sun set on my first night in Neustadt, everywhere there were bodies entangled in hungry embraces. Here a caress, there a punch, and everywhere moaning.

Mama Paraska and I left the field with a few other women from the work camp and found a dorm room large enough for us to share. She called us together and immediately took charge to ensure the safety of "her girls."

"These men," Mama Paraska said, walking back and forth, "are like pigs and dogs in heat, locked away for so long without women. It will not be safe for you, especially at night. So if you want to stay here with me, you follow my rules, and I will try to keep you safe."

The work camps had been divided into male and female sections, closely monitored by guards and separated by barbed wire. Yet now that the war was over, danger and possibility lurked around every dark corner. Mama Paraska set down her rules: curfew at dusk, no walking alone with a man, no men back in the dorm, no smoking in the room, and—unless a girl was sick—everyone was required to dine together in the evening. If any of us broke any one of her rules, we would lose the privilege of staying in her dorm.

"This is going to be a crazy time, now that the war is over." Mama Paraska shook her head. "My daughters, you must be careful. Men are worthless. And men in heat are dangerous. They fight or rape without a thought because they have been shamed and beaten. And broken. Beware the broken man who sings sweetly but punches after his caress. Remember, they are all lovers and poets before the first kiss."

She looked each of us in the eye as she spoke, this tiny woman with her rosy cheeks who knew our deepest fears and desires.

There were eight of us then, but two girls left that night and didn't come back. Mama Paraska shook her head and said only, "Pity, like the good Lord, I too must lose some sheep."

To further ensure our well-being—physical and spiritual—Mama Paraska made arrangements with Father Petro Petrenko, an Orthodox priest whom she had met while in line waiting to record her name in the books. She had been leaning over the shoulder of the old man in front of her to hear how he answered his questions. Afterwards, she said it was because he looked so familiar. It turned out they came from neighboring villages near Kyiv.

I had been trembling and sweating as I stood in the registration line, trying to decide what to say, how to answer the soldiers' questions. All the rumors I heard rushed through my mind: that the Americans were going to force us all to go home; that the Russians were having us sent to Siberia; that we would "disappear" en route to Ukraine and turn up in ditches; that Ukraine had been demolished in the War, and there were few people left alive. So many nightmares, and we had no way of knowing the truth.

Standing in line, I thought I saw Liliana, the vorozhka, in the distance, walking toward the barracks. She walked with that same sway of her hips, her long hair down around her waist. I stepped out of line and rushed over to her. I could smell berries and mint, her distinct smell. Of course she had survived; she was a warrior! I had so many questions to ask her. I reached out to touch her elbow, and Liliana turned around to look at me, her face thinner; her eyes still bright.

"You survived, farmer girl," she said. "Now it's time to start living."

"Nadya!" A voice called and I looked back. Mama Paraska had been saving my place in line. "It's your turn."

I looked back toward Liliana, but she was gone. I hurried back to my place. When it came time for me to give my name, I lied. I gave Stephan's last name as my own. Nadya Palyvoda. It was the same name I had given in Slovakia, before they took him away. I decided never again to use my father's name. I wanted no connection made to my family. If any of them were still somehow alive, I wanted them to be safe. To have family alive in Germany could only mean one thing to the Russians: Treason.

After I wiped away traces of my past, Mama Paraska began working to convince Father Petrenko and his traveling companion, Brother Taras Moroz, to stay in the room beside ours to be on hand if there was any trouble. In return, she promised to embroider some vestments for Father for Sunday services. She impressed Father Petro with her spiritual pedigree, and in time the two of them grew to be good friends, spending endless Saturday afternoons arguing about the authorship of the Gospels and other spiritual mysteries.

Word of our little safe haven spread, and more Ukrainian girls sought refuge in Mama Paraska's dorm. By the end of that first week, she was responsible for a dozen girls. But Mama was overjoyed, not overwhelmed. She was happiest when taking care of other people; and as for us, the motherless daughters, we craved someone to look out for us, to worry if we didn't come home, to hold us when we wept. Given the choice between freedom or safety, we twelve chose safety. The war had already provided us with a lifetime of adventures.

One of the oldest girls, Natalia, had also come with us from the women's barracks. She had been a poet and teacher; the only one of seven daughters to survive the war. Left for dead among her sisters' corpses in the schoolyard, she had awoken to wild dogs gnawing on her fingers. Despite her own disfigurement—or maybe because of it—Natalia insisted that we "create beauty" around us and suggested that we find a name for our new home. We called our dorm "Nebo," or Sky, and referred to each other as "the Star Sisters."

Even though everyone ate together in the great dining hall, we were each responsible for preparing our own dinners. Eventually, the Red Cross came and relieved us of that chore, but in those first few weeks, we prepared our food outside in pots and garbage cans, using whatever we could find in the dirty abandoned kitchen. Because everyone was looking for supplies and utensils, people fought over ladles and knives. The Star Sisters worked together and took turns preparing meals. As a result, we survived better than many around us, thanks to Mama Paraska and Father Petro.

"The secret to peace is sharing meals," Mama Paraska said before our first official camp dinner of mashed potatoes and spinach. "We will always gather together for the last meal of the day. With food, we feed our bodies. With family, we feed our spirits. And we are family." Then Father Petrenko would bless our meal with a prayer of thanks.

After each meal, Father would stretch back, rub his belly, and say, "The bread of life, the bread of life."

He became for us like a kindly grandfather, full of stories and advice. As time passed, he eventually performed marriages for nine Star Sisters and baptized several of our children.

If he was our new grandfather, his traveling companion, Brother Taras, was our godfather. In a camp filled with "heat-stricken pigs and dogs," Brother Taras and his bright blue eyes, thick blonde curls and strong shoulders was for us an untouchable saint: someone whom we could confide in, dream about, and never fear. He called us his sisters and kissed our cheeks each morning. The first few weeks, he even slept outside our door to keep us safe and in doing so, forever endeared himself to us. Several times, when drunken admirers came searching for "their girls," Brother Taras chased them away, risking stolen guns, dull knives and bloody fists. To us he was the gentlest of men, but to anyone who troubled us, he was our avenger. Many of the Star Sisters swore to name firstborn sons after him.

Together with Mama Paraska, Father Petro, Brother Taras and the Star Sisters, I had a family. It could not replace all I had lost, but I was safe and loved and cared for. Even the nightmares seemed less frightening, and for a while, even the ghosts seemed to be at peace.

But Mama Paraska never gave up hope that she would be reunited with her precious Andriy. Each morning as the sun rose, she and I would take a walk around the camp to the Wall of Words. An outside wall of the cafeteria, it had been transformed with messages and photos left by wives looking for husbands, sons looking for fathers, mothers looking for daughters. Refugees wrote their names and home villages with the hope that someone might find them with news, good or bad:

"This is my uncle, he was taken from the village of Tallinn. Is he alive?"

"Is there anyone here from Drohobych?"

"Here is my wife and son. I have not seen them in four years. Has anyone?"

Eventually these efforts would become more sophisticated as the camp put together a newspaper and began receiving radio broadcasts. But during those first few months, we had nothing but that wall. So we walked and read and hoped.

It was through the wall that Mama Paraska got word of her son's whereabouts. I helped her write a letter and then asked a kind American soldier to send it for us. Together we waited; and as we waited, summer turned to fall, fall turned to winter, and then one glorious day, winter teased us with a taste of spring.

The unexpected February sun had set the snow aglow, and that radiance soaked into our skins, into our moods. After weeks of gray skies and icy winds, the midday rays breaking through the clouds brought a change to all our attitudes. Around me I heard hints of singing, humming, and whistling. The change was soft and subtle, like a whisper in a cathedral, but it was amazing because in the DP camps people were still grieving. Those who had lost loved ones or had lost hope put most of their energy into work and forgetting. Some chose to try and erase time with drinking, fighting, weeping, and empty embraces. Others buried the past in silence.

But this winter sun reminded us of spring, of hope, of things stirring somewhere deep beneath frozen soil, of things that could possibly still stir somewhere deep within our hearts.

That warm February night, the light still lingered in our spirits, and after dining, we remained in our seats in the dining hall. The air was heavy with sweat and cigarettes, onions and burnt butter. The floors were sticky with smeared potatoes and spilt coffee and beer. Hundreds of breaths, old and stale, young and fresh, were caught in half-open mouths, their lips on the verge of song.

Waiting.

Not wanting this brightness to somehow fade away with sleep.

We knew that in the morning, nothing would have changed. Greeted with the same gray skies, the same backdrop of dirty snow and ashen barracks, the same shadows of people, we would go about our work, afraid to get close to anyone. But that night, we found shreds of courage.

It began with a violin, a haunting melody that I recognized as the song I heard at the Gypsy camp, the night I had run off into the woods. I scanned the crowd for Liliana, but she was nowhere to be found. Soon other players joined in. Someone had a guitar, another a flute, and out of the silence came songs from home. A few older men and women wept through their words, words we all knew, some singing, some humming, a few clapping their hands. Several of the younger ones cleared an area in the corner and began to dance. Still others stared off into their memories.

"The guitar player keeps looking at you, Nadya," said Nina, one of the Star Sisters. She nudged me again with her pudgy elbow, her irritation obvious, her voice melodramatic, as usual. "Look at him. If I had a man like that looking at me, you'd better believe that I'd look back at him."

To annoy her further, I looked instead at her. She shook out her braid and tossed her long blond hair around her shoulders. Nina assumed that she and I were destined to be best friends because she had the bed to my right, so each night I was forced to listen to her rattle on and on about her unfortunate engagement and her plan for a better future.

Back in her small village outside of Kyiv, Nina Ochumelov had been promised to a scholar of religion, a handsome older man with a distinguished graying beard, a large house, and several of his own cows. But during one of Stalin's purges, the scholar had been taken away, presumably sent to Siberia. He never returned, and Nina never found a replacement.

When the War reached Ukraine, Nina and her sisters were taken to be laborers in Germany. Her sisters both married

German soldiers and left Nina alone to "toil in the factory" as she would say, each time throwing her hands over her head for emphasis.

Nina felt that God owed her either a rich or a handsome husband to make up for her misfortune. Because we were in the DP camps, she decided to settle for handsome.

"Nadya, if you don't want him, can I have him?" Nina asked while pinching her round cheeks for color. I wasn't sure how she managed to remain so plump; she ate the same as I did. Yet while I remained thin, her hips continued to soften. I knew she was friendly with some of the American soldiers stationed in camp, but I couldn't imagine them giving up any of their food.

I finally turned to look at the man Nina was referring to. No sooner had I turned my head, then he caught my gaze and held it until I realized that I had stopped breathing. He smiled.

I looked back at Nina who was studying my face. She frowned and said, "So you do fancy him, hmm? Okay, fine. But his friend, the cute little blonde man with the long whiskers, he's mine. Besides, I was never one to like musicians—" She kept talking, but I turned back to the guitarist and watched him tune his strings. He started to play the chords for a slow, sad, love song. Glancing up at me, he smiled and began to sing.

I blushed when I realized his seduction: The careful way he stroked and plucked and caressed the guitar strings, while peering at me from the corners of his eyes. As if I was watching something private. As if he was performing only for me.

I suddenly felt as if my breath was pulled from me and a heavy sadness filled me instead. The loneliness of the melody caught in my throat and held my heart from beating. Then and only then did I truly understand the power of the Gypsy music I had heard on the wind. I had thought the music haunting and magical. It was, but it was so much more than that. A longing was echoed in the chords the guitarist played. It would forever echo in any song I heard from home, a rhythm like my mother's heartbeat.

When the guitarist was finished, he bowed his head and sat for a moment. After a long silence, he brushed his light brown hair from his eyes and looked over in my direction. After whispering something to his friend, the guitarist walked over and sat down at my table directly across from me. I hadn't wiped away my tears. I had long since abandoned vanity.

We stared at one another. His gaze steady; his eyebrow raised in a question. He had the look of a man who just devoured a feast and was still hungry.

"Good evening."

"Good evening," I replied and looked down at my hands.

"Shared joy is double joy," he said brushing a tear from my cheek, "and shared sorrow is half the sorrow."

I looked into his eyes. I had always been good at reading people, and the war had been a great teacher, giving me daily lessons about the nightmares people carry in their eyes: pain and fear and hopelessness. Worst of all was the hopelessness, because it felt like razor blades inside my belly every time I looked into hopeless eyes. That was where madness crept in. I learned that it was better not to look, so I avoided people's eyes in camp. Better to look down than to feel that loss, to touch that madness, to see myself reflected.

But I looked into his eyes, and they were guarded. So, the handsome guitarist had learned that walls keep you safe, that trust makes you vulnerable. I found myself wondering if I could ever earn that trust. I found myself wanting to earn it.

But his were also kind eyes, and I smiled despite myself.

"My name is Pavlo. Would you like to dance?" He stood up and stretched out his hand.

I didn't hesitate. I wanted to touch him. I wanted to talk to him, to thank him for the music, to share with him my loneliness, to tell him about the past year of my life. All because of what he made me feel with his music.

And in the end, I told him nothing.

One hand pressed hard against my back, the other holding my own, we moved out onto the floor. Nina glared, her thick lips tight. Others nodded and smiled as we danced by them.

"You are beautiful," he said.

I watched his face for signs of insincerity, of trickery. I saw none. Yet I recognized something in his face, in his eyes, and then it was gone. I tried to look deeper into that blue, but he kept his secrets buried so well.

The room seemed to spin around us, and all the time Pavlo whispered sweet words, his breath scented with cigarettes, whiskey, and coffee. "I think, I think we understand each other. I saw it in your eyes when I played. I think you are the only person in all the world who can understand me."

And I thought I could.

We stopped for a drink, he smoked another cigarette, and then more dancing. Drinking, smoking, dancing—we whirled round and round in a room filled with lonely people, all trying to keep awake the feeling of hope.

"You are the loveliest women I have ever seen." His words slightly slurring, his tongue loose, his cheeks rosy, "Someday, I am going to take you away from all this, to a place worthy of you and your beauty."

I was not looking for this, not looking to be swept up into some stranger's arms.

"You belong in Paris, where I can buy you a bright red beret for your hair, and we can drink wine on the river."

For months I had been asleep, wanting only to work, to sort out the past, to find a way to deal with death and loneliness. Here was someone who touched me, who made me want something more.

"Hand in hand, we could walk along the boulevard, and all the men would stop and stare at my beautiful beloved."

Such sweet words.

Such sweet music.

I should have remembered to look at his hands.

So much is revealed in the hands: future, present, past. All there. But I did not think of the vorozhka or Baba Lena or poor Miriam. I did not remember their words of caution, their wisdom. I should have paid attention to the way he gripped my right hand so tight that my littlest finger went numb. I should have noticed the way that he held my back, pressing me to him so there was no space between us, making a deep breath impossible. And as we strolled past the elders who watched from their benches, I should have heeded Mama Paraska's frown and shaking head. I should have remembered: They are all lovers and poets before the first kiss.

But all I heard were his sweet words.

And although I could not admit it then, I was happy for the attention.

That night he walked me to the door of my barracks, a perfect gentleman, and for the first time since Stephan, I wanted to be kissed. But he only smiled, that one cocked eyebrow teasing me with mischievous unspoken promises. That night I slept soundly, my dreams filled with guitar music and dancing.

CHAPTER EIGHT

There were more dances. Spring teased us with her warm nights, prompting us to find excuses to forget ourselves. So we did. I did, and each time I came to dance, Pavlo was there playing his beautiful music. As soon as I walked in the door, he would set his guitar down and approach me with his arms outstretched, looking to spin me around—much to the envy of the other young women.

One warm night, after weeks of dancing and hours of drinking, Pavlo took me to see the gardens he tended for the camp. He beamed with pride as he pointed out the different vegetables. He touched them so tenderly that I mistook him for gentle. I had not yet seen his temper, only his passion.

"This is a safe place. My place." He slurred his whisper.

He lightly caressed the cucumber vine. "They are so fragile." He looked to the ground.

I knew from the way he had leaned against me as we walked, that he had drunk too much.

"I-I am ashamed," he said and sat down heavily on the ground, dropping his face into his hands.

"I don't deserve this. I don't . . ." He shook his head back and forth. I stood by, helpless.

"What? What's wrong, Pavlo?"

I went to touch his shoulder, but he pulled away from me.

"Don't touch me!" he whispered harshly, then louder: "Leave me alone."

I stepped back, uncertain what to do or say.

"Pavlo?" I squatted down in front of him, speaking as softly as I could. "Pavlo, what's the matter?"

He looked at me, full of fear and anger . . . and sadness. Such sadness.

I could feel it all coming off of him, so strong that it caught in my gut and I felt sick.

"I deserve to die. Just let me die. Let me die."

I felt helpless, so I reached out again to touch him. "Pavlo, you can tell me."

"Nooo," he whispered, but he allowed me to rest my hand on his shoulders

"Please."

He looked at me. Looked into me with wide eyes, and I was afraid of the words that were coming.

So quietly he whispered. "You'll leave me if I tell you, Nadya. You'll leave me, and I don't want to lose you."

"I won't leave you, Pavlo," I said.

He sat up and rushed over to the bushes, heaving. I could hear him throwing up, and then a howl that chilled me. I had heard that cry before. When the animals were trapped in the barn and burning alive. That was the cry to call Death. I ran to him.

He had crawled away from the bushes and lay curled in a ball on the ground.

"Please just sit near me," he whispered.

I lay down beside him, resting my arm gently around his shoulders. He began to rant. He would not look at me. "You need to know . . . why they come for me . . . need to know why . . . so afraid . . . time keeps going back and I see it . . . again and again . . . I am alone with the dead . . . the train is full of corpses . . . ."

Then he looked up at me. "You wouldn't believe what I've seen; what I've had to do to survive. My time as a prisoner in the camps was filled with nightmares I can never forget. The things they did, to men, to women. To children!"

For a few moments, nothing but silence. I think that neither of us took a breath, we just sat there curled together as he shook ever so slightly.

"Pavlo, I—" I tried to find something to say. I had seen death, experienced loss, but not like the stories I had heard from the concentration camps. Those horrors went beyond war, they were pure evil. What could I say when I really didn't understand?

He stopped me with more jumbled words: "Why am I alive? Everyone else was dead . . . the barbed wire . . . the train car . . . so many ghosts always around me . . . I am not worthy of you . . . I deserve only to die . . . to die alone . . . leave me alone . . . ."

I held him tightly as he tried to push me away again, and then he finally stopped pushing. I wanted to say something, but I said nothing, asked nothing.

After what seemed like hours, he pulled away and stared at me. "Never ask me about this," he said.

I nodded.

"Never. Promise me."

"I promise," I said and watched him close his eyes. My chest felt so heavy, I wanted to do something: to scream, to break something, to run away. But I was afraid to move, afraid even to wipe away his tears, and yet it hurt me to just sit there, unable to comfort him. I looked up at the sky, full of the moon. Perhaps if I could remember the words, the old words.

That night was powerful, the moon completely full of the milk of heaven. It was that milk that could soothe dreamers. I closed my eyes, trying to remember and heard Baba's whisper: "Moon Mother's milk. Good to chase away nightmares. All you need to do is ask. What mother would deny her child peace?"

I stroked his forehead, tracing my fingers along his eyebrows, his cheeks, his jaw. Gently forming circles of pressure. I looked up at the moon until my eyes formed tears for not blinking. I stared until light was all I saw, all I breathed. I let it fill me up and gave it to him with each gentle touch. When I looked down, he had fallen asleep.

I lay there, keeping watch. Holding him and keeping Death away, for I knew Death would not answer Pavlo's call if I stayed near and remained awake. I tried to understand his words, tried to make sense of his pain and anger, but I had so many questions that I could never ask him. Could I love such a man?

I watched the stars and moon and blackness. The same sky can look so different when you look with different eyes. I knew that to be with Pavlo would be to share his ghosts. Could I see him as he was, not as he saw himself or as others saw him?

Before the next full moon, Pavlo claimed me for his own and insisted that we stay together in the married couples' barracks. He insisted that marriage itself was only a formality, and he would rather wait to have the ceremony in a real church, not in a camp courtyard. As I stood in Nebo, the girls' barracks, and gathered Stephan's overcoat, my shirt and skirt, shoes and journal, Mama Paraska begged me to stay with her, promising that Brother Taras would protect me until Andriy came to take us both back home. But fear and love kept me blind.

Pavlo didn't trust Mama Paraska's influence. He was jealous of any time I spent away from his careful gaze. He tried to forbid me to see her, but I refused. After a few slaps of warning, he finally commanded that I spend as little time with her as possible. I learned that with Pavlo, punctuation marks came in the form of shaking, slaps, and punches. The greater the emphasis, the harder the blow.

Mama Paraska and I still met in the evenings after work to talk, usually in Nebo under the protection of Brother Taras. At least there I knew I would be safe for an hour or two.

One night, many months after we sent the letter to Andriy, I sat on Mama Paraska's bed waiting for her to join me. Normally she was on time, but that night she was fifteen minutes late. Suddenly I saw her, running up the stairs waving a letter, her face flushed with excitement, her cheeks even rosier.

"It came!" Mama Paraska shouted, her wide grin revealing the gap where the German soldiers had stolen her gold tooth.

"Andriyko got my letter. He's coming. He's coming!" She tossed the letter into my lap, lifted up her long skirts, and began to dance around, singing over and over again: "My son is coming, my son is coming."

I looked down at the letter in my hand, quickly scanned a few lines. He was obviously well-educated by his vocabulary and style. But his handwriting said even more than his words. The writing was tiny and neat. Nothing ran together, neither word nor letter. Everything calculated, everything careful. He was a man in control of the image he put out into the world. Yet he wrote his letters close to the line, not open or tall. He was a man with secrets.

> *"My Beloved Mama,*
>
> *I am so happy to hear that you are alive and well. I am also well; you need not worry about my health or well being. In fact, I will be coming to see you in a few weeks' time. I have made important friends in the Army and have explained to them that you were captured by the Germans. They have granted me time to come and bring you back to Ukraine. I am to receive land as repayment for my time served. So you see, it will all be set right again—our family name, our legacy."*

Andriy went on to describe medals he had won in the Battle at Stalingrad, under General Volsky's 4th Mechanized Corps. He wrote about his nickname among the soldiers—"Soldat Spivak," the Singing Soldier—because of his beautiful voice. On rare nights when someone had a guitar or a bandura, his comrades would ask him to sing the old songs, and Andriy would bring them all to tears.

"Oh, how I wish you would leave that Pavlo and come back with me," Mama Paraska said, stopping her dance and staring into my eyes. "I won't tell my son that you've been living with him. I know that it wasn't your choice."

I shook my head. I could not leave Pavlo. When he drank, his temper flared, but he did have a soft and loving side—the part of him that was tender, that cultivated life in the gardens. I was ripped apart by my emotions for Pavlo. I was curious about Andriy though. After all, he was Mama Paraska's son. After hearing about him for so long, I had painted quite a picture in my mind and I wanted to meet him.

One Friday night, many weeks later, Pavlo came home drunk again after work, and we got into another terrible fight. He accused me of being too friendly with Sonny, an American soldier stationed in the camp. I told him that the soldier was only a friend, but Pavlo insisted that we had been having an affair. I threatened to leave him, and Pavlo hit me. He left me weeping in the corner and went off to drink some more.

Soft knocking on the door. When I didn't answer, Mama Paraska let herself in.

"My son is here, Nadya," she said, lifting me to my feet. "I want him to meet you."

Sobbing hysterically, I would not look at her. I felt so helpless, so lost. She wet a rag and wiped my face. Then she looked me straight in the eye that was not swollen.

"You're coming with me to meet my son. It's dark, and he won't see the bruise. Besides, Pavlo will be gone until morning, no doubt drinking himself to sleep in some hole somewhere. Who knows what other trouble he will find."

I was ashamed. I didn't want her son to see me, to know that I allowed myself to be treated in such a way, but I followed her, my spirit broken.

We walked over to the campfire, where I could only see the shadow of a man. As we came closer, firelight began to reveal his face. He stood up and extended his hand.

"Hello, my name is Andr—"suddenly he stopped and took a step back.

I looked down, embarrassed. I must have looked horrible. Tears formed again, and I ran back toward my barracks.

"Nadya, wait! Please!" he cried out, and I could hear his footsteps behind me.

I stopped at my door and turned around to face him.

"I'm sorry," I said. "I know I must look terrible." I looked down at the dirt.

He shook his head and stared at me, eyes wide.

"No, that's not it at all. You will probably not believe this, but I've seen you before."

I looked up at him, trying to recognize him.

Interrupting my memories of Andriy, Pavlo tossed a tiny green tomato at my legs.

"Hey, old woman, what are you doing there?" he asked. "Are you sleeping?"

"Just taking a break, Pavlo, and thinking." I looked at my husband's white knees poking out from his shorts. His socks stood out black inside his brown sandals.

"The garden looks nice, no?" he asked.

I nodded, staring at his big toe poking through the hole in his right sock. I need to mend that, I thought.

"Yes. It's beautiful this year, Pavlo," I said. "Do you remember when we first met?"

I looked up at his face. His grin stretched wider. "Of course I do. It was that beautiful winter night when I was playing my guitar in the dining hall. You couldn't look away from me."

"What? You were staring at me!" I protested, still watching his mouth.

"But that wasn't the first time I saw you," he said, his left eyebrow peaking to match his crooked grin.

I searched my memory. I could not remember ever seeing him before that night.

"Remember? We had been in camp for a few months. It was the last warm harvest night, and I watched you creep up to my gardens not knowing I was there." He laughed, walking toward me. "I saw your ankles because you had bare feet. I told myself, 'This girl has beautiful ankles.'" He reached down and touched my ankle. "You still do, even for an old woman." He didn't take his hand away.

I never knew he liked my ankles, and I could not believe he saw me before the dance, in the garden where I would go to escape before I knew it was his handiwork.

I looked for you after that," he said, "but once the snows came, many people chose to eat in their own barracks. I did see you a few times, though. You were so beautiful; how could I miss you?" He winked at me. "But you were always talking with the girls in your barracks or with that old woman. I never knew how to get your attention."

I still could not believe that he had seen me before, that he had been looking for me. "That was you?"

He stroked my ankle. "That was me. I could be quiet when I wanted to. I would often go there to calm down. I overheard many interesting things in my garden."

He laughed, and I tried to picture my first night in the garden, before I knew it was Pavlo's. "What I remember is a man covered in mud jumping up and scaring me. I almost lost my skin. I thought you were a poliovyk."

"You thought I was a field spirit?" He laughed that deep, roaring laugh of his. "Well, Nadya, this field spirit is too hot outside. I'm going to have some lemonade. Don't stay outside too long. Remember, Taras is coming soon." He turned around, still laughing, and went back inside the house. Khvostyk was sitting in the window, batting at something he thought he saw.

A week earlier, for Pavlo's birthday, our children put their money together and bought him a new television and video machine. It had just arrived at the store, so Taras told us that he would bring it over. I looked again at the tomatoes, then back toward the porch window where I saw Pavlo teasing Khvostyk, tugging at his tail. Khvostyk hissed and batted him with his paw. He never really liked Pavlo. He was always my cat. But then again, cats usually didn't like Pavlo. I closed my eyes to remember that night in camp more vividly.

No matter how long I stared at Andriy, I could not recognize him. His face was smooth, his features delicate, as if sculpted by a skillful hand. He reminded me of an icon of the angel Michael in St. Sophia's back home, before the Communists had stripped the church of all her treasures and boarded it shut. But other than that, I could not recognize him.

"I'm sorry, but I do not know you," I said. "I feel like I should, from all that Mama Para—um, from all your mother has said about you, but I don't recognize you."

"We've never met," he said, "not really." He took a step back. "Is there any place we can talk? I don't wish to wake anyone."

I looked around. The lights were on all over the camp. Music was playing, people were singing. Not many people would have been sleeping, but this was Mama Paraska's son, and I did not want to offend him.

"All right," I said. "Follow me."

We walked in silence to the section of camp where they kept

the gardens—those for the soldiers and those for the rest of us. Andriy and I sat down on a patch of grass.

"Nadya . . . may I call you Nadya?" he whispered, his voice smooth and slow, each word carefully rolling off his tongue, onto his lips, into the night. I only nodded, feeling slightly light in the head.

He looked at me so intently, almost without blinking. It was then that I first noticed his uniform, so familiar. Could we have met? Then something struck in my memory. His uniform. I realized why his uniform seemed familiar. The soldiers who had taken Stephan wore the same uniform, although theirs had been dirty and torn. His was clean and fresh. What if he—could he have been? Gray flashed before my eyes, breath pulled from my lungs. I suddenly felt faint.

"Were you ever in Slovakia?" I asked, desperate. "Were you?' I searched his face for clues, but his face was not familiar. Could I have forgotten? No. Never!

"Only on the train ride here," he answered, looking at me strangely. "Are you all right?" He reached out to touch my forehead. "You are very cold."

"I'm fine," I said, suddenly wanting my bed, my blanket, the safety of sleep. "What were you saying?"

His eyebrows lowered in concern. He went on. "I have had vivid dreams ever since I was a boy. My mother said that they were messages from God, but I never believed very much in any god. Especially not after the things I have seen."

He plucked a leaf off a tomato plant and continued, "This will sound strange, but it is true. I swear it on my father's grave. I have dreamt of you, Nadya. I've seen your face so clearly in my dreams. Sometimes you were crying, holding my mother's hand. Sometimes you were smiling. I would watch your lips, wishing I could hear what you had to say.

"On the nights after battle, after burying comrades, friends, I would pray that you would enter into my dreams. I would wish that I could hear the stories you were telling, instead of just watching your lips move. Many nights, you did return, but I never heard your voice. But on those nights when I saw your face, I cannot tell you how much peace you brought me. I thought that you must be my guardian angel."

I looked down at my hands: nails caked with dirt from helping in the gardens earlier that day. Then I glanced at his hands: clean, trimmed smooth.

"Many months ago, the dreams stopped coming. I waited, prayed each night to a God I lost faith in, that the angel who appeared in my dreams would visit me again. Only once more did I see you, and that was ten weeks ago."

I looked up at him. As he talked, he never stopped looking at my lips. It was the same way Stephan used to look at me.

"You were crying. I wanted to comfort you but could not. The next morning, the letter from my mother arrived. I took it as a sign.

"You brought me such hope on those nights. If I *could* have named you, it would have been Nadya. How perfect that your name means hope, because that is what you have been to me. My hope."

This man had such a gentleness to his voice. Somewhere off in the camp, Pavlo was surely drinking more, and here this man was sharing his soul with me. What had happened to my life? I looked down. Everything was spinning out of control. I fell backward, caught by his strong hands. Darkness . . . and then his face.

"Nadya?" Andriy whispered. "Nadya, are you hurt?"

Rage filled my mouth, bringing up the words I had been burying for months.

"I hate him," I whispered.

"Who?" Andriy asked.

"I hate him. I hate my life." I sat up, my voice growing louder as I shouted into the night. "I hate you, Pavlo! For all that you've done to me. For ruining my life!"

In the near distance, a stray cat hissed and darted past.

If only Pavlo were before me at that moment, I would finally have bared my soul. I would have told him how much he hurt and disappointed me.

If only I could escape. If only I had another choice. If only I were a man. I wished that I had the strength to match my rage. Why did I always have to stand by with arms twisted behind my back, my mouth held shut, choking on silence?

This war had silenced the women and released a poison inside the men, something that changed their eyes and twisted their vision. I didn't know where it came from, but it broke us.

I had seen it in Pavlo's eyes, in his anger. It was the same poison in the Germans who burned my family, the Nazis who murdered Miriam's mother and destroyed her, the Russians who raped the vorozhka, Stephan with all his lies and betrayal, the Slovak Partisans who beat me, and all the other beasts who ripped and clawed and thrust and spit and burned. Wolves wild with blood lust. This was a man's war.

If only I were a man.

I would rip off the lips that had curled around lies and accusations. Tear out a heart that pumped only poison. Pluck out those eyes and crush them in my palms until the poison ran out over my fingers and onto the ground, staining it red. Like the wise witches who could read the future in a black pond or candlelit mirror, maybe in that thick pool of poison I could see the horrors in all their eyes. Maybe then I could understand war.

Andriy tried to brush tears away from my face, but I wanted no man near me then. My hands in fists, I began to beat at my belly and rock back and forth. Wailing. No more words. I slipped into a dark, empty place far away, where the only thing I saw was blood red rage all around me. And the only thing I heard was moaning in the distance, a sound I did not recognize as my own voice. Andriy held my shoulders and shook me gently. I could smell the tomato plant on his fingers. A clean, green smell. Somehow that smell brought me back into my body. He held my hand and let my cry.

After I had no more tears, I sat staring in silence at the moon.

"Come on, Nadya," Andriy said. "Let's walk away from here. Leave your sorrow with the tomatoes."

I started to laugh and couldn't stop. What a ridiculous thing to say, as if I could lose my sorrow. As if the tomatoes could hold it. I stopped, bent over with laughter that came from deep inside my belly. A laugh I had not felt in a very long time.

"What's so funny?" Andriy looked concerned again, which only made me laugh harder. Who was this man to listen when no man did, to advise me on the healing powers of tomatoes?

After I lost the laughter, I walked with him toward the edge of camp in silence, the smell of the garden still on our clothes. After a moment, Andriy said, "Leave him."

He stopped and looked me in the eyes. "Leave him and come with me and my mother. You will always be safe, always taken care of."

I started to shake my head, but he reached out and gently put his hand on my forearm.

"Don't worry; my intentions are honorable."

I watched his face for signs of insincerity, but there were none. How could he care so much?

"I would always make sure that you were taken care of," he said.

A wave of nausea, sharp pains. I put my hand on my side.

"I can't," I said, although his offer held more promise than any dream I had dreamed since I left Ukraine: a family. I already loved his mother. But I could never return there. What if they found out about Stephan? And Pavlo, I could not leave him—

"Why not?" he asked. "You don't love him."

I inhaled a deep breath, then exhaled long and heavy. I stared at my feet and said, "I think I'm pregnant, Andriy."

It was the first time I had said the words out loud.

Silence. Then he took my hand again.

"I'll marry you, Nadya," he said. Again the sincerity. Again the kindness.

I laughed again, this time bitterly. "You don't know me."

"I believe I do," he answered.

How different my life would have been had I gone with Andriy. I would surely not be here in Chicago, in a backyard sitting against a garage with peeling blue paint. I stared at the tomato plant in Pavlo's garden, watching the thick worms crawl on the stalks.

I heard the screen door slam against the side of the house, and Pavlo walked toward me, his face red, troubled. He didn't look right. I panicked and began to rise. Pavlo stretched out his hand, motioned that I stay seated. I looked up at him,

"What's the matter, Pavlo? Don't you feel well? Are you having chest pains?"

He walked over to me and sat down. His knees creaked. He let out a groan as he leaned back against the garage, next to me.

"Nadya," he said, "I've been thinking about something. I'm not sure why, maybe it's because you look so pretty sitting here in the garden. Maybe it's just the games our minds play with us when we get old."

I gazed intently at him. "What is it?" I asked. I was getting angry. Was he gambling with the old men in the bar again? I was saving that money for a new coat. "What have you done now, Pavlo?"

"I never told you," his voice cracked.

Pavlo was not an outwardly emotional man. As I looked away, staring straight ahead, I heard him take a deep breath.

"I don't know if you remember that night back in the camp when we got into a fight, something about an American soldier. I was angry and drunk. We fought. Back then I was always afraid, afraid of losing you. I had nothing else. I loved you so much—"

What triggered this memory for him? I looked at his face, but he avoided my eyes, staring at the grass while brushing his hand along the surface.

"I'm sorry we fought," Pavlo said looking at his fingertips.

I said nothing and watched Khvostyk hitting the screen with his paw. Pavlo continued, "I left you crying in the barrack and went to drink, but I had no more money. So I went to the garden to think. To sleep. I couldn't face you. I fell asleep there, and then I dreamed that I heard your voice, and you were crying. I thought I woke up, but I must have been dreaming. I heard you talking to someone, a man. First I was angry again, but I kept listening.

"You said you hated me. You said you cursed the day you met me. Nadya, something inside my heart was squeezed so tight I couldn't breathe. I promised that night never to hurt you again. I promised God. I promised to make you happy. I promised—"

He stopped talking. I looked down at the grass. I couldn't believe Pavlo was there. Couldn't grasp the possibility.

"I'm sorry. Nadya, I loved you. I knew the first time I saw your face that I would marry you. I knew." He reached for my hand. "I just wanted to tell you."

For a few minutes we sat in silence. Then Pavlo looked at me, as if there was something more he wanted to say, then shook his head and kissed me on the cheek. He let go of my hand as he stood up and reached for the side of the garage for support. Flakes fell apart under his hand as he looked down at me and said, "Maybe tomorrow I'll buy fresh paint."

How like him to change the subject. How like him to stir me up, then back away.

"Another shade of blue," he continued. "I know it's your favorite color." He smiled. "Remember when you told me you always dreamt of a blue barn with a brown speckled cow named Zorya. Well, we never did get that cow, but we have a nice brown car." He walked back to the house.

So quickly the seasons changed, the wheel of life turning. Sometimes I cannot believe that I have surpassed my grandmother's age, that I have lived a lifetime and am closer to the end than the beginning. Sometimes I feel as if just yesterday I was five years old sitting in my Dido's garden. Just yesterday, I held Stephan's hand as we walked through the woods, naming our future children. Just yesterday, I buried my secrets under a grove of dead trees. The closer I get to the end, the more I turn back to the beginning. Just waiting for tomorrow to become yesterday.

I missed Ana. If only she were here, I could talk with her. She would have known exactly the right thing to say and do. I waited, but all I heard was a cat in the neighbor's trashcan and a siren in the distance.

Just as I thought my life had reached a calm, a peace that comes with age, that cursed envelope arrived to haunt me with thoughts of what might have been. Still, I had no answers. I continued to wait for something to happen, for something to change.

My Baba always told me that when you needed a teacher, the Universe would send you one. When you needed an angel, you needed only to look around. I keep looking and listening. I suppose I had been lucky in my past, blessed with many angels in my life. If Andriy was one such angel, should I have gone with him? Americans say "Hindsight is 20/20," but even looking back, I didn't know if I made the right decisions.

I collapsed at Andriy's feet, exhausted and heavy with pain and guilt and confusion and regret and shame. Andriy knelt down beside me and extended an arm, which I pushed away. Rushing at me were the events of the last two years, they raged inside like wildfire. I felt again the deaths of those I left behind: Mama, Tato, Laryssa, little Halya, Stephan, Miriam. I felt again Pavlo's cruel accusations. They were like a fist around my heart, squeezing. Yet, I could do nothing but cry and pound the earth. I thought nothing of the child in my womb, nothing of my own health, nothing of the future.

I wanted to die.

I awoke, having cried myself to sleep, my face in the grass, my hands still in fists. Andriy sat beside me, hands folded in his lap, watching me. The sky was still dark; I could not have slept for long.

"I'm so sorry," I said, my throat raw from crying.

"I would do anything for you," He said.

"How, Andriy?" I asked, angry and suspicious. "How can I believe you? You don't know me. You don't know anything about who I am." I looked at him.

"You have a choice," Andriy whispered in darkness.

"No. It's not that simple." At least the pounding in my chest had stopped.

Then I remembered. Choice. I did have a choice. Mama Paraska knew all about herbs. If I didn't want this baby—

"You're right Andriy. We need to go see your mama." And I leapt to my feet.

After I explained to her my plan, Mama leapt shook her head. Andriy stood behind her, his right hand on her shoulder, his left hand tugging at his eyebrows. They looked like a biblical icon, standing there together. The angel standing behind the saint. If only I had the patience for painting. Or the freedom.

Mama Paraska just stared at me, eyes unblinking, and said, "Kill your child?"

She looked up at her son, "Kill her child? You can't approve of this."

Andriy said nothing. He just kept tugging at those caterpillar eyebrows. He hadn't said anything since we left the gardens.

"Mama Paraska, I don't want a child made in hatred—"

"It's a child!" Her eyes bright, her voice even stronger, "A human child, Nadya." She stood up and rushed at me, placing her strong arms on my upper arms. Her cheeks were white, her hands shaking, she brought her face right up to mine. Standing up on her toes a little, she glared at me, and I could feel power from this woman. I could feel it like heat coming off her body.

"Above all else, life is sacred," Mama Paraska continued. "Have you learned nothing in this war? How can you ask this of me?"

I looked away. "Will you help me?" I wanted no child conceived in War.

Silence. I walked over to where someone had left a fire to burn itself out. I stared into the embers, feeling glares on my back. The snap and pop of the fire called to mind Miriam from the train, whose lovely hands had been burned by the German soldiers. Why create more children for this horrible place? To die at the hands of cruel men, or worse. To live lives filled with pain, suffering, deception, death. I thought of Halya, of Mama, of Baba Lena. Or worse yet, to give birth to a son who could someday treat women in such a way. No. A child conceived in hatred would only live out that hatred in his life.

I looked over at mother and son. Mama Paraska stared at me. Andriy stared at me. Waiting.

"I will not give birth to this child. I will not. If you won't help me, I'll find someone who will."

Mama Paraska walked closer to the fire and again reached out to touch me. I shook her away. She reached up and grabbed my chin, pulling it down so I could not help but look her in the eye.

"If you kill this child, I can never again call you daughter. If you kill this child, I can never again call you friend. You kill this child, I can never speak to you again, Nadya. Never."

"Thank you," I said.

"Do not ever thank me, not for this." She walked away, and I went back to the barrack.

An hour later, Mama Paraska walked to my door with a cup of warm, dark liquid and said, "Eat nothing. Drink this and go to sleep. The pain will wake you." She slowly handed me the cup, and as I took it, she said, "Nadya, you can still change your mind. Listen to your heart."

She held both of her hands out in front of her, palms facing upward, and took a step toward me. As I stepped back, she reached out and cupped my cheeks in her warm hands, holding my head still so she could peer up into my eyes.

"Nadya, know this: there is balance in the universe."

But I shook her hands off. "Paraska, I can't birth this child. I can't."

She let go and took a step back, her cheeks flushed, her eyes tearing.

"At least bury him," she said, "and give him a name." Mama Paraska wrapped her arms tightly around herself. "I put in a little milk of the poppy to help you, to dull the pain a little." She looked up at the sky, crossed herself, and walked away,

I closed the door, then lit a candle beside my bed to protect me from any evil spirits who might smell death and come to call. The other couples who shared the barracks were still out dancing, drinking, and enjoying this, one of the last warm nights of summer. Pavlo was undoubtedly passed out somewhere, so I had the room to myself for a few hours. I drank down the warm liquid, tasting honey and a hint of mint, then closed my eyes and lay down to sleep.

Crying, not pain, woke me from a dreamless sleep. A soft

whimpering from the darkest corner of the room, and a tiny voice: "Mama, why is there no love for me?"

I sat up in bed, suddenly shivering, and looked around for my blanket. Seeing it on the floor, I reached over the edge to lift it up and felt a cold breeze brush against my arm. I quickly drew my hand back and pulled my knees up to my chest. Nothing moved in the room, and for what seemed like hours, I sat there. My eyes grew heavy, I must have drifted back to sleep. Again the voice: "Mama, why did you take away my breath?"

"Who-who's there?" I asked, afraid. Only silence.

A breeze must have burned the candle out, so I reached for matches. I felt a tight cold grip on my wrist in the dark, and for a moment I hesitated, afraid. When I finally lit the candle with shaking fingers, the light cast no shadow on my arm. Still that icy pressure around my wrist.

"Leave me in peace," I cried out. "Leave me; I have no choice."

Tears were forming in my eyes. Pain, like a deep throb in my belly, forced me to lurch forward on the bed. I was chilled except for the fire beginning to burn in my womb. I rested my chin against my thighs, trying to rid myself of the chill, but still that icy pressure on my wrist.

"Leave me in peace, please." I begged. I wept. No longer in control

"Mama, why? Why is there no love for me?" Again that sweet voice.

"I have no love," I said aloud. "I have no love left. It died inside of me, and there's nothing I can do."

I sat back up and shook my hands, trying to rid myself of the grip. Then a stab, like nails scraping against the inside of my belly.

I fell over onto my side and wrapped my hands around my stomach, my eyes squeezed shut.

"Mama." A whisper, closer to my face.

I refused to open my eyes, the pain intensified.

"Mama?"

I bit the inside of my cheek and tried to picture myself anywhere else. Still, the ripping. Still, the stabbing. Still, the feeling that I was not alone.

"Mama. I chose you."

Another stab and burning and pounding in my head behind my eyes. My heart was beating so quickly. I opened my eyes and saw on the ground the shadow of a little boy standing at the foot of my bed.

"Stephan," I whispered.

I closed my eyes. Fluid gushed from between my legs. Then the painful throbbing. Suddenly, the chill was gone, replaced with a fire of pain. Then a black and heavy silence.

CHAPTER NINE

"It's time to burn them," she said.

My dearest Ana often appeared to me in my dreams. The night before the Feast of the Triytsya, I had a particularly vivid dream of Ana, so I knew she was sending me a message. In it, Ana was standing beneath a tree with falling leaves. She beckoned me closer, and when I came, I saw that the leaves were really envelopes falling to the ground.

"It's time to burn them," Ana repeated.

That morning before having my coffee, I set fire to the envelope over the stove and watched it burn. I had learned nothing from it, and there was nothing left to learn. I felt sadness as I swept the ashes into the sink. Then I went to Mass at St. Volodymyr's Cemetery to honor my dead. After Mass, everyone went off to lay flowers on the graves of family and friends. The feast day was popularly called Zeleni Sviata, "The Green Holidays," another religious tradition that we continued from the old country. I often wondered if the souls of the dead still entered the flowers and trees in this foreign soil. I suppose they do. But many of my dead are not resting in this American ground.

On the first Zeleni Sviata after Baba died, I was so anxious to receive a visit from her, to be able to somehow touch her again. I stood beside Mama during the service, and as soon as we finished singing, I ran around to each of the trees. Knocking gently on the bark of each tree, I'd whisper, "Baba, are you in there? It's Nadya. I came to find you. Where are you? Are you here?"

Mama told me it was impossible to know which tree held Baba's soul, but I insisted. For what seemed like hours, I ran from oak to pine to maple to sycamore, until I saw a white hare sitting quietly in the shadow of a fir tree. Forgetting everything, I crept up to the hare. As I approached, it just sat there twitching its whiskers, looking at me.

I stopped within steps of the hare and put out my hand, expecting it to run away. Instead it hopped over and smelled my palm. With my other hand, I gently petted its fur. Then it scurried around the tree and disappeared. For a moment I smelled lilacs on the air. That was when I knew this was Baba's tree.

I couldn't reach the branches, so I called Mama over and asked her to break a branch for me.

"This is Baba's tree." I told her.

She smiled at me and broke off the branch, but I knew she didn't believe me.

Later we went home with the branches and flowers we had collected and spread them all over the house, so the ancestors were all around us. The house felt full, like it did on holidays when so many visitors would pile into the tiny room that I couldn't see the other side. And it smelled wonderful, as if a forest had sprouted in our home.

Mama prepared a seven-course supper, and before we ate, Tato greeted all the ancestors:

"Oh, shining Sun, radiant Sun,

Oh, Blessed Mother of all life,

Holiest of ancestors,

Spirits of the forest, waters, fields,

We greet your visit with the coming of summer.

We honor you. We welcome you."

It was not quite the same celebration here in Chicago. But at least it survived. As part of the tradition, I first went to the grave of Mykola, my youngest son. Tracing the numbers on the tombstone with my finger—1952-1971—I thought, *He was just a baby. Too young.* I lifted the tiny American flag that had fallen over. The sun had bleached it, and I forgot to bring a new one. Kneeling down, I kissed the stone and rested my cheek against it. It was so cold. At least the flowers were growing nicely. I knew Katya came here often to tend to them. She and Mykola were so close, even with the large span of years between them.

Katya had tried to convince him not to enlist in the army, but he said it was his duty. I remember sitting in the kitchen that day as they argued in his bedroom.

"Mykola, you're not violent. In the fifth grade, you wouldn't hit Tony Malaniuk even after he gave you a black eye and called you a sissy."

"Yeah, it did wonders for my reputation to have my older sister come over and yell at the class bully. I thought you were going to hit him. So did he."

"I was just looking out for you, Kolya. Tell me, what have the Vietnamese ever done to you? It's not like you'd be fighting the Russians."

"Katya, what else can I do?" He lowered his voice. "I can't go to college. You know there's no money. I'll end up being drafted anyway."

"No, I'll help you—"

"Katya, I've made up my mind."

"Kolya, think of what you're doing to Mama. She's crying in the kitchen right now."

"I'll be okay. I'll come back a hero. You'll see."

"If you come back."

"I will come back."

I went to church every single day that he was gone. Three hundred and fifty days in Vietnam, and I lit a candle for him each morning and said a prayer. Every night before I went to sleep, I prayed to the Blessed Mother to keep him safe, to keep all our boys safe.

But the soldier still came, the chaplain standing behind him, trying to offer solace, offering no explanation. Later, a metal box was sent with an army medal and Mykola's watch.

I looked again at the dates on the tombstone. It's not right that a mother should bury her child. I wouldn't speak to God for a long time after that—a very long time.

After visiting Mykola's grave, I walked over to see Ana and her husband, Nicholas. Sitting down, I stared at their photo on the headstone.

"Hello, old friends," I whispered. "I miss you."

We had met them on the boat to America, the *General Stuart*. Like so many other couples, Pavlo and I slept huddled next to each other in the darkness, while our children were curled up beneath Pavlo's heavy coat and a tattered bed sheet. I was pregnant with Mark, and he was already keeping me up at night. The pregnancy, combined with Pavlo's snoring, made my seasickness unbearable.

I remember waking up to the sound of moaning. While my eyes adjusted, I expected the darkness to reveal a seasick passenger. Instead, I saw an attractive dark-haired woman passionately kissing a tiny, fair-skinned man. He had his hand inside her shirt, on her right breast. Her eyes were closed.

I looked around, but it seemed that everyone else was sound asleep. I knew I should look away, but I sat there amazed; staring. I watched as she stroked his head gently, playing with his fine blonde hair. I watched as he switched his hand to her left breast.

What kind of people were they to have no sense of shame, no pride? Suddenly she opened her eyes, looked up and met my gaze. Embarrassed, I looked away. But not before she smiled.

The next morning the smiling woman came over, introduced herself as Ana, and offered me sweet bread. At first I refused, but she sat down next to me and would not leave until I had tasted some of her husband's bread. I had never met a man who could cook, so I tried the bread out of curiosity. I shared the soft honey-flavored loaf with my children while listening to Ana explain her remedy for my obvious seasickness.

"It's a purple kiss you need," she said with a glance in Pavlo's direction. He was sitting with a few of the other Ukrainian men.

I must have blushed, because she touched my cheek and laughed. Her fingers were cool and smelled of peppermint. And that laugh—a deep and round "hahaha" her mouth wide open, large teeth showing.

"Oh, my darling, it's not what you think. Although there are other remedies I could suggest."

I could feel the heat spreading down my neck and across my chest.

She continued, "But this is quite ordinary. It's a flower. Wait, I think—" and she hurried over to her things, mumbling to herself along the way, a habit that I would eventually pick up, much to Pavlo's dismay.

I watched her walk. A tall woman, she didn't slouch to hide her height but stood proudly erect. She was older than I was, in her late twenties or early thirties. Everything about this woman seemed too much: her shoulders too broad, her breasts too large, her hips too full, her hair too wild, her voice too loud. She commanded attention and always looked into your eyes.

Ana came back with a brown woven bag. As she opened it, I was struck by the many unusual smells that I could not identify.

Over time, she would teach me to recognize and utilize the different scents.

Her long fingers reached into the bag and poked around until she exclaimed,

"Ah, hah!" Everyone nearby turned their heads.

She smiled at me. Yes, everything about her seemed to take up too much space, except her mouth. It was perfect: lips like a heart, full and red. Small on her face, they worked together with her deep blue eyes to balance out her nose. I smiled despite myself.

"Oh, we're going to be good friends," she said, "Whether you like it or not."

And my own self-conscious giggle highlighted her robust laugh.

"Okay. Now, here we go. This is marjoram." She pulled out a tiny sprig of purple flowers.

"See, they have two lips. I call it 'purple kiss' because if they have lips, why not use them? Plants are quite erotic, you know."

I glanced down at my children, who had fallen asleep despite the early morning hour.

"Don't worry so much, darling. Now take this and steep it in a cup of hot water twice a day. You'll feel much better. It's good for cramps, too. It will calm your stomach."

She reached over and took my hand. Looking at my palm, she placed the dried flowers in it.

"Trust me." she said. "What's your name, darling? We're going to be friends, so I should know your name."

"Nadya," I said, placing the flowers in my handkerchief.

"Perfect." she said shuffling around in her bag.

"Where are you going, Nadya?" she asked, pulling another cluster of flowers out of her bag.

"Chicago." I answered.

"Then, that's where we're going."

We shared our first apartment with them and two other couples. Eventually, we bought a house, and Ana and her husband Nicholas, or Niki, as she liked to call him, bought the house next door. For a few years Ana and I worked together as cleaning ladies in some of the big office buildings downtown. After our shift we would sometimes stop for coffee at Chuck's 24-Hour Diner, down the street from our work.

The coffee was too strong and reminded me of the coffee we were served in the camps, so I would add milk and sugar to try and cover the taste. Ana always drank hers black.

"Nadya darling, I heard you telling the kids stories out on the stoop. You have a bit of the author in you. You should write down your stories."

I blushed, as I always did, hearing her compliments.

"Ana, don't be silly. Those are just little fairy tales to keep the children quiet." I looked down at the menu, even though we never ordered anything but coffee.

"You're gifted, dear. Like Lesya Ukrainka or Olena Teliha."

"Olena who?" I asked, ashamed of my ignorance.

My schooling had ended with the war, but as a young woman, Ana had been sent away to school in Kyiv. Her family had been very wealthy, something to do with oil. Once the war began, she returned home to be with her family. When the Germans arrived in Lviv, they executed her parents and other wealthy business people, and their property and investments were transferred into German hands. Ana was a survivor.

"Olena Teliha. In Kyiv she was the head of a writer's group and edited the journal *Litaures*. Oh, she was very good, and beautiful, too." Ana sighed and patted her black curls.

"What a waste. I heard rumors that she died at the hands of the Gestapo." Ana gazed out the window, her eyes glazed. After a moment she looked back at me.

"You know, dear, you shouldn't keep silent."

I shook my head, "What do you mean?"

"You have stories. I know: I've heard them. What does Pavlo think about it?"

I laughed. "Pavlo? He doesn't think anything about them. "

Ana frowned at me, her eyebrows meeting in the middle.

"You're still not talking?" She began to chew on a hangnail.

When I shook my head, she slammed her palms down on the table.

"You have to talk to him. He should be your best friend, you know."

"Ana, we don't have the kind of relationship you and Nicholas have."

"I'm not talking about the sex matters again."

"Neither am I." I looked around to see who was watching, but the only other people in the diner at four o'clock that morning were an old homeless man sleeping in the corner and the waitress and cook laughing in the back. I was still embarrassed.

"Nadya, things are not perfect between Niki and me. We disagree, but we talk. Just the other day, he told me not to work as a cleaning lady. He said I was above it, that we didn't need the money so badly. Well, I told him, I like it. I like having my own money."

"It's so different with us, Ana. We almost never see each other. He works days, I work nights. He's not like Nicholas. He won't help me cook or clean. That's my job, he says. This won't change with talk. Besides, I don't mind. It was good enough for my mother."

She sighed, "I'm not talking about the cleaning. I'm talking about your souls. They should get the chance to see each other sometime. Darling, you both have to open up a little. Forget about everything else and talk with your hearts."

She reached over and took my hand. "You're all locked up,

Nadya. Sometimes it's hard even for me to reach inside and see who's hiding there."

Turning my hand over, she softly traced the lines with her finger.

"At least your hands give me a little clue," she said.

I smiled at her, "So that's why you look at my hands from time to time?"

She looked up and stared into my eyes. "Yes,' she said seriously. "Hands can reveal so much about a person. If you won't tell me, I have to find out the truth somehow."

I started to pull my hand away, but she held it tightly.

"What do you want to hide from me?" Ana asked. "Have we not been friends forever?"

"What could you possibly see?" I asked her. "If you see anything at all; what do you see?"

She shifted her attention back to my hand. "Oh, I see, darling. I see too much pain and regret. I see that you are surrounded by love, but you keep a wall around yourself. Nadya, you need to learn how to open your heart again, now that the silence has slipped in."

She winked at me. "I've got a little Gypsy in me."

Her words were so familiar, and they made my heart heavy.

Picking up her coffee cup, she said, "Remember this, my sweet, silence is not the only option."

Ana had found me curled up in a ball in the garden behind the garage. We had buried Mykola's uniform that morning. That night, sleep rescued Pavlo first, while I lay there drowning in the stale air. Suddenly I had to run away, so I slipped out of his arms and went outside.

The night was so cruel. The skies were clear, the winds cool, and the ground warm. I lay flat on the ground, smelling the greenery, feeling quiet, hearing hunger inside and out. If only we had lived closer to the cemetery, I would have slept on his grave to keep him warm.

But he wasn't there. Only an empty box. He was alone in foreign soil, like me.

Suddenly chilled, I curled up against the side of the garage, rocking back and forth to the rhythm of the twisting in my gut. I felt like it was my fault. I remembered Mama Paraska's words: *"There will be a price. There is balance in the universe."*

Ana must have seen me from her back porch, because she came outside and walked into my yard. She had a coat in her arms, which she put around my shoulders. I smelled peppermint and only then looked up.

"Nadya, dear, come with me."

She drove us to the beach and we sat on the hood of her car facing Lake Michigan.

"It's really beautiful," she said. "Looks more like an ocean than a lake."

I couldn't speak. I just sat, leaning my head on her shoulder as she gently stroked my hair.

"You know, I think that we should do something special," she said, hopping off the hood. I heard her footsteps behind me. After rustling around in the trunk, she came back with a white votive candle. Then she walked over to a bush and plucked off a bunch of green branches. Taking my hand, she led me to the sand.

"Sit down, Nadya. Weave these into a wreath, like you used to at home."

My fingers began to work in a pattern I hadn't practiced since I was a girl. The coolness of the leaves soothed my fingers, drawing me out of my thoughts until all I saw was the pattern of twisting branches. Soon it was finished.

I looked up to see Ana. She stood facing the water and held the candle in both her hands rubbing her palms back and forth along the short base. After a time, she turned around, knelt in front of me, and buried the bottom of the candle in the sand between us. I could smell sandalwood. Ana took the wreath from me and placed it around the candle. Then she pulled a prayer card from Mykola's funeral out from her pocket. She wrapped it around the candle, blocking the wind and securing it with sand.

"My dear Nadya, take this lighter and say his name as you light the candle. Picture his face. Remember."

I whispered, "Mykola." The lighter licked wax off the wick until orange and blue light sprang up filling the entire candle with a soft glow. I watched the flame sway and flicker, drawn to the bright white light in the center of the fire's tongue. Some flames will stand calmly, only shimmer as they burn. But this candle's dance was an up and down jump, an anxious child bouncing on his father's knee. I watched its steady bobbing, hearing my breath settle into the same rhythm, the tides a distant echo.

Ana walked over to me and took my hand, helping me stand. She led me closer to the edge of the water, and together we knelt on the sand.

"Cup your hands and scoop up some water," she said, doing the same.

"Hold it, even as the droplets fall between the cracks. These are the precious Waters of Life, Nadya. They are the same ones that flow underground and from the clouds. They connect us all, no matter how many miles we are from home. This is not our native shore, but the waters still make their way home, just like our tears.

"Waters are the womb of the earth. As you hold these waters, think about Mykola. Think about his life and all he brought into yours. These waters can hold your grief..."

I closed my eyes and pictured his smiling face. I heard Ana's words somewhere in the distance, like a song in a dream. But closer was the smell of oranges and leather, two of Mykola's favorite things.

"Death is a part of the cycle of life. It has always been this way. Death is a story we remember in our hearts and retell in our bones when we rejoin the Earth . . ."

But I have had too much death, too many sacrifices. Why did I have to continue to lose those dearest to me, my Mykola, my little angel who wanted to save the world? Who at ten years old gave his favorite Christmas sled to Vinnie across the street after Widow Ostromohylska backed her rusted Ford Fairlane over Vinnie's dog Rocco. Mykola, who blushed when that pretty Lusia girl blew him kisses in church, who braved the German Shepherd in Mr. Cantonini's yard each year to bring me lilacs on Mother's Day.

"He has always been a part of you, no matter how far away. Even while in Vietnam, when he slept there and you slept here, you were connected. You are still connected. The Earth holds you both, and she can hold your tears like all the waters of the world. Let them go, Nadya. Let them flow into the water."

I let the last of the water flow from my fingers into the lake, but I had no tears. Inside I felt as if I were scorched dry, as if my heart would never feel again. We knelt there in silence.

Driven by a longing for the moon, the waves created a rhythm to match my pulse. The pounding of blood in my head echoed their slap against the sand. Their seductive caress against my knees and ankles made me think of my Aunt Katia, the rusalka who succumbed to the water's sweet escape. But somewhere underneath their hushed prayer, inside the rhythm of my own heartbeat, one word whispered near my ear:

"Mama."

At that moment, when my only thought was to join the waters, to dissolve and be carried away, to lose my pain in their promise, Mykola was there. I could feel him. Somehow I knew that to speak would break the spell. To open my eyes would sever the connection of blood, of water, of heartbeat. But I knew in my bones that he was standing next to me.

"Mykola is your child. He is a part of you, always—a part of everything. To come here is to heal, to connect, to remember." Ana's voice flowed through the water, through my blood. I could feel her words like the spray against my neck, like the sand under my nails—a part of everything. Her voice came from beneath the sand, above the clouds, on drops of water, inside my own head. Maybe she said nothing at all. Maybe it was just the wind.

I kissed my fingers and ran them along the ground in front of her tombstone. Ana was the first person I learned to trust in America.

"Why is it that you and Pavlo never celebrate your wedding anniversary, Nadya?" Ana asked one night while we stood talking over the fence between our houses. She and Niki had just come back from a trip to Mexico, where they had celebrated their tenth anniversary.

I was holding a picture of Ana wearing a two-piece bathing suit; her husband was in colorful shorts decorated with dancing mice, his skinny legs white against the sand. I exhaled long, and we stood there in silence for a while. Then I glanced over to the house and turned back to Ana.

"Well, those were hard times." I said, feeling instantly foolish. She had lived through the same war.

She looked at me, not saying a word, the question in her eyes. Ana spoke sentences with her face.

"I didn't want to marry him," I said quickly, then looked toward the Chicago skyline. "I had no choice."

We spent so many nights talking over that fence. She knew me better than anyone else. She was my best friend, my sister.

Five years earlier, when she and Niki moved into the new condominiums near the church, I thought my heart would break.

She smiled at me and said, "But it's only three blocks down, Nadya. I'm not moving to California. These condominiums are new and shiny. And no more mowing the lawn or shoveling snow. You know, Niki isn't as young as he used to be. It's getting to be too much for him, although he would never admit it." She winked at me and gave me some seeds from her last herb garden to plant in my own, wrapped in an embroidered handkerchief.

But it was no longer the same. I couldn't just step outside and call her name through the screen door. I had to call her on the telephone, because if I just stopped by, she might not be home. Three blocks might have well been thirty miles because we began to see each other less and less. She and Niki began traveling more and more: Spain, Italy, New Mexico, Argentina, Greece, Egypt, Arizona. After each trip she would call me over, and we would have one of her homemade fruity drinks and look through her latest photo album filled with places I had never even heard of.

"Nadya, Look at this. This is the Grand Canyon."

"Is it in Europe?" I asked, gazing at a photo of enormous red rocks set against a sky of impossible blue.

"No, it's right here in America, but far west. It's so beautiful, dear. It makes you feel so small. We rode donkeys all the way down to the bottom. Niki almost fell off three times. It was breathtaking."

She set the book down on her lap and looked at me.

"You know, we should go on a trip together. Just you and I. No men. What do think?"

For a moment I savored the thought of traveling to someplace exotic. But I couldn't leave Pavlo and the kids. Who would prepare Sunday morning breakfast? Besides, we didn't have that kind of money to spend on a vacation. We had just lent Mark money for his new house.

"No, Ana, I couldn't do that." I shook my head and turned the page on her album. Niki was holding her hand while she stood atop a stone fence overlooking the canyon. "I'm needed here," I whispered.

"Nadya darling, you have never done a single thing just for yourself as long as I've known you. Pamper yourself once in a while. Family is important, darling, but so are you. Think of the fun we'd have. We'd flirt with all the old men, and if we go to Europe they would chase after you because you have aged very well and most European women look like the grave. The Italians say they look like "la morte in vacanza," which means death on vacation. Come on Nadya. It would be our grand adventure, something to hold onto.

Still, I refused.

Later, when Lesya's younger sister Tanya went to visit her boyfriend in Kyiv, an exchange student she had met through the Ukrainian Club at her high school, Ana tried to convince me to go with Tanya. In all their travels, Ana had never gone back to our motherland. Niki refused.

"Imagine going back after all this time?" she said while mixing our weekly Saturday night cocktails.

I could not imagine going back. I didn't dare. There were too many secrets that I was not prepared to face.

Sipping my drink that night, I wanted to tell her everything—about the camp, Andriy, the vorozhka, Stephan, and my family, but I was so afraid to speak it aloud.

I searched my memory for something safe, something I could share with her, and so I told her about Andriy Polotsky and Mama Paraska. I told her about that fork in the road, when I had chosen Pavlo and let Andriy and his mother walk out of my life forever. I didn't tell her why, that would have been too painful. Because of Ana's miscarriage—caused by kicks from the boots of German soldiers—she and Niki had never been able to have children. When I finished telling her about Andriy, she walked over to me and gave me a big hug.

Kissing the top of my head, she said, "Thank you for telling me this, Nadya." She smiled at me, "What if you could see him again after all these years? Aren't you curious?"

I shook my head, "That was a long time ago. There's nothing to revisit."

"Maybe, maybe not," she said with a coy smile. "Darling, sometimes life presents you with an unimaginable surprise. Look at our meeting. Who would have thought? Remember, purple kisses are everywhere, but unless you pluck them and make tea, there is no magic."

Living in the condo, Ana came to miss her lush garden and decided to grow marjoram, rosemary, sage, rue, and chamomile in her window box. When she and Niki traveled to the Ukrainian Festival in Dauphin, Manitoba, Ana asked me to water her seedlings.

I unlocked the door and took off my shoes. Laying the mail on the table by the door, I walked straight to the kitchen window, determined to water the plants and go home. Pavlo had a chess game with Yuri Radchenko, and I had the morning to myself. The truth was, without Ana, I had little else to occupy my time. I wanted nothing more than to hide in this sanctuary, but I felt awkward about being alone in their home. Of course, Ana told me she had no secrets from me, her home was my home. I wished I could be as open with her.

I filled the watering can and walked over to the window box. Ana's green thumb always rewarded her with healthy plants, and her herbs were growing beautifully. She said her secret was the songs she sang to them every sunrise while she brewed her tea. I think it was because she loved them.

The herbs watered, I looked around. My Baba always said

that you could feel the happiness of a family in their home, that their joy filled the rooms and lightened the air like spring flowers and baking bread. Ana and Niki's home certainly felt cheerful, passionate, and welcoming. I fought with myself to stay, to look around for clues into their happiness, the happiness that I was missing. Walking slowly through the rooms, my fingertips grazed the surfaces of counters, tables, chairs, feeling for secrets.

I looked down at their Oriental rugs and big, fluffy jewel-toned pillows scattered about the room. As if any moment, you might find yourself sinking to the ground and would be greeted with soft luxury. Ana and Niki didn't really collect knickknacks, but it seemed that every possible surface was covered with candles, half-melted and hinting at romantic evenings. Traces of their scent still lingered in the air.

Growing bolder, I walked into their bedroom. Leaning with my back against the dresser, I looked around at the mismatched woods and textures. So different from my own blue and white flowered bedspread and carefully matched dresser and chest. The purple satin sheets and crimson blanket were slightly tousled, but everything else was in perfect order. I walked over to the bed and sat down, running my hands along the covers—such softness.

I lay down on my stomach and closed my eyes, inhaling the scent of lily of the valley and something deeper, like wine. Wondering if this was Ana's side of the bed. Wondering if this is what passion smelled like. I rubbed my cheek along the blanket, as if somehow it would share their embraces with me. My fingers searched the pillow for their breath, the secrets of their lips. On the nightstand, Ana's reading glasses stood beside a single black feather and a rose petal, like relics of a religion into which I was not initiated.

I stood up and walked over to the closet and stepped inside. Ana had told me how much she loved lingerie, even showing me a nightgown here and there, but I had never seen her entire collection. Everywhere silks and satin and lace. I stretched out my hands to touch them, my fingers alive with sensations. I brushed my cheeks along the fabrics, smelled the powder-fresh fabric softener.

What would Pavlo think if I brought home one of these nightgowns? He would probably laugh or think I had a fever, or that I was having an affair. Well, he would not have to think because I would not do it. This old body in lace and ribbons? I would have to be crazy. That had never been me. Perhaps if I had walked a different path?

I spied their slippers, scattered like footsteps in a dance near the bed. Both sets were men's brown leather—Ana's feet were too big for most women's styles. Walking over to her dresser, I reached for the heavy French perfume that she always wore and dabbed it on my wrists. Bolder with her scent on me, I now opened their drawers with a quiet hunger.

Plain white briefs for him, for her—underwear of many different colors and patterns. "For different moods, darling," she told me once while we were shopping, "or else to create different moods. Color is very powerful. Never take color for granted. Back home, during the war, so much was gray. Here colors are delicious, and so I devour them."

This philosophy played out in everything, from her clothes to her home. Never had I seen so many mismatched colors in one place: her walls, her rugs, her furniture—different shades of every color and fabric.

"What about matching, Ana?" I once asked her. "Certain colors go together very well."

"Who can decide what goes well together?" she asked with a wink. "Look at Niki and me: Do we match?"

I searched through the underwear and found treasures: beads, a silver ring, chains and bracelets, silk handkerchiefs. I raised the scarves to my face, soft and sweet-smelling. Ana had started wearing them when her hair began to thin.

Suddenly their eyes were upon me. Everywhere, black and white photos of Ana and Niki in exotic places peered over at me standing guilty, my hands rooting about in their underwear. I tossed the silk scarves under the underwear, slammed the drawer, and turned back to the photos of their adventures.

Every time they went on a trip, Ana brought me back a spoon. I never told her that I liked or wanted them, but she had decided that I needed something to collect. So I have spoons from Cairo, Rome, Las Vegas, Mexico City, Paris, New Orleans, Seville, and Malta. Pavlo hates them. He says they're a waste of space because you can't actually use them for coffee or tea. I think that's why I decided to buy a little cabinet to hold them all in the kitchen. I don't have many things that are mine alone. Let him have his garden, I will have my spoons.

I walked back to the front room, stopping to look at their antique globe next to their wine rack. On it were little slips of red and green paper pinned to different countries. The red for places they've seen, the green for places they were going to visit next. There were many red tabs, but only one green one left.

The cuckoo clock brought me back to reality, and with a final glance I locked the door and went on my way to the bakery for rye bread. I would make borshch for dinner. Maybe I could find a way to make it a little spicy?

After they returned home, I waited to see if Ana would notice any disruption in their house, but she never mentioned anything. The morning after they flew home, she just handed me a spoon decorated with pair of red boots and poppies. She went on and on about the wonderful Ukrainian dance groups and delicious varenyky and borshch, "just like from home."

Right around that time Ana started getting more and more headaches, and each one seemed worse than the one before. She tried taking the medicinal herb feverfew, which had worked in the past. When that failed, she switched to magnesium and then aspirin, but nothing helped. Eventually Niki and I convinced her to see a doctor, who recommended a series of tests—injecting dye into her head and taking pictures of her brain. Ana went into the hospital for a special scan right before their final trip together to Ireland. "The land of myth and magic," Ana called it. "The perfect place to celebrate life and find the strength for a miracle."

I once asked Ana why she and Niki traveled to the places they did. Their albums were filled with pictures of ancient ruins, tombs of kings and queens, stone circles and monuments, pyramids and temples. All of their pictures were of places long gone and civilizations buried by time.

"It's a mystery, darling, and I love a mystery. These ancient peoples have secrets we can never learn, wisdom buried under earth and stone and sand. When we travel, I look for clues. Sometimes, if you stand very still in the shadows of those places, you can hear songs on the wind, whispers in the trees. That is why I travel.

"Someday, when we are dead and buried, someone will walk past our gravestones and wonder about my secrets, your secrets. Will our wisdom be buried with us? Or will it somehow survive?"

One week after their return from Ireland, I was called to identify their bodies. They had no other family and few friends, so I was the one called to the morgue. A sheet was draped over their nude bodies. My neighbor's son Ihor was the officer assigned to the case. Ihor told me that he had found them naked in bed. A Cheremshyna CD, set on repeat disk, was playing softly.

Apparently Niki had prepared a large, fancy dinner for the two of them. Ihor had found the remains of a feast on the dining room table: borshch, mashed potatoes, smoked salmon, stuffed mushrooms, and fresh baked rye bread. They must have consumed three bottles of expensive wine between the two of them, because two empty bottles were on the table and one beside the bed. The tub had been filled with soapy water and rose petals, and there were a few strawberries dipped in chocolate lying on the floor of their bathroom. The chocolate had been mixed with poison.

Niki had thought of everything. The gas had been left on, so when their neighbors, the Jaworskys, came home to their condo across the hall, they smelled gas and knocked on the door. When there was no answer, they called the fire department. To avoid scandal, I bribed Ihor to arrange it so their death certificates read "died of natural causes." He told me that it was going to be quite a lot of trouble. Five hundred dollars bought them a proper death.

Many in the Ukrainian community hadn't liked the couple in life and would have been only too happy to disgrace their deaths. Judge and jury, the Ukrainian gossips had long condemned their many sins. Ana and Nicholas were too affectionate in public. How dare they hold hands and kiss like newlyweds? They traveled too much. They never went to church. They drank too much wine. They danced like young people, to boogie-woogie music!

So many outrageous theories had been whispered by gossiping babas over fences, on telephones, and in bathroom stalls at church: Ana and Niki were really Jews, or Gypsies, or Nazis. They never had children because they were really brother and sister. They were Soviet spies, who often had to return home to get new assignments.

I had talked with Ana the day before they died, after she came back from the hospital to find out the test results. She had been diagnosed with a high-grade astrocytoma, a cancer in her brain stem. The doctors said that there was nothing they could do.

Ana tried to explain it to me over the phone that day. "This cancer, it's like an invasive weed in my precious garden. It has infected the low, stemlike part of my brain and has also put out roots into my healthy brain tissue."

Suddenly there was panic in her voice, "Why my brain? I don't want to die like this. I don't want to lose my mind. Slowly fall apart." I heard her fighting away tears. "Nadya, I don't want Niki to watch me die."

She gave in to tears. "We had so many more trips planned; so many adventures. If only there were some miracle."

Ana asked me to light a candle for her in church. She had only been to church twice since I met her, once for Mykola's funeral and once for Taras' wedding.

That night she called again. Her voice was calmer.

"Darling, I'm sorry I was so upset before. It was just the shock of it all. Thank you for listening."

I reassured her, told her I understood, and asked to see her the next day.

She replied happily, "Oh, Nadya, not tomorrow. Tomorrow is a special day. It's our anniversary."

Suddenly she laughed; a girlish giggle.

"Stop that, Niki," she said away from the phone, and then to me, "I have to go. I love you, Nadya dear."

"I love you, too, Ana. See you—" but before I could finish, I heard a click, then silence.

I made arrangements for their funeral. My family and I were the only ones who attended. At the gravesite I planted daisies, Ana's favorite. I didn't visit them at the cemetery often, choosing instead to talk with Ana in my garden, along the fence. That was "our spot." Here I felt Niki's presence as well as hers. Maybe it was their photograph on the headstone, but I felt more self-conscious speaking candidly. However, because of the dream Ana sent me, I now felt the need to speak with her right then and there. I sat down on the grass in front of the tombstone.

"Ana, I burned the envelope. I'm not sure what good it will do. My mind will still wander back and forth, wondering who is out there, but I trust your wisdom, as always."

I felt such an ache in my heart. I should have her there with me in person, not in the ground. I wanted to hold her hand, not stroke the grass. I fought back tears.

"It was good to see you, even in my dreams. I miss you, Ana."

Just one sentence, one thought entered my head, *Go home; kiss Pavlo.*

I hesitated, wanting to sit with her a little longer, but again the voice, *Go home; kiss Pavlo.*

I went home. Pavlo was sitting on the bench in the backyard, drinking tea in the shade. I walked over to him and kissed the top of his head.

"Did you have a nice visit at the cemetery?" he asked.

"I did." I answered, "but I'm tired of burying people I love."

He patted the seat next to him on the wooden bench, and I sat down.

"It's going to get harder," he said after a few minutes of silence. "More of our friends are dying."

"That's not what I wanted to hear, Pavlo," I said.

"But it's the truth, Nadya. We can't wish it away or pretend it's not happening. Our lives have been long and full."

I looked at my husband. He looked tired, but still handsome. Ours was not a passionate or easy life, but overall, it was a good life. I put my hands on his cheeks and kissed him on the lips. His eyes were wide when I pulled away.

"What was that for?" he asked. "Tell me so I can do it again."

I smiled. "Just because."

We sat there in silence until the sun set.

CHAPTER TEN

Pavlo walked in from the wind, smelling of the rain. He went to the cupboard to get a mug and sat down across from me at the table. I could feel him staring at me as I went through some paperwork. I ignored his gaze and kept sorting. I had been trying to move on, but even after burning the envelope, I was plagued by "what ifs?" Had it not been for the rain, would I have gone with Stephan and abandoned everyone and everything? Or did the rain somehow protect me from an even worse fate? What if I had never left the house?

"Can you stop what you're doing and talk with me?" Pavlo asked.

"What?" I looked up at my husband.

"Talk with me."

Could he be sick? "What's wrong, Pavlo?"

I put aside my papers and poured his coffee.

"Nothing's wrong," he said. "I just wanted you to sit and talk with me. We don't do much of that anymore."

He was right. When the kids still lived in the house, every Saturday morning we would sit and drink coffee and talk. I would come home from work, and he'd have the coffee ready for me, along with some kind of fresh baked sweets that he had picked up at the bakery, usually chocolate.

We talked about work and our friends, the house and our kids. We compared notes about how they were doing in school, what their challenges and accomplishments were that week.

When the kids moved away, we still talked about work and eventually our grandchildren. Then we both retired, and the ritual stopped.

The kids were the glue that kept us together. Without them to discuss, we only had work. Without work to discuss, we stopped making an effort. I would talk with Ana or the neighborhood ladies. He would talk with his chess buddies and the other old men in the neighborhood. The years passed, and we stopped talking to each other. Really talking.

I hadn't thought about our Saturday coffees in years.

"What's on your mind, Pavlo?"

"Do you think the domovyk is angry at us?" he asked, reaching for the sugar.

I laughed. "Why do you ask such a question?" I spread honey on my bread.

"Well, I can't find my glasses, my left slipper, or my toenail clippers."

"You've probably just misplaced them, old man, like you 'lost' your keys next to the bathtub, or your umbrella under the couch."

"Listen here, old lady. I'm not convinced those were my fault either. See, I've been thinking about this. I have determined that too many disappearing things are blamed on old age. I believe they are really taken by mischievous house spirits to get our attention, to remind us of something."

"That's what you believe, eh?" I said, in between bites of bread. Wiping my mouth, I asked, "Do you feel your hair being pulled when you're alone? Have you heard groans or moans in the night?"

"Only yours," he said, reaching for my hand.

I felt myself redden and pulled away. "And what are we being reminded of? The domovyk would have no reason to be disturbed. I still honor our traditions. I always toss the first crumbs of bread into the stove."

For a minute he just sat there, staring into his chipped blue mug decorated with a cartoon picture of a farmer. It had been Mykola's favorite. I wondered why Pavlo had chosen it.

He saw me looking at the mug and sighed. "I miss him. Sometimes I wonder what he would have grown up to be."

"Me too, Pavlo. All the time."

"He was my best friend."

"Who? Mykola?"

Pavlo smiled. "Yes." He leaned back in his chair. "Mykola and I would talk while he helped me in the garden. He would tell me about his dreams, about school, about how the other kids sometimes picked on him because he stuttered a little when he was nervous."

I felt jealousy stirring inside. I never knew this.

"He would ask me questions about my life, the war. I even told him a little about home, about my mother and my sister."

More jealousy.

"Pavlo, you've never even talked to me about these things."

"Bah, what do you want to hear about this for? You always tell me the past is past. No need to dig it up. But Mykola really wanted to hear about everything. Before he left, he asked me about the war. Our war. He asked me if I had any advice for him. I told him to do whatever he could to come back home alive and in one piece. Then he gave me a hug and told me he loved me.

"I miss him. I should have given him better advice." Pavlo looked at me. "You know, I still talk to him. All the time, especially in the garden."

This time I reached for Pavlo's hand.

Time stretched out and reversed. I was sixty, then forty, then thirty. The same chairs, the same kitchen, the same hand in mine. We were not unhappy then. Our small house was filled with children and laughter and shouting, all of which kept my ghosts at bay. There was just too much to worry about: Mark needed buttons sewed, and Katya needed her hair braided, and baby Mykola needed his bedtime story. There was no time for the past.

Again time shifted in a breath, a groan, and the wrinkles settled back into my skin, leaving my younger self buried.

"Sometimes it feels like just yesterday that I was changing our babies' diapers, or yelling at Mark and Taras to stop picking on Mykola." I said. "We were so busy then, but happy. So happy. I can't believe how quickly time has passed."

"That's exactly what I was talking about." Pavlo said.

"About the kids?"

"Yes ... no, about being happy." He reached again for his coffee. "Don't laugh at me, but that is what I think."

He looked shy, embarrassed. Pavlo was never a philosopher. He was a farmer at heart and a machinist by trade, a man of the earth with a practical mind.

"I was thinking that the domovyk likes to have a happy house, right?" he asked.

We were back to the domovyk then. He waited for me to respond. I was surprised by his sense of drama and smiled: "Right."

"Well, when we had a houseful of kids, we were happy and he was happy. There were crazy jokes and good times. Now that it's just you and me, and the kids and their families don't visit as much, the house is missing something. That got me thinking about us, and how we don't sit together anymore, we don't laugh together."

I began to protest and he interrupted. "I know what you're going to say. Yes, there are moments. And I'm not unhappy. But let me ask you, are you happy? Happy like you were back then?"

Back then? My heart beat quickly in my chest. But back when? I stood up and walked to the sink. I needed to get something. I opened the cabinet and pretended to look through the spices. Cinnamon.

"Nadya? Are you happy?"

"Sure. Sure," I said. "What's not to be happy about? We have a nice house, a big family, good health." I heard his knock on wood echoing my own.

I didn't want to sit down, so I continued looking in the cabinet. I felt Pavlo's eyes on my back.

"What's wrong? Why are you getting upset?" He asked.

"I'm not getting upset. I'm looking for something. For nutmeg."

"But I just asked you a simple question, and you're getting angry. Why?"

I sat back down and poured too much cinnamon and nutmeg into my coffee.

"Why are you pestering me?" I asked him, stirring.

"I thought we were trying to have a nice conversation."

"Sure. But you don't like my answers." I tasted the coffee. Ruined.

"What's wrong? Did I do something to make you mad?"

A list of complaints jumped to mind: not replacing the toilet paper roll, leaving toenail clippings all over the bathroom floor, forgetting to unplug the toaster, that one nose hair he never seems to clip, leaving the porch window open all night, opening my mail.

"Why did you open my mail yesterday?"

"What are you talking about?" Pavlo looked like I slapped him.

"I had a letter from the doctor, and you opened it."

"You open my mail all the time. It was just a bill from your last appointment. Besides, I didn't know it was a secret." His face was starting to get red.

"It's not, it wasn't. Forget about it." I took another sip of coffee.

The house was quiet except for Khvostyk scratching in the

litter on the porch. I could feel rage inside, but I wasn't sure why.

"No, actually, Pavlo, I have a question for you. I received an envelope from Ukraine several months ago. It had been opened, and was empty. Did you take it?"

He stared at me, not blinking. "What?"

"Did you open the envelope? Take the letter?"

"A letter from Ukraine? I don't even remember any letter from Ukraine?"

"Think back. It was spring, and you brought in the mail. Before Palm Sunday. The envelope was there, but the letter was missing."

"Nadya, how could you think such a thing of me? Who was it from?"

A sob in my chest stretched up my throat and let loose so many tears, "I don't know. I don't know who could be left alive. I don't know how they could find me. I just don't know—"

Pavlo walked over and tried to hug me in my chair, but I shrugged him away.

"Why would I take your letter?" He kissed the top of my head. "I didn't take away that letter you got from that Andriy Polotsky last year, did I?"

I didn't know Pavlo knew about the letter. He had heard of Andriy Polotsky. All the Ukrainians knew who he was. He gained the American spotlight in the 1970s. I first heard about him on the Ukrainian radio program in Chicago. Apparently, after Mama Paraska died, Andriy immigrated to New York. He started out as a stagehand, became an actor, and eventually started up a successful theater company. In time he became a wealthy man, who gave generously to help others with scholarships and charities. A good man.

When someone of Ukrainian ancestry became famous, his fame would spread around the country until everyone Ukrainian knew about his success. We cheered them on, our brothers and sisters who had proudly declared their heritage in the public spotlight. Whether they were actors, athletes, writers, or politicians, their names were learned by the entire community: the cubist sculptor Alexander Archipenko, the actors Jack Palance and George Dzundza, the Olympic figure skating champion Oksana Baiul, Illinois State Senator Walter Dudycz, the NFL football player and coach Mike Ditka, and many others. *To nash, to nasha*, we would say. He's one of ours. She's one of ours.

Andriy, *to nash.*

I thought about calling him, but never did. When I told Ana about him and his mother, she urged me to contact him, but I didn't have the nerve. What could I say that he would care to hear?

Then, last year Andriy somehow found me. In the mail I received a plane ticket to New York and a theater ticket for the opening night of one of his plays. There was no note or letter attached. I burned both tickets on the stove. I suspected that Ana must have contacted him. Maybe if she had still been alive we could have gone together. But she died a month earlier, and I would not go alone.

I never received another ticket. I would read Ukrainian newspapers and listen to Ukrainian radio programs for stories about Andriy, his adventures, his generosity. He was one of the most eligible Ukrainian bachelors. Women, young and old, sent him pictures and love offerings. I heard about it on a special St. Valentine's Day radio program, and I tried to keep up with the latest gossip.

But Pavlo knew! What else did he know? I crossed my arms and asked, "How did you know, Pavlo? I burned those tickets."

"I saw the envelope. Besides, Ana told me that he was once your friend. I think I remember his mother from the camp. Mama Paraska, right? Crazy old woman."

"She wasn't crazy."

"Sure she was. She thought she could talk to God. She once told me that you were promised to her son and I should walk away. Imagine that! Like I would listen to some crazy old woman."

"She wasn't crazy," but I smiled. So she went to Pavlo. She never told me.

"Anyway, years ago, when Ana and Niki were in New York, they went to see a play at his theater and they met him, that Andriy," he said. "You know how Ana liked to talk to everybody. Well, she and Niki loved the play and asked to meet him, to talk with him and all that. They all had dinner at some fancy restaurant, and they found out that they both knew you."

"But why didn't she tell me?"

"It was supposed to be a surprise. See, Ana came to me and told me that she had the perfect idea for a present for you. She told me I should surprise you and take you to New York to see one of Andriy's plays. But I know how much you hate to travel. So I bought you the new coffeemaker, and we went to the Polish all-you-can-eat buffet instead, remember?"

Ana met Andriy? So that was how he found me. That was why he had sent the tickets. She never told me.

"Well, Ana said she would take you there someday and surprise you, but she must have forgotten. I guess after a few years that Andriy got curious, because I remember seeing the envelope from him on the table. I never even opened it or asked you about it. See?"

He knew about that letter?

"What else did Ana say?"

"Nothing. She just wanted it to be a special birthday for you. She was upset with me that I didn't get you the tickets, but we weren't like them. We don't just get up and travel all around the world."

He's right. We were not like them. I knew he didn't take it. It was not something he could do now.

"Nadya, I trust you. After all these years, I better trust you." His voice became softer. "I did some bad things when I was young. But times were so different then."

Times were so different.

He sat back down and said, "Do you know how lucky we are?"

"Yes, we are lucky, Pavlo. Lucky to have lived as long as we have, survived all we have. But do you ever wonder what could have been? If we had never met? If we had chosen different lives?"

"No."

"No?"

"No, I don't. You see, Nadya, you're a romantic. You try to deny it, pretend to be practical, but you're not. That is why you are always disappointed.

But me? I have few expectations, so when things go well, I'm surprised. I never expected to live beyond my teens. I have, and I'm happy. I never expected to find love, but I found you. I never expected to have a good life, but look at us. We have a nice house, a good family. It hasn't always been easy, but we've survived so many things . . . together. Who else has been so lucky?"

I thought about the other people I knew, couples who stayed together for their children and were now too old to start looking for something different. Some husbands had wandering eyes and crafty lies. Some women were obsessed with gossip and excuses, they hid from their husbands except for meals and family visits. There were alcoholics, abusers and abused, and so many lonely people. So many people had no one to love. So many people had forgotten how to love, or maybe never learned how. During the war, we needed to hold onto something, someone. Often we turned to the person next to us, and the next thing we knew we were seventy-five years old and alone.

"Ana and Niki were happy together." I said.

"Sure, but their relationship wasn't perfect. They were never able to have children, and all their traveling couldn't fill that space. And look at Ana's illness. They had their share of problems.

"Nadya, we even sleep in the same bed, the same room, after all these years. Most couples we know, as soon as the kids moved out, they each got their own room. But not us, we're still together."

He was right. I couldn't imagine falling asleep without Pavlo next to me. For so many years I worked the night shift, and he worked the day shift, and we never slept together except on the weekends. In our old age, I had grown spoiled by his body next to mine.

"That's just because you keep my feet warm." I said. "As soon as they make an electric blanket that doesn't catch fire, I'll take over the guest room. You hog so much of the bed anyway, I'm surprised you even notice I'm there."

"How can I not notice that big behind of yours? Besides, you would miss my hugging at night and in the morning. No blanket can do that."

As he talked, I stood up and went to brew another pot of coffee.

"Sometimes I don't know how I've ended up in this old body," I said.

"You have a lifetime of memories." He said

"To replace a lifetime of dreams," I said.

Memories: one for every wrinkle, every gray hair.

"But how did it happen so fast, Pavlo? I want more time, I want fifty more years."

"And what would we do with fifty more years?"

"Have adventures. Something meaningful."

"Look there," Pavlo pointed to the photographs on the wall. "We have done something meaningful with them."

"But is that enough?" I asked.

"It is for me," he answered. "Is it enough for you?"

We both looked around the room, at the walls, the table, and the photographs.

"Look at the time," I said to break the spell. "I need to clean up the house. Lesya is coming by to ask me questions about her homework."

As I was talking, Pavlo walked over, gave me a hug, and kissed the top of my head.

"I love you," he said. "Thank you for talking with me."

"Aren't you going to have more coffee?" I asked.

"Maybe after my cigarettes," he answered and walked outside.

I stood watching the coffee fill the pot, a steady stream of dark brown. Khvostyk rubbed against my legs.

"How can one lifetime be enough?" I asked him, scratching his head while he rubbed against my legs.

Katya told me that in America cats have nine lives. If only we all had that luxury.

"So Khvostyk, is the domovyk upset with us?"

Khvostyk looked at me in earnest and let out a long meow. He must have thought I was asking him if he wanted a can of tuna. Pavlo's theory was interesting, but I think that after living in our house for fifty years, our domovyk was probably grateful for the peace and quiet. House spirits liked a clean but peaceful house. When I was young, before my Baba died, she often complained that we sisters made such a racket that the domovyk was sure to be upset with our family.

"Halya, Nadya, Maria, Laryssa," shouted our Baba. "Stop fighting right now. And clean up those dolls on the floor before your mother gets home. Don't you know that the domovyk likes a nice, clean house? That way when he walks around at night nothing is in his way. You don't want to make him angry."

"Why, Baba?" asked Maria. "What happens if he's upset?"

"If he's angry, he can bring bad luck to the house." She motioned for us to sit next to her. "Come here, my little ones. Come sit next to Baba near the fire. It's cold, and we'll help keep each other warm as I tell you a story about the domovyk."

Laryssa spread our big brown blanket on the floor by Baba's feet, and we sat close together bundled in layers of softness. Mama got the goose-filled comforters by trading her embroidery with the widow Moroz. We giggled as we pressed closer to the fire, watching the flames dance.

"All settled now, girls?" Baba asked, stroking my hair.

We nodded, excited to hear another of Baba's stories.

"Are you sure you're feeling well enough to tell a story, Baba?" asked Laryssa, always considerate.

"Shhh. Of course I am, it's only a little cough, and I've drunk plenty of nice hot tea and honey. So I should be just fine."

"Once upon a time there was a little girl who lived with her mother and father in a house outside of Kyiv."

"Didn't she have any brothers or sisters?" asked Maria.

"No, she was their only child. But she did have a lot of goats to play with. She lived in a house like this one. She was a good little girl, but she was lonely. Her mama and tato would work all day and night, leaving her alone in the house most of the time. She decided that she would try to meet the domovyk so she would have a friend in the house.

"Now, this is not completely unknown, because the domovyk can communicate with us. You just have to pay attention and know how to read the signs. If you hear shrieking or moaning, crying or wailing, then it is a bad omen, and you need to be careful. He will often cry when he knows that someone in the household is going to die. But if you hear laughter or singing, giggling or music, it is a good omen, and you should feel honored that the domovyk is sharing something with you.

"Sometimes the domovyk will even touch you to give you a message. This usually happens if you are a sound sleeper and haven't heard his earlier communications. If you feel a warm, gentle touch, like a cat's fur or a dog's breath, then it is a sign of good things to come. But if you feel an icy touch or a rough, prickly one, then your luck is turning for the worse. The domovyk will sometimes pull the hair of wives to warn them that their husbands are going to beat them. But only if they like the wife.

"The domovyk is involved in everything that happens in the house. He watches the bread baking, the water boiling, the floor being swept, and everything in between. But at night the domovyk has special responsibilities.

"Why, Baba?"

"Because that's what the domovyk does. Cats meow. Cows make milk. Foxes try to steal chickens. And the domovyk watches over the house. That's life. We all have our place.

"So the little girl, her name was Motrya, knew that the domovyk had a lot of chores to do at night, and they kept him very busy. He had to keep an eye on the goats, watch out that the neighbors didn't steal any food or animals, and also protect the house from other spirits. Motrya decided that she would help him, so he could finish his chores more quickly and have time to talk with her."

"How could she help him if she couldn't see him, Baba?" I asked.

"Little mouse, the domovyk doesn't like to be seen directly, but it is not impossible to see him. Sometimes he looks like the previous owner of the house, other times he might look like a dog or a cat, or a furry little creature with an old man's face. The domovyk can change his shape depending on how he wants to be seen.

"So one night Motrya crept out to the yard and watched the barn for hours to make sure the goats were safe. Then she walked around and around the house to make sure no one was trying to steal anything. Finally, she sat on the threshold of the house and waited for any mischievous spirits that might try to come in."

"But Baba, the threshold is the domovyk's special place," said Laryssa.

"That's right, and of course the domovyk was watching Motrya all night to see what she was up to. When he saw her sitting on the threshold, he tapped her on the shoulder and she turned around to see a young boy with brown fur all over his body.

'What are you doing?' the domovyk asked her.

'I'm helping the domovyk so that he will be my friend.' Motrya replied.

'The domovyk doesn't have friends. He just lives alone and takes care of the house.'

'But why?'

'Because that's the way it is, Motrya. That's the way of the world. Now, thank you for your help, but you should get some sleep, the sun will soon be rising,' the young boy said and then disappeared.

"Motrya went to sleep, but she repeated these chores every night for one month, hoping to see the little boy again. But the domovyk never appeared. She eventually gave up and grew up, alone and without many friends. Motrya spent most of her time inside the house or on the farm. She helped her mother around the house, but mostly kept to herself, reading books and telling stories to the goats. She always hoped to see the domovyk, but she never did. But every year on her birthday Motrya would hear music at night and wake up with her hair braided.

"When she turned sixteen, her parents decided that they were going to send her to a convent because they didn't have enough money for a dowry. They knew no one would want to marry the poor lonely girl whom the neighbors considered odd because she talked to goats and kept to herself. Motrya didn't want to leave her home or the goats, or the trees or flowers. She loved the land on her family's farm. She knew every rock, every patch of poppies and cornflowers. She was so upset that she sat up that night crying.

'You're sitting on my threshold again,' said a voice behind her.

She hadn't noticed that she had sat down on the threshold to cry. Motrya turned around to find a handsome man with long brown hair standing behind her.

'I'm sorry, I wasn't paying attention. Are you the domovyk?' she asked him.

'I am,' he answered. "And I am sad that you're leaving. I've enjoyed listening to your stories, and you always keep the house so nice and clean.'

'Then help me to stay here. I want to stay here. Maybe you have some magic that we can do to help me stay here?'

'I told you once a long time ago, there's no way. I must be alone.'

'But why?' Motrya asked. 'You deserve to have someone to love you.'

'Could you love me?' he asked, his brown eyes changing to blue.

'You are the spirit of this house, and I love this house, so I already love you.' Motrya answered and kissed the domovyk on the lips.

"There was a bright flash of light and Motrya was transformed into a new spirit, the domovykha. The two of them fell instantly in love and were married under the birch tree in the backyard on the night of Ivana Kupala, Midsummer Eve. All the spirits came to celebrate, the rusalky, bannyky, dvorovyky, and even the lisovyk.

"So sometimes a house has two spirits living in them, and this brings the family much luck and happiness . . . if they keep the domovyk happy by keeping everything in order."

Baba kissed us all on the top of our heads.

"Now, can one of you four mistresses of this nice, clean house make me some tea?" she asked.

"I will," said Maria and ran to get some water.

"Baba," Laryssa said shyly, "I want to become a domovykha and stay here in this house."

"Shh!" Baba said and knocked on wood, "Be careful what you wish for. It might come true. You must always be careful of your wishes, little ones. The Universe will make your dreams come true, but often not in the way that you expect."

What did I want after all this time? Did I want adventures? Did I want to travel? Was I too old to even think about making changes? Pavlo was content. Maybe I needed to try and follow his example. Was I too greedy?

I needed to put my energy back into my family. Lesya was coming over. Was she still seeing that boy? She said she loved him, that German. She was caught up in the illusion that so often ensnares the young into notions of invincibility and a love that conquers all.

I loved Stephan with that same burning, foolish, young love. I wondered about the promises we had made when we were young. Did we somehow tie our souls together with our early declarations of love? Or was the Universe more forgiving? I had many chances for love, but did I choose wisely?

I loved Stephan, but death made the choice for me. The German colonel loved me with a cold adoration. He would have turned me into a rich lady, but nationality and loyalty made that choice for me. And sweet Andriy would have loved me, cherished me with kindness and devotion, but I could not make the choice to follow him. I could only bury my regret and watch him and Mama Paraska leave the village, leave my life.

Once in a while, I allowed myself to fantasize about what my life could have been. A different life, a different love. What else does an old woman have but memories and fantasies?

CHAPTER ELEVEN

"Hi, Baba. Sorry I'm late," Lesya shouted from the porch. I heard her shaking off her umbrella and kicking off her boots.

"It's okay, Lesya. I'm making coffee. Would you like some?"

I got her favorite mug from the cupboard and set it on the table. She walked into the kitchen looking guilty. She wasn't that late. Then I knew. She was late because of him.

I tried to stay calm. I bit the inside of my cheek and poured the coffee. "So, how is your tato? Your mama?"

"Good. Tato has a conference coming up in California," Lesya said while spooning sugar into her cup. "But you know Mama, she doesn't want to go because she hates to fly."

"Who can blame her?" I set a plate of toast on the table. "We were born on the earth, not in the air. What else is new?"

"Oh, nothing much. Natalie and Jerry have their hands full with little Pavlyk, but I think they're going to try for baby number two soon." Lesya buttered her toast, avoiding my eyes. "Tanya is lovesick about her long-distance boyfriend in Kyiv. She wants to go visit him again. Maybe you can go this time?"

"I'm too old to travel," I said spooning too much blackberry jam on my toast, my favorite. "Maybe if Ana were still here we could have gone together, but I can't go by myself."

"What about Dido? Neither of you have been back for so long."

Like Ana's husband Nicholas, Pavlo had sworn that he would never return. It would be too much for him. Besides, he knew nothing of where I came from. I could not revisit my past with him.

"No, Lesya. Your Dido does not wish to return. It was a bitter exit from our homeland, and he would rather leave the dead sleeping."

I gave her a look that meant this subject is over. "So what can I help you with today?"

She reached into her backpack and took out a pad of paper and pen. "Baba, I'm writing a paper about the history of Jewish and Ukrainian relations before and after World War II. Could you tell me a little about your experiences?"

Faces flashed across my memory: Miriam, My teacher, Sonny . . . and many others without names. Panic caught in my throat. I took a deep breath. "Where will this article be published, Lesya?"

She looked over her notes, "It's just for school, Baba. Don't worry about it. Nothing public."

"Because you know that we are private people," I told her sternly. "I cannot have my life shared with the whole world."
I suddenly had nightmare visions of the Soviets tracking down my family and friends and sending them to Siberia.

"Baba, it's not like that anymore. Things have changed."

I sighed. She was so young, trusting and foolish. The seeds planted by Stalin were still growing, even if quietly and hidden under rocks.

"You're asking me a difficult question, Lesya. Things back home were not like they are here. They were . . . complicated. There are old prejudices that remain deep within our people. During our long history, we have been trespassed upon by so many hordes that we are wary of all strangers and slow to trust anyone not Ukrainian on our soil. During the Austro-Hungarian Empire, which controlled Western Ukraine, the Jews were the stewards of the Poles. Even a socially lowly Jew was above a poor

Ukrainian peasant. The Ukrainians were at the mercy of Jewish merchants and Polish landlords. Did this fuel tension? Probably. Certainly some Ukrainians were unkind to the Jews during the war. But other Ukrainians risked their lives to help them. It's complicated.

"My first experience with someone Jewish was positive, but it was secret. You see, when I was a girl, I had a burning curiosity. My mama and tato were so relieved when I started going to school because it gave them a break from all my questions. I wanted to learn everything I could.

"My teacher was called Danylo Zhytomyrsky, a kind and brilliant man who nurtured my love of books and stories. For five years I studied with him, and he taught me many lessons: Russian and Latin, history and art, grammar and literature, philosophy and poetry.

"When I was nine years old, Danylo came as a stranger to our village from the university in Lviv. We had only an old woman who taught the young children, and no one to teach the older ones, so Danylo was welcomed.

"Everyone just assumed that he was Christian. We had been forbidden to go to any religious service for so long after Stalin's purges, and then during the German occupation, that most families celebrated religious holidays in private, in their homes. This is the way of our people anyway. The church is a meeting place for the community to celebrate, but the home is the heart of the family and traditions. For hundreds of years it is where people were born, married, celebrated, grieved, and died.

"Once when I was looking around in the teacher's library, I found some books buried behind others. They were written in a language I couldn't understand. I asked him about it, and he swore me to secrecy first, then told me his story.

"Danylo had left Lviv after a pogrom. Immediately following the German occupation of Lviv, the Einsatzgruppen—German task forces—organized a pogrom. Danylo was the only one of his family left alive. His parents had long been dead, and his older brother, Jacob, died in the pogrom. As his brother lay dying in Danylo's arms because of a terrible beating, he whispered the name of a young woman he had loved and the village she had come from. It sounded like our village, so Danylo came to find her.

"He never did. He told me her name, but it was not one that I recognized. He had nowhere else to go, so he stayed and became a part of our community. Although he kept mostly to himself, he was well liked by his students and their parents.

"I was the only one he ever trusted with his secret. He was afraid that if anyone found out, he would be forced to leave, or worse. Even at that age, I knew the importance of such a secret.

"Danylo taught me that stories are the lifeblood of a culture. He even shared with me some of the special stories of his people, such as the legend of the golem who protects the Jews, and the mysteries of the Tree of Life. Perhaps most importantly, he taught me about tolerance, showing me that people who are different can be trusted and can enrich your life with their differences."

"I think you've forgotten that lesson," Lesya said quietly.

I chose to ignore her and continued, "When I was fifteen, Danylo was taken by the German police. They were rounding up the intellectuals, priests, teachers, and politicians. We never saw him again. My Uncle Vasyl said that he was certainly killed. I always wondered if somehow someone had found out his secret. From Danylo I learned that stories can kill if they are not properly guarded. Not all stories can be shared, Lesya."

I stopped to pour myself and Lesya some more coffee, watching as she carefully took notes in her notebook. When she looked up, she asked, "What about during the war? In the camps? What was that like?"

I took a deep breath and closed my eyes.

Tell her, darling.

A whisper beside my ear? Inside my mind?

For a moment I could see Ana in my memory, hands on her round hips. She was the only one I had ever told about my life, in bits and pieces at that.

It is time to tell the story . . .

I wanted to.

I was afraid to.

I began.

"Our people are not without blame, Lesya," I said, then hesitated. But I was gently urged on, as if there were hands on my shoulder, comforting and pushing me. I looked down at my hands. When did they get so wrinkled?

"I'm going to tell you a little about the DP camp. The same one where I met your dido, in Neustadt, but this happened earlier, before he had joined our camp.

I was living in an all-women's barracks. There was a lovely old woman who was in charge of us twelve. Her name was—"

I was still afraid to say their names.

"—We called her Mama P., because so many of us had lost our own mothers during the war. We followed her rules, which were very strict, and she made sure that we were safe. Well, just outside of Mama's dorm, there was a small cluster of ancient trees. Further away was a grove of oak trees that had already died from disease or heartache, but this particular cluster was fighting to stay alive. I had 'adopted' one of them and used to sit outside and write—"

"You used to write, Baba?" Lesya asked. "Really? What did you write? Where is it now?"

"Shush," I said. "Long gone, everything is long gone. Now let me continue my story."

If she only knew how hard it was, how easy it would have

been to turn back and bury those words in more silence.

Tell her.

A trace of familiar French perfume in the air.

I turned back to Lesya.

"Back home, it is said that each tree has a spirit who lives inside. Very often those who die pick a tree near their family's home and stay there as a guardian. I truly believe this, Lesya. My own Baba picked a tree near my house, and I felt her whenever I was there. On full-moon nights I could see a shape shimmering inside the tree, like something dancing. And I would hear her voice on the wind when it rushed through the leaves. Praising. Guiding. Warning."

"Have you?" Lesya interrupted.

"Have I what?" I asked her.

"Have you picked a tree?"

"What?! I haven't decided to die yet." I couldn't believe she was asking me this, but then I saw a grin stretch across her face. She was teasing me. Fine, then I would tease her back.

"You see, Lesya, I am waiting until you buy a house, then I can choose the tree closest to your bedroom window. That way I can scratch against the glass to get your attention and send you dreams whenever you need my advice." I smiled at the image, "Not that you would listen. Young people never listen. But I was the same once.

"My first night in the DP camp, I walked out into the center of those trees and sat down. Of course, it was not safe for a woman to be out alone, but I knew that Brother Taras had followed me to make sure that nothing would happen. I saw him hiding behind a nearby building, watching over me."

I smiled with the memory. "He was like my personal bodyguard and a dear friend. I named your father after him.

"I sat down to escape all the madness of the camp. It was crazy that first night; people were going wild from the unfamiliar freedom. But in that grove of trees, with Taras nearby, I felt safe. I returned to that place almost every day, usually in the mornings, and I got to know those trees well: the shape of their trunks, the stretch of their branches, the patterns of their leaves.

"They were the saddest trees I had ever known. They had stood through the war, and it seemed to me that whenever the wind blew through their aching branches, the air was full of weeping. You see, they were forever forced to gaze upon their dead brothers and sisters who had not survived the war. A tree cannot run and hide in the face of pain or terror. A tree must stand and face each storm as it comes. And those trees had seen so much death.

"That first night, I leaned against an ancient linden tree, maybe 300 or 400 years old. Most of the other trees were oak, also ancient. The Germans called them "Knorr-Eiche," or knotty oak, because their trunks were gnarled with age. Each oak had many round protrusions on its trunks; they looked like heads. Some had dozens of these heads. Most of the other people in camp found them a little unnerving, so they avoided the grove. I was often the only one there.

"When I leaned against the linden tree in the company of the oaks, they whispered in the wind. Like the rest of us, the trees were too drunk on death. The spirits in them had twisted and churned as if trapped, trying to escape their own skins. I would sit and look at the heads on the knotty oaks, and sometimes the faces would weep.

"But the spirits of those trees did not let the trees die. They stood and waited for better, brighter days to come, days when the cranes would return to fly through their branches, and the white-tailed eagle and the osprey would take refuge in their cool leaves."

I realized that I was rambling, and I was suddenly embarrassed for having revealed so much to my granddaughter.

After all, she had come for facts, and I was giving her fancy. I avoided her gaze and reached for a napkin to twist in my hands. I continued,

"Lesya, I'm sorry. You see, it is so easy to get an old woman off the subject."

But to myself I wondered: Had the birds ever returned?

"I do have a point," I said. "I had claimed for myself that ancient linden tree because it was closest to Mama P.'s dorm room, within sight so she and Brother Taras could see that I was obeying the rules. But I wasn't the only one who liked these trees. After many months at the camp, an American soldier started coming in the little grove to read.

"Everyone called him Sonny, because even at age twenty, he had about him a boyishness, a young face that appealed to the mother in most women and the father in most men. Even Mama P. liked him, and she didn't like any men, except for her son, the priest Father Petro, and Brother Taras. But there was something kind about Sonny; he put us at ease.

"Sonny had adopted the oak with the smoothest trunk. Later, he told me that most of the knotty oaks unnerved him. He said that when he sat next to all those heads, he felt as if someone were trying to read over his shoulder. So on his breaks Sonny would sit beside the smooth oak, and I would watch him from my own chosen tree, just a few feet to the southwest.

"Sonny had a ritual that he would perform each afternoon, as the sun began its journey westward. I would watch him lift his pack onto his lap, carefully pull out three books and spread them on the ground in front of him. It was always the same: Sonny first stroked the cover of the first book, tracing the letters with his fingertips. He lifted the book up to his face and drew in a deep breath as he flipped the pages . . . smelling the breath of old books.

"I knew that smell. I remembered it from the old books that

had once filled my teacher Danylo's shelves back home. I loved those books, and I admired their owner for his scholarly devotion. When we were younger, my sisters always teased me, saying that someday I would marry my teacher. I think he was the first man I cared for after my father, and I adored Danylo with that sweet love of youth. But he was my father's age and his passions were only for books and music.

"I thought of Danylo often when I saw Sonny; they had a similar nature. Usually Sonny sat as still as his tree, silently tracing the words, his face determined over the pages. But sometimes, after touching the binding, he would pull his fingers back, burned by the leather. Then he'd fling the book away from him, his cheeks flushed, his hands bunched up in fists with which he would pull at his thick black hair and shake his head, as if to ward off some terrible evil.

"After a few minutes, he would look up at the sky still shaking his head, walk over to the book and carefully pick it up. His head heavy, he would sit down and lean back against the trunk, asleep? Praying? I pretended to write while watching him there, wondering what he was thinking about.

"One night, he put his head down on his helmet, buried his hands in his hair and sobs shook his thin, muscled body. The setting sun faded into violet, then black. I wanted to go to him, to comfort him. After weeks of watching him in the silence of the trees, I wanted to say something. I don't know what compelled me. I was usually content to stay safe inside my own head, trying not to reach out to anyone, afraid of people being taken away.

"Perhaps it was the way he reminded me of Danylo that aroused an innocent adoration. Perhaps it was the way he relished the books that reminded me of home, of safe times when Tato would captivate me with fairy tales. Whatever the reason, I walked over and sat down across from him in the grass. He looked up at me, surprised. At that moment panic struck, as I realized that he probably did not speak Ukrainian, and I did not speak English. German was our only option.

"'Wie gehts?' I asked him if he was all right.

"'Gut,' he replied, I'm fine, but the German words seemed to catch in his throat as he struggled with them. He continued, 'Ironic. We can only speak in German. Even after defeating them, they still hold a certain power.'

"He looked around toward the camp. 'It's the only language most of the people here have in common, the only language that allows us to communicate. Hitler must be laughing in hell.'

"I couldn't find the words. Now that I was sitting in front of him, I just wanted to run away. Then I saw that the young soldier was not so very young. His shaking hands belied the rest of his strong body. His haunted eyes betrayed his bare cheeks. He had the look of a young dog that had been beaten and left for dead— angry and afraid and hungry. It was a look I had seen on many others during the war, but somehow I had expected the Americans to be invincible.

"'Are you all right?' I asked again.

"He shook his head, then rested his face in his hands and said, 'I have seen so many monsters this last year that I am afraid I will never sleep soundly again.'

"I stayed quiet, afraid that any interruption would silence him.

"I have seen ovens with human bones in them, and so many dead waiting to be burned, the smell of their decaying bodies thick on the air. I have seen thousands of corpses not yet dead and watched hundreds of people deny their involvement. I am angry. So angry. And sickened.'

"After a few minutes of silence, he looked up at me, eyes red and wet, 'This war has bred so many monsters. But I'm sure that you have seen your share. My name is David Goodman. Thank you for coming over. What is your story?'

"'My name is Nadya Palyvoda,' I responded, 'and I'm just another DP who is afraid to go home.'

"'Where is home?' he asked.

"Without thinking, I answered, 'A little village outside of Lviv.'

"He looked at his watch and gathered up his things, 'Me? I can't wait to get home. To scrub this death off my skin, kiss my parents and little sister, hug my girl, and try to sleep without dreams.'"

"Was this another admirer, Baba?" Lesya asked.

"No," I said, smiling. "We were just strangers who shared the same grove for a time. After that day, whenever we saw each other, we would say hello and goodbye, sometimes just nodding, I think, to avoid the German words. It took many more weeks before we struck up another conversation, and it was our last one. After that he disappeared; transferred to somewhere else."

"So he saw a concentration camp? Which one?" she asked, writing notes in her notebook.

"He was one of the soldiers who liberated Buchenwald, and the things he told me are still clear in my mind. The last time I saw him, he had just pulled out the three books from his bag when he called me over,

"'Nadya Palyvoda, come sit with me. I am leaving tomorrow.'

"'Your oak will miss you,' I told him, sitting down across from him. I did not tell him that I would also miss seeing him. 'May I ask you a question?' I felt bolder, knowing I would never see him again.

"'Of course.'

"'What are those three books? I've watched you with them, and I'm curious.'

"He smiled wryly and told me his story:

"'My squad was stationed in a castle, Saxe-Colburg. It had

remained untouched by the occupying Germans because it was allied with the House of Windsor. I had never been in such a palace, surrounded by such wealth. The contrast with the war was painful, like staring into the sun after having lived in darkness.

"'In the castle there was this library. I have always loved books, and so it was my favorite room. It was enormous, with bookshelves from the floor to the ceiling, and a ladder that slid along the top. The wood was dark and polished, and the floor was covered with expensive Oriental rugs.

"'We were instructed not to touch anything while we were there, to leave everything in perfect order because of the British connection. But I had to take something with me. I couldn't leave that place with nothing. I figured that they couldn't possibly miss a few books. So when we were leaving, I went back to the library and grabbed three books off the lower shelves and threw them into my bag. I have carried them with me ever since. I have kept them safe, and I will take them home.'

"'What books are they?' I asked.

"'That is the great irony,' he answered. 'One is by Goethe. Do you know that Goethe spent a lot of time in Weimar, the village just outside of Buchenwald? That's where he died. Inside the camp there was actually a tree called the Goethe Oak. It was destroyed in a bombing, but the stump is carefully preserved.

"'The second is *Nathan der Weise* by Gotthold Ephraim Lessing. It is a play on the theme of religious tolerance. And the last book was a religious text, a book of Christian prayers. So you know my secret. These are my three companions. I have never told anyone.'

"'At home, will you tell them what you have seen?' I asked.

"'I don't know. Not yet.' he answered."

"And I understood, Lesya. It is so hard for us to speak of that time. I know you cannot understand," I said looking at her.

"Here in the safety of this house in America, you want to know everything. You want to learn everything, but there was a time and place when knowledge meant death."

"I am so happy that none of my grandchildren have had to be in a war," I said, looking at her. Looking toward the wall in my kitchen adorned with photographs of my children and their children.

"My life has been a life of soldiers. My grandfather Mykola. My father Ivan. My childhood friends . . ." I stopped. I was treading too close to the truth. "My sons."

"So many times I wished that I were a man, Lesya, so I could bring them all to justice. Men have revenge as an option. We have only silence."

"Baba," Lesya said gently, walking over to give me a hug, "Silence is not your only option."

For a minute she sounded like Ana.

Suddenly Lesya looked down at her watch.

"Shoot," she said, closing her notebook. "I've got to run. I have a . . . an appointment."

There was something she was not saying. She avoided my eyes when she talked to me.

"You lie to your Baba now?" I asked her.

"I didn't want to get into a fight, Baba. I have a date. It's Luke's birthday."

"So that's his name, the German boyfriend? Luke?" I tried to stay calm. Deep breaths, Katya told me. Something she learned in her Yoga classes. So I took deep breaths.

"Lukas actually. Lukas Neumann."

I needed to come up with a new strategy. I needed to think about it some more.

"Fine. Go on your date. We'll talk again later." I stood up and started to gather the dishes for the sink.

Lesya walked over to me and kissed my cheek.

"I love you, Baba. Thank you."

Then she left, and I watched her through the window.

I ran the water so it got hot in the sink, hot enough to kill the germs. Baba always used to say that cool water soothes, but hot water can wash away everything, from dirt to heartaches. Well, Baba wasn't always right. I remembered after I lost my baby in the camp. I felt dirty for months. So many months of scrubbing myself, always feeling as though blood were staining my hands and thighs. Pavlo never knew about the baby lost to him.

A few weeks after I buried the baby in Stephan's overcoat under that grove of trees, Mama Paraska left with Andriy. Sonny left soon after. I was feeling alone again and trapped. Pavlo tried to mend his ways, but between us there was so much pain and regret that it seemed like nothing could bridge the gap. The wounds only started to heal after Katya was born. That was when something in Pavlo softened. She was his angel, his redemption. When the nurse put her into Pavlo's arms, he stared at little Katya and said in a faraway voice, "The only things that can save our souls in these times are children."

The hot water felt good on my hands, but I would have to put cream on them later. They got so dry as the weather began to get cooler.

So Lesya's love was Lukas. At least it wasn't Adolf or Fritz or Hans. I didn't know what to do with my granddaughter. She was a good girl. How could I make her understand? What could I tell her?

"You better be careful."

I turned to see my daughter, Katya, standing in the doorway.

"What?" I asked her.

"You better be careful with that mug," she said walking over to give me a hug. "That's the antique I brought you back from England. It's fragile and can't handle extreme temperatures for long. And I know how you like to wash your dishes with super-hot water. So where's Tato?"

"He went for a walk. He should be back soon. He probably stopped by Marko Somovych's house," I smiled at my daughter. "Did you come to see your tato? What about your mama? What brings you to the neighborhood on a Wednesday night? Maybe you have a date later?"

She was so pretty, I didn't understand why she hadn't married. "You know, Katya, Yuri has been a widower now for three years. He's a kind man with a good head of hair."

"Mama, I'm happy without a husband, okay? Now, do I need an excuse to visit my own mother?"

"Well, I usually only see you for Sunday lunch. This is a treat for me. So what brings you here?"

"I came over because I had an odd dream last night, really vivid, and I wanted to share it with you. Tell me what you think."

My children always came to me with their dreams for interpretation. They used to do it much more when they were younger. I wondered: Had they had stopped dreaming?

I turned off the water, wiped my hands and walked over to the icebox.

"Okay, but only if you let me fix you something to eat."

"I ate, Mama. I ate before I came."

"Coffee then."

"Okay, coffee." She sat down at the table.

Preparing the coffee, I asked her, "Well, then, what is this dream?"

"It was a dream about Mykola. He was in the war, but not in Vietnam—in Germany. I was in this house, and I could hear bullets and bombs exploding all around me. I was waiting for Mykola to come home. I was sitting in a rocking chair, embroidering a black shirt for him with brown thread.

"All of a sudden I heard shouting, so I ran outside. There was a terrible rainstorm with thunder and lightening. I could make out that the cries were Kolya's, and I followed them to a forest where I found him buried to the waist in mud. He was so thin, and he kept asking me for water, saying that he was dying from thirst. I realized that although it was raining, it was not raining on him. I looked up to see why, and I saw you sitting in the trees, although you were much younger, and you were holding an umbrella over his head. And you were crying, Mama. Your tears were mingling with the rain. When I looked back toward the house, I saw a wolf slowly walking toward us. Then I woke up."

It was an omen dream. My Baba taught me that when you hear about a dream and it made the hair on your neck prickle and an icy breath run down your spine, then that was an omen dream. Like the dream that Uncle Vasyl had about the screeching owl sitting on a stack of books that forewarned us about my teacher Danylo being taken away.

"How did you feel during this dream, Katya?"

"In the beginning, I felt hopeful. Then, when I saw Mykola, I felt terrible sadness, and when I saw you, Mama, I was angry. And also sad. I hated to see you cry."

She had not often seen me cry.

"Your dream is telling you many things. You believe I am preventing you from achieving something important to you, something dear to your heart. There is something about an obstruction—"

The phone rang, and Katya went to answer it. I watched her face grow pale. Something was wrong. She hung up and walked over to me.

"Tato had a heart attack at Slavko's Bar. They've taken him to the hospital."

My chest felt tight. "What does that mean? Is he all right? We have to go."

I didn't want to be left all alone.

"I'll call everyone from the car as we drive to the hospital," Katya said. "Let's go, Mama."

I couldn't move. I stared at the black and white picture on my kitchen wall. It was my favorite portrait of my children, taken at Mykola's First Holy Communion. In the back stood Taras and Mark, heads shaved by Pavlo that morning. Mark was pouting, his lower lips jutting out. He held Ivanka, who refused to sit still on the floor. Taras was smiling with all of his teeth showing. In front of them, sitting on chairs, Katya and Zirka held hands, their hair pulled back in neat little braids. And standing in the very front, between the girls, Mykola held a candle in his right hand and a prayer book in his left. All of them were dressed in Ukrainian embroidered shirts and blouses that I had made for them.

After Mykola died, both Mark and Taras felt such guilt for surviving, for not being able to do anything to help their brother. My two oldest sons were always close, but Mykola's death brought them even closer. They were lucky to have each other. It was easier in this life if you had someone to lean on. What would I do without Pavlo?

CHAPTER TWELVE

Pavlo was in surgery; we could do nothing but wait. The full moon was visible outside the window of the waiting room. It would probably have been bright enough without the overhead lamps. I wished we could have turned them off, those horrible lights that bounced off the terrible white walls. In the middle of the night, who wanted bright lights? I decided to turn them off soon. It would have been better to have candles. Candles were a soft, hopeful light. Besides, candles carried prayers up to heaven. The waiting room was heavy with prayers; it would have been good for some of them to go directly to heaven.

I couldn't think about Pavlo this way, could not imagine him with his chest cut open. I had to think about other things. The waiting room was filled with family—my children. Mark and Christina sat with their daughters on the couch. The girls were watching television and Mark's eyes were red. Taras had been calling the nurse's station in the ICU every fifteen minutes to find out his father's status, while Anna stood next to him, her arm on his elbow. Zirka leafed through a fashion magazine, and Katya sat next to her staring at the pages. Even Ivanka was here.

Tragedy has a way of bringing people together, making them forget their petty differences. I hadn't seen Zirka and Katya sit next to each other without fighting since they were kids. And there was Ivanka. Ivanka had pulled away from the family, preferring the icy, polite company of her extremely formal in-laws to the intense, fiery tempers of her brothers and sisters.

Ivanka chose to keep everything inside, instead of arguing like the rest of us. Growing up, she was almost invisible—speaking quietly, stepping softly.

Her sisters were much older and had their own interests. Katya and Zirka had made little time for their baby sister. Ivanka and Mykola were closest in age; when they were kids, she would follow him around the house, worshipping his every move. They used to play "Pretend Church." Mykola would be the priest, and Ivanka would be the person coming for communion. Sometimes I would bake special little loaves for their games.

When Mykola and Ivanka were older, Pavlo was able to spend more time at home. While I was sleeping or at work, the three of them went to the park or did some work around the house. Pavlo was closer to Mykola and Ivanka than to the others. He had to work so many odd jobs when the older kids were growing up that he never really had a chance to spend time with them. So Pavlo made an effort to be there for the two youngest, teaching them how to carve wood and fix things around the house. Eventually Mykola started spending more time with his brothers, and Ivanka alone helped Pavlo with his projects. Even then she liked to build things. Now she was an architect, building huge office buildings and hospitals. She had dreamed of building houses.

"I'm going to build a castle someday," she told me as a teenager. "It will be my dream house. And I'll build you a dream house too."

I would have been happy just to see her more often.

After Mykola's death, Pavlo became distant, and I think Ivanka felt betrayed. She needed her father to be there for her, but he was lost in his own grieving. That's when she moved out of the house and distanced herself from the family.

Even as an adult, Ivanka kept it all carefully hidden: her happiness and her sadness. I couldn't read her emotions; my youngest living child had such defenses. It used to bother me. I would try to reach out, to break down her walls. Instead, she pulled farther away. At least Roman was a good husband.

I tried to catch her eye, but she avoided my gaze and stared instead at the muted television, her hands tightly gripping her tea. She and Roman had brought pastries and fancy coffees for everyone. I tried my first cappuccino and liked it.

I know Pavlo missed his little Ivanka. I hoped he knew that she was here, that we were all here waiting for him, praying for him.

An hour before, a doctor came out to give us an update. He looked far too young to be operating on my husband, but Taras assured me that he was only one of a team of surgeons. The doctors had to take veins from Pavlo's legs and arm, and also repair his leaking mitral valve. The surgery was amazing, that they could get his heart beating again and fix it so this problem wouldn't recur. I just wished they didn't have to crack open his ribs. He was an old man—not frail, but old nevertheless. I kept imagining his ribs cracking and being pulled apart. It was a terrible sound and image.

I looked at my two sons standing by the telephone. Taras had his arm around Mark's shoulders. They were always close, and I was glad they had each other to lean on. I didn't think I could help anyone. I felt faint. As I watched my boys, I thought about how they were as children. In high school, the boys decided to form a Ukrainian motorcycle gang. It was Taras' idea, but Mark was his biggest supporter.

In the early 60s, many of the area's teenage boys belonged to a variety of neighborhood "clubs." The motorcycle gang seemed to be the toughest type, so my boys were determined to start their own.

One Friday afternoon, Mark and Taras gathered ten of their

friends, calling themselves the "Ukie Dukes," a Ukrainian "motorcycle gang" of boys with names like Stash, Dirty Wally, Vasyl, and Myron. These young Ukrainian James Deans would meet in our garage, confident that their greased hair and white T-shirts with a pack of cigarettes rolled in the sleeve would make them cool and tough.

The Ukie Dukes were ready to take on the neighborhood. Unfortunately, they only had one motorcycle among the twelve of them: Stash's Uncle Ted's old "Zundapp" motor bike. The boys took turns riding around the block, two at a time. When it was Mark and Taras' turn, Mark tumbled off as they went around the corner onto Western Avenue. Fortunately, all he got were minor scrapes and bruises.

At the time, I was working nights and was supposed to be home sleeping, but my gut instinct warned me that the boys were up to no good. I got up from bed to watch them from the porch window. They were all so brave back then, before Vietnam. Before Stash came back in a wheelchair, and Myron didn't come back at all. When Mark and Taras whizzed off on the motorcycle, I went back to my room to listen to the radio.

The boys tried to be so quiet coming home, but failed miserably. I sent them to their room and spent the rest of the afternoon cleaning blood off the bathroom rug. That was the last day of their glorious gang, because when Pavlo got home he punished them with old-world discipline—not for the motorcycle ride, but for smoking at such a young age.

Both boys continued smoking until they were grown. Taras quit fifteen years ago, but Mark still smoked. I didn't think Pavlo could ever quit. He always told me that it was one of the few pleasures he had left.

I needed to go for a walk. Katya wanted join me, but I shook my head. I needed to be by myself. I needed to have a talk with God.

The hallways were empty, except for a Latino woman watering the plants. Another woman was wiping the pictures in their frames. Both women wore neat blue and white uniforms, white kerchiefs tied around their heads. That used to be me. And Ana. I wondered how long they had been in this country. Why did they come here? What secrets had they left behind? Did they get together at the diner after their shift to talk about children and husbands and dreams left at home? I missed Ana, her advice, holding her hand.

I turned down another hall and was struck by the heavy silence—surrounded by the dead, not just the sick. How many wives had walked these halls praying for their husbands? How many had their prayers answered? Each step was like the tick of the clock when time was moving too slowly.

I had to be strong. The kids looked to me to see if everything would be all right. Of course I said yes. Pavlo was strong. He was a fighter. He would put off death this time. He had survived the war, after all.

Not like my Mykola.

"Not another one, God," I whispered. "I can't lose someone else I love."

If Mykola had lived, I think he would have become a priest. It would have been nice having a priest in the family; nice to have connections. He would have been sincere and kind and compassionate. Katya used to call him the Wizard Monk, because he loved Bible stories and fairy tales in equal measure.

I walked into to the hospital chapel and looked around. It was so different from our elaborately painted churches, where you were never alone because of all the icons on the walls. This room was empty, simple. Just wooden pews and candles. I knew what Ana would say: It's not about the place, it's about the intention.

I stood by the flickering candlelight and watched the flames.

How many other prayers were burning there tonight? How many would be answered?

My Baba always taught us to light each candle with a prayer. "When you light the candle, the smoke sends your prayers directly to God," she explained. "So make sure you think carefully before you light the wick."

Think carefully. But my prayer was so simple: I wanted my husband to live. I wasn't sure how to pray this time. When I had prayed for my son's life, it hadn't gone very well.

"I'm not sure how to ask this," I whispered into the candlelight, "and I am afraid. I know that I've made bad choices, but I've always tried to live a good life . . ."

I felt awkward, clumsy. Afraid. I lit my candle.

"Please give Pavlo the strength to come through this operation. His family needs him. I need him."

I remembered the candle I had lit for Mykola. It seemed so long ago. I smelled a hint of oranges and leather. Mykola's smell. It was too much to bear; my knees got weak. I closed my eyes and leaned against the wall for support.

"My dear Mykola," I said. "I'm so sorry for everything. I'm sorry I couldn't save you. I'm sorry for all the things you never got to do. For all the things I never got to say."

I remembered how he looked in his uniform, standing at the doorway before he left for training. So handsome. So young.

"It's not too late to change your mind," I told him. But it was. Too late. We both knew. He leaned over and kissed my cheek.

"I have to go," he said to me. "It's my destiny. I'm going to help people, and I'll be back soon."

But he never came back.

Mama Paraska told me, "There is balance in the Universe." But how was this balance? I kept losing people that I cared about;

that was not balance. I wish I could let it go. Just let go of all this heartache and be happy. I wished I could be free like when I was a young girl. But I had lost that too.

I asked aloud: "Why don't you give me any answers? How do I let go?"

Then I sat down in a pew, rested my head in my hands, and cried.

"Mama?"

Katya startled me, putting her hand on my shoulder.

"Shh," I said, wiping my eyes.

"You okay?"

She walked around and sat down next to me.

"I'm fine," I said. "I just needed to cry. All better. Are you okay?"

"Sure. I'm fine." But her eyes were red too.

"Any news?" I asked her, looking in my purse for a handkerchief.

"No." She stared at the candles. "Mama, what are you doing here?"

"I don't know. I just ended up here somehow."

"But who were you talking to?" she said, not looking at me.

"Mykola. God. I don't know."

"But you're crying," she said and turned to look at me.

"It's okay. I cry sometimes."

"But my dream—" she began, but I interrupted her.

"Don't worry about your dream," I said.

"You know it was an omen, you said so yourself." She looked past me at the wall. "Ma, why can't we talk?"

"We talk all the time. I see you more than any of my other children. We talk almost three times a week."

"That's not what I mean." Katya stared behind me. "Why can't we talk like women? Like adults? We always carry on these general conversations, these snappy remarks, this defensive posturing—"

"I don't understand."

"Always skirting around the real conversation."

"No, I mean you're using words that I don't understand. Remember, I am not a Ph.D."

"See, you're finding ways to change the subject."

I saw she was getting upset because she started rubbing her hands together, "I'm not changing the subject. I'm just not sure that I know what you mean."

"It makes me sad, Mama. So sad that you don't know me—"

"Of course, I know you. You're my daughter."

"—and I don't know you. You are such a mystery to me, all locked up with so many secrets. From you, I learned that some things are best kept to oneself. That we need to protect the ones we love from truths that will hurt them. From you, I learned that silence is an acceptable alternative." She was sobbing through her words, as if each one was growing more difficult for her to say. "But it's not okay, Mama. It's not okay. I want to know you, the real you. Before you die."

I moved closer to her and put my arm around her.

"What do you want to know?" My words terrified me, because I was afraid of what she would ask. "What is there left to know about an old woman, a Baba?"

"Everything."

Everything. There was too much.

"Tell me about the girl you once were. The one you lost."

So, she'd listened to me pray, but I didn't have the energy to get angry.

Katya pulled away from my embrace and continued, "Tell me about your Mama, about your life and why you left home. Tell me about the war, about your dreams, about your secrets."

"This is not the time or place—"

"Don't!" she said, her eyes bright. "Don't put it off any more."

"But what if there is news?"

"Zirka will find us. She knows where I am. Please, Mama."

I sighed and sat there for a moment. How could I find the words? Could I really tell my daughter this?

Part of me wanted to be rid of the weight on my heart, to allow someone else to carry it with me, but another part was so afraid to let it go.

"What for, Katya?" I asked her. "What is the point? It won't change the past. It can't bring back the dead."

Katya looked at me and said, "But it can change things, Ma. It can teach me something about you, and it can help you to let go of some of that pain you carry around."

Of course, she was right. I buried my face in my hands and rubbed my eyes and my cheeks. It would change things. It would change how my daughter saw me, and I was afraid of what she would think of her mama. I had worked hard to create a life for myself, for my family. I was supposed to be a strong and wise old woman. Like my Baba. Like my Mama.

"Katya, what do you see . . . what do you see when you look at your mama?" I bit the inside of my cheek to keep from crying.

She stared at me for a moment and said, "I see a woman who has lived her whole life trying to be strong, trying to carry the world around so life will be easier for her family. Mama, what are you so afraid of?"

My intuitive daughter asked the right question. I *was* afraid.

"I'm afraid of being found out," I said with a sob. "I am a phony, Katya. I am living the wrong life. I left them all, my family. I should have been there. I should have been dead. I should have never left, but I did, and it's all my fault!" The tears were hot on my cheeks, and I was ashamed of crying in front of my child. I couldn't look at her, but I continued. "This isn't the life I was supposed to live, and so I have to be someone else. That's my secret. That's what I carry around." And I told her about the stone and the river and going to see the vorozhka and finding the barn on fire ". . . the cries of the sheep, like children, the sound of the flames like raging, angry winds rushing through the barn."

I hadn't told her about Stephan yet. Through my tears I saw Zirka walk into the chapel.

"The doctors are there with an update," she said, stepping towards us. Then she changed her mind, turned around, and left.

Katya looked me in the eye. "Thank you, Mama." She stood up and offered me her hand. "I would really like to hear more."

She hugged me, and we walked together. I was terrified to hear what the doctors would say. We walked up to the waiting room, where the doctors were explaining things to Anna and Taras. The others were standing nearby, listening. Why hadn't they waited for me? I was Pavlo's wife. I'm sure they figured I could not understand. My sons would explain it to me later. The doctors said that the surgery had gone well, and Pavlo was in the ICU. They needed to monitor him, but he seemed to be doing well. Because of his age, they had to watch him carefully.

"I recommend that you go home and get some rest," the young doctor said. "You can see him in the morning."

"I want to see my husband." I said stubbornly. "I will wait."

Everyone went home, except for Katya, who stayed with me. We dozed on each other's shoulders in the waiting room. When Pavlo finally came out of the anesthesia, a nurse came to get me.

Pavlo was connected to so many machines that he didn't look like himself at all. He looked so weak, so bruised, so old. I wanted to cry when I saw him, but I smiled at him instead and took his hand.

"You're going to be all right," I said to him. "Rest now. I love you."

He looked me in the eye and nodded. Then he squeezed my hand lightly and closed his eyes.

Pavlo fell asleep and Katya drove me home, promising to pick me up in a few hours. It was already morning. I sat on the back steps to watch shades of plum and salmon reach beyond the horizon, crawl up the sky behind the birch, toward the moon.

I almost lost Pavlo.

I looked at the birch tree, and I couldn't believe that she was thirty years old. Pavlo and I planted her in the backyard after I started to come to terms with Mykola's death. She kept me rooted to this place. I would never leave our house, our yard. Never move away because I was tied to that land, like I was once tied to the land of my birth.

The birch was so young, so different from the ancient trees back home and the trees in the DP camp. The trees at home taught me to find strength in my roots, to rely on my foundation. From the trees in camp I learned about peace and healing. Those trees echoed the lessons of my Baba, that we are all connected.

Back home, these lessons were taught in songs and stories passed along by grandmothers, wise women who held a cherished place in the circle of community. I thought someday to take my place among them. But the war had broken the cycle and torn millions of people away from the bosoms of their mothers. We were forever searching to recapture all that we had lost . . . connections to blood, to bones, to earth.

And connections resurface . . . refuse to be denied.

Soon it would be Halloween, the night when American children ran around with bags of candy and faces that are not their own. The night when spirits walked on the Earth to deliver messages and remind the living. My dead were no exception. Even buried so far away they had found me. What messages would they bring me this year?

Pavlo.

I couldn't bring myself to go to sleep; I felt unsettled, so I sat for a while longer, just listening to the birds begin their songs. Pavlo always hated their early cries. He swore they sang outside our window just to torment him. How he could hear them through all his snoring I would never know.

I heard the phone ringing and ran inside.

"Mama . . . Tato's dead," Katya said. "He died a few minutes ago. His heart just stopped."

PART THREE

Lullaby

Crawling in the sheets, I fear
burying you in my dreams where
your tears drop as water
trickling from the sky, and I am
an instant of devastating white.

—Fiona Sze-Lorrain, "Fragile"
from *Water the Moon*
(Marick Press, 2009)

CHAPTER THIRTEEN

The first few weeks after Pavlo died, the business of death kept me calm and focused. I was so busy with the particulars that I didn't have time to think. I had to notify his friends and acquaintances, pick out his burial clothes, and buy his tombstone. There was the wake and the burial. I was touched by the little details attended to by family and friends, details I couldn't remember.

Taras placed a pack of cigarettes in the pocket of Pavlo's burial suit, and Zirka brought a beautiful framed photo of the entire family, taken at the last family wedding, which was placed in his hands. Ivanka hid her first wood carving—a tiny wooden dove—in the coffin beside him. Pavlo's friend Yuri Radchenko brought a handful of soil carried from Ukraine to toss on the coffin as we watched it being lowered into the ground. It would have made Pavlo happy to be buried with a little earth from home. Katya prepared a large batch of kutia, the ancient porridge of wheat and honey, to be served at the meal in the cultural center following the burial.

At the cultural center, friends and family reminisced about Pavlo, sharing stories and laughing at his pranks. They applauded his garden and tomatoes; they praised his large, beautiful family; and during solemn moments, they broke into several, spontaneous chants of "Vichnaya Pamyat," Eternal Memory. I sat in a fog, smiling and nodding but not really participating.

The phone kept ringing every day for weeks, as friends and family expressed their sympathy and offered comfort. Sorting through Pavlo's clothes, I gave things away to our children and grandchildren. It was the details, the busy work, that initially kept me from grieving.

Then one morning, I woke up early and prepared to get out of bed before I heard Pavlo's snoring. That was when it hit me. There would be no more snoring. I didn't have to get out of bed. What did I have to get up for? I didn't need to make Pavlo's breakfast or wash his clothes. The house was clean because there was no one around to dirty it up. I was alone. I wept because I would never hear Pavlo snore again.

I stayed in bed all day. I couldn't eat. I wouldn't answer the phone. Mark let himself in that afternoon because he worried when I didn't answer the phone. He found me in bed and panicked.

"What's wrong, Mama? Are you hurt? Sick?"

"I'm fine. Just leave me alone. Go away."

Eventually, he fed Khvostyk and left, but he must have told his brother and sisters what he had seen because one of them came by to check on me every day for the next several weeks. Some days, I made it out of bed; other days, I didn't. Poor Khvostyk was grateful for the automatic feeders Katya brought to the house. When I did eat, it was mostly tea and bread with butter. The kids kept my fridge well stocked, but so much went to waste. I lost a lot of weight, and I think I was preparing myself to die, to join Pavlo, Mykola, and the rest of my late family members.

On one of her visits, Katya asked me to make her a new scarf: black with red embroidery. She bought material—so soft to the touch—and ruby red thread, and she left them on my nightstand. When I woke the next morning, I saw Ana sitting at the foot of my bed. She looked young, like she when I met her on the boat.

It's not your time, darling. You have to get out of bed.

"I'm not ready," I said. "What am I supposed to do? The kids all have their lives, their families. No one needs me anymore. I am alone. What am I supposed to do with my time?"

Find things you love to do, people you want to share your time with.

"But Ana, you chose to leave . . . together with Niki. You didn't go through it alone."

I was dying. I didn't want to spend it fading away. I wanted to live until the last moment, and we did.

Then she looked as she had the last time I saw her, with her purple scarf tied around her thinning hair. *There's more joy for you here, I promise, Ana said, pointing at the embroidery. Start with one stitch and go from there. See what happens. Just start.*

Then she was gone. For a minute, I toyed with the idea of closing my eyes and going back to sleep. Instead I stood up, took the cloth and thread with me into the kitchen and brewed a pot of coffee. I lit the candle in front of the Blessed Virgin Mary for the first time since Pavlo died.

I had a pile of bills and envelopes to go through on the table. Instead, I threaded a needle and started embroidering. The material was soft, like silk. My fingers knew their work so well that I could do this in the dark. I had done it in the dark. I finished the scarf later that night and gave it to Katya.

Over the next few months, I tried to get involved with other people. I volunteered at the church and the cultural center but never really connected with any of the women there. I was looking for a kindred spirit, but none of them really fit. The old women had their own cliques of friends, and I always felt like an outsider. I was also afraid to let down my guard. I wasn't ready to talk about Pavlo, and everyone kept asking me how I was doing, how I was feeling.

In reality, I was trying not to feel anything because I felt too many things too intensely: loneliness, sadness, anger, and guilt. The day Pavlo died I was thinking about escaping, having adventures. I had never answered his question. He had asked if it —our life together—was enough. I couldn't say yes to put his mind at ease. What if our talk is what gave him a heart attack? Maybe I upset him. Maybe I let him down. Maybe it was my fault.

Maybe I broke his heart.

Most of all, I missed him. I kept looking for Pavlo in his chair. I thought I saw him sitting in the kitchen. I expected to smell his cigarette smoke wafting in the kitchen window. I kept looking for cookie crumbs on the counter and ice cream drips on the floor. I reached for him at night to warm my feet and put his arm around me. But he was gone.

The seasons changed, and I continued going through the motions. Somehow we managed through that first Christmas. My girls helped me prepare the traditional feast, but our mood was somber. We were all actors in a bad play, performing our roles without enthusiasm. Winter turned into spring, and spring into summer. Lesya continued to see her German boy, although she wouldn't talk about him with me. I heard snippets from her mother. Everything else carried on as it does. The children grew older, the grandchildren grew taller, and life went on around me.

On the first anniversary of Pavlo's death, I went to the cemetery in the morning to lay flowers on his grave and then to church for his memorial service. Our entire family was there, and they sought to take me out for dinner afterwards. I didn't want to talk and socialize, so instead I went home and prepared Pavlo's favorite dishes for myself. I set the table for two, toasted Pavlo's memory with a glass of wine—which turned into a bottle—and I ate his favorites: breaded pork chops, mashed potatoes, cucumbers and sour cream, and an apple strudel for dessert. For a while I just sat in the kitchen, staring at the photos on the wall. I wasn't sure what I was supposed to do. How does one honor her husband's memory? Suddenly the house felt too small, too stuffy, too confining. I needed to get outside for fresh air.

I walked into the garden and sat down in Pavlo's favorite spot, where he often smoked his "morning cigarette." I heard the faintest hint of music—violins and guitar in a sad duet—coming from the alley. The melody sounded strangely familiar. As a car sped through the alley and past my backyard, I recognized the song as the same music from the vorozhka's camp, the same melody that once drew me away from my parent's farm. The same song!

The music got louder and then fade again as the car sped down the alley. When I looked toward the gate, the vorozhka, Liliana, walked toward me, dressed in the beautiful skirts and scarves that she was wearing the first time I saw her—not the tattered, bloody clothes from the night of my reading. She smelled of berries and mint, and she stopped in front of me and extended her hand.

It's a night for dreams and dreamers, she said. *Are you brave enough?*

I took her hand and walked with her through the dimly lit alley to the small park near my house. There was no moon; the park was dark and empty.

"Why am I here?" I asked her.

Three questions. Three visits.

Three questions? I searched my memory for stories of visitations from the dead. I knew that the dead could play tricks or speak in riddles. And then there were the unquiet dead, whose intention was to bring misfortune. Why tonight? Why three questions?

Your first question? Liliana asked me.

I answered quickly, without thinking, "Is Pavlo at peace?"

The question determines the visitor, the vorozhka said. *The visitor determines the answer.*

Liliana smiled and pointed to my left where Ana was dancing toward me, young and lovely like the day I met her on the boat. My heart hurt. I missed her.

As Ana came closer, I saw a sprig of marjoram behind her ear.

He is, Darling, Ana answered. *Pavlo is content.* Ana looked as if she wanted to say more. She looked at Liliana, then back to me.

Later, she said, then winked before dancing back into the trees.

My Ana. I knew she'd return.

My thoughts turned to the envelope.

"Did I make a mistake?" I asked Liliana for my second question. "Should I have stayed?"

Out from behind Liliana stepped a middle-aged woman. Pani Orysia: Stephan's mother. I almost didn't recognize her but for her eyes.

Pani Orysia had once invited me to dinner. I was in awe back then, sitting with Stephan's family at the table. They were such a beautiful family, so intelligent. After dinner they all sang together, each brother playing guitar, Stephan's mother on the bandura. Stephan had his mother's eyes, her smile. She was beautiful, cultured, and strong. She was everything I hoped to someday become. I loved them and the way they welcomed me. Life was always a feast in their home, a celebration. At least, until the Germans took away Stephan and his brother Bohdan. After that, I was no longer invited. Pani Orysia would not leave her bed. She wouldn't eat. They found her one morning, drowned in the river.

There in the park, Stephan's mother looked ragged. Her skin

hung on her once round body, and her lips were blue, as if she were frozen.

Stephan died with your name on his lips. Where were you? You should be with us.

She smiled, revealing only two teeth where once there had been a brilliant smile. She looked hungry, licked her lips, and motioned for me to follow. I felt drawn to pursue her. Liliana stretched her hand out to block my path. Then Pani Orysia was gone. I felt a chill up and down my spine, and I crossed myself. Her visit left me feeling exposed and vulnerable. I wanted to run home to the safety of my house. And what of her answer? It was not an answer but an accusation. My name on Stephan's lips?

"What do I do now?" I asked, because I didn't know what to do. I didn't know what to do that night, next week, or next year. My children were grown. My grandchildren were nearly grown. What was there left for me to do?

I smelled lilacs, and Baba Hanusia stepped out from behind me with open arms. I wanted to lay my head on her chest, like a child, and lose myself in her voice, in her strong heartbeat.

Stories are the connection, little mouse, Baba answered. *Find someone to share them with.*

When I stepped forward to embrace her, Baba vanished. I looked at Liliana.

"What about Pavlo?" I asked her. "Why not him?"

The question determined the visitor, she repeated.

"It is all true?" I asked her.

The visitor determined the answer, she replied.

"Why you?" I asked her.

We are connected, Liliana answered.

Once again I heard the Gypsy music approaching. A silver station wagon pulled up in front of the park, windows down and music playing loudly on the speakers. I couldn't see through the darkened windows, but somehow I knew that the vorozhka's brothers were inside. Liliana walked over to the car and got in the backseat. The car drove away, the melody getting softer and softer.

I walked back home alone.

CHAPTER FOURTEEN

The next morning, I woke up and placed a small framed photo of Pavlo on the table in my icon corner. The house felt particularly cold and damp, and there was a musty smell in the air. I would need to do a thorough cleaning soon, open all the windows and doors to welcome light and life back into the house.

I realized that I had not covered the stove with an embroidered cloth after Pavlo died, to prevent the domovyk from leaving. I had not only neglected myself, Khvostyk, and the house, but I had forgotten to make an offering to the house spirit. There would be nothing but bad luck and sadness in the house if the domovyk left. I could not bear more misfortune.

I took a loaf of bread from the icebox and put it on a plate. I poured salt into a small dish and, for good measure, I opened a bottle of honey wine and poured it into a small bowl. I set the bowls on the plate, which I then placed in the stove. I draped a beautiful embroidered cloth across the handle of the stove, to cover the glass window.

"Domovyk, little grandfather, I have been lost in grief," I said. "Accept this offering and please do not leave my home. I promise to invite happiness in, so that you will once again enjoy laughter and warmth in this household."

Khvostyk rubbed against my legs and then curled up in front of the stove, which I took to be a good sign. I brewed coffee, made toast with butter and blackberry jam, and sat down with the mound of mail I had been avoiding for the last few weeks. Mark had gone through the mail during his visits, picking out obvious bills that needed my attention. I had paid those, but I still had cards, letters, and other mail to sort through.

After going through condolence cards, newspapers and advertisements, I came upon two envelopes: one from Andriy Polotsky and the other, a familiar envelope from Ukraine. My chest felt tight, and I sat frozen for a long time, trying to decide which to read first. I picked up the envelope from Ukraine. It was the same handwriting, the same village, but this one was still sealed. With trembling hands, I opened it and carefully pulled out the white lined pages.

"My Dearest Nadya,

This is my second letter to you. I assume the first one didn't reach you last year. They still check the mail here, opening the envelopes to read the contents as if we had anything of value. So I must assume that the letter was lost. I cannot imagine that you would not respond to me, Halya, your own sister.

I'm sure it will come as a shock to hear from me after all these years, but I only recently found out that you were still alive. It is quite a story about how I found you in Chicago, in America!

An American who called himself Sonny came to our village, looking for you. He was a soldier during the war and had met you in the DP camps. Imagine our surprise to hear that you were alive! That you had somehow survived. You must have changed your identity, using Stephan's last name instead of Tato's, because Sonny came to the village asking for Nadya Palyvoda. The villagers knew of no one by that name, but brought him to me, since I am Halya Palyvoda.

You must be wondering how I came to have the

name of your old sweetheart. It's a difficult story to reveal, and I'm sorry that I have to write it here, but you must know the truth.

That last night when you left, I remember I was sleeping soundly. I never heard you leave. I woke to the sound of pounding on the door. Tato got up and let them in. It was the German soldiers, and they began shouting at us to get up and get out. We scrambled out of our beds, and that's when Mama noticed you were gone. She panicked and began screaming, asking for you. The soldiers kept telling her to shut up, but she was so upset. I thought it was another bad dream and kept hoping that you'd wake me up and hold me and sing me a song, but I couldn't wake up. And you were gone.

I was crying and covering my eyes and ears. They took Tato and me outside. Some of the soldiers stayed in the house with Mama and Laryssa. I heard screaming and much noise. Tato tried to get inside, but there were too many soldiers and they beat him unconscious. After some time, the soldiers came out, but Mama and Laryssa never did. They set the house on fire and dragged Tato and me away.

I never found out where they took Tato, but I never saw him again. I was taken to the town center with some other women and children. As we prepared to ship off to some kind of camp, the Russians arrived, and the world turned upside down again. The Germans were shooting everyone in sight. The Russians were shooting everyone in sight. So many people died all around me, in front of me.

Your friend Sonya and her mother survived and took me in, and we lived together like family. When the war ended, we started to rebuild. One day, ten years later, a thin, scraggly stranger arrived in town and began asking about our family. Sonya's mama found me and brought me to the church where this man waited. He looked so old and sick that I didn't recognize him at first. When I gazed at him closer, I saw that it was Stephan! Somehow, he had escaped the soldiers in Slovakia and fled, but he didn't get very far. Soon after, he was captured and sent to prison in Siberia. When he was finally released, he could only think of returning home, to find you.

I told him that we had never heard from you and assumed that you had died during the war. Stephan refused to believe that you perished while he had survived. He told us how you and he fled to Slovakia, how he was taken, had escaped, and was recaptured. He said thoughts of you were what had kept him alive during the war and in prison. He was praying that you had returned home. He had nowhere to stay, having lost his entire family in the war, so Sonya's mother took him in until he could find work and a place to live. You see, Sonya married a Russian soldier and had moved with him to St. Petersburg, so it was only the two of us in her home.

Stephan stayed with us and together we mourned for you, for our families, for everything we had lost. We were two orphans who had turned to each other for support and comfort. We became friends, and after a year we decided to marry.

I gave birth to one child, our son Mykola, named after Dido. He was our future: so good, so handsome. But he died in military service during the Soviet occupation of Afghanistan.

When Sonny came, Stefko and I were surprised to

hear that you had survived the war and made it to the DP camps in Germany. Of course, we had no way of knowing if you were still alive. Sonny left the village and promised to contact us if he found you. He said he had one more person to find: a Ukrainian named Andriy Polotsky who had been in the Soviet army during the war. He told us that Andriy was quite famous in the United States. Sonny thought that you two may have stayed in contact, since you were such good friends with Andriy's mother.

Two months later, we received a letter with your name and address inside. As it turned out, Sonny found Andriy, who had your address. I wrote to you that same day and Stefko even attached a short note.

Sadly, there is no note from Stephan this time. He died in his sleep last month. Sonya's mama passed away long ago, and Sonya herself died last year. Now you are all I have left. So once again I write, hoping to reach you.

If this letter should find you before Christmas, I pray your holidays are blessed with happiness, as I eagerly wait with hope to hear from you soon.

With love,
Your sister Halya"

My sister was alive? Stephan died a month ago? My heart was beating quickly. Stephan had attached a note. I could have had a note from Stephan after all these years. My sister and Stephan? But I never returned home. It was my fault. I left him for dead. They found each other. He was looking for me. My Stephan, not hers. Mine. Sonny found her? Him? Me? Andriy found me? I never found anyone. Maybe if I'd gone back? My

littlest sister with her thin braids and bad dreams. I wasn't there
to protect her, to protect them. To warn them: Mama, Tato,
Laryssa. I wasn't there. I left them. Her handwriting was neat,
careful. It was a woman's writing, not a little girl's. Not my little
Halya. Stephan came back. He took care of her. She took care of
him. They had no one else. They should have had me. Me. It
should have been my life. It could have been my life. Siberia? He
was in prison in Siberia? I was in America, eating instant noodle
soup and soft white bread, while he was in Siberia. My poor
Stephan. But he wasn't mine. He was hers. He came back. But he
found Halya. My littlest sister was alive? And she was alone now.
Like me.

I didn't know what to do next. Who could I tell? What would
I say? I wanted to tell Pavlo, but he was gone. Like Stephan. I
had lost them both. Not knowing what else to do, I decided to
clean the house with the fervor of a madwoman. I hadn't really
given it a thorough cleaning in over a year, and I needed to work
with my hands to avoid thinking.

I changed into old clothes, pulled up my hair, and put on
some loud Ukrainian folk music. Then I began in the kitchen and
cleaned everything in sight, determined to scour the smell of
death and sadness from everything in my home. I cleaned out
cabinets, dusted china and knickknacks, emptied out the icebox,
washed the floor on my hands and knees, scrubbed the toilet,
vacuumed, and washed mirrors and windows. I worked from
morning until night, stopping only to drink some tea.

I left my bedroom for last. I had already gone through
Pavlo's drawers and closet, so there wasn't much to do except
strip the sheets, flip the mattress, and change the bedding. Time
to put away the light summer quilt and replace it with the warm
down blanket for the coming winter.

When I pulled up the mattress, I found a squished pack of
cigarettes with only two remaining, and an envelope addressed

"To Nadya."

It was not sealed. I thought it was from Pavlo, a note he had written but never had the nerve to give me. I sat on the bed to read it.

> "Dear Nadya,
>   Halya and I..."

The writing was not Pavlo's. I stopped reading. This was Stephan's note. Pavlo had hidden it from me. I had been sleeping on it all this time? He had lied to me. He had robbed me of the chance to say goodbye. Pavlo had stood there and told me he did not open the envelope. What else had he lied about? That moment I felt like I had never really known my husband. What else had he been capable of?

For a moment, I thought about throwing the letter away. What would it change to read his words? He was dead. But my curiosity was too strong, so I continued:

> "Dear Nadya,
>   Halya and I were so relieved to hear from the American named Sonny that you were alive and had a family in Chicago. I'm sure that Halya explained our situation in her letter. It's a blessing that I found her. We have a good life together, a happy life. Your sister, my wife, is a passionate, amazing woman. She reminds me of how you were: brave and adventurous. We had a son named Mykola, who died too young. He was our joy, and a part of us died with him. The rest has been filled with the ups and downs of life. We work, we play, we dance, and we laugh. What more is there, really?
>   I hope that you have been happy in America and that you found love and friendship. Perhaps someday

our paths will cross again, and we can share old stories.

Yours truly,
Stephan"

That was all. No declarations of love. No heartfelt apologies. Just a quick note about how happy he was with my sister. I felt betrayed and sad. I had carried a torch in my heart for him for all these years. All along, he had been alive and making a happy life with my sister. I should have been happy for her, for them. I should have been relieved that Halya found someone to care for her. She lost everyone that night too. It wasn't her fault, but still I felt jealous. It was my own fault. If I had only gone back, I could have taken care of Halya and been there when Stephan returned. If only—

My chest felt tight, my nerves raw and exposed. I looked again at the note, the neat handwriting. "Dear Nadya". *My* Stephan. But not mine. Can you ever really let go of a love that shapes you, that changes your destiny? Maybe it was just because he reminded me of a time when I was younger, full of hopes and dreams. Maybe it was because I promised to love him forever. Maybe it was okay to love him still. Ana used to say that love is one of the greatest natural resources we have on the planet.

"Darling, love isn't exclusive. You don't run out of it," Ana once said while slipping garlic and basil into a dark blue glass container of olive oil on her counter. Ana said that blue glass was the best because it kept things fresher.

Because Niki was out of town on business, I had come over for pizza. We had been talking about old lovers. Actually, Ana had been talking about her old lovers. I hadn't specifically mentioned Stephan.

"It's like this olive oil," she continued. "Old lovers are the spices that give life flavor."

"But I feel guilty thinking about someone from my past," I said. "Someone I had loved before Pavlo."

"Was he your first true love?" she asked me.

"Yes," I said with a sigh.

"Well, you shouldn't feel guilty for thinking about him. I would guess that he probably symbolized something in your current relationship now that's missing. Maybe it's the romance?"

"Maybe." I said. "But I still feel guilty. Don't you have any kind of herbal concoction to make me forget?"

"I'm an herbalist, Nadya, not a sorceress."

"Same thing, really," I said, sipping my cocktail. Ana had tried her hand at making a fruity pineapple drink. It was sweet and sour. I loved it.

"Don't feel guilty, Nadya. I think about old flames from time to time. I even fantasize sometimes." She winked at me and continued, "I love each of them for the things they taught me . . . about love, about the world, about myself."

"Each of them? So many?" I asked.

Ana pulled back her shoulders, stretched her neck proudly, and said, "I am not ashamed of my past. I didn't meet Niki until I was much older, and in the meantime, I had a lot of fun. Niki and I have talked about all this. He knows everything." She looked me in the eye. "Maybe you should talk to Pavlo?"

I burst into laughter, imagining the conversation. "No, Ana, I don't think so. You and Niki are unusual; you're lucky." I said.

"Yes, he's a soul mate. No question. But I loved others before him, and I didn't stop loving them when we were married. Sure, there are shades of love, but don't think that the minute you have a ring on your finger, the past is erased and the future is sealed."

She sat down next to me and continued, "My theory is that

the happier you are, the more love you have to give. If there's one thing I'm sure of, it's that human beings were put on this earth to love."

Ana smiled that big toothy grin. "That's what gives life meaning, darling. The rest of it passes the time and creates drama, but love . . . love is what makes it all worthwhile. Think about it, you have such a big family, so many kids and grandkids . . . you love them all, yes?"

"Yes, but that's different—"

"Shush. Not so different. Listen, I'm making a point. You aren't afraid of running out of love for them?" She took my hand. Her fingers smelled of garlic. "And you love me, right?"

I felt myself blush, "Of course, Ana. You're my best friend, my sister."

"And I love you . . . as much as I love Niki, Nadya. If you were a man, I probably would have run away with you years ago." She winked at me and let out that loud, unapologetic laugh of hers. "My point is that love doesn't have limits. It's people who set limits for love."

"What about marriage?" I asked, determined to make my point.

"Marriage?" She laughed again. "Think about all the couples we know who are miserable in their marriages. Everyone's kids have grown up. Just see how many of them split up—or at least have separate bedrooms—once their kids are out of the house "

"No, marriage doesn't guarantee love. Marriage is about creating a partnership for all kinds of practical reasons—like raising a family, which is easier if you know your partner is going to stay around. It's also a way to make sure that we don't die alone. Ultimately, that's what we're all afraid of: being left alone. So marriage seeks to quell that fear. Hopefully you grow old together. If you're lucky, you marry your friend."

Ana stood up to make us some more drinks. "Or in cases like

yours, dear heart, you need to make friends with the man you married. Unless you want a divorce?"

I could feel the warmth from the alcohol in my head. It made me feel freer, more confident. The words flowed a little more easily. "No, Ana. Divorce is not for me. Pavlo is a good man, a kind man. He's a good father. And he . . . is my friend. We have our Saturday morning coffees. We talk about the week, and he actually makes the coffee."

"And he loves you, Nadya," Ana said, bringing over another drink. "I don't think you see how much he loves you."

"He loves the way I take care of him," I said.

"No, he loves you, darling." Ana sat down again. "I don't know about this man from the past, who he was or what he meant to you. But I do know that Pavlo loves you right now, albeit in his own way."

She took my hand again. "Let yourself love the past, but live the present."

My Mama used to say that marriage is a way for two souls to be united for eternity. But was it marriage that united the souls? What was it about a ritual that could make it so? Maybe it was a silent declaration in your heart that united the souls. What happened if you made that unspoken promise, but then married another? Could you ever break that covenant? What happened when your beloved died? Could your soul be joined to more than one person?

I was exhausted. It was too much to think about. Pavlo had lied to me. Halya was alive. Stephan had been alive. They had loved one another. Now we were both widows. At least I had a large family; Halya was truly alone. I would have to call her, but not yet. I wasn't ready.

I got ready for bed and crawled under the warm blanket. I lay there thinking about the letters. Stephan had written that

Halya was a brave and adventurous woman, like I had been. But I wasn't that girl anymore. I had lost touch with my adventurous spirit, and I didn't know how to get it back.

I lay with my back to the wall. If Pavlo had been alive, he would have been curled behind me. He always slept closest to the wall so I wouldn't disturb him when I crawled out of bed in the morning. If I closed my eyes, I could imagine that he was still there in the darkness.

"Pavlo, why did you lie to me?"

His voice whispered from the darkness: *I'm not the one who's guilty here. Ever since I met you, I loved only you. I never wanted to be anywhere else but by your side.*

"But I would never deny you anything that you cared about," I said. "I would never steal from you."

Oh no? Never?

"No. Never." I responded, but I felt a stab of guilt in my belly.

I saw you, Nadya.

"What? When?" I was afraid. But he couldn't know. He was drunk that night.

I saw you burying something that night.

Oh my God. This was too much for one night. Too much.

I saw the bloodstained rags. You went to the grove of dead oak trees and dug with your bare hands. Why didn't you tell me, Nadya?

"I didn't know how," I answered. "Why didn't you tell me you knew?"

I kept hoping some day you would tell me yourself.

"Oh, Pavlo." I wanted to turn around, to see if he were really there. To touch him, but I was afraid. Afraid of what I would see. Afraid he would vanish.

"All these years, you never told me," I said.

All these years you never told me.

"So you kept the letter to punish me? Is that why?"

The envelope was already open. The letter from your sister was not there. Only the note addressed: 'Dear Nadya.' You ask why I took it. Curiosity? Jealousy? I could say it was to protect you, but in fact, it was to protect me.

"You robbed me of the chance to say goodbye," I whispered.

And what did you rob me of, Nadya?

His words stung, and I began to weep. "I'm sorry, Pavlo."

I felt a kiss on the top of my head, and I knew he was gone.

My sleep was fitful again that night, filled with disturbing dreams. In the morning, I woke early and returned to the pile of mail on the table. The letter from Halya was still there, as was the envelope from Andriy Polotsky. I opened it, and inside was a ticket to see his latest play *Angel's Lullaby*, this time in Chicago. No note, just a single ticket for opening night on the following week. I set it aside, not planning to go. I had had enough brushes with the past. I was ready to start living in the present.

If only my Baba were alive, I could ask her for some herbs or an incantation to chase away the sadness and doubt, to rid me of ghosts and regrets. Baba always knew the right thing to say or do.

I remembered that when we went to visit her, just after our Dido Mykola died, Baba would sometimes light a red candle and recite the following verse while gazing into the flame:

"Dear Father, Holy Spirit of Fire, be kind and gentle to me. Burn away my heartache and sorrow, so my heart can be free."

Baba did this ritual nightly, to help ease the pain of her grief. I once asked her if it really worked.

"Of course it works, little mouse," she answered, collecting the melted wax to place in a bowl of water. The shape it took would give her hints about the future. "The Holy Spirit of Fire is powerful," Baba continues. "He can create and destroy. Fire is one of the greatest gifts we have been given. It brings us life, and we must honor it."

I decided to try for myself. I took out a new candle, a red one, and set it on the table in front of me. I drew the curtains and turned off the lights. Because the day was overcast, the room was quite dark. I lit the candle with a match and imagined the pain being burned away from my heart. I repeated the incantation:

"Dear Father, Holy Spirit of Fire, be kind and gentle to me. Burn away my heartache and sorrow—"

I wasn't able to complete the verse because suddenly a bird flew into the glass of my kitchen window, and the candle flame I had lit shot up to the ceiling, burning a dark spot in the shape of a cloud onto the plaster. I crossed myself and threw the candle into the sink.

I wasn't sure what to do next. I was shaken and unsure of what had transpired. I only knew that it was a bad omen, a sign that all was not well in my home and my life. I needed help. I decided to call Katya.

"Are you busy?" I asked her over the telephone.

"What's wrong Mama?" she asked, her voice anxious.

"I need help. You have all kinds of strange friends, don't you?"

"What kind of a question is that?"

"I just mean that they have a wide range of interests, right?"

"I guess so, Mama. What's this all about?"

"I've had a rough day and a weird omen. My house has an unpleasant feeling, and I need some help, some advice."

"You think the domovyk is unhappy?" she asked.

"Worse, Katya. He may have left, and I'm not sure if something else has come in his place."

"Do you mind if I bring a friend? She has experience with this kind of thing," Katya said.

"Yes, please do. The more help, the better. I'll make some tea." I walked over to the cupboard.

"We'll be right over." She said.

CHAPTER FIFTEEN

Within the hour the doorbell rang. I opened the door and standing beside Katya was a tall, striking woman with long, black hair streaked with grey. For a minute, I thought it was Ana. There was something about her that reminded me of my friend. Maybe it was the mischief in her smile or the intensity of her eyes.

"Hi, Kat's mom. I'm Robin. So you have an icky vibe in your house and we need to get it out, eh?"

I kissed Katya and said, "Hello Robin. Please, come in. Let's talk in the kitchen."

The women entered, removed their shoes and followed me into the kitchen. Robin had brought a bag filled with an assortment of objects. I was curious about the contents. She saw me looking at it and smiled.

"I wasn't sure what we would need, so I threw a few things together." Robin sat down at the table and looked around the kitchen. "So, what's been happening here? I'm sensing a lot of emotion, sadness especially. You have any unusual visitors in the night?"

I wasn't prepared to share this with my daughter, let alone a stranger. I thought of the night when the vorozhka came. Did this Robin need to know my secrets in order to help me? I took a deep breath and explained Pavlo's death, the letters and my feelings of guilt, anger, and betrayal. While I talked, both women watched me carefully, listening attentively. I realized that it was the first time I had talked openly like this since Ana died. It felt good to get some of my thoughts out. I missed the company of female friends. After I finished, Robin stood up.

"Well, we can talk more later," she said, "but I need to get started, now that I have some perspective."

From her bag she removed a large jar of sea salt, three large pillar candles, a bag of herbs, a small bowl of sand, disks of charcoal, some black stones, a rattle, a few sticks of incense, and some matches.

"When did you last thoroughly cleaned the house?" she asked.

"Just yesterday," I answered.

"Perfect. That's important. We need to turn off all the lights, and you'll have to do exactly as I say. Please don't interrupt or ask questions. You must trust me. Do you trust me?"

I didn't know this woman, but the facts that she was Katya's dear friend and she reminded me of Ana allowed me to trust her.

"I trust you."

"Good. Let's begin." We went around the house shutting off lights and closing curtains. Then Robin lit three candles, giving one to me and the second to Katya. The third she left burning in the kitchen. She lit the incense, and a warm, spicy scent filled the room. She set the incense holder next to that candle and made a circle of the black stones around both. She put the rattle beside them.

Then Robin lit the charcoal and set it on the sand. On the burning disk she placed several pinches of the herbs from the bag. New smells emerged, sweet and earthy, heavy and thick. She handed the salt to Katya and took the bowl in her hand. We walked into the living room and stood in the darkness. I could barely see Robin's figure as she scattered salt in the corners of the rooms and created shapes in smoke from the burning herbs.

I saw shadows in the corners, heard creaking and scratching. There, in the darkness, I felt like I was a child at home again, afraid of creatures in the dark.

Don't be afraid, a voice whispered. It sounded like Liliana, the vorozhka.

Ahead of me, Robin had become transformed in the firelight. I saw her spirit as fierce and strong, like the vorozhka. This woman also had the spirit of a warrior. I had no doubt she could vanquish whatever had entered my home. She looked even taller in the dark. Her eyes reflected the candlelight, and her movements seemed bold and larger than life. It was like a terrible dance, the swaying of her arm, the way the smoke wrapped around her like a serpent, the sound of salt hitting the windowsills. I watched as something scurried across the floor. It must have been Khvostyk, but moments later I saw him dozing on the kitchen chair.

We returned to the kitchen and set down the salt and burning herbs. Robin handed me the rattle.

"Now I want you to go from room to room, and in every corner and at every threshold I need you to shake this rattle with all your strength. Hold firm to the intention that you want all negative energies to leave your home and never to return. You have to do this alone. We'll wait here for you. Do you understand?"

I nodded and walked back into the living room. I followed her directions and shook the rattle at the corners and thresholds, commanding the negative energies as she called them—evil spirits as I thought of them—to leave and never return. I felt cold, and the hairs on my neck began to prickle. Again, I saw the corpse of Stephan's mother, this time standing in the doorway to my bedroom. She was one of the unquiet dead and must have followed me home.

I shook the rattle and she laughed. I closed my eyes and blew with my breath, bidding her to leave. When I opened my eyes she was gone, and I felt somehow lighter. I crossed myself three times and continued through the other rooms, but I knew that with her departure, my home would return to its happy state.

When I went back to the kitchen, Robin pinched the candle flames with her fingers and we sat in darkness for a few minutes. I felt myself getting tired as the drama of the last few days took its toll on my body.

"Now let's turn on all the lights and open all the windows." Robin instructed. "It is night, but the light of the full moon will help clear away any residual negativity."

We did as she asked, and then sat huddled in our jackets drinking hot tea in the kitchen for an hour.

"These stones are for you. Place them in your icon corner along with this pouch." She filled a small bag with the herbs and added a pinch of black pepper and one black stone. "The herbs are angelica and sage; the stone is black tourmaline. I don't think you'll have any more trouble, but they will help protect you, just in case."

"Do you have a priest from your church that you trust?"

It had been a while since I had talked with any of them, but yes, I trusted our pastor, so I nodded.

"I would call him and ask him to come with holy water to do a proper house blessing."

I agreed and made a mental note to call first thing in the morning.

"So what was it?" Katya asked, speaking for the first time since her arrival. "I felt something sweep by us at the end, then the room felt brighter and lighter."

"Back home, we called it the unquiet dead," I answered. "Spirits, who for many reasons refuse to move on and instead choose to remain here and torment the living."

"I call them negative entities," Robin said. "They are often attracted to people who are discouraged, afraid, depressed. They feed off guilt, doubt, despair." Robin looked at me. "Have you been feeling particularly sensitive lately?"

"What do you mean?" I asked.

"Prophetic dreams, whispers, visions? I get the sense that there's been a lot of activity around you lately. Your guides have been sending you messages."

"My guides?" I asked, thinking of Ana, Liliana, Baba.

"Yes, spirits who are there to help you in life, like guardian angels. They may be here to teach you, advise you, warn you. Sometimes they were people you knew, sometimes not."

"Oh, yes." I answered.

"Well, I hope you've been paying attention because they're all worried about you."

"I think I've gotten the message. How do you know all those things?" I asked Robin, curious about this woman.

She smiled. "I got my Ph.D. in Comparative Religion, so I've studied mythologies and folklore from around the world. I also studied with shamans, wise women, and teachers from many countries. There's so much to learn, and I'm fascinated by all of it."

I saw Katya looking at her with admiration. She really cared for this woman, like I loved Ana. Ana would have really enjoyed our conversation. I could just imagine her sitting with us, and for a moment, she was there and winked at me. Then she was gone.

We talked for a little while and then closed the windows. Katya and Robin got ready to leave. I walked them to the door.

"I'll call you tomorrow, Ma." Katya said. "Are you going to be okay?"

"I am, thank you—for everything." I gave her a hug. Then I hugged Robin. "Thank you, too. I owe you a fabulous home-cooked meal."

Robin laughed a great big laugh. "You've got yourself a deal." She looked serious for a minute. "One last message: Use the ticket. I don't know what that means, but it's important."

I nodded at her and watched them walk down the stairs. I locked up and walked back to the kitchen to look at Andriy's ticket, which I had tossed in a pile. The show opened in three nights. I went to bed and slept soundly for the first time in over a year.

CHAPTER SIXTEEN

Three days later, I dressed in my nicest black dress and took a taxi to the theater. I arrived early and found my seat: in the center of the third row. It appeared to be the best seat in the house, and the seats all around me soon filled. The theater was sold out, and every last seat was occupied. I listened to the voices of people around me praising Andriy's work and expressing their excitement over this latest piece.

"He's influenced by Mary Zimmerman, combining mythic qualities with a Slavic twist."

"But he also draws so much from his war experiences."

"Have you ever met him? He's kinda sexy for an old guy. Like Captain Picard."

"I've heard that he's really sad in person, and he uses theater as his escape."

"No way. He's always laughing and smiling."

"Ah, the sad clown."

"This play is supposed to be really dark, almost gothic . . ."

Listening to the anonymous voices, I wondered about Andriy. It was hard to imagine that he was responsible for all these people being here. I had never been to this kind of theatrical production, only school plays in which the kids or grandkids performed. I had seen *The Nutcracker* once with Zirka and her family, and the kids bought Pavlo and me tickets to see the Ice Capades a few times. But never anything like this.

The lights dimmed, and I watched a lone soldier in a Red

Army uniform appear on stage. Behind him were the shadows of
men who had fallen on the battlefield. The soldier spoke:

"Follow me on a journey into heaven and hell,
past angels and devils, into the realm of dreams.
That is where our souls go when we sleep,
to meet up with our soul mate, to love without abandon,
without regret. For in the morning we must return
to life and all its painful illusions."

The soldier stepped back into the darkness, and his shadow
merged with those of the other soldiers. A new shadow stepped
forward, a man in a Nazi uniform, who said:

"Into this realm of mortal men once fell dread angels
from heaven, driven out by Michael and forced
to live on earth. The fiercest fell beneath the ground,
devils already. Others fell into trees   and streams,
homes and bath-houses—spirits content to live
in peace, with occasional mischief in their hearts.
Still others, lusty for blood and fear, hid and waited
to stir the hearts of men to wage wars,
so they could harvest hatred and feast on flesh."

As he turned around to view the still life of the battle, we saw
a small tail poking out from his uniform, a sign that he was not
quite human. The Nazi walked off stage as the light gradually
illuminated the battle scene on stage, which sprang to life with
our young warrior among the other soldiers.

The youthful soldier from the Soviet army, whose name was
Petro, fought with fervor but lost everyone in his platoon. He
realized that he was the only one left alive just as some
nonhuman shapes and cries began to crawl onto the battlefield.
Petro hid among the corpses and watched as the bodies of both
sides were devoured by creatures of darkness: vampires and
werewolves. As the sun came up, the creatures sank back into the
earth. Petro ran toward the bunker and reported on the battle to

his superiors. He did not tell them about the creatures. His reward for surviving was assignment to another squad, where he witnessed even more atrocities.

Each night, he and the other soldiers wept silently into their pillows. Each night, we traveled with Petro into the land of dreams, where he met and talked with his mother. He also saw another woman, a beautiful young woman who shared the room with his mother and sung a lullaby every night. Petro fell in love with her; she gave him hope, when all around him was death.

Meanwhile, far away from the soldiers, his mother and the woman, whose name was Vira, were living in a women's prison camp. Each day, all the women were chained together and forced to cut down trees with small axes. The wood was used by men in a men's prison camp to build a large fence around both camps. At night, the trees would grow back again, under the spell of the chaklun, an evil wizard.

Dressed in Nazi garb, the chaklun strolled through the forest of dead trees each night, his small tail poking out of his uniform. Each night, he sprinkled the blood of a sacrificed maiden onto the land so the trees would grow back. A woman had to die so the trees would live again. Each morning, the surviving women would cut down the same trees. If a woman tried to leave, she became the next sacrifice. If none tried to escape, the chaklun chose a woman at random.

American soldiers came to liberate the camps, and the chaklun hid among the male prisoners. He saw the beautiful Vira and wanted her for his own. The chaklun cast a spell on her so Vira would be devoted to him and return to his barracks each night. While she lay sleeping, he would drink her blood to keep her weak and under his spell.

Eventually, Petro found his mother and came to the liberated camp to bring her home. He arrived at night and saw the beautiful Vira weeping in a garden. He told her that he loved her and dreamed about her, that she had given him hope when he had nothing to live for. He begged Vira to leave with him and his mother. He told her that he would care for her always, expecting nothing from her in return. She had already given him the greatest gifts: hope and faith. In fact, Vira meant "faith" in Ukrainian.

Vira knew that she was under the chaklun's spell, but she couldn't free herself. She tearfully told Petro to leave for his own safety because she had to return to the chaklun. But Petro would not leave her. He followed her and watched as the chaklun drank her blood and chanted over her sleeping body. Petro begged his mother for her precious silver cross. The mother protested at first, afraid to be without its protection, but eventually agreed. Petro then melted down the cross into a bullet.

The next night, Petro followed the chaklun into the forest, where he saw the evil one enter a glowing yellow circle that appeared on the ground. Engrossed in his chanting, the chaklun didn't notice Petro's approach. Only the hoot of an owl, his guardian, alerted him to danger. The chaklun opened his eyes, saw Petro approaching, he turned himself into a bear, and lunged at Petro. Knocked to the ground Petro lost his gun in the brush.

Meanwhile, Petro's mother ran out of the forest with a silver knife and charged the bear, ready to save her son at any cost. The bear killed her with one sweep of his powerful paw. Then we heard a shot and saw Vira standing with a smoking gun in her hands. The bear, which had been shot to death, turned back into a man.

Petro came to his senses and quickly cut off the chaklun's head. The couple buried him with a silver thunderbolt and a wooden cross to keep him from becoming one of the unquiet dead.

The play ended with Vira and Petro embracing and walking

into the sunrise. In the distance, we heard the hooting of an owl.

Petro's Mama spoke the final verse of the play:

"Though pain and vice roam this world,
the soul seeks its partner above all else,
if only in dreams. The souls will join
to celebrate their ageless love.
In life, illusions may keep us imprisoned
and unwilling to change. In dreams,
the truth strips us bare and innocent,
Our lullaby: the sound of two hearts
beating in harmony."

The applause kept coming in waves as the curtains closed. The actors came back on stage, and eventually Andriy came out to take a bow. Everyone jumped to their feet to honor him for his work. I tried to see in him the man I had once met. He did seem to stare right at me and nod. I wasn't sure how to react.

As everyone left the stage and the spectators began filing out of the theater, I sat back in my seat. Everywhere around me, I heard critiques of the play.

"The sets were gorgeous. I love how the lighting engineer used light to evoke the mood."

"The music was excellent. It really captured the angst of the characters. Even the trees seemed to cry out. That violin was haunting."

"Polotsky did it again. What a commentary on the human condition, using characters from folklore to amplify the inhumanity of war."

I thought the play was beautiful, but I didn't understand all the nuances to which these people were referring. I was also a little upset that Andriy had chosen to use our encounter as the cornerstone of his play. Thankfully, he hadn't mentioned the baby; that would have been unforgivable. Even so, his portrayal of Pavlo as a chaklun was harsh. Is that how he saw us? Saw me? Why did he send me a ticket?

Soon I was the only one left sitting in the theater. I half expected Andriy to emerge from the stage and was a little disappointed when he didn't. After all, I had made the trip downtown to see his play. All dressed up with nowhere to go, I thought to myself. It had been so long since I went out and it seemed a shame to go home so early in the night.

Someone sat down behind me. I assumed one of the ushers had come to tell me that I had to leave.

"I'm sorry, I was just—" I turned around and stopped when I saw it was Andriy. I could finally see what he looked like nearly six decades later. He was handsome: old age clearly suited him. His thick hair had turned grey, but his eyes still had the same intensity. He put out his hand, and I gave him mine, which he kissed. Something in me stirred, and the warmth in my body traveled up to my cheeks.

"I am so happy that you came, Nadya." He spoke each word slowly, carefully, looking deep into my eyes.

I looked away, "Of course, it was my pleasure. Thank you for the ticket." I played with my purse to avoid looking at him. I was a widow. Was he trying to seduce me? Was he, as the rumors reported, a gigolo? Is that why he invited me?

"I would love the chance to talk with you and catch up after all these years. Would you like to join me for drinks at the lounge down the street? I have to make an appearance there, but then we can go someplace and have coffee."

A drink? I felt as if I were watching television. This kind of thing didn't happen to me. Better that I go home, feed Khvostyk, and curl up with the remote control.

Bah, it's time to start living, Ana whispered in my ear.

"I will," I whispered back.

"You will? You'll join me? Wonderful! Let me help you with

your coat. My car is waiting outside."

I didn't know what to do. I followed him outside to his shiny silver Mercedes. He opened the door like a gentleman, and we drove in silence to the lounge.

As we pulled up in front, Andriy said, "I'm sorry if we're not able to talk much here, but I have to stop in to see the cast and crew. I have to thank them for their hard work."

We entered the Black Hat Lounge, and everyone cheered. I would have been content to stand in a corner somewhere while Andriy mingled, but he was very attentive, holding my elbow and making introductions. So many people were involved in the production. Men in tuxedoes walked around with silver plates offering snacks and drinks. I tried tiny meatballs, little pies, and other foods I couldn't identify, but they were delicious.

Andriy led me to the bar. "Are you all right? We'll leave in a minute. Can I get you a drink?"

I honestly didn't know what to order. My most exotic mixed drink was a screwdriver, introduced to me by Ana at a Ukrainian New Year's dinner dance many years ago.

"Whatever you're having," I said, not wanting to sound ignorant or sheltered.

"You're in luck because I prefer the so-called girly drinks."

He ordered two Cosmopolitans, which came in frosty blue glasses with sugar around the rim. Delicious, but strong. I tried to drink slowly, but nervousness made me drink quickly.

After the drink, I felt more relaxed and looked around the room with awe at the beautiful men and women dressed in sharp suits and sparkling dresses. I felt like I was part of a play. The people I knew didn't dress like this, drink like this, or talk like this. Tonight was unreal, like something from a movie or a dream.

"Are you ready to go?" Andriy asked. "I certainly am."

I nodded, and we said our goodbyes as we left the party.

Once we were in his car, Andriy asked, "Where would you like to go next? Do you have a favorite coffee-shop or late-night restaurant?"

The only place Pavlo ever took me was to Slavko's Bar or the all-you-can-eat Polish Buffet. The only coffee shop I knew was the one Ana and I used to go to after our shift, but that was years ago. I didn't even know if it still existed. I would have offered him some tea at my house, but I didn't want him to misinterpret my intentions. Plus, I wasn't sure what he'd think of my simple home, after seeing the kind of life he lived and the class of people he worked with.

"Nadya?" He asked.

"Sorry, I was just thinking. Honestly, I'm not sure if the diner I know is still open; it's been years since I've gone there."

"Well, let's give it a try."

I directed him to what used to be a highly industrial area but was now filled with converted lofts and new homes. Everything had changed; instead of homeless people, well-dressed couples walked the streets, but Chuck's 24-Hour Diner was still there and looked largely untouched.

We drove around looking for parking and luckily found a spot across the street. The temperature had dropped and the wind was biting. We ran across the street to the diner, where there were a few couples and groups even at that hour. Fortunately, we were able to sit in my and Ana's regular booth. I took it as a good omen.

"Do you mind if I eat something?" he asked. "I had to skip dinner."

"Of course I don't mind."

"What do you recommend?" he asked, looking at the menu. I thought he might have felt out of place in his tailored suit and shiny shoes, but he looked completely at ease.

"I usually only ordered coffee." I answered.

"Is it any good?" he asked. Just then the waitress came by with a pot. We both turned over our cups and she promptly filled them.

"Not really," I answered after she walked away. I added cream and sugar, but Andriy drank his black.

"It's not bad," He said.

I tasted it and agreed. Chuck must have switched his coffee. Maybe the young diners had more discriminating tastes. I laughed and Andriy smiled, his face lighting up.

I was suddenly self-conscious again. I felt comfortable with him, but we were strangers.

The waitress came back, and he ordered the Greek omelet.

"Anything for you, ma'am?" she asked.

"No, thank you," I answered, suddenly feeling self-conscious about my age. The alcohol must have started to wear off because I began to worry about how I looked. Had my powder caked up around my wrinkles? Did my neck look flabby? Andriy was looking at me so intently that I wondered if I had spinach in my teeth from the puff pastry I had tried back at the Black Hat Lounge.

"So what did you—"

"I thought the play—"

We both started talking at the same time and laughed.

"Please, you go ahead," he said.

"I thought the play was beautiful," I said, looking at his watch. It looked like it had diamonds on the face.

"Thank you. You weren't angry?" he asked.

"Not angry, but surprised," I said. "Do you often use real life to inspire your plays?"

"Always," he said and went on to talk about how he had returned to Ukraine with his mother, then moved to England to study after she died, and eventually to America. While he was still living in Ukraine, he collected material about folklore and superstitions from the small villages, recording songs and poems and taking photographs.

"I wanted to preserve the old ways which were disappearing. I have given much of my collected material to Slavic folklorists, but it left a lasting impression on me, as did the war. As did you."

I blushed, not sure of what to say.

"Was Mama Paraska—was your mother furious with me? Did she ever forgive me?" I asked him, trying to change the subject.

"She was. She did. Mama was simply disappointed that you hadn't come with us. She loved you like a daughter, and she could tell that I cared for you."

"I loved her, too," I said. "She was an amazing woman."

"I heard about your husband; I am sorry for your loss," Andriy said as the waitress set his food in front of him. "Uh oh, now it's your turn to talk so I can eat all this food." He winked at the waitress, who gave him a big smile in return. He was so charming.

"I'm not sure what to talk about." I stopped and searched for something to say. Then, I don't know if it was because of the alcohol, because we were in the booth where Ana and I used to talk, or because I felt connected to this stranger from my past, but I opened up to him. I told him about the envelope from my sister, about Pavlo hiding the letter from Stephan, and even about Katya and Robin's purification of my house. I told him how sad I had been, how afraid and guilty, how lonely I had been feeling.

While I was talking, he watched me carefully, spooning food into his mouth like an afterthought. Andriy sat so straight at the table, his shoulders back, his head held high and cocked slightly to the right. He was an attentive listener. I never felt like he was bored or drifting in thought.

When I finished my story, he wiped his mouth with his

napkin, set it on his empty plate, and said, "You're an amazing woman, Nadya. I can't believe you're here with me in this place having coffee. Thank you for sharing that with me." He stood up.

For a minute, I thought that was his sign for ending the evening. Had I talked too much? Was he disappointed with me? Had I bored him after all?

"May I sit beside you in the booth?" he asked.

I was too surprised to say no, so I nodded.

"I didn't want to have to shout over the noise of the diner," he said, and only then did I notice that all the tables and booths were full, and the voices around us had gotten louder.

"Nadya, I don't want to scare you away. I don't want you to think me too forward, but you really did save my life during the war, and I never forgot you. For most of my life I've been hoping that you and I would meet again."

"I know it's getting late, and you're probably tired, but can I see you again? I think we have more to talk about, and it would make me very happy."

I nodded. "All right, I would like that."

He leaned over and kissed my cheek before getting up to pay at the counter. I touched my cheek after he walked away.

Snowflakes had begun to fall outside; the first of the season. Andriy insisted that he bring the car around so I didn't have to walk outside in the snow. Driving to my house, I looked at the Chicago skyline in the distance, obscured by the light snowfall. It was a beautiful night, and I felt like a princess. Maybe it was the cold or the late hour, but I felt exhilarated and bold. When Andriy walked me up to my door, I gave him a hug and whispered, "thank you" in his ear.

He smiled at me and then slipped down the stairs and fell.

"I'm okay!" he shouted.

Andriy stood up, spun around, and bowed in my direction. I laughed out loud and applauded, and he walked a little more carefully to his car. I smiled in the window as his car drove away, and then I sat down on the couch and looked around the room. I almost wished I had invited him in just so the evening would not end. Then I could have lived in the fantasy a little longer. Unless it wasn't a fantasy? I was afraid to consider the possibility. Then I felt guilty for even thinking that. What would Pavlo think? Would he be angry? Jealous? I remembered my vision of Pavlo in the park. He had said, "It's never too late," but what did he mean?

CHAPTER SEVENTEEN

Winter settled into Chicago, the temperatures dropped, and the sun spent more time behind the clouds. It was a winter without snow. None had fallen since November, and anticipation hung heavy in the air. Over the next few weeks, Andriy and I spoke frequently on the phone, but we hadn't seen each other. He was busy with his play most of the time and also had to fly back to New York on business.

I remembered my Baba's words, that I find someone to share my stories with. I hoped to share them with Andriy, but I also wanted to reconnect with my family. I invited Katya and Lesya to come by and help me bake bread. I was glad that Lesya's mother had other plans, because I wanted to spend the time alone with my oldest daughter and my favorite granddaughter. I wanted to share my life with them, and even though I was afraid, I knew I had to take this step. Katya knew some of the story; Lesya knew very little. If I had any hope of putting the past behind me, then I would have to entrust my memories with those I loved.

They came by after breakfast, letting themselves in with the spare key I always kept under my statue of Mary in the front yard. I had them sit at the table with cups of coffee and my freshly made almond torte.

"Wow, Mama. A torte? You haven't made one in years. What's the occasion?" Katya asked playfully, but she was right. The torte took hours to make, and it was created with the sole intention of honoring my life, a life that I was going to start enjoying again.

"I'm celebrating my return to the land of the living," I answered, "and I wanted to share this moment with both of you."

First, I handed Katya the letter from my sister, watching as she read it, tears forming in her eyes. Then I gave her Stephan's note. When she finished reading, she passed the letters to Lesya.

Watching her read, I felt as though I were standing outside myself, as though I were viewing this scene from far, far away: a mother, daughter, and granddaughter in a play or a movie: The kitchen was pretty, neat, yellow. There were plants all around, decorated with silk flowers. Cheerful. Everything was in its place except for a throw rug lying crooked on the floor, a tiny coffee stain on one corner. The oven was preheating, releasing a faint smell of old cheese burning on the bottom. The aging cat slept under the grandmother's chair. The clock ticked, ticked, ticked too loudly, exaggerating the seconds, creating a heartbeat in the room to match the old woman's heart. An army of pictures arranged on the wall tried to fight off time—to freeze the past, to rekindle happier moments. A life in pictures from every decade, some black and white, some color. The counter of the hutch was cluttered with birthday cards and a vase with dying flowers. The smells of yeast and cinnamon lingered in the air from unkneaded dough on the counter. Light focused on the letter—written on white lined stationary—in the granddaughter's hand. Everyone was still, barely moving, only breathing, and the clock ticked, ticked, ticked. Except there were things the camera couldn't see. Things the daughter and granddaughter almost sensed, but could not see—ghosts that lingered in the corners of the room. An old man and an old woman with a scarf around her head stood with their arms around one another, just behind the grandmother. A handsome young man in uniform sat on the radiator, holding his heart. A tiny old woman with rosy cheeks carried a laughing baby. A girl wearing gloves rubbed her hands together, healed and whole. And still the clock ticked, ticked, ticked. The camera didn't see the visitors, couldn't capture them except as a shimmer in the shadows, or a streak of light on the lens. But they were there watching them—watching the grandmother—watching me.

"It's an amazing story, Baba." Lesya said, putting the letters back on the table.

"Are you okay, Mama?" Katya asked.

"I left them behind." I said.

"What happened?"

"So much. I was young. I wanted to know the future, and instead I lost everything."

"But what happened?"

For a minute I felt the familiar sensation that the earth beneath me was slipping away, like I was going to slide into a deep dark hole. This was usually the point when I stopped talking, but this time I felt as if I were supported. I felt as if my roots were dug deep into the earth, too deep to be washed away. Ana would have said I felt grounded, and I did.

I remembered my conversation with Katya in the chapel on the night of Pavlo's heart attack. I was afraid of how I would be judged by those I loved the most. I was afraid that the life I had lived had somehow not been authentic. As if Halya and I had switched places. Maybe she should have been in Chicago with a large happy family. Maybe I should have been in Ukraine, alone.

"I sometimes feel like I don't deserve this life," I said to Katya and Lesya. "I feel like I should have been there when the Germans came."

They had both read the letters, so I had no choice but to fill in some of the blanks in the story. When all was said and done, I didn't know who they would see when they looked at me. I was like that black pysanka, covered in wax and layers of paint. The letters had come to melt it all away. Then it would come together—the story revealed.

Katya had already heard the beginning of this story, but I had to start at the beginning for Lesya.

"At the age of sixteen, more than anything, I wanted to have my fortune told," I said, and I told them about Stephan, about the vorozhka, about the soldiers.

"If I had only been there, maybe I could have saved them. Maybe I could have been there for Halya," I said in between tears. I avoided their eyes, afraid of what might be reflected there.

But when I cried, they both cried with me.

"I hated myself for leaving them. I hated myself for living." I said.

Katya hugged me, stroking my hair. Our roles had reversed.

"Baba, if you had stayed and died, none of us would be here today." Lesya said, holding my hand. "Maybe it wasn't a curse on you that you left. Maybe it was a blessing, like someone was looking out for you because you had something special to do in this lifetime."

A blessing? Certainly my family had been blessed, but how much of that was because of me?

"Mama, I do believe that we are put on this earth to do something special," Katya said, still stroking my hair. "We all have a destiny, something that our souls need to do. Maybe yours was to be a mother and grandmother to us. You have been a wonderful matriarch, holding this family together, especially after Tato died. I never knew your sister, but I don't think anyone else could have done that."

Morning turned to afternoon, and although the first loaf of bread in the oven burned, I introduced Katya to her Baba and Dido, her aunts and uncles. I shared my happy childhood memories, and when I laughed, they laughed with me. I searched their faces for signs of condemnation but found only love.

I told them about Mama Paraska and her son Andriy while we pounded the remaining dough, careful not to cry and bring sadness to the bread.

"I still can't believe that you know Andriy Polotsky," said Lesya, adding more flour to the countertop.

"That was a very long time ago." I said, drying bread pans at the sink. I wasn't ready to discuss my visit with Andriy after his show.

"But didn't you go see his play last month," Katya asked, as I glared in her direction.

"I did. He sent me a ticket, and I went to see the show," I answered, trying to be nonchalant.

"I heard it was fantastic, Baba. What did you think?"

"What do I know about plays? I've only seen your school productions, but this was different. The sets, the costumes, the acting—they were all beautiful."

"How about the story, Ma?" Katya asked, slipping dough into the pans.

"It was a . . . familiar story, set during the war but with some fantastic additions." I said, "You should both go see it. I bet your German-American boyfriend would like it too, if he loves history as much as you."

"His *name* is Lukas, Baba."

"Yes, yes. I forgot." Then I winked at her. "I'm an old lady. My memory is not so good."

Lesya laughed, then changed the subject, "I wonder about the soldier, Sonny. He's never contacted you, even though he found your address from Andriy?"

"No, I never heard from him. Maybe he wanted to give Halya time to contact me." I answered, wondering if he were still alive. "Maybe he got busy with other things."

"Maybe he'll still call. If he does, can I please talk with him? I would love to listen to his stories about being a soldier." Lesya looked so excited. Like the little girl she once was, the same little girl who ran into the house to tell me that the worm she had cut in the garden magically had turned into two worms. She must have been thinking of her next paper for those history magazines.

"If he wants to talk about it, sure. But don't be disappointed if he doesn't. It's not so easy." I told her.

I watched Katya's long fingers in the dough. She looked so thoughtful. She caught my gaze and smiled.

"Are you okay with all this, Ma? It's a lot to handle."

"I wasn't okay, but I am now." I told her. "I'm beginning to make my peace; it's just hard to do. In time, I will be all right. There is so much more to tell."

So I did, and I shared more memories that I had kept buried, memories of the dead. As I spoke each of their names and recounted their stories, I felt their ghosts leave me with a cool breath on my cheek like a kiss, or a light touch on my shoulder.

Through the kitchen curtains I saw a sky without clouds. And as we sat drinking coffee, our eyes and noses red from crying to match the streaks of sunset in the sky, I was reminded of a time when I was young and hopeful.

"I have never told you the story of the tsvit paporot, have I?" I asked them.

"The feast of Ivana Kupala, Mama?" Katya asked. "I've read about it, but no, you haven't."

"In the camp I had a few friends, but one of the dearest was a girl called Natalia. She came over from the women's barracks to the DP camp with Mama Paraska and me. Natalia was a poet, and even though she had lived through so many terrible things during the war, she still insisted that we try to find beauty around us. She's the one who named our bunk Nebo, and she called us the Star Sisters."

"Like the three Zorya sisters who watched over the sky throughout the day?" Katya asked.

"Yes, like that," I replied. "You would have liked her, Katya. You are kindred spirits. Natalia and I would sit and compare stories from home. One day, right around midsummer, Natalia decided that we needed a little magic. This was before I met your Tato, when my heart was still broken and lonely and aching for home. We were both pining for romance.

"She asked me if I knew about the legend of the paporot, the red fern that blooms only on Midsummer Eve, the night of Ivana Kupala. My Baba had told me about the old Midsummer celebrations, the dances held in the fields for Ivana Kupala, dances of life and light and love. But I didn't know much about the paporot.

"Natalia told me about some of the legends, about how if you found the tsvit paporot, you were given a wish. She explained that some people believed if you found it, you could understand the animals' speech for the whole evening. Others said that you could make anyone fall madly in love with you if you found it. There were many beliefs.

"Well, we decided to sneak off and look for the tsvit paporot on the upcoming midsummer night. We walked in darkness through the trees, listening for the rusalky singing and looking for flickering lights. When we couldn't find any clues, we sat down across from one another next to a patch of wild flowers and held hands. We closed our eyes and listened for any sounds on the wind. I remember that it felt almost like home, with the leaves rustling, the birds singing, the grass against our legs, the scent of flowers in the air. I almost believed that if I opened my eyes, I would be in the forest by my Tato's house.

"'Make a wish,' Natalia whispered.

"'But we didn't find the paporot,' I replied.

"'It's okay, it's still a magical night,' she said.

"So, holding hands in the dark, we made our wishes. Then a howling wolf broke the spell, and we ran back to camp."

"So, what did you wish for, Baba?" Lesya asked me.

"It's not right to ask someone about their wishes," Katya said. "It means they won't come true."

"But it's been over fifty years," Lesya replied. "I think it's okay."

I smiled. It felt good to talk with them and tell them my stories. It was as if I were more fully connected to these women, having shared a little of my soul with them.

I remembered Mama Paraska, and I brought together my thumb and first two fingers, kissed them and then lifted them first to Katya's cheek, then to Lesya's cheek.

"I give you a piece of my soul," I said. "It's something I learned from Andriy's mama. It will keep us strongly connected, no matter what."

Katya looked exhausted, but Lesya couldn't stop asking questions, about my family, Stephan, the war. "Did you wish for Stephan? To be reunited?" she asked. "I just can't believe he was still alive. Or maybe you wished to see your family again? What were the chances of your sister and your ex-boyfriend falling in love? It must have been fate—"

In the distance, or maybe in my heart, I heard a baby crying.

"—and you both had a son named Mykola. That's just wild."

Had she heard the cry?

"Well, our dido's name was Mykola," I said.

"I wonder what else you've had in common," Lesya said.

"Halya left her phone number on the back of her letter," said Katya, sipping her coffee. "Will you call her?"

"I don't know; maybe on our Christmas Eve," I answered. "She has no other family now. We are all she has."

"Mama, do you think Halya will come to visit?" Katya asked.

"I don't know. I don't know if she could."

I caught Katya peeking at her watch, and Lesya was starting

to fidget. It was time for me to release them. They had been a good audience.

"All right, girls. I'm exhausted. It's time for you to go and do young people things so that I can rest."

"I'm not so young anymore, Mama," Katya said, smiling, "but I'm planning on meeting Robin for a movie."

"Which one?" Lesya asked, standing up.

"We haven't decided, something at the Fine Arts."

"Why did Robin call you Kat?" I asked Katya.

"It's a nickname. Because I love cats." Katya answered.

I watched as she and Lesya exchanged a look. There was something they weren't telling me.

"Oh," I said

"It's kind of a joke . . . Kat and Robin . . . both animal names."

"Of course." I didn't get the joke. I would have to ask her another day.

"So who will come and help me before Sviat Vechir? I can't do Christmas Eve dinner by myself."

"Weren't we all here last year helping?" Lesya asked defensively.

"Shhh, yes. I know you were. I was only teasing." I said, giving her a hug.

"My mom and I will come," she said.

"Me too, Mama," Katya answered.

"Well, why don't you invite your Lukas; and Katya, I owe Robin a dinner. Maybe she would like to come, since she is interested in folklore and traditions."

Both women lit up and smiled.

"Thank you, Baba." Lesya said hugging me tightly.

"Robin would really like that, Mama," Katya said, taking her turn to hug me as well.

Both left, and I sat down in the kitchen to wait for the bread to finish baking. I didn't want to risk another batch burning. I knew that if I sat on the couch, I'd fall asleep again. It had become a bad habit over the last few weeks. Somehow it was easier sleeping there alone than in our big bed. I think I was afraid of facing Pavlo or his ghost. I still felt guilty for seeing Andriy and talking with him, although our relationship was only friendly. But I couldn't help my fantasies and daydreams. Those were what I felt most guilty about.

As if he were reading my mind, Andriy called from New York at that very moment. We exchanged small talk about our day, and I told him how I had shared the letters and my story with Katya and Lesya. I could hear that he was happy for me, but he sounded tired.

"It must be hard for you to split your time between two cities like this," I said.

"It is," he replied, his voice strange, distant.

"Are you all right?" I asked. He was usually so chatty on the phone, but he sounded weary and uncomfortable.

"I've had an unpleasant day, and I'm eager to get back to Chicago. I've been living in New York for a long time, but it's never felt like home."

"When do you get back?" I asked.

"Tomorrow. Would you like to spend New Year's Eve with me? We can do anything you like. I just need a break from the drama of the theater."

I hesitated. I could rationalize away our relationship more easily if we only spoke on the phone. To see him again would make it more real, more dangerous. I was a widow, and I was still grieving the loss of Pavlo, but I wanted to see Andriy. Hadn't I promised myself that morning while making the torte that I would start living my life again?

"Okay, I'd like that. Do you think we could maybe have dinner at a French restaurant? I've always wanted to try a soufflé'."

He laughed. "Last-minute reservations are my specialty. I'll see what I can do. I'll pick you up around eight o'clock."

"Have a safe flight." I said.

"Thank you. Sweet dreams."

I never answered Lesya about my wish on Ivana Kupala because I truly believed that if you reveal a wish, you destroy the spell. I could only reveal it once it came true, and I was still waiting for my wish to come true. I would hopefully wait for a little while longer. On that magical night I had wished for a happy ending. I wasn't specific. I didn't know what it would look like in the end. I still don't. Throughout my life it had comforted me to think that whatever the heartbreak, whatever the trials, I might still have a happy ending. It gave me hope.

On New Year's Eve I was nervous. I didn't know what to wear. I didn't like my hair, my shoes, my face. Everything looked frumpy. I felt old and unattractive, and I wanted to look beautiful. For once, I wished that I had been using the anti-aging cream that Zirka had given me.

I was ready an hour early and kept pacing around the house, talking to Khvostyk, talking to Ana, talking to myself. I was excited and anxious, and angry at myself for feeling like a young girl when I was really a great-grandmother, and according to Lesya, her older sister hoped to soon be pregnant with her second child. Maybe a girl this time? Little Pavlik could use a sister.

Khvostyk just looked at me and said nothing. He sat curled up on my slippers, watching my pacing with one eye open.

Ana whispered playfully. *Darling, have fun, and kiss him if he doesn't kiss you first. Remember, if you have lips, why not use them?*

I ignored her. My mind was filled with so many thoughts and emotions. At least the snow had finally decided to fall, relieving some of the pressure and expectation in the air. I hoped it was a good omen.

Andriy arrived early, standing at the door holding a single beautiful red poppy. I hadn't seen such a poppy since I was a child, and I took it with wonder and kissed his cheek without thinking.

"It's magnificent, Andriy. Where in the world did you get it?"

Stepping inside the doorway he smiled. "I have a friend who grows exotic flowers from around the world. I wanted something special for you."

"It's marvelous. Let me go put it in water and I'll be right back. Please have a seat on the couch."

I filled up a vase and placed the poppy on the kitchen table. When I turned around, I saw Pavlo's picture staring at me from the icon corner. I walked over and whispered, "I hope that you're not angry, Pavlo, but I need to do this. I need to find reasons to live." I kissed my fingers and touched them to the picture.

When I walked back into the living room, I saw that Andriy had taken off his shoes, and that made me smile. I always appreciated when guests removed their shoes without my asking. It showed that they respected my home.

Andriy was looking around the room, and again I felt self-conscious.

"You have a lovely home," he said. "Very warm and inviting."

"Thank you, I try," I said, putting on my coat. Andriy sprang up to help me. I was embarrassed, unaccustomed to this type of courtesy. We put on our shoes and stepped outside.

Andriy had ordered a limo for the evening. I had only ridden in a limo once before, for Zirka's wedding. This was a small, elegant car, with a moon roof that we left open to watch the snow falling. We rode to Mon Cheri in silence, listening to classical music on the radio.

At the small, elegant restaurant we were seated in the back, closest to the fireplace. The interior was beautiful, with white Christmas lights interwoven with white silk drapery and suspended from the ceiling. There were silver candlesticks and lace tablecloths on every table. Lovely music played softly in the background, and around us were couples at different stages of their meals.

I looked at the menu and was overwhelmed. Most of the dishes were in French, so I was grateful for the detailed descriptions. We began with cocktails, and we had warm bread with real French butter. It was the best butter I had ever tasted in my life.

As we waited for the waitress to bring our food, we talked like old friends, discussing the past few days.

"What had you so upset the other day?" I asked without thinking, just because I was concerned for him.

He sighed and looked away. I instantly regretted bringing up the subject.

"I'm sorry, I didn't mean to upset you."

"No, it's all right. I was going to tell you. You see, I had been casually seeing this woman, Margaret, for the last five years."

My heart sank. Perhaps his intentions were not so honorable after all. Or maybe he was only looking for friendship with me.

He continued. "It was never serious, at least not for me. She knew I traveled a lot, and I wasn't interested in a commitment. I tried to end things with her before I came to Chicago to do 'Angel's Lullaby,' but she didn't give up.

"When I went back to New York, Margaret was waiting for me outside my apartment. I told her we'd talk later, and she went home. I had a lot of business and, frankly, I tried to put off the conversation as long as I could, until the day I spoke with you. We had lunch and once again I tried to explain things to her. She made a big scene and said she'd go to the press with rumors and gossip. I didn't care. I told her I wished her well but didn't want to see her again. That was it. I stopped taking her calls, and I'm planning on changing my phone number."

"I had heard that you were a bit of a gigolo," I said, trying to make a joke.

Andriy looked angry, "I'm not. I just haven't been as lucky in love as you have."

"I'm sorry. I didn't mean it like that," I said. The evening was turning into a disaster. He'd probably never want to talk to me again either.

The waitress brought our food, and it looked incredible. I had never seen food so artfully presented.

Andriy wasn't touching his food.

"I'm sorry, Andriy," I said again and reached for his arm.

"It's all right. I don't mean to be defensive, least of all with you." He paused. "I've just spent my whole life looking for true love, the kind of love that lasts, and I had essentially given up. I figured I would probably die alone."

"I was married," I said, "but I'm no expert on love. I spent much of my married life wondering about a love I had lost during the war."

Andriy made a sound like a cough, or a bitter laugh.

"At least we have that in common," he said quietly.

I didn't know what to say. I tried to remember what Ana had told me about love.

"My dearest friend, Ana, once said, 'Let yourself love the past, but live the present.' I am trying to live that philosophy right now."

"It's a good philosophy," Andriy said, taking the hand that I had rested on his arm and holding it in his. His palm was warm, dry, soft. These were not hands that had spent a lifetime doing manual labor. His only calluses were from writing. He lightly traced his fingertips along my wrist and palm. I got goosebumps and blushed. I couldn't help but think that he must have had many lovers in his lifetime.

"We should eat before our food gets cold," I said.

Andriy nodded, his face serious. He poured more wine into my glass and said, "First I'd like to make a toast—to living the present and perhaps finding love, too."

We toasted and ate our meals. I often caught Andriy watching me, and I would blush. I wasn't sure what the rest of the evening had in store, but the meal was unforgettable. The food was delicious. I decided that beef bourguignon was my new favorite food.

As I finished my meal, I looked around and noticed that we were the oldest couple in the trendy restaurant. I caught the eye of a young pregnant woman whose husband had gone to the bathroom. She smiled at me. I smiled in return. I silently wished her a long and happy life.

"Save some room for dessert. They have chocolate soufflé." Andriy said, interrupting our silent exchange.

"Hm. Oh, yes. Right, of course," I said, setting down my fork and knife.

"What were you daydreaming about?" he asked.

"That young woman there," I said with a toss of my head. "I hope she has a happy life, a healthy baby."

The waitress cleared our plates, and I leaned forward, resting my chin on my hands.

"I also realized that we are the oldest couple here," I said.

Andriy smiled again. "Oh, we're a couple, are we?"

I blushed again, "I only meant—"

"I know; I'm teasing. Go on." He reached out to touch my arm.

I was grateful that at least my skin was not too flabby. I had never developed the age spots that some women get. Thank God for good genes, my daughters always said.

"I forgot what I was saying," I said, realizing that the wine was beginning to make me feel giddy.

"Well, I've been waiting to tell you something all evening," Andriy said.

I pulled away and folded my hands in my lap.

"You look even more beautiful now than you did when I first saw you," he said.

I shook my head. "Your eyesight must be failing you in your old age, Andriy."

"I'm serious, Nadya. You're beautiful. You don't know how hard it's been not to kiss you. It's all I've been thinking about since you came to see the play." He got a mischievous grin. "Well, not all."

I took a breath to say something clever in return, but I couldn't think of anything, so I closed my mouth and bit my lip. At that moment, the young pregnant woman came up to our table, her husband standing behind her looking embarrassed and a little drunk.

"Excuse me," she said. "I'm sorry to interrupt, but I just wanted to say how nice it is to see a couple your age that's obviously very much in love. It gives me a lot of hope. Congratulations."

I smiled at Andriy, not having the heart to correct her.

"I've loved this woman from the first time I saw her more than fifty years ago," Andriy said, "and tonight I am the happiest man in the world."

I felt a knot in my throat. I smiled at the girl and said, "Thank you." I couldn't look at Andriy.

The girl smiled a big grin in return and walked away with her husband.

The waitress brought our desserts, and I devoured mine, afraid to meet Andriy's eyes. The soufflé was amazing, like a gooey, chocolate cloud served with fresh whipped cream. As we drank our coffees, Andriy asked, "Are you all right? Did I upset you?"

"This coffee is much better than the coffee at Chuck's." I tried to change the subject.

"Nadya, that doesn't work with me. I'm sorry if I said too much, if I embarrassed you. I just couldn't lie to that girl."

"It's okay," I said, staring into my cup. "I just don't know what to say."

"You don't have to say anything. I'm just happy to sit here with you."

"Thank you for tonight," I said. "It's been an amazing meal."

"The company was pretty good, too," he said, and I looked into his eyes.

He had become more handsome with age, and there was such depth in his eyes. My Baba would have said they had too much water, from a life of too many unspent tears. He had lived through rough times during the war, too. The scenes in his play were certainly only a shadow of the pain and horrors he had witnessed. I had been so self-contered, thinking only about my own sacrifices.

"Are you ready to go?" He asked, a little sadly.

But I wasn't. I wasn't ready to re-enter the real world.

"Not really," I answered. "How about an after-dinner cocktail?"

He lit up. "You surprise me, Madame," he said in a playful French accent. "I would love to have one."

Andriy ordered two after-dinner drinks, sweet and thick. It was the perfect ending to our meal. We sat sipping them as the snow began to fall more heavily outside.

"So, what's next?" he asked.

"I don't know." I honestly didn't know what I wanted.

"Do you want to go dancing? See a movie? Go for a carriage ride?" he asked.

I would have loved to have done any of those things . . . twenty-five years ago. But my body was achy and getting sleepy with all the food and drink.

"Those all sound nice," I said, "but I'm getting a little tired. I was on my feet all day, and I don't think I could stay awake for a movie. Maybe another time?"

"Of course," he said, a little disappointed.

"You can come back to the house for a little while," I said in a voice I didn't recognize. "I can make us some tea."

"Tea is nice, but it's New Year's Eve," he said. "How about we buy a bottle of champagne to toast the New Year?"

"Bubbly wine always goes right to my head," I said. "It makes me a bit silly."

"That's not a bad thing," he said with a wink, and then he ordered the bottle of champagne.

We held hands in the back of the limo, watching the snow covering the city. It would be a dangerous night for driving, and I wished a silent blessing for any of my family members who were on the road that night.

CHAPTER EIGHTEEN

Andriy sent the limo home when we got to the house. He said he'd call a cab later. Once inside, we kicked off our shoes. I hadn't worn heels since the funeral, and it felt good to walk flat-footed again. I rubbed my feet on the carpet, enjoying the sensation.

"You know, I can rub them for you, if you like."

For a minute, I wasn't sure what he meant.

"My feet?" I laughed. "That's okay. No one has ever touched these feet."

I walked into the kitchen to find glasses for the champagne. I heard the pop of the bottle, and when I came back into the living room, Andriy was sitting on the couch holding the opened bottle. He had also plugged in the Christmas tree lights, removed his suit jacket and tie, and unbuttoned the top button of his shirt. I was surprised to see gray hair at the top of his chest. I never imagined that he was a hairy man. Pavlo had always been so smooth, not much hair on his face or body. Then I looked at his arms and saw that the hair was thick there as well.

"You have a lovely tree," he said as he poured the champagne.

"Thank you. My granddaughters helped me put it up the weekend after Thanksgiving."

Andriy set the glasses on coasters, placed them on the table, and patted his lap.

"Come on, put your feet here. I'll give you a foot rub you'll never forget." He winked at me.

Again, I'm sure the wine made me bolder than usual, but I sat down and lifted my feet. He pulled at my pantyhose.

"Sorry, they're knee highs," I said.

"May I?" and before I could answer, he had lifted my long skirt and begun to pull down my stockings.

"Um, okay," I said, since one stocking was already off.

"Close your eyes and relax, Nadya. I'll take care of you."

I shut my eyes, and he started rubbing the heel and ball of my foot. No one had ever rubbed my feet before. I didn't even think about my unpainted toes, gnarled from having broken them on chair legs and doors too many times in my life. Katya tried to get me to have a pedicure once, but I refused, telling her that no one would touch my ugly feet. Apparently I was wrong. Blissfully wrong. Andriy had wonderful hands, strong and gentle. I think I moaned, because Andriy asked, "Are you all right? Too much pressure?"

"No, it's good. Even better than rubbing my feet on the carpet." I opened my eyes and watched as Khvostyk walked over to sniff Andriy's shoes. Satisfied, Khvostyk returned to his spot on my slippers. I was afraid to close my eyes again, for fear of falling asleep. All I needed was to start snoring.

His fingers moved up to each toe, and he paid them equal attention: pinching, pulling, and squeezing in a way that made me warm all over.

"Where did you learn how to do that?" I asked him.

"Honestly, I just pay attention. I listen to your body and feel where you need pressure. Plus I've picked up a few tricks here and there. I give an excellent massage as well."

"I'm sure you do," I said, thinking that I had never had a massage either.

"Do you mind if we turn on the television?" I asked. "They'll be doing the countdown soon."

"Not at all," he answered, rubbing my calf.

I watched as young people jumped around to some music.

"Is it just me, or do those announcers look drunk?" Andriy asked.

We flipped through the channels, and all the announcers did look drunk. I didn't think I had ever seen that before. It must have been something in the air. Apparently I wasn't the only one who had indulged that night.

As the clock edged toward midnight, I began to get nervous. Andriy had stopped rubbing my feet as we both watched the television. I wondered what he was thinking. I wondered if he would try to kiss me. I licked my lips, they felt so dry. What if he didn't try? What if he was a bad kisser? What if he thought I was?

"8 . . . 7 . . . 6"

Andriy handed me my glass.

"4 . . . 3 . . . 2 . . . 1 . . . Happy New Year!"

He gently brought his glass to mine and we toasted.

"To the New Year and a new friendship," he said.

We watched each other over the rims of our glasses as we took our sips. I took several, afraid to put the glass down. He reached for my glass to set it on the table. He inched over to me and leaned over to kiss me. I could taste the champagne. I started to pull away, but he put his arm around me and pulled me closer. He stroked my hair and kissed me more hungrily. Pavlo had never kissed me like that. Ours were always loving pecks, but these were deep passionate kisses, like the ones I had seen in the movies.

My heart was racing after we pulled away. We drank more champagne and then Andriy excused himself to go to the bathroom. When he came back, I took my turn, stumbling a little on my way. After washing my hands, I checked myself in the mirror: nothing in my teeth. I still looked the same. I hadn't transformed into a young vixen during our meal. My thoughts kept racing as I walked back into the living room.

Andriy had turned off the television and dimmed the lights. He stood up when I walked in the room and wrapped his arms around me. He felt strong, and I felt safe. I rested my forehead on his shoulder and he kissed my neck, my weak spot.

I tilted my head up to kiss him, when I heard a crash in the kitchen. I rushed in just ahead of Andriy, stubbing my toe on the table. Looking around, I saw that Pavlo's picture had fallen to the ground. Fortunately, the glass hadn't broken.

"Jealous husband," Andriy said from behind me.

I sat down at the table and started to cry. I felt out of control, I didn't know what I was doing. I wasn't a child, yet there I was acting young and spontaneous. I was lonely, and yet I felt like things were moving so fast.

Andriy just put his hand on my shoulder and kissed the top of my head.

"I'm sorry for moving quickly, Nadya. I didn't mean to rush you."

"I know, I know," I said in between sobs. Andriy handed me his handkerchief, and I wiped my face. So much for looking beautiful. I laughed at my vanity.

"I never forgave myself for letting you go," Andriy said, "and I always wondered if you were okay; if your life was happy."

"I was. It was. I'm sorry so much of your life was spent alone."

"Don't be sorry. I have lived a rich life, and I'm proud of what I've done," he said, looking away. "It just would have been nice to have someone special to share it all with." He turned back to me. "I don't play games, Nadya. I say it like it is. I'm hoping that with time something can grow between us. I feel like I've been given a second chance, and I'm not going to let you slip away easily. Not again.

"That said, if you know that you will never have feelings for me, please tell me now. It would kill me to get close to you and have you pull away."

I didn't know what to say. I did feel something for him already, but I needed time to sort this out. I needed time to let Pavlo go.

"I need you to give me a little time," I said.

"That I can do."

I stood up, setting Pavlo's picture face down on the table. We walked in silence back to the living room, where he helped me clean up the bottle and glasses.

"May I use your phone to call a cab?" he asked.

"You don't have to leave. The weather is terrible," I said, looking at the snowstorm outside my window. "You can sleep on the couch."

"Thank you. I accept."

I brought him a blanket and pillow, and then got ready for bed. I walked over to say goodnight, but he had already fallen asleep. I turned off the lamp and walked back to my room.

"I'm sorry, Pavlo." I whispered quietly.

Just as I was drifting off to sleep, I heard, *It's okay, Nadya. It's okay.*

I dreamed that I was flying in the snow-filled sky, the city below lit up with lights. In the distance I heard the Gypsy music of my youth, tugging at me to follow.

In the morning I woke up late with a dull headache. The clock said 8 o'clock. For a minute I thought I had dreamt the whole evening, until I smelled coffee and butter burning in the kitchen. I grabbed my robe off the back of the bedroom door and walked out to the kitchen. Andriy was standing there in his wrinkled suit pants and T-shirt, making French toast.

He smiled at me. It was odd seeing a man cook for me in my kitchen. I thought of Ana and Niki. So this is what it must have been like for them. I smiled.

"Good morning," he said. "I thought I would keep the French theme going. Do you like French toast?"

"I do," I said. "But you didn't have to. I would have made breakfast."

"Nonsense. It's my pleasure. I was up early anyway. I'm still on New York time."

I pulled out a mug, choosing the one Katya had brought me from Ireland.

"Are you okay?" he asked, as I poured myself some coffee and took an aspirin.

"I feel shy," I told him honestly, "and I have a headache."

"Don't feel shy with me, Nadya. You look lovely in the morning." He put the French toast on two plates and walked over to the table. He kissed my cheek, and I could feel myself blushing.

"Morning, Baba. This is Luke." I heard Lesya's voice from the living room. It was too late to hide. I looked at Andriy. He raised his eyebrows and shrugged.

Lesya and Luke walked into the kitchen.

"Baba!" she said in surprise. She pushed Luke back into the dining room and motioned with her head for me to join her.

"Happy New Year!" Andriy said.

"I'll be right back," I said, following Lesya out of the kitchen.

"It's not what you think, Lesya. He stayed overnight because of the snowstorm. He slept on the couch."

"Baba, you don't have to explain to me." Lesya said smiling.

"But you have to understand," I said. "I'm not betraying your Dido."

"Baba," Lesya said quietly, "I never thought that. I'm just sorry that we didn't ring the doorbell. I didn't mean to embarrass you. I figured you'd be up and back from church. I thought I'd bring Luke so he'd be the first man in the house, according to tradition. But I guess you already have a man in the house." She winked at me playfully.

"Lesya!" I said. "That's no way to talk to your Baba. I told you, it wasn't safe for him to go out, the snowstorm—"

"Yes, yes. I know," she said, walking toward Luke, who was sitting on the floor scratching Khvostyk's ears. Khvostyk seemed to like him.

"Luke, I think we're going to go and get some breakfast, and come back later, if that's okay?" She looked from Luke to me.

"That would be fine," I said.

"It was nice to finally meet you," Luke said. I nodded.

"See you later, Baba," Lesya said, giving me a kiss before they walked out to their car.

After Lesya and Luke left, I went back to the kitchen and sat down at the table, resting my head in my hands. What if she called her father? Worse yet, her mother? Soon everyone would know, and gossip would start spreading.

"Do you want me to warm those up in the microwave?" Andriy asked, pointing to the French toast.

"No, this will be fine." I said taking a bite. It was delicious. "I'm sorry about that. My house is always open to family. I don't usually have anything—or anyone—to hide."

"You want to hide me?" he asked.

"That's not what I meant. I just didn't want you to be embarrassed."

"I have nothing to be embarrassed about. I'm an old man. This is the kind of thing that keeps me going." He winked.

"Thank you for the French toast," I said. "You're full of surprises."

"You have no idea," Andriy said playfully.

After breakfast, he phoned for a cab. We waited in the living room, sitting on the couch in comfortable silence. My headache was getting better, and I felt more calm, more clear than I had the night before.

"Thank you for everything, Andriy."

"Thank you, for giving me hope," he said. "Not just now, but fifty years ago."

The cab driver honked his horn, and Andriy got up to put on his shoes. At the door he kissed my cheek. "I hope to see you again soon."

"I'd like that," I answered, then closed the door behind him.

I thought about Andriy as I stirred honey into the wheat for kutia, the most ancient of Ukrainian dishes and the cornerstone of Sviata Vecheria. I would leave some out as an offering for the ancestors. For my Pavlo. My Mykola. For the rest of my departed family, since I knew their fate. And even for Stephan. Although I was sure his spirit would visit Halya, not me.

A week had passed since New Year's Eve. I had spoken with Andriy every day but chose not to see him. I needed to give myself a little time, to think about what I wanted.

After Andriy went home, Lesya came by, and I formally met her boyfriend, or rather her fiancé. Luke had proposed on New Year's Eve. He seemed like a good boy, but it was hard not to look at him and see the sins of his grandfathers. Only time would reveal him to be a man of integrity.

I placed walnuts in a bag and began to smash them into small pieces with a rolling pin. I reminded myself to think only of happy things when cooking, so I thought about Andriy. In the past week I had resisted the urge to invite him over. My heart raced each time the phone rang, and I smiled during all our conversations.

On impulse, I invited Andriy to join my family for Sviata Vecheria, and he agreed. He told me that the last time he had celebrated Ukrainian Christmas Eve was before his mother died, and even then it was a quiet affair for the two of them. I was not sure how to prepare him for the boisterous and colorful evening that awaited him in my home.

I added the walnuts to the wheat mixture and then spooned in the poppy seeds, raisins, and honey. Mixing the kutia, I thought about the rest of the day's schedule. Even though I had most of the dishes prepared, there was much left to do before dusk.

I put the kutia in the refrigerator so the flavors would blend. Then I bundled up in my long, down coat and tied a kerchief tightly around my head. Before doing any more preparations, I needed to release some spirits to try and make room in my life for happiness and hope. I stepped outside into the early January morning and looked around. The frost on the trees and fences had given everything a glassy sparkle in the bright sunlight. I rode the bus down to the lakefront and walked down a familiar path to the shores of Lake Michigan.

The spot that Ana had brought me to after Mykola's death was still a sacred place for me; my sanctuary so close to the center of the city and so far from my home across the ocean. I settled into my favorite spot, against a stone wall facing Lake Michigan. I was often tempted to leave my name among the other letters and years etched into stone, but I was afraid that when I died, it might tie me to that place, and I would rather choose a spot closer to my family.

Still, so many had chosen to leave their mark there:

Bob loves Sandy 1969
E+D Forever
Wally was here March 1964

Their names are monuments to love, to youth, to hope. I wondered how their lives had turned out. Were their endings happy or filled with heartache? I reached into my pocket and pulled out Stephan's note.

It was time to let him go, to let go of the illusion of young love. To let go of my younger self which I had clung for years as a beacon—showing my way home, revealing my guilt, stifling my heart. I reached into my pocket and pulled out Stephan's letter. Then I took a book of matches, struck one and set the letter ablaze. Holding one corner, I watched the paper turn orange, then black. All around me the smell of burning paper. When the flame went out, I cast the letter on the wind toward Lake Michigan, and watched as it flew toward the waves.

"Dear Stephan, I'm glad that you found peace and love. I'm glad that you did not die alone," I whispered to the wind. "May the earth be light above you, and may your spirit rest in peace."

I watched the paper smolder, and I thought of Halya. What would my sister need now that she was alone? Should I bring her to live with me? Could I bear to spend time with the woman who had married my first true love? Did she hate me for being alive? What would she think of the life I lived?

Would she forgive me?

Could I forgive her?

One time we girls—Halya and I—were left alone in the house, just Halya and I. I was lonely and sad because the other girls in the village had made fun of my clumsiness when I had fallen off a fence earlier that day, and I wanted Halya to hug me, to show me that she loved me. But Halya was always frugal with her emotions, sharing them only when it suited her: when she was afraid or needed something. I told her a story, vivid in detail, about a ghost who lived in our house, and then I hid inside the cupboard, under some rags.

She ran around the house, giggling at first because she thought it was a game. One minute turned into ten, then twenty, and she began to cry because she was afraid the ghost had taken me away. I sat inside the cupboard listening to her running around the room until her wailing became so loud I was afraid she would actually summon some lonely spirit. I slipped out and called to her, proud of my performance and reveling in the affection I knew would come. And it did, she hugged me tighter than ever before and slept that night, curled into my back, her arm around my shoulders. In fact, my plan worked so well that she spent the next few days by my side, afraid to let me out of her sight.

But I could not sleep that night, or the next, or the one after that, because hidden in the cupboard I had actually evoked a ghostly visitor, a spirit who plagued my dreams and teased me with bumps in the night. The stronger that Halya hugged me or told me she loved me, the worse the nightmares. The more she begged for me to sit beside her or offered her own dessert and sweet milk, the stronger the voices in the dark and rustlings under the bed.

Finally, it got so bad that I told my mother what I had done. She was kneading dough, always kneading, and she shook her head at me.

"Nadya," she said, "you can't trick someone into loving you. Remember Old Man Lesych, who went to talk to the witch in the mountains? He had her cast a love spell on the Widow Vasylchenko?" Mama pounded the dough harder for emphasis. "It worked too well, and they were married, but she drove him crazy because she wouldn't leave him alone. Not even when he went to the bathhouse! One night when he went outside to do his business, she quietly followed him. When he walked out, she stepped in front of him, and he thought she was the devil and died right there."

"That's not true, Mama."

"It is true. Don't you dare call your Mama a liar!"

And my mama, who ordinarily remained calm in the face of stress and exhaustion, looked fierce, like a warrior or a bear. I stepped back from her and she continued, "If your Baba were here, you could ask her, but she's gone. Goodness knows you believed everything she told you. Well, she also taught me a thing or two. The only way you can be rid of this spirit is to tell your sister what you did and ask her forgiveness. Then you must leave your favorite dessert, my special makivnyk, behind the barn, as an offering for the spirit."

"You made makivnyk?"

"Yes, I made it fresh this morning, but none for you. You need to sacrifice something to gain something, Nadya."

So I told Halya what I had done, and she was upset with me . . . for a few hours. She never held grudges for long, and soon she was asking me to play with her again. That night, after I left my piece of makivnyk outside for the demon, Halya snuck me a small piece.

"Because I know it's your favorite," she whispered, carrying it in her small hands. "And because I love you."

Waves crashed and whirled around me, struggling against the ice that formed in the more shallow parts of Lake Michigan. The roaring pushed aside my thoughts, and all was still inside my head, the kind of silence that only occurs when a sudden surge of noise drowns out everything else—even regret.

I slipped into it, the rolling hush of waves and wind. It echoed in the pulse throbbing inside my veins, the rush of wind through the trees, the steady hum beneath my boots, the waters slapping against stone. Those sounds joined and blended to become the same rhythm, a steady heartbeat that reached inside and outside, across the ocean and over time. The pulse of life, Baba would say, the rhythm of the universe, the heartbeat of the Mother.

I reached again into my pocket and pulled out the cigarettes I had found beside Stephan's letter. Pavlo's. I never smoked a single cigarette, but I watched Pavlo light and relish many in his lifetime. My hands attempted to mimic his as I lit the match and held it to the end, waiting for it to catch as I puffed. The smoke was warm and slightly bitter in my throat. I held it up, protecting it from the wind.

"This is for you, Pavlo. I'm sorry for never giving myself to you wholly. I'm sorry for keeping things from you, and I forgive you for the same thing. No matter what, we had each other, and we made a beautiful family. Rest in peace, my love, and I pray that you let me go to live the rest of my life."

I sat and smoked my first and last cigarette, enjoying the slight buzz in my head even as I coughed occasionally.

"I think I can see why you liked this filthy habit, Pavlo." I said aloud. "This one is for you."

As the cigarette burned down to the end, I stood up and flicked it onto the winds and watched as it fell into the waters. I missed the slight warmth, and once again I became aware of the cold.

I closed my eyes and saw Pavlo's face, heard his voice, tasted his breath on my lips.

"I'm not sure what's going to happen next, but I miss you, Pavlo, more than I ever thought I would."

Because of the cold, my senses seemed more acute than normal. Everything felt so alive that it almost hurt, a fine line between pain and pleasure. Goosebumps on my skin and hairs on my arms, so sensitive to the feel of all my layers of clothes. The silky pantyhose against my thighs. The warm, coarse knit of my sweater on the back of my shoulders, the tops of my arms. Lace against my breasts. Heavy wool scratching my neck, my hands. An illusion of warmth against this cool arousal of winter. I could only stay a short time, before my aches began to shout out reminders of my age.

If only the wind could reach inside me, wipe clean my heartache, my guilt, my confusion. If only the waves could wash away this heartache, this jealousy and rage, this guilt and sadness. If only the rocks could lend me their stability, their strength, so I might choose wisely. If only the sun could burn away my past, so I would not have to live with any regrets.

I stood still and listened for the answer on the waves.

Just let it go. Let it go. Go.

It was a voice inside me, and all around me. No, not one, but many voices: Baba's, Mama's, the vorozhka's, Mama Paraska's, Ana's. Maybe even my own?

"Goodbye," I whispered.

But that was not the end. I had one more goodbye to make; one more offering to leave. From my pocket I removed the little black stone that I had carried for over seventy years. It was the only thing I had left of my parents, my family, my home. I was afraid to let it go, to let it rest on the bottom of the lake, a little piece of my old home there in my new home. Without it, I feared I would have nothing to hold onto. Without it, I would be forced to tell my stories because they would be all I had left.

I held the stone in the cup of my hands and blew my breath onto it. Baba taught me that the breath is powerful. It carries with it a tiny spark of your soul. To blow on something is to imbue it with your essence and emphasize your intention.

"My intention is to let it go . . . to love the past . . . to live in the present . . . and to look forward to the future," I said aloud. To the stone. To the lake. To myself.

I visualized all those whom I held onto, and I fought the tears that threatened to spill out. "I will share your stories, and you will live on in their memories."

I blew once more and summoned all my strength to toss the black stone into the water. I heard the tinkling of bells. I closed my eyes and made a prayer, giving thanks for all I had and asking for strength. Then I tossed the stone into the waters and released the past.

CHAPTER NINETEEN

On the way home, I stopped at a local flower shop to pick up some wheat and hay. Back home, people believed that our Ukrainian ancestors lived among the fields and crops, the trees and flowers, helping to ensure that each harvest was prosperous, that the lives of their descendants were happy. During the Feast of Obzhynky, the harvest, the best stalks of wheat were gathered into a sheaf called the didukh. On Christmas Eve, the didukh was placed in a special corner for the winter holidays. The ancestors would make their entrance into the family's home with the arrival of the didukh.

In America, I had had to settle for store-bought wheat, and I hoped that my intention when I was fashioning the didukh would please the ancestors. This year I would be inviting many more than before into my home, and I wanted their arrival to be happy.

Once I was home, I put on a pot of coffee and lit a candle in the icon corner. I checked on the kutia, added a bit more honey, and then got to work preparing the dinner. The dishes were meatless to honor the animals that had given so much during the year. Each dish had its own special meaning. They were the same dishes my Mama used to make, and my Baba before her. Twelve ancient dishes—one for each apostle and each full moon in the year, my Baba used to say.

"These dishes have magical properties, little mouse. They were once served on the longest night of the year," Baba said, while peeling potatoes for the varenyky. "Each one has a story, and when you make them, you should remember the story like a prayer for your family."

"A prayer, Baba? Like the 'Our Father'?" I asked, while playing with the hay we were going to spread under the table for dinner.

"A little bit. But these prayers are older than that. They are like the prayers of a pine tree when a bird makes a nest in her branches, or the prayers of a river when she is full of fish. These are prayers of the spirit, blessings that the mistress of the house prepares for her entire family. You must make each dish with intention. It is a special job, to be taken seriously—" Baba stooped down to tickle me. "—but also with much joy. That's why it's good to cook in a house filled with laughter. Some of that joy will get passed into the food and will help the meal be happy."

So as I prepared the foods, I made my silent blessings— ancient prayers that joined me to a chain of women stretching backward and forward in time. With each sacred ingredient, I blessed my children and their children and their children, on into the future:

Kolachi: Three loaves of bread, each braided into a circle. Everything is interconnected. May they honor life in all its forms.

Kutia: Wheat sweetened by Baba's wisdom. May they remember their roots,

Borshch: May these tart beets brighten their cheeks and bring them passion.

Baked fish: May they swim in a sea filled with love.

Pickled herring: May they find compassion in times of sorrow.

Pidpenky mushrooms: Let them remember to find beauty in all creation.

Holubtsi: As these cabbage rolls are bursting with rice, may their minds be filled with inspiration.

Varenyky: May they always be grounded, their bellies filled with good food and good sense.

Beans: May they also soar, with active imaginations and open minds.

Cabbage: When times are sour, may they turn to one another for comfort.

Beets with mushrooms: May they find a balance of desire and stability.

Fruit compote: May they not wait until the end of their lives to find the sweetness of joy.

Makivnyk: Cake swirled with poppies and sweetened with honey, like life's spiral of joy and sadness. At the end of their days, may they have the courage to face their ghosts and dreams, their successes and disappointments.

I thought to myself, when I am gone, who will continue the traditions? Katya? She has no children of her own. Zirka has decided that Ukrainian foods are too high in calories, so she prepares bland versions of some dishes and completely avoids others. Maybe Ivanka. And Lesya, what will Lesya do with her German husband? Will they incorporate his traditions with hers?

Eager to rest my feet, I sat down at the table to fashion the didukh, which I tied with a pretty blue and yellow embroidered ribbon. It had always been Pavlo's job to make the didukh, and the year before we did not have one.

I went outside to walk clockwise around the house three times before coming back in and placing the didukh in the eastern corner of the dining room, beside the icons, on top of an embroidered cloth. Then I arranged the leftover wheat stalks in a vase and carefully placed hay under the dining room table, hiding nuts, candy, and coins inside the hay for the children to find after the meal.

While I was arranging the treats under the table, Katya arrived at the back door. I heard her unloading things on the kitchen table.

"Are you here, Ma?" she asked.

"Under the table. Did you buy the kolach?"

"Of course."

"Would you spread out the tablecloths and put the kolach on the table? Place a white candle in the center,"

"You forget I've been doing this my whole life," she said, bending down to show me the loaf of braided bread with a candle already in its center. "And you should have waited for me to do the hay. You don't need to be bending down under tables."

"I'm not so old, Katya."

I walked back to the kitchen and handed her four cloves of garlic to place under the four corners of the tablecloth, to ward off any evil spirits. Together we set out all the candles I had around the house, leaving one in the window to welcome travelers. We warmed the food on the stove and changed our clothes. Then I opened a window to cool off the kitchen, and we sat down to have some tea as we waited for the family to arrive.

"Katya, I invited Andriy Polotsky to come to Sviata Vecheria. He has no one else, and I thought it would be nice for him to spend the evening with us—"

"I think that's great," she said with a smile. "I'm glad that you've reconnected."

"He's just my friend."

"Don't be defensive. Whatever he turns out to be, it's okay." Katya reached for my hand and squeezed it. "I just want you to be happy."

"Thank you, Katya. I want you to be happy, too. I worry about you. I don't want you to be all alone."

"I'm not alone, Ma. One can never be alone with a family like ours."

"You know that's not what I meant," I said, but I let it drop. I didn't want her to be sad.

"Robin is really sorry that she can't make it," Katya said after a moment. "But she thanks you for the invitation,"

"Is everything all right?" I asked her.

"She had to be with a friend at the hospital," Katya said.

"I'm sorry," I said. "I really like her. I hope her friend is okay. Maybe she can come next year. It's nice that she has such an interest in our traditions."

Mark and Christina and their girls came through the open door, and the calm was broken. My youngest granddaughters each gave me a kiss and then ran to the living room to peek at the presents under the tree.

"How are you, my beautiful mother?" asked Mark, hugging me from behind.

I turned around and looked at my son. He looked so much like his father. Christina walked over to me, holding a torte.

"Mama, just a little something for dessert."

"Christina." I shook my head. "Next time, just bring yourself. We already have too much food." But she looked offended, so I added, "Put it in the icebox, and we'll have it for dessert. It looks delicious."

She smiled and headed toward the icebox. So much for my diet.

Ivanka and Roman came in from the front, and directly behind them were Zirka, Pete, and the twins. After getting a kiss from each of them, I snuck the twins over to the pantry and gave them each ten dollars, for ice cream. They rushed out to join the men in the living room watching television.

"Let the party begin; I'm here," announced Taras with arms full of presents. Anna came over, hugged me, and then immediately started stirring the borshch on the stove. I cautioned her not to add any salt when I wasn't looking. Tanya came in carrying a wreath and went to hang it on the front door.

Taras followed her into the living room to set the presents beside the tree. This year's theme was an all-natural tree, complete with berries, acorns, and popcorn garlands. Khvostyk loved lying underneath when I had the white Christmas lights turned on.

"Mama, you're looking beautiful today. Is that a new apron?" Taras asked when he got back into the kitchen. He poured himself some coffee.

"Taras, it's the same apron I've been wearing every year since you were married."

"A new haircut then?" he asked.

"Is my brother kissing up to you again, Mama?" asked Mark, coming into the kitchen.

"It's not kissing up, it's called complimenting. You should take some lessons."

"Is that your secret to success, Taras? Brown-nosing?"

The two men hugged and patted each other on the back. Then they went off to the dining room to tease the twins. Each was a godfather to one of the boys, and they had decided that this allowed them the special privilege of relentless teasing. It was also another source of competition, as each of my sons claimed the superiority of his godson.

"Is Lesya here yet?" asked Anna.

Katya hugged her sister-in-law and said, "She mentioned something about stopping by Natalie and Jerry's to see if they needed any help with the baby."

As if on cue the doorbell rang, and I rushed into the living room to answer the door. The room smelled like pine and mulberry from all the candles.

First Natalie came in carrying my great-grandson.

"Hi Baba," she said, kissing my cheek. As she handed little Pavlyk to me, I noticed that she had a little belly. She caught my eye and nodded, smiling.

"Another one?" I asked, handing the little one to his grandfather.

"Another what?" asked Taras loudly.

"Another baby, Tato," said Natalie quietly. Of course everyone heard her, and she was ushered into the house with good wishes and blessings.

Jerry walked up to the door and shook off his boots, "Hi, Baba."

"Congratulations, Jerry." I said, and he smiled, his arms full of baby supplies and presents.

Lesya stood behind him and behind her was a tall silhouette.

"Hi, Baba," she said, pulling off her mittens, "You remember Luke."

Luke stepped into the hallway and handed me a bottle of wine.

I paused, then smiled as he greeted me. "It's nice to see you again," he said. "Merry Christmas. Thank you for inviting me."

I went back to the front door and peered into the darkness. I wasn't sure when Andriy would arrive, but I hoped he wouldn't be late. Looking for Mark's daughters, I spied them on the couch and walked over. As the youngest, they had an important responsibility.

"Girls, you must look out the window and watch for the first star. Only when you spot the first star in the sky can we begin to eat. This is important. As soon as you see it, you have to let us all know. Do you understand?"

The girls nodded seriously and ran over to the window in the living room. I walked back to the kitchen and asked Tanya to set the table.

"Baba, maybe next year I'll have a boyfriend here too," she

said, carrying plates. "I'm not much younger than Lesya, and I've been writing to Borys in Ukraine for almost seven years now. Hey, maybe next year he can come here for Sviata?"

"If he comes to America, Tanya, then he'll be welcome," I said and put my arm around her. "Now get to work, and don't forget to set an extra plate for the ancestors."

The doorbell rang and I caught the puzzled glances from some of the kids. As far as they knew, everyone had arrived.

"Is that the carolers already?" asked Mark.

"No, we have a special guest coming." Katya answered. "Mama reconnected with an old friend from home—the famous playwright Andriy Polotsk— and she's invited him to dinner. Let's be on our best behavior, everyone."

"Then we won't be ourselves." Mark said playfully.

"Maybe he's looking for inspiration for a new play?" asked Christina fixing her hair. "Or maybe he's on the lookout for new talent?"

"No, no, no," I said, shaking my head. "He's just my friend from a long time ago. He had nowhere else to spend the holiday, so I invited him to join us."

"Just be yourselves," I said as I walked toward the front door, trying to appear calm.

Andriy looked handsome in his coat and suit, and he was carrying a big bouquet of poppies, wheat, and blue cornflowers.

"You look lovely," he said, kissing both my cheeks.

When he entered the house, there was silence as everyone stood around watching us.

"This isn't the noisy crowd you described, Nadya," he said playfully.

He turned to everyone, "Khrystos Razhdaietsia!"

To his traditional Ukrainian Christmas greeting of "Christ is born," everyone responded in unison, "Slavite Yoho!" Let us praise Him.

I took his coat and set it on the bed with the other coats. When I came back to the living room, someone had handed Andriy a cocktail, and he was chatting with Christina and Anna. They were positively glowing in his company. I watched him for a moment, admiring again how charming he was.

"Your friend seems nice," Lesya teased playfully, putting an arm on my shoulder. "Don't worry. I've never said a word." She smiled at me and walked back to where Luke was sitting, discussing politics with Lesya's father.

I went to the kitchen to check on the food. Andriy looked like he could take care of himself.

"We see it! We see it! It's the first star, Baba!" the girls shouted as they ran into the kitchen.

"Good, good," I said to them. "Tell everyone to find their seats. We'll be eating soon."

I heard their high voices commanding everyone to the dining room, and I smiled. It was always nice to have little ones in the house for the holidays.

"It's time to sit down. Everyone to the dining room, come on," Katya said, herding everyone to their seats, leaving me alone in the kitchen.

I took the *prosfora*, bread blessed in church, cut it into enough pieces for everyone in the family, and coated the pieces with honey. Holding the plate, I walked over to the icon corner, crossed myself and said, "Bless this meal and all who share it." Then I added, "And please give me strength."

I scooped the last of the kutia into a serving dish and entered the dining room with the kutia and the bread. Everyone was sitting in his or her seat. The chair at the head of the table where Pavlo always sat was left empty, it would serve as the one seat we leave reserved for the ancestors. Beside it was my seat, and next to it sat Andriy. He winked at me and I smiled.

Everyone stopped talking when I entered. My family. When had it become so large? How had we been so blessed? Pavlo was always so proud of his children and grandchildren. I set the kutia and prosfora on the table and touched Pavlo's empty seat, dusting away the many ancestors who had been invited to join our feast. I wanted to make sure that there was room for Pavlo. This was his family first and foremost. Our family.

I smelled a hint of tobacco and felt Pavlo there beside me. Taking a deep breath, I lit the white candle in the braided kolach. We would leave it burning through the night.

It was always Pavlo's job to circle the inside of the house three times with the kutia, but this year the ritual fell to me. In the old days, the head of the household would throw a spoonful of kutia onto the ceiling. If it stuck, it meant that the family would be blessed with a bountiful harvest in the year to come.

The kutia was always the first dish, as it has been for thousands of years. I went first to the empty seat, scooping a helping of kutia onto the plate set for the ancestors: for Pavlo and Mykola, Ana and Niki, and for those who couldn't be with us.

As I did this, I took a deep breath and said, "We have a few more guests on this night than we have had before."

I looked around at my family, my sons and daughters, my grandchildren. We'd our share of arguments and dramas over the years. I remembered one Christmas Eve dinner when Taras and Mark refused to talk to one another because of some disagreement about the best way to fix Mark's computer. They sat on opposite sides of the table and glared at one another over the borshch. But by the end of the night they were laughing together and wrestling with their godsons.

It was always like that. We argued with passion, but we made up with passion, too. When it came down to it, my children were always there for each other. They had accomplished much in their individual lives, but I think I was most proud of them for their commitment to each other. I knew that it was a rare gift in this age of divorce and scandal. At least, that was what they showed on television talk shows.

I passed the bowl of kutia to Katya, who was sitting next to her father's empty chair. She took over my job of spooning out the portions onto everyone's plates.

"I recently received a letter from my sister in Ukraine," I said. "I did not know that she was alive. Somehow she survived the war and was married . . . to an old friend. She told me what I had always feared, that my mother, father, and older sister Laryssa were killed by the Ger—" I looked at Luke. " —in the war. My sister's son, Mykola, died during the Soviet war in Afghanistan, and her husband, Stephan, died last fall."

I felt the tears in my eyes, but I kept talking. "So tonight we open our home to them. We welcome my family and Pavlo's family. We welcome all those we have loved and lost. My beloved Pavlo, our dearest Mykola, Ana and Nicholas. My Baba and Dido, and all the ancestors who share with us blood and tradition."

Katya finished serving the kutia and set the bowl down in front of me before returning to her seat. As she returned to her seat, a gust of wind came through the window I had left open in the kitchen. I could hear the wind chimes shaking outside. They had come. The house felt more full; the light a little different. I knew that if I peered in the corners, I would see their eyes peering out at me, my family. We were together.

I didn't know if anyone else sensed the change, because I was afraid to look in their eyes. Instead, I focused on the candle burning bright in the kolach, and I continued, "My Baba always taught me the importance of names. They carry power. They are connected to our spirit, to our blood. Our names reveal a great deal about us, and they carry with them the power of our ancestors.

"Many of you know that when people came to America, their

names were often changed—by themselves or by others who could not pronounce the unusual surnames. Some chose to make a new start by shedding their old names. To protect others or themselves from a past they had to leave behind.

"I have never told you my true names: the names of my father and his father before him. The name of my mother, which is my own. To protect my family, I changed my name during the war. I didn't want anyone to be able to trace me. I felt I needed to hide. Those were different times, and it's hard to make sense of this logic now, but I did what I thought was right.

"Looking back, I now know that I lost something then. I lost a connection. So I want—I need to share this with you, because it is also *your* history. To tell you their names, my name, is to reconnect you to that blood, that history.

"The name I gave, the name you know as my maiden name is Nadya Ivanivna Palyvoda. My real name is Nadya Ivanivna Rozumna. My parents were Ivan and Nadya. I had two older sisters, Laryssa and Maria, who died; and one younger sister, Halya, who is still alive."

Only then did I look at my children. Some had tears in their eyes, others were smiling, and I felt a weight lifted off my shoulders. I heard Ana's voice whisper: *You did it, darling.*

"So tonight we welcome them, our ancestors, and we give them their due honor at this table. Vitaiemo. Welcome."

Taras raised his glass of vodka and said, "To our ancestors!"

Everyone raised their glasses and replied, "To our ancestors!"

I lifted the plate of bread soaked in honey and offered the first piece to Katya. Then I went around the table, offering a piece to the rest of my family. Everyone took the bread and gave me a hug or kiss. Andriy was last, and when I approached him, it was the first time I had looked at him since I walked in the room.

"Thank you for letting me be a part of this," he said, kissing my cheek.

I returned to my seat and cleared my throat to lead the prayer. "Dear God, we ask that You bless this meal and this celebration. We thank You for our health and good fortune, and we hope that next year we will all be gathered here again. Amen." Everyone echoed, "Amen."

Andriy began to sing "Boh Predvichny," the traditional Ukrainian carol "God Eternal." His voice was low and rich, and after a moment of enjoying his singing, the rest of my family joined in. We finished singing and sat down to eat our kutia. Afterwards, Katya and Zirka walked around to give everyone a ladle of hot borshch. I heard Luke ask Lesya why there was hay under the table.

"It's supposed to promote fertility," she answered, "and the wheat is on the table to show that there has been a bountiful harvest."

"It sure has been," he said and kissed her cheek.

I liked the way he looked at her, as if she was the only thing in the world that mattered. I caught his eye and smiled.

I watched my daughters pass around the rest of the dishes. It was nice to sit back and see them do this. The dishes had turned out well, and everyone ate their fill, smiling wider with each bite and laughing more with every sip of wine. My Baba always said that a meal was successfully prepared if the guests had a second helping and ended the meal with a glow on their cheeks. She said it meant that the cook had worked her kitchen magic well. My intention certainly had been for a happy meal. My magic had worked.

I looked at Andriy, who had remained quiet throughout most of the meal, occasionally chatting with Anna, who was seated on his other side. He sat back and patted his belly absentmindedly. I wondered if he felt sad that he had never been a part of a family like this, that he had never had children of his own. I supposed that his plays were like his children, born of his imagination.

"You've been so quiet," he said to me.

"Funny, I was thinking the same of you," I said.

"I'm just taking it all in," he replied. Then Anna asked him another question, and he turned her way.

When everyone finished eating, Mark's daughters crawled under the table to find the nuts and candy and coins hidden in the hay. They left the nuts and money on the table. The candy they hoarded for later. We all crowded into the living room to open the gifts, and then returned to the table for dessert, relaxing as the children played with their new presents.

Luke and Lesya still sat together on the floor, her head on his shoulder. He looked up at me, and I got up to walk toward them. I sat down next to them. Little Pavlyk was giggling nearby.

"So what do you think of our Christmas?" I asked Luke.

"I think it's marvelous," he answered, and he took my hand. "Your speech tonight at dinner was beautiful and brave. I can see where Lesya gets her strength."

Embarrassed by the gesture, I blushed. "Thank you." I didn't know what else to say.

For a few minutes we all sat in silence, watching Jerry play with little Pavlyk on the floor.

I heard the echo of guitar music and closed my eyes. I was remembering the young man who had spun me around the dance floor, how he had swept me off my feet with sweet kisses and sweet words. We never did make it to Paris.

Let yourself love the past, but live the present. Ana's words echoed in my head.

I looked around for Andriy, who was sitting at the dining room table watching me. Maybe it wasn't too late to have a few more adventures. I thought of Ana and Niki, who lived every moment until the end.

From the kitchen Katya waved to get my attention, so I headed over.

"What is it, Katya? Is everything okay?" I asked.

"I have a present for you, Mama," she said and handed me a box wrapped in a silver ribbon.

Inside the box was a pysanka. I took it out and turned it around in my hands. The egg was decorated with a circle of trees. On one side of the egg were three women: a grandmother, daughter, and granddaughter. On the opposite side was a circle of stones, within it stood two women holding hands.

"Katya, it's beautiful."

"I made it that night after you and I and Lesya talked. It's my wish for you. See? The women are all dancing. I want you to be happy, Mama. I love you."

"I love you too, Katya. Thank you." I said. "We'll keep talking, okay? I want to get to know you better, my daughter."

Katya had tears in her eyes. She nodded and smiled, then went back to the sink to wash dishes. I looked at my gift.

I needed to call my sister. I waited for everyone to bundle up and head home. A few headed off to midnight mass. Most would be back in my neighborhood the next morning for the Christmas Day service at church. They took their gifts, exchanged hugs and thank you's, and drove away. I waved goodbye to the last of them and turned to face my house, suddenly quiet and empty except for Andriy, who was sitting on the couch in the dark living room, lit only by the Christmas tree lights.

At least the domovyk would be happy. No major disagreements that night, mostly happiness.

"You're welcome to stay a while longer, but I have a phone call I need to make," I said to him, walking toward the kitchen.

"Certainly. As long as you don't mind my sitting here."

I walked into the kitchen and pulled my sister's letter out of the wooden box Pavlo had made for me. I took a deep breath and dialed her phone number.

"Happy Holidays," answered a voice in Ukrainian.

"Halya?"

"Yes. Who is this?"

"Halya, it's Nadya."

"Oh, my God!" Then there were a few moments of silence. "You received my second letter. Nadya, how are you?"

"I'm well. The first letter must have been lost in the mail, but I did get the second one. I don't even know where to begin. There's so much to say."

"Nadya." I heard her weeping. "What a gift you have given me. I thought I was all alone in the world."

"You are not. You have me and my five children, and so many grandchildren. Even one great-grandchild, and another on the way."

"Such a big family," she said. "So time has been good to you. You are happy?"

For a minute, I hesitated. "Yes, I'm happy. I've had a good life in America, although my husband also died last year. His name was Pavlo. He was a good man. But you . . . how are you?"

"All right. It's been hard since Stefko died," Halya paused. I heard her blow her nose. "Do you forgive me, Nadya? Do you forgive him?"

For a moment I waited to feel the familiar pangs in my chest.

"Of course," I said. "I'm happy that you found each other. It is good that two people I loved so much found comfort in one another."

Ans it was not a lie. Better that they had each other than no one at all.

She was crying. "Thank you, Nadya. It would have made him happy to hear that. He cared so much for you. You were always dear to his heart, like a sister. When he heard you were alive, he wept."

Stephan wept for me. Dear Stephan, I hoped he'd been happy.

"Were you happy, Halya? Happy together?" I asked her.

"Yes, I think we were. Times were hard. They are still hard here, but it helped to have each other. And he adored Mykola, our son," she said. Her voice quavered. "It almost killed Stefko when Mykola died in Afghanistan. Of course, it was devastating for me too, but I had to be the strong one. He was so fragile when he came back from Siberia. Not like the man you knew.

"After Mykola's death he used to say, 'Now I have nothing left of my soul.' He was depressed for a long time. But we had each other. And he was lucky that he always had good work to keep him busy. Of course, you remember how smart he was.

"Before he died, he told me to tell you something. It didn't make any sense, but he told me to tell you that he never forgot the smell of the raspberries. Does that mean anything to you?"

I closed my eyes and remembered that last night in Slovakia, before the soldiers came to take him away. The strong sweetness of raspberries crushed underfoot and the dark, moist smell of sweat and dirt. Stephan's fingers on my lips, my neck, the hollow above my collarbone.

But I said, "No, I'm sorry."

"That's what I figured," Halya said. "He was so lost at that time. I figured it had something to do with his mother's cooking. Then again, he always liked it when I made him berry tortes." She sighed. "We have so much to talk about, so much to share, but I am tired ... so tired."

She sounded so old, exhausted. So I said, "Of course. I understand. It's early morning there. We will talk again soon. Take care of yourself. And thank you for writing."

"You too, my sister. Veselykh Sviat."

"Veselykh Sviat, Halya."

I hung up the phone and turned off the light in the kitchen to sit in darkness.

Raspberries.

"Are you all right?" asked a voice from the darkness. For a

minute I expected Pavlo, but it was Andriy's silhouette in the doorway.

"Did you call your sister?" he asked.

"I did."

"How is she?" he asked, coming closer.

"She sounded so old, Andriy. She sounded so sad." Then I started to cry.

Andriy came over to me and pulled me up by the hand until we were facing each other. He put his arms around me. I couldn't stop myself from crying. Andriy didn't say anything. He just held me and let me cry.

"Why isn't life fair, Andriy? Why do the people we care about have to suffer? Why do we have to lose those we love?"

"I don't know," he said. "But think of all the people that you still have in your life."

He was right. I felt so selfish then, knowing I had so much. My poor sister was all alone. "Andriy?"

"Yes?" he answered.

"Thank you."

"For what?" he asked, slowly starting to sway side to side.

"For being here."

He pulled me in closer and started to hum under his breath. We kept swaying until we were dancing in slow circles in the middle of the kitchen floor. I closed my eyes and tried to remember what he looked like when we first met in the DP camp, but all I could see was his face now.

Andriy spun me around and started to sing a slow Ukrainian love song, and we continued to dance in the kitchen. Khvostyk watched us from under the table. I pressed closer to Andriy and kissed him, interrupting the song.

After the kiss, I put my head on his shoulder, and we kept dancing.

"Andriy?"

"Mmhm?"

"Maybe you could make French toast in the morning?" I asked him.

"Absolutely," he replied.

My legs were getting tired, and I was sure his feet were hurting, but neither of us made any move to stop. By dancing we could remain in the moment. By dancing we could avoid talking, dwelling on the past, or thinking about the future. We were connected in a way that was neither threatening nor complicated; just circling and swaying, following the oldest rhythms of breath and heartbeat.

Baba always said that dancing united the entire Universe. We moved in circles, all of us together. The sun and moon danced, as did the wind and the leaves, fire, and even falling waters. Each animal had its own dance, and each human couple found its own rhythm. So there in the kitchen, among the smells of fried potatoes, cinnamon, pine, and honey, Andriy and I held onto each other, and we kept dancing.

ACKNOWLEDGEMENTS

In 1996, I was taking classes at the School of the Art Institute of Chicago as part of the inaugural class of the MFA in Writing Program. I began writing this novel there, working to flush out the story and characters with the support of my peers and our excellent faculty (Stuart Dybek, Jim McManus, Michael Collins, Carol Becker, Carol Anshaw, George H. Roeder Jr., Peter Brown, Janet Desaulniers, Rosellen Brown, and others).

The journey to complete this novel spanned into the next century and stretched across two continents. Along the way, friends and family have read many versions of *The Silence of Trees*, providing valuable edits and critique. I am grateful for each and every question and comment.

I want to thank the Ukrainian American elders who have over the years allowed me to listen to their stories of life before, during, and after WWII. I hope that I have honored them here. I also want to thank Abner Ganet for sharing his experiences as a Jewish American soldier involved in the D-Day Normandy landing and the liberation of Buchenwald.

In 2008, Amazon.com had its first Breakthrough Novel Award contest. As one of 836 Semifinalists, *The Silence of Trees* received more than 200 customer reviews from all over the world! I was touched by the support of friends and strangers. To all of you who read and reviewed my entry, you have my sincere gratitude. Thanks also to my fellow ABNA semifinalists, many of whom have become friends and supporters. I hope to someday have all their books on my bookshelf.

I would like to thank Marta D. Olynyk, who was my proofreader of all things Ukrainian; my amazing editor Laura Bridgewater; and my talented cover artist Madeline Carol Matz.

In *The Silence of Trees*, family is integral to the protagonist, Nadya. I thank my own extended family—grandparents, aunts and uncles, and cousins. While the events and characters of this novel are fictional, they have been inspired by the love, humor, passion, and challenges I've witnessed in my own family.

I thank my parents, Walter and Oksana Dudycz, for always supporting my drive to write, and for being readers, editors, critics, chauffeurs, babysitters, and cheerleaders during the writing of this book. Thanks also to my sister, Nadya, whose eye for detail caught many inconsistencies and errors, and who has always remained one of my dearest friends and supporters. It is no coincidence that she shares the same name as the central character.

I am a mother, wife, friend, and writer. I would not be able to juggle all these things without the assistance of my family and friends, and most of all the unconditional support of my husband, Mark. In the last ten years, we have lived in three cities, two countries, and on two continents. We have had three children, three cats, and three gardens. We have traveled across Europe, started a literary magazine, and shared adventures. Through it all, Mark has supported me as I carve out time from our lives to write and edit. His faith, patience, and generosity have made it possible for me to finish this book and share it with you.

I also thank you, my readers, for allowing me to share this story with you. In this evolving world of social networking, I welcome a conversation with you on twitter (@Valya) or on my blog (www.vdlupescu.com/journal).

THE SILENCE OF TREES

VALYA DUDYCZ LUPESCU

A Reader's Companion

THE STORY BEHIND *THE SILENCE OF TREES*

When I was a child, my parents took turns reading stories to me before bedtime. I've wanted to be a writer since that first moment sitting under a pink patchwork blanket with my little sister, my mother's voice creating a new world in my mind's eye. I knew then that words were magic, that stories could transform ordinary reality, if only for a few hours.

As I grew older, I discovered that I had at my disposal a wealth of new stories, tales unwritten in books. My grandparents would share stories with me from their childhood in Western Ukraine. After Ukrainian school on Saturdays, many of my visits would consist of fresh potato varenyky, rye bread and butter, and folk tales passed down for generations.

My novel is fiction, but I was inspired by their stories and the tales I heard from other Ukrainian American elders. While many were eager to share anecdotes from their youth and stories from home, it has only been in the last two decades that these elders have begun to speak out about their experiences during World War II. Fear has kept many of their voices silent for over half a century.

Only after Ukraine achieved independence on August 24, 1991, did some begin to feel safe enough to talk about their experiences. They began to open up the doors to the past; doors that remained tightly sealed for over fifty years. Their trend of self-revelation and reclaiming the past were my inspiration.

My novel is written from 70-year-old Nadya Lysenko's perspective. Hers is a woman's experience of war and sacrifice, a story of revelation and resolution. Nadya has secrets that she never shared with her husband or family. Hers is a past ridden with guilt and regret. Yet Nadya realizes that if she dies without disclosing the secrets of her youth, her memories will die with her. Only by sharing the stories of her family and friends can she allow them to live on in the hearts of her children and grandchildren. Nadya chooses to remain silent...but sometimes the Universe has a different plan.

I brought to this novel my love of mythology and appreciation of folklore. The Ukrainian people have a rich cultural heritage that serves as the backdrop for Nadya's story. Thus it also became a story about myth—both cultural and personal. The mythic qualities create a sense of magic realism in the story, for Nadya's daily reality is rich in old superstitions and traditions: She still tosses the first crumb of bread into the stove for the hearth spirits and knocks on woods to avoid tempting fate. In her world, dreams can come true, ghosts do whisper in the night, and a fortuneteller's cards can predict the future.

The relationship of humanity with nature is also critical in the novel. It is not a supernatural experience; rather it is a hyper-natural reality. The Divine is present in the world, and everything is interconnected. Ancient Ukrainian people believed that the forces in the spiritual world affect human beings and their relationships. Even after Christianity was brought to Ukraine in the 10th century, the Old Ways still survived alongside the new religion. These traditions were filtered into the holidays and remained a part of everyday life. Many survived the immigration to America and are still a part of Ukrainian American culture.

To this day I don't allow whistling in the house for fear of attracting malevolent spirits, and I light candles along with my prayers. I hope to show that there is wisdom and beauty in the old ways and in the old stories. We have much to learn from them and from the elders in our community who are the trustees of this wisdom.

I wrote this book to honor my grandmothers and all women who have lived through war and lost themselves in the struggle to survive. Too often they have been silenced, their stories unrecorded in the annals of history. It is my hope that this novel speaks with their voices, preserves their legacy, and reveals the power of stories—to remind, to heal, to connect, to teach, and to transform.

Valya Dudycz Lupescu, 2010

QUESTIONS AND TOPICS FOR DISCUSSION

1) Stories are an integral part of *The Silence of Trees*. What are some of the stories that Nadya recounts and what is their importance to the larger story?

2) Review the vorozhka's prediction? Did it come true? Discuss the role and importance of dreams, signs, and omens in the book.

3) What are the important trees in the book? Why do you think the author chose to title her book, *The Silence of Trees*?

4) Discuss the dynamics of each of Nadya's romantic relationships. How are they similar and different?

5) Female relationships figure prominently in *The Silence of Trees*. Discuss the dynamics of Nadya's relationship with her Baba Hanusia, Mama Paraska, Ana, Katya, and Lesya.

6) In *The Silence of Trees*, we watch Nadya grow from adolescence to old age. Discuss how she changes and matures. What lessons does she learn as a young woman and as an older woman.

7) If you had to pick one word to describe her life from the time she left home until she receives the first empty envelope, what word would you choose? How does Nadya's life change after she receives the envelope?

8) How might Nadya's life have been different if she had fled alone without Stephan after visiting the vorozhka? What if she had stayed in the village?

9) Is it important that Nadya is a peasant and cleaning lady, not a teacher or professional woman? How does her status shape her life and experience of the world? With what result?

10) Is the story told in chronological order? Why do you think the author chose to write it in this way?

11) What does Nadya care most deeply about in her life? How does this shape her character and world view?

12) What is the significance of the various spirits who appear to Nadya in the story?

13) What is the story's central conflict? Is it between characters, a character and society, a character and nature? Is it internal—an emotional struggle within the character? Does the conflict create tension, even suspense, to hold your interest?

14) Can you identify any symbols in the book—people, actions or objects that stand for something greater than themselves?

15) Which character do you most identify with and why?

16) Discuss the significance of Nadya's acts of letting go of the past. How might you have acted differently?

17) Each of the three sections begins with an epigraph. Discuss their significance.

18) Who did you think sent the first letter? Were you surprised to find out that it was from Nadya's sister? What other letters are important in the story?

19) When they are talking on the telephone, Halya tells Nadya that Stephan told her that "he never forgot the smell of the raspberries." What do you think he meant?

20) If you were going to have another character from *The Silence of Trees* tell us the story, whom would you choose? How might the story be different?

VALYA DUDYCZ LUPESCU is a writer and the founding editor of *Conclave: A Journal of Character*. Born and raised in Chicago, she received her degree in English at DePaul University and earned her MFA in Writing as part of the inaugural class at the School of the Art Institute of Chicago (where she began working on *The Silence of Trees*). Her novel, *The Silence of Trees*, was selected as a Semifinalist in the 2008 Amazon Breakthrough Novel Award. She occasionally teaches workshops around Chicago and online, and helps to facilitate a monthly gathering of writers and artists. For the last seven years, she and her husband, along with their three children, have been dividing their time between the United States and Germany. They currently reside in Chicago. Visit her website at: www.vdlupescu.com

7378990R0

Made in the USA
Charleston, SC
25 February 2011